Wendy Oberman is a journalist who has worked in television and films. *Family of Strangers* is her first novel and she is now at work on her second. She lives in North London with her young son.

D0620600

WENDY OBERMAN

Family of Strangers

GRAFTON BOOKS

A Division of the Collins Publishing Group

LONDON GLASGOW
TORONTO SYDNEY AUCKLAND

Grafton Books
A Division of the Collins Publishing Group
8 Grafton Street, London W1X 3LA

Published by Grafton Books 1987
Reprinted 1987, 1988, 1989

First published in Great Britain by
William Collins Sons & Co Ltd 1986

Copyright © Wendy Oberman 1986

ISBN 0-586-06841-4

Printed and bound in Great Britain by
Collins, Glasgow

Set in Plantin

FOR BENJAMIN

And for Lily and Barney Oberman
and Bella Sherman

There are so many people to thank, but mostly

My agent Gill Coleridge
and my editors Susan Watt and Laura Longrigg
and
John Scarborough without whom there would be no
Family of Strangers.

'To go away is to die a little, it is to die to that which one loves: everywhere and always, one leaves behind a part of oneself.'

RAYMOND HARAUCOURT *Seul* (1891)

Rozia's Story

—PART 1—

A Polish Princess

Chapter One

In September 1923, five years after the birth of the independent state of Poland, the new academic year began at the University of Warsaw. It was the day of registration. The new students were conspicuous and proud like the children some of them still were; they wore their new white hats, with the narrow brims and high crowns trimmed in red braid as a badge of honour; for in Poland those who learnt were indeed an honoured band.

They hurried past the neat railings, through imposing white pillars into the cobbled courtyard, jostling each other; most accidentally, a few apologetically, some quite deliberately. In a country that so prized its past, the longed-for independence prompted ideals of patriotism and service and the students saw themselves as restorers of the golden heritage that had been robbed from them. They would make their country whole again, one nation, rid of the Austrians, the Prussians and most sweetest of all, the Russians. Poland would once more be powerful and liberal.

But the Poland of 1923 was not the same nation as it had been under Boleslaw the Pious in the twelfth century. Hatred and jealousy fuelled by the oppressor had left its mark, and the three million Jews, many of whom did not speak the mother tongue, who feared and shunned their fellow Poles, were not to be tolerated easily. Resistance may have made strange bedfellows but freedom allowed prejudice; and in the name of God that prejudice found a home in the hearts of the Jews and the Poles.

There were those who would have wished otherwise, but that was the way in Poland in 1923.

In the surge of students anxious not be late the onlooker might well have noticed a pretty girl, slim with almost porcelain skin, her long red hair unfettered by pins or combs, holding her student's hat with one hand, whilst trying to balance her books in the other. This was Rozia Mezeurska, who was to join the faculty of chemistry, and eventually specialize in physical chemistry. Unusual for a woman, even more unusual for a Jewess – but Rozia Mezeurska never saw herself as ordinary.

She was a true inheritor of the dreams of the new Poland. Fuelled by her father's unfulfilled dreams of being a doctor Rozia believed, in her wilder moments of fantasy, that she might arise, like Marie Curie, a heroine of the state, clutching the flag of Poland and offering the antidote to pain and death.

She was not comfortable with the separateness of a different culture in a host land. She was a Pole and she was Jewish. She could not see how the two worlds could not come together; but Rozia did not know many Poles, she lived in the tightly fettered warmth of orthodox Jewish middle-class life. Her decision to go to university had been bitterly opposed by her parents, who wanted a safe marriage for their child, but Rozia had a powerful ally – one whom her parents had to obey – her grandmother.

In the early hours of that first morning she had lain in her bed and listened to her father's mother snoring rhythmically in the next bed. She had turned on her side away from the noise. Rozia hated the sound of snoring. It had dominated the nights of all of her eighteen years. She always thought that paradise must be a room of one's own, where the rustle of sheets and the sound of breathing were not an intrusion; where she could read when she wanted, dream when the

16

want was there. But still she loved the old lady. Rozia turned on to her other side and watched the body as it rose and fell under the crisp white covers. She could just make out the line of steel grey hair, braided into one plait for the night. The gaunt features were stretched over the bones, the nose jutted out from under bushy grey eyebrows, the mouth was small but full.

Instinctively Rozia touched her own mouth; she liked her face, she knew she was pretty with big brown eyes and wide flaring nostrils that could make her seem a little haughty – but did she look like her grandmother? Would she be like her when she was old, when she was sixty-five? She wondered if Booba, as they called her father's mother, felt as if she were on the other side, slipping towards the end of her life. Rozia took in the flaccid body, relaxed without its stays. She remembered the first time she had been aware of her grandmother being laced into her corsets. Every morning at seven-thirty, including the Sabbath, Biruta, the Polish maid who helped in the apartment, would lace Booba in. The strong young hands pulled the corsets tighter and tighter so that the sparse flesh swelled into seemingly attractive moulds. Booba would hang grimly on to a chair for support and nod as each pull constricted her until, finally satisfied or unable to bear any more, she would put up a hand and the strings were tied. Sometimes at night Rozia caught a glimpse of the red bruised flesh before a vast nightgown concealed the body. She remembered that she had once asked, when she was quite young, 'Does it hurt, Booba?'

And her grandmother had replied: 'Yes, I suppose it does, but I don't think about it. It is how I look that matters.'

It was just such a discipline that Booba installed in Rozia.

Booba was untypical of her name. Such a derivative implied a vast Jewish grandmother who smelt of chicken soup and soap. Booba swished in soft silks and declined to wear the obligatory wig of her generation. Rozia was glad, for she despised the tradition that on marriage the bride's hair was cut and the short ends hidden beneath a scarf or a wig for the rest of her life. It was to no avail that Rozia's mother, Hannah, told her of *Jus Primae Noctis* which allowed the local landowner the right to deflower a virgin before her marriage, and that, by cutting her hair, Jews believed they could prevent such an atrocity. Rozia had never cared for such protection. She moulded herself on Booba.

It was Booba who decreed that the family speak Polish and not Yiddish as was customary in so many observant Jewish families. She would gladly remind whoever inquired that her own family – not her husband's side, of course, '. . . God rest his dear soul . . .' – had come to Poland some four hundred years before. It was Booba's money which enabled the family to find an apartment in a location such as Elektoralna, her money that paid for the maid; and it was Booba who said, despite the resistance of her parents, that Rozia could go to university and study chemistry.

Samuel, Booba's son, would sit in his little office above his leather shop and imagine the great things he would have achieved – if only! Rozia knew he wasted hours, but she would never accept any criticism of Samuel. She adored him, he was the centre of her world. She loved to sit at his feet while he stroked her auburn tresses. Her mother used to say that it would be more seemly if she wore her hair in a chignon. But Rozia loved the way her thick red hair hung down her back, its tendrils licking her waist. When she washed it she could feel its heavy weight on her shoulders and she would move her back and sway her head, enjoying the sensations as the strands slithered across her skin. She knew that all the men of her acquaintance found her requests or favours difficult to refuse, especially when she put her head on one side and cajoled. And the most vulnerable of all was Samuel, but even he had been against her going to the University.

'Rozia,' he had said quietly, 'our laws are there to protect you. It may seem ridiculous to you to forbid contact between young people of the opposite sex without a chaperone, but it is better not to invite temptation.'

'But I am not going to a party, Papa, I am going to university. To study.'

Samuel put his hand up. 'Marriage is a sacred and beautiful thing, between Jew and Jewess and, of course, between Christian and Christian, but the two can never mix. Don't allow yourself to forget that.'

'Papa, I don't want a husband, I want a career. I want to understand the human body, I want to learn about hereditary behaviour, I want –'

'Rozia, Rozia, you want everything. You want the world,' her mother interrupted. 'What you need is a good man and a home to take care of, you are of age now.'

'There is more to my world than stuffed carp,' she snapped.

Hannah hadn't been angry, she had merely touched Rozia's hair. She knew Rozia loved the stuffed carp she always prepared for Friday night. She filled it to overflowing with a ground mixture of fish and onions, flavoured with sugar and pepper to give it the sweetish taste so favoured by Polish Jews. Rozia would invariably come back for a second helping and Hannah would pile her plate – happy that the food was there to give her child. She had come from a region of Poland near the Russian border where there had been dreadful poverty. The crops would sometimes be burnt just because they had been farmed by Jews. Mama was fearful of the non-Jew. She had seen him murder in her village and she lived with the knowledge that it could happen again, even in Warsaw. She bitterly opposed Rozia going to the University.

'No good will come of this,' she told her husband in Yiddish.

'Booba wants her to have an education,' Samuel replied in Polish.

And now Rozia was here at the University, ready to begin her new world; she glanced around her, looking for a friendly face, searching for someone who would smile back.

In the press of the students she noticed two religious Jews, their long gaberdine coats sweeping the ground, their little side curls proclaiming just who they were. She wondered what they were doing at the University, why they were not at their houses of prayer or study, and she looked away, not wanted to be associated with them and then, suddenly ashamed, looked back just as a group of boys barged past, shoving them rudely out of the way.

'Hey, Yids, don't block the path,' they shouted in unison, and Rozia watched as one reached out and pulled one of the Jewish students' hats off, trampling it in the dirt. Tears stung her eyes, her cheeks went red, she stumbled, her books dropped out of her arms and on to the cobbles. She bent down to pick them up.

A boy asked, 'Can I help you?'

She didn't look at him as he gathered the books into a pile and offered them to her.

'My name is Stefan Gordanski,' he said. She took the books from his outstretched hands.

'My name is Stefan,' he said again. She saw that he was blond with blue eyes and she thought him quite beautiful, but still she couldn't speak to him. He was so different from the youths of her own acquaintance, even those who shunned the side curls and the head coverings had a familiar almost heavy quality that was quite unlike this Polish young man with his wide open eyes, and full, upturned mouth.

'Tell me your name,' he insisted.

'Rozia Mezeurska,' she managed to say as she turned away.

'Wait a minute, what's your subject?'

'Chemistry.'

'I'm doing law. What societies are you going to join? I am going to be in the debating group – and you?'

Rozia bit her lip and shrugged. The thought of joining a society had never occurred to her.

Stefan continued as if he hadn't noticed her gesture. 'And a fraternity, I want to be accepted by "My Country" – they wear sashes in red and white.'

Rozia wanted to say, 'Do they let Jews in?' but instead she said in a small voice, 'the debating society.'

'Good. So we'll meet again,' he said, and was gone.

The hundreds of new students gathered in the vast lecture hall; some sat on the floor, on the window ledges, other stood or squatted wherever there was room. The august heads of the University inspired, cajoled and warned them –

'University is for working, not for playing, you, the elite of your year at school, have a responsibility to Poland, to yourselves, to your families . . .'

Rozia would have been uplifted had she absorbed the words, but she heard nothing; her head was full of the boy she had just met. She saw his face in front of her and she held on to his image – not wanting to lose it.

She saw him again, on the way out. He was with a group of friends, boys and some girls. They were laughing. Rozia felt a pang of envy – she wanted to be with them, she wanted to have her friends with her – but her two best friends Mordechai and Shosha had no desire to be part of the new Polish state. All Shosha wanted was to get married, and Mordechai – well Mordechai had once wanted to be a chemist too. Every morning he had left the family home in the heart of the Jewish quarter and gone to a friend's apartment close to the University. He had taken off his long coat and black hat, changed his trousers, worn a different jacket and scraped his hair back, pulling his side curls out of sight; he told Rozia that he had even thought of cutting off those ritual curls, but Mordechai could not do that, his faith and his rituals were part of him, so in the end he had forsaken his studies rather than risk the humiliation of antisemitism. Instead he dreamed of a hot, strange homeland for the Jews and learned how to deal in diamonds, following his father in a trade that had no interest for him.

Rozia felt slightly guilty about Mordechai, allowing him to believe that she might not be adverse to a match with him, but she had never cared for him in the same way as her friend Shosha, who thought him wonderful.

'Rozia Mezeurska,' a voice interrupted her thoughts. 'Come with us, we are going for a coffee.' Had she dreamt it? But no, Stefan was there in front of her saying again, 'Come for a coffee?'

A gentile boy, a beautiful gentile boy with dancing eyes and a soft mouth and blond curls enticing and inviting her.

'Yes,' she said inside her head, but 'No, I am afraid I can't,' was what she said aloud. 'I have some things to do.' She didn't want to say, 'I have to be home for the Sabbath tonight.'

'Well then,' said the prince; did she imagine it or was there disappointment in his voice?

On impulse she smiled at him, putting her head on one side. 'But I could always come for just a quick coffee . . . and then do my tasks afterwards, if you would like.' She had time; sunset was not until seven o'clock.

'Yes, I would.' Stefan Gordanski ushered her towards his friends. There was Jan, Alekander, and Robert; there was Joanna and Wanda. Open and friendly, no one appraised her, no one judged her, they took her in as one of them . . . a student on the first day.

The café was like dozens of others in Warsaw. Marble-topped tables, the smell of *rouki* cooking over the hot fire, the steel rods for curling the cooked mixture into a horn shape, the cream whipped and ready to be stuffed into the hot pastries, the smell of coffee, the newspapers on long sticks, the student clatter and laughter – for this was a students' meeting place. Rozia took her place, a coffee was put in front of her.

'Have you heard that the Communists are holding out an olive branch?' Jan asked Stefan.

'Don't ever trust them,' Stefan replied. 'Marxist doctrine is for world domination and Warsaw is the gateway to the West. They want us, they need us, if they are to fulfil their dream.'

'And one day, the danger is that if we do not form cohesion between us, between all groups, they will exploit our differences and take over our country,' Rozia found herself saying.

'Yes,' Stefan said.

'Poland is fragmented, some of us have lived under the Russians, some under the Germans, some under the Austrians . . . for 120 years we have been partitioned. And, of course, we have to cope with the Jewish situation,' Jan said, pouring a lot of sugar into his coffee; he was a small, thin man with neatly combed black hair and he liked sweet things.

Rozia blushed, she felt herself tense – what did he mean?

'I am going to have a *rouki*, anyone else?' Jan asked, calling the waitress over. 'The Jews are entitled to their own religious structures, and those who don't wish to be part of Poland should leave!'

Rozia digested his words. She wanted to speak, but she couldn't, the words were lost in her throat. She wanted to say, 'It is you who have outlawed us,' but she could not, for perhaps Jan was right.

'I can only say that,' the young man continued, smiling into her face, 'because I am a Jew.'

Rozia laughed, they all laughed. Suddenly she was comfortable. Too comfortable; she didn't want to go, but it was getting late and she had to leave. Almost guiltily Rozia glanced down at the little watch on her blouse.

As she scraped her chair back and got up, Joanna said, 'I have to go too. I'll walk with you.'

Rozia saw that she was pretty with blonde hair cut short in the new style, and that her blue shirt emphasized the blue of her eyes, a different blue to Stefan's, paler.

'I am in the law faculty,' Joanna told her, 'but I doubt if I'll qualify.'

'Don't be pessimistic – I am sure you'll do better than you think.'

Joanna laughed and Rozia noticed she had dimples. 'I don't want a law degree, I want a husband,' she said, smiling.

'Is that why you came to the University?'

'Yes. Of course. Didn't you?'

'No. I want to be a chemist,' Rozia said simply.

'You are a surprise. I am going to join the drama society – I want to act, and I hear the men are very attractive. Stefan is already going to audition for a part in a play and he'll get it. He's wonderful don't you think?'

Rozia could feel herself blushing. She hated it, she always seemed to blush at the wrong moment.

Joanna laughed. 'You like him. Good, he likes you. I know. We have known each other since we were children. My parents and his mother are friends.'

'Tell me about the others,' Rozia said quickly, wanting to change the subject.

'Robert is an independent thinker. His father is an aristocrat, very, very rich – but you wouldn't know it unless you went to his parents' house. Unlike you, Jan is an assimilated Jew so it is easier for him.'

Rozia looked up sharply. Had her discomfort been so obvious; was that what had marked her as a Jewess?

'Stefan, well Stefan will tell you about himself. And Wanda is studying history. She wants to be a teacher, and she is very serious and very political. We think she is a Communist but of course she will not say.'

Rozia thought briefly of the quiet young woman with curly black hair who had said so little.

'It's her parents, you see,' Joanna continued. 'Her father is a member of Pilsudski's inner sanctum, and they could hardly countenance a Communist daughter could they? And then there is Alekander – he too is studying law. As you probably noticed, he is a flirt. It is so funny to think that such a dilettante could attract Wanda.'

'What do you mean?' Rozia was curious, she had hardly registered Alekander at all.

'His father is a lawyer, not very well off. Alekander concentrates much more on his looks than on his law, so his father may well be disappointed if he thinks the family fortunes will be repaired by his son's legal abilities. Of course, if he keeps that carefully coiffured hair in shape and doesn't put on weight he may well find a rich lady.' Joanna giggled.

Rozia immediately saw Alekander in her mind. He was tall, could be called plump, and he did have beautiful, thick black hair which curled in just the right places. He had nice eyes too, now that she thought about it, brown with flecks of gold, and they were kind eyes that didn't match the flashy quality of his face.

By now the two girls had crossed the wide Krakowskie Przedmiescie and reached the Saxony Gardens. As they were about to bid each other farewell, hot clammy hands touched each of their shoulders.

'You've been gossiping, both of you. I was watching as I walked behind you.'

'You didn't walk,' Joanna said, smiling. 'You ran.' Playfully she punched Stefan's shoulder. She turned to Rozia. 'I'll come with you to join the debating society. I'll meet you by the main notice board on Monday after our lectures have finished. And now I'll leave you with Stefan.' She grinned and was gone.

Rozia could feel that awful blush again.

'Will you walk with me?' Stefan said, indicating the park with his hand.

'I can't. I have to be home now. The Sabbath, you see.'

'Of course.'

'How did you know I was Jewish?'

'I watched you,' he said quietly, 'when those thugs abused the two religious Jews.'

Rozia looked sharply at the ground.

Stefan paused for a moment. 'You are very beautiful,' he almost whispered.

And Rozia experienced a new sensation – was it joy, was it happiness? – and she embraced the sheer pleasure of it for a moment before she spoke.

'Can we walk in the park next week?' she asked, unaware of her forwardness.

'Yes.' Stefan bowed and kissed the inside of her wrist.

She felt as if she were scorched by hot flames as his mouth touched her skin.

'Good night,' he said quietly.

'Good night,' she said.

Rozia walked along the narrow pavements that led to the densely populated Jewish area of Warsaw. The normal bustle of life had taken on an extra urgency with all the tasks which had to be completed before the dusk that would mark the beginning of the Sabbath. There were pedlars selling steaming potato cakes, porters with enormous baskets of coal or wood strapped to their backs, weaving amongst the beggars and undernourished children sprawled in doorways. Rozia didn't notice any of them. As she ran down the road that led her to her own apartment building, scampering past children, tripping over cobbles, she didn't feel the ground under her feet. Rozia Mezeurska was flying on wings . . . silken gossamer shot with silver, they transported her to regions of pleasure she had never imagined. A boy had kissed her skin and she was shivering with delight; as soon as she got home she hid in the heat of the bathroom, relishing the memory whilst she bathed for the Sabbath.

Friday night, the eve of the Sabbath, spun its own magic in the Mezeurski family. As the hour drew close to sunset, an atmosphere that was almost tangible, a mist that softened reality, permeated the household. The smell of the food that had been cooked during the day – for on the Sabbath no fire could be lit and all the preparations had to be made before the sacred hour – the gleaming white tablecloth, the ritual silver candlesticks that would be kindled to signify the commencement of the day of rest, the wine that would bless, the bread that was for sustenance: they were all intrinsic to the play. And the actors took up their parts, happy to let go of the pressures of normality for just one day. Mrs Mezeurska, powdered and pretty, dressed in her best black dress, would fluster around the table. Booba would sit in her chair, her lips pinkened and her cheeks just slightly rouged.

Samuel, cleansed from his bath, would stand in the hall waiting for his son Jonathon to go with him to the synagogue and for the evening prayers that marked the commencement of the day of rest. Since the ceremony of bar mitzvah on his thirteenth birthday, Jonathon had become a man in the eyes of the community, and was expected to play a man's role alongside his father. The balm of the Sabbath would be severely stretched by his tardiness. Jonathon didn't like going to synagogue and his protests would be heard even after the front door had been shut.

'Rozia doesn't have to go, and if I am a man then I am entitled to make a man's decision.'

'You will do as you are told,' Papa would be heard to say every Friday.

And every Friday Jonathon would say, 'How can you tell me I am a man and then treat me like a child?'

Hannah would smile, Booba would smile, and Rozia would purse her lips in irritation. She agreed with Jonathon, but on this Friday she didn't even hear the argument. Stefan filled her; she could feel him, smell him, and she was ecstatic.

Later, after the men had returned from the synagogue, the family ate stuffed carp. Between eating and offering up prayers to the glory of God, they talked.

'How was it today?' Samuel asked Rozia.

'Marvellous,' she replied and then glanced down at her plate. 'It is so wonderful to be at the University. You see so many people, so many things. Why today . . .' Rozia suddenly felt guilty – Jewish girls were not supposed to hold hands with a boy until they were married. She had let one kiss her wrist, something that was unheard of in her life and she hadn't even thought it wrong. Well, it wasn't wrong but there was no point discussing it with them because they wouldn't understand. Inadvertently she glanced at Booba. Perhaps she might, but the look on her face was impassive, disinterested almost. Rozia had seen that look on Booba's face quite often. She flicked her hair, unaware that for the first time she had set herself apart from the family.

'Today what?' Jonathon asked, hungry for information. Since he had known that Rozia was to go to university, he had felt so stifled within his strict Yeshiva school.

'Today, a gentile boy asked for my name,' Rozia said quietly, wishing she hadn't said anything.

Her family stared at her, except for Jonathon who couldn't see anything interesting in someone asking for someone's name.

'Oh,' he said, disappointed, 'I thought you were going to tell us something exciting.'

After a moment Samuel spoke. 'Rozia, please remember

that you are Jewish. I do not want to have to remind you again.'

Rozia looked at her father, her face was flushed.

'I am not rebuking you,' he said, 'for talking with a boy. I can understand how it happened. I just want you to realize that it is wrong to tempt oneself to travel where one must not go.'

She hung her head. She loved Papa so much. He was so wise. How could she contemplate going out with a Polish boy? She should try to be more like her friend Shosha, who only wanted a husband and children. Her future should be with a boy like Mordechai who was of her world. Rozia looked back at her plate. She must change the subject.

'Mama, I'd love some more,' she said.

Rozia chewed her second helping slowly. Even the most favourite food is difficult to digest when there is no hunger.

She decided to placate her parents and invite Mordechai to tea after the Sabbath, even though it would mean a boring evening listening to the delights of turning a desert into a land for men.

The Sabbath day was passed in a ritual that was set, as if it were inscribed in a law. The men went to synagogue in the morning, the women prepared the lunch; there was a thanksgiving for the food – and then for the elders an obligatory sleep, while the younger ones talked or walked – until Saturday evening when at sunset the Mezeurski family assembled in the salon where Samuel attended to the ceremony that marked the closing of the day. He lit a candle, invited his family to smell incense that was kept in a small, highly embellished silver box, recited the prayers and sang the songs. The traditional greeting, 'Have a good week, have a healthy week,' was given to each member of the family in turn, and the day of rest was over.

Rozia sent Jonathon to Mordechai's home with a note inviting him to come and visit her. He came back with him;

she knew he would. She had dressed carefully in a white blouse, a black skirt, and her hair was brushed neatly so it hung down her back like a piece of silk.

Mordechai took off his coat, his pale face and curly hair merging with his suit. His shoulders were slightly rounded and his slender fingers were linked together, one hand into the other as if he did not know what to do with them.

'Mordechai, you've come,' Rozia said. 'I knew you would.'

'If you ask me, I am happy,' he answered.

Rozia noticed her parents glance at each other, a satisfied look on both their faces. He sat down at the dining room table which was now covered with a velvet cloth. He took some tea and cakes. She could see that he was embarrassed.

'I cannot stay, I have arrangements this evening,' he said.

'Oh but –'

'Rozia, you must thank Mordechai for coming,' Hannah interrupted from where she sat in her chair. She had her embroidery on her knee, her glasses on the end of her nose. Rozia looked at her sharply.

'Thank you, Mordechai,' she said with as much charm as she could muster.

Mordechai just nodded, bowed to Mr Mezeurski who sat dozing in his chair, a bowl of fruit and a lemon tea by his side, then to Mrs Mezeurska, and Rozia walked him to the front door.

Jonathon burst out of his bedroom. 'Are you going out, Mordechai – can I come with you?'

'No, you can't. I am going visiting.'

Rozia moved forward slightly . . . where was he going? She couldn't ask.

'A girl, I suppose,' Jonathon said in disgust.

Mordechai smiled and cuffed his ear. 'That's not your business,' he said.

Rozia smiled stiffly. She didn't like Mordechai in that

way, but she had expected him to stay, even for just one hour. Suddenly curiosity overcame good manners.

'Where are you going?' she heard herself say.

'To see Shosha.'

'Shosha,' Rozia repeated, suddenly feeling rather left out. 'But she is my friend.'

'Yes, I know. Rozia, we like each other very much.'

Mordechai was looking at her and his white skin was not quite so white. Rozia could detect some spots of red colouring the flat cheekbones, and she saw that the eyes danced a little.

'Oh, Mordechai,' she said, 'that is wonderful. Be good to her, I love her very much.'

'I have been so worried about telling you, I didn't think you would be pleased for us.' He bent close to her. 'I knew you never – cared for me in that way, but you were always so possessive of me.'

'It's because I like you,' Rozia said hurriedly.

'We want to go to Palestine, to the kibbutz. Hopefully I will eventually work in a university, but before –'

'I know,' she said, suddenly bored, 'you want to make the desert bloom.'

'It is the place for the young. We don't have to be ashamed there.'

'I am not ashamed now! But don't let's argue.' Impulsively she put her arms around his neck and kissed his cheek. '*Muzletov*,' she whispered.

Mordechai literally jumped. No woman, except his mother, had ever touched him before.

Rozia giggled. 'I am the first girl to kiss you,' she said gaily. 'You had better go to Shosha and put that right.'

She closed the door after him, pushing it shut with her back, thinking about Stefan's kiss which she could still feel scalding her wrist.

'You kissed Mordechai,' Jonathon said accusingly.

31

'Yes. I am happy for him. I was not doing anything wrong, just congratulating him,' she snapped.

'I don't care what you do,' Jonathon snapped back. 'You always do what you want anyway.'

'I suppose I do,' Rozia said quietly.

Chapter Two

On Monday morning an excited Rozia chose to walk through
the Saxony Gardens to the University. She stopped for a few
moments by the fountain near Zmyciestwa Place, wondering
if she might walk there with Stefan, imagining how it would
be, letting her mind play tricks as she watched a boy and a
girl pass by, their shoulders almost touching, their fingers
so close they were nearly linked.

She had brushed her hair a hundred times that morning,
telling herself she didn't mind whether she saw Stefan or
not, but knowing that she would look at every face, and
around every corner.

All the students enrolled in the faculty of chemistry were
gathered in the vast lecture hall. Rozia found a place right
at the front. She was a little late, so she had no time to look
around and examine her fellow students. Dr Oberski, the
head of the faculty, was about to arrive.

Rozia tried hard to concentrate as he outlined the form
their studies would take, but Stefan kept jumping into her
mind, blocking out the sound of Professor Oberski's patient
voice. At the end of the talk Rozia was about to leave the
hall when she heard someone call her name. Startled, she
turned around and saw that it was the great Professor Oberski himself. How had he remembered her name? she wondered. They had met only once when he had orally examined
her to ascertain her suitability for acceptance as one of his
students. Hesitantly, she walked over to the big brown table,
her heart beating a little faster as she approached him. He
was a tall man and he had a kind face – she had noticed that

at her examination. His hazel eyes were magnified by glasses whose steel frames did nothing to harden his features. A shock of untidy brown hair crowned his head.

'You were not concentrating,' he said.

Rozia bit her lip. 'No, sir.'

'See that it doesn't happen again. If I remember correctly, you wanted very much to be accepted on this course. Others too wanted a place; you were the one who was awarded the chance. It would be a shame if you abused that opportunity. As you well know, Miss Mezeurska, we are now forced, many of us against our will, to operate the *numerus clausus* in respect of our Jewish students, so you have a special responsibility.'

Rozia felt the rebuke as if she had been slapped. The *numerus clausus* had exploded into the lives of the Jewish community in June of that very year. It meant that only a proportionate number of Jews to the population, not to those at the University, could be admitted to study there.

Still smarting, Rozia went to the little grassed area near the lecture hall. She had brought some food with her for her second breakfast of the day. Being an orthodox Jewess there was no question of her eating with the other students. Suddenly she felt lonely and cut off by her religion. She saw a group sitting together not far from her, and they were all laughing. One of the girls was cuddled up to a boy. Then she noticed that one of the group was Stefan. Rozia wished she was with them.

She turned away, suddenly not wanting him to see her. He was talking to one of the girls, his face close to hers, almost intimate in his proximity. Rozia felt the hot flush of jealousy. He looked strong and confident. Deliberately she turned her back on the group and opened one of her text-books, trying not to hear them. A shadow fell over the printed page, it began to dance like fingers making patterns. Rozia looked up to find Stefan looking down at her.

'Why are you sitting on your own?'

'I am working.'

'Can I stop you?'

'Yes,' she said, and threw the book to one side.

He sat down beside her. He looked at her little pile of food, some fish, bread and an orange.

'Are you hungry? Would you like some?' Rozia asked him.

He nodded. She tore off some bread, put some pickled fish on it and handed it to him. He gobbled it down.

'More?'

'Errum . . .'

She gave him all of it. She was a little hungry, but she didn't want to appear churlish.

'Stefan – come on!' a dark-haired boy called out; it wasn't one of the boys Rozia had met and liked the day before. This student was more poised, and his voice was clipped.

'Have you classes?' she asked Stefan.

'No, we're going sailing. Come with us.'

Rozia wanted to go, but she said, 'No, I have to do my work.'

'Why? It's a beautiful day and winter will come soon and we won't be able to go out into the sunlight. You have such beautiful hair – it shouldn't be locked in a classroom. I won't allow it.'

She smiled at him, but shook her head. 'I had to fight my family to get here. I had to fight for my place within the Jewish quota. I can't go out on a boat instead of going to class.'

Stefan pursed his lips. 'You'll still come to the park though?'

'Yes, of course.'

'Tomorrow – after classes, I'll wait for you on this bench.'

Rozia could scarcely speak, she was so excited. Alone with a boy, with Stefan – just as she had imagined that morning!

35

But at the same time there was a sense of wrongdoing that made it even more exciting. She sucked her cheeks in, feeling her tongue. Would he kiss her? No, she must not allow such a liberty, but all the same she did wonder how it would feel.

Later, when she met Joanna she mentioned that she had seen Stefan and that he had gone sailing.

'With Piotr Zahorski and his cronies I have no doubt.' Rozia could almost taste the dislike in Joanna's voice. 'He's a count, his father is a friend of Stefan's uncle. Rozia, he is an antisemite, stay away from him.'

'And he is a friend of Stefan?'

'No, he is not a friend of Stefan. Stefan doesn't like him, nor does he approve of his politics, but his uncle is a lawyer and Piotr's father is an important client. He says it is expediency.'

'I don't think I like – what is it you said?' Rozia turned to face Joanna. 'Expediency.'

Joanna touched her face gently. 'Don't judge Stefan by his uncle, he is his own person. You will see.'

Rozia tried to enjoy herself with Joanna. They registered their names with the debating society, they indulged in the thought of joining the folk dancing society, but it was obvious from a few introductory remarks that it would all be too serious for them. Joanna put her name down for the dramatic society and arranged an audition for herself; she and the young man sitting at a desk tried to persuade Rozia to join, but she refused. They met Robert in the forecourt, who invited them to go for a coffee. Alekander joined them and Rozia saw that he was a flirt, but without Stefan it was not the same for her. Even the *rouki* did not have the same smell.

'What is the matter with pretty Rozia today?' Robert asked. He was a tall slender young man, who kept himself in excellent shape because he was an athlete.

'She saw Stefan with Piotr Zahorski and I told her of his racial preferences,' Joanna said.

'I have known Stefan all my life,' he interjected, 'and I know he is not an antisemite. I give you my word.'

Slightly mollified, Rozia allowed herself to look forward to a walk in the park.

It was raining the next day. Rozia felt cheated, for she had planned to wear a white dress – and no one wears white in the rain. Angry, she snatched her navy skirt from her wardrobe. Without even looking at herself, she pulled on a pale pink blouse. Almost instantaneously she took them off again and defiantly put on the white dress. The rain might clear. She wrapped her coat around her, holding it shut, not wanting her mother to see what she was wearing. She was careful, on her way, to avoid puddles. She didn't want to spoil the dress.

At lunchtime, as if bidden by Rozia's prayers, the sun came out, peeping from behind white cottonwool clouds that raced across the blue sky, playing hide-and-seek with each other.

Rozia saw him first. He sat, or rather lolled against the bench, waiting for her. His cap was perched on the back of his head, his blond hair dishevelled.

'Hello,' she said.

'Hello.' Stefan looked up, smiling. 'I thought we might go to Lazienki Park. We could walk by the Palace on the Island.'

'That would be lovely.' She hoped her voice didn't sound unnaturally high. She had only been to the park once and she remembered the visit very well. She had gone there with Booba, when she was about twelve years old, and had clung on to her hand – the Russians controlled Warsaw then and Rozia was frightened of the soldiers; but the moment she saw the tiny island with its fairyland palace, she had forgotten any fears. She thought it was the most romantic place in all of Warsaw. And now she was going there with her prince! As they climbed into the droshki she was so excited, she could hardly breathe.

Usually she loved to ride in the little open-air carriage. The team of horses harnessed together clip-clopped over the cobbled streets and, when they reached Ujazdowskie Avenue, the sound changed as their hooves beat a muffled tune on the wooden slats that paved the entire length of the street. But Rozia was too nervous, too conscious of Stefan sitting beside her to enjoy anything. She could almost feel a heat coming from him.

'How were your classes?' she said in a breathless voice, wanting to say something – anything.

'All right, but I don't like them very much. I don't have the same aptitude as you. Law was forced on me, it wasn't a question of choice.'

'By your uncle?'

'Yes. How do you know about him?'

She turned away embarrassed. Perhaps she had been too forward. 'Joanna told me that student – the one you went sailing with – is the son of one of his clients.'

'Yes,' Stefan said, his voice unexpectedly soft. Then he changed his tone, quickly so that Rozia had no time to question him. 'So you see why I don't have the same feelings as you.'

'Probably not the same need.'

'Probably, and I am curious about that. I don't know you well yet, but even I have understood that your work seems to be the most important thing in your life. Don't you ever have fun? What about boyfriends?'

'Boyfriends?' Rozia smiled to herself, she liked his use of the word 'yet' when describing their relationship. 'I can see you know little of the Jewish way.'

'I know nothing about Jews,' he said.

The droshki rounded the corner and set them down

outside the great iron gates of the park. Stefan helped her out, holding her fingers easily. They walked down the gently sloping paths carved neatly between the great spaces of grass. Rozia would have liked to throw off her shoes and dance on the grass, but she quickly controlled the impulse; it was not allowed.

'But,' he continued as if there had been no break in the conversation, 'I would like to know about you – what kind of person you are.'

Rozia smiled at him out of the corner of her eye and put her head slightly on one side. She felt herself colour a little as he looked back at her, and quickly averted her eyes.

'There are five of us in our family. My grandmother, we call her "Booba", my mother and father, my brother and myself.' She cleared her throat, still feeling a little embarrassed. 'There would have been more children, but my mother was unwell.'

'There is only one of me. My father died,' Stefan told her. 'Hey, look,' he said, grabbing her hand.

Rozia gasped. In the sunshine the white Palace seemed to be shimmering in an almost emerald green sea. The giant trees swayed gently as if on duty, guarding the little white house with its colonnades and statues.

'It's so wonderful,' Rozia said quietly, 'I think I shall make it my special place.' In the sheer pleasure of the moment she even forgot Stefan.

'Come,' he said, and they walked across the little bridge and into the fairyland itself. Stefan held her hand, cupping the fingers between his own. Rozia wanted to climb the steps and look in the windows, but even though the Palace was deserted good manners forbade her from such a lapse. Instead she allowed Stefan to guide her to the steps that led down to the water's edge. They sat down.

'Go on,' he said, 'you were telling me about your life.'

'It is expected, normally that is,' Rozia stopped and cleared her throat, 'for Jewish girls to complete a modicum of education, to learn how to make a home from their mother and then to marry someone from their own background.'

'Faith you mean?' Stefan interrupted.

'More than that. The Jews are practical.' She smiled, laughed almost.

'But what happens if you fall in love with someone else?'

'Normally, it would not be possible for someone to fall in love with someone who was not suitable, or at least it would be very unusual. Parents are very protective. We don't mix with boys without a chaperone until we are married.'

'Why did you want to be different? Why not be the same as everyone else?' Stefan's voice had an insistence, as if he were challenging her. Rozia was curious about that.

'Why do you want to know?'

'I would have thought it would have been easier for you to follow the traditions of your family.'

'Oh yes, it would have been much easier. This way is very lonely. But I have a dream and whilst I have that dream within me, I must fight for it.' She slammed her fist on the grass as if to reinforce her words.

'What's the dream?' He moved a strand of hair out of her eyes. She shivered at his touch.

'You would laugh,' she said.

'No.'

'I want to find a cure for tuberculosis.' She turned away from him, embarrassed in case he should laugh.

'That would be wonderful. I have a dream too. I want to be a sort of politician – to unite Poland, to free it from prejudice.'

'A sort of politician?' Rozia repeated.

'Yes, a sort of politician. I want to be an actor.'

'How wonderful. Why didn't you go to drama school?'

'My uncle thinks I would make a better living as a lawyer . . .'

They both giggled, lightly.

'Tell me,' Stefan continued. 'Was it difficult for you to get a place at the University?'

She nodded, remembering the disagreement with her parents, the guilt at her mother's tears, the remorse at her father's worries and how she had almost despaired until Booba had said that she must go.

'I suppose you and I are very different,' she heard Stefan say.

'No, I –' Rozia began to say, but then stopped herself. Disconcerted, she drew her feet up under her dress; he didn't like her, she had said or done something wrong. Perhaps it was because she was Jewish.

'But then perhaps I don't have the same disadvantages. I am neither a woman, nor am I Jewish.'

'It isn't a disadvantage being a woman,' Rozia said hotly.

'But it is to be Jewish,' Stefan said quietly, and he reached over and gently touched her forehead. She felt as if she had been stung, not only from his flesh. She couldn't answer him.

They were quiet, neither able to speak. Stefan sat with his weight on one hip, leaning towards Rozia. He gnawed on his thumb, a habit from childhood, one which only reappeared when he was nervous. And he did feel nervous. He couldn't understand his feelings for this Rozia, this wild, passionate, intense Jewish girl. Part of him, the sensible part, said run . . . go back to Piotr and his world, to the drinking and sailing with the girls. A few adventures would enrich his sexual fantasies and then he would marry a girl from his own class and his own faith. A tryst with this extraordinary Jewish girl would only cause problems, he could hardly expect his mother to welcome her into his home. Like most Poles, himself included, his mother had an intense mistrust, perhaps even dislike of the Jews.

41

'What happened to your father?' he heard Rozia ask, as if she was searching for something to say.

'He was killed in a battle somewhere.'

'Aren't you lonely without him?'

'No. We have a good life. My uncle is really my mother's boyfriend, she just calls him my uncle. He is a bachelor. I don't know why they haven't married. Perhaps it is because they both enjoy their freedom.'

'And will you practise law?'

'I expect so.'

'Somehow I didn't see you as a servant of injustice.'

'What do you mean injustice? Don't devalue the law, Rozia, without it there would be anarchy.'

'For the Jews sometimes it is anarchy.'

'You are very aggressive. All you Jews are like that.' The words came so quickly, and he hadn't wanted to say them, but Rozia had drawn that response. The wind over the water felt cold and he wanted to go.

Rozia stood up. There was nothing else for her to do; she needed to run home, back to her room, to shut out the world.

'I am sorry,' Stefan said, 'I got too deep, too quickly. Neither of us were ready for it.' He felt so sad. He had just wanted to walk in the park with a pretty girl.

They crossed back over the bridge, not walking together but merely parallel with each other. Just before the great iron gates Stefan looked at Rozia and he knew he didn't want her to go away, he wanted her to stay with him. He took her hand, cupping it in his as he had done at the beginning of their walk. Rozia knew she should pull away but she didn't, she let her finger curl around his in an act of defiance to her faith and its protections.

'I don't want to be different to you,' she whispered. 'I am tired of hearing of willing and unwilling martyrs of two thousand years of persecution. I just want to live.'

Stefan nodded, wanting to hold her close, to kiss her. Instead he said, 'I'd like to see you again.'

'Yes,' she replied.

Rozia's life began to take on a new pattern. After an early breakfast at home – mostly some bread and cream cheese and a coffee – she would go to the University, always walking through the park, always stopping at the little fountain, but now someone waited for her there. A young man who would dip his hand into the water, turning circles this way and that, sending ripples out to the ripples that she would make with her hand in the same water until the ripples touched the other's skin, like a kiss, one from the other, and the hands would get nearer and nearer and the ripples stronger until they became little waves and then their hands would touch and link.

Rozia and Joanna had become friends, not like it was with Shosha of course, but still companions. Wanda, Rozia discovered, was agonizingly shy, but clever and kind, never failing to say hello or to pass a comment to someone who might be standing alone. The little clique of friends solidified. Robert was their extrovert, Jan their politician, Alekander was their flirt and Stefan was their star. Often when they were sitting in the refectory during the break for second breakfast, Piotr and some of his friends would try to entice Stefan away, but he would stay, an arm on Jan's shoulder, a hand on Robert's neck, eyes only for Rozia. She blossomed, she glowed, she grew.

On the day after their walk in Lazienki Park, Stefan had come and searched for Rozia on the benches outside the University. He had taken her food and her books and ushered her into the refectory.

'Eat with us, you are one of us,' he told her.

Wanda had got up and fetched her a coffee. Joanna had moved over and made room. But as she unwrapped her

43

chopped herring on bread, she had seen displeasure on Jan's face.

'Don't you like herring?' she asked him.

'I can't understand why you can't eat here. It's the attitude that non-Jewish food is unclean that offends so many people.'

'You know it is not that,' Rozia said hotly. 'It's our dietary laws – we may not eat milk and meat together.'

'Well, it's ridiculous in today's society to impose those kind of rules. It was different in the desert.'

'Why is it,' the gentle Wanda remarked, 'that the Jews are so much more intolerant of their own people than anyone else?'

'Because we know that we are hypocritical. Most of us are pretending –'

'Maybe, my friend,' Robert interrupted, 'you are a little guilty that you don't observe the laws and Rozia does.'

'Why should I feel guilty? I have never had anything to do with orthodox Jews. Their rituals have nothing to do with me.'

'Well,' Rozia said, 'you are having something to do with one of them now.' She was surprised to find she was laughing and not offended.

'That argument was won by Rozia,' said Robert. 'Who says Yes?'

Hands banged the table. 'Yes, yes, yes . . .' they all said, including Helene, a small blonde who was Alekander's girl of the day, much to Wanda's distress. Rozia stood up and made a small bow.

'Now we launch her on the debating society,' Stefan said.

'Yes,' Rozia agreed to her amazement.

From that time on Rozia went to the refectory – but took only a coffee; she ate her second breakfast on her way back to the laboratory, swallowing it quickly behind a wall or a tree, anxious in case anyone she knew should see her. Rozia discovered that the debating society met on Fridays after

44

classes at five o'clock. She would not be able to attend; the Sabbath would be in at six-ten that week and would come in earlier and earlier as the days grew shorter. There was no question of her not being at home. As Rozia walked back to her family home on that particular Friday, she was for the very first time resentful of the stricture that kept her apart from others.

On the Saturday afternoon when the family was sleeping, Rozia walked the narrow streets that took her to the heart of the Jewish section of Warsaw. She had not seen Shosha properly since she began her course at the University – there hadn't been time – so she had arranged to meet her that particular day.

Shosha's father was a rabbi, her mother, Bashela, had come from the same village as Rozia's mother and the women were best friends. Bashela assumed that Hannah had made the better match. She was not envious, she just accepted that Hannah Mezeurska lived in a nicer apartment, that she had a maid, and a washerwoman who came twice a month to wash the family's linen in great iron baths over the stove, and then carried them to the drying rooms at the top of the house where she would hang the huge white sheets and pillowcases to dry on long rope lines. Hannah even had a sewing woman who would come and do any repairs that might be required, stitching delicate underwear, mending tiny holes. There was not enough money in the Mezeurski household to replace consistently what was worn, but there was enough to visit a dressmaker for one good dress in the winter and one good dress in the summer for both Hannah and Rozia, and those visits were a high point in Hannah's life.

None of these embellishments improved the quality of Bashela's life. She had no maid, just a washerwoman who came every two months; there was no sewing woman, just Bashela. But her children, three boys and Shosha, adored her and her husband loved her as much as he had when she was a young girl.

And Hannah envied her – there was no Booba to run the family's affairs, no illness to dry a womb and prevent conception, but what was most painful to Hannah was the knowledge that Bashela still had the loving she no longer enjoyed.

Shosha was waiting for Rozia in Nalewki, the main shopping street in the heart of the Jewish area. She was standing under the sign for the umbrella shop, which had a drawing of a black, rather smart umbrella above a pointed hand, the longest finger almost touched the twenty-four which was the number of the shop. Rozia and Shosha always met under the sign and the two of them, Rozia with her wild red hair and Shosha with her wiry black untidy curls, would link arms and bend their heads together, giggle and share secrets. But today Rozia did not link arms. She just kissed her friend's face, appraising the deep-set dark brown eyes, the firm nose, the soft mouth. Shosha had a plump face that could never be described as pretty, but her warmth, her caring were so clearly stamped on it that one could easily be forgiven for thinking that she was.

'What is it?' Shosha said immediately.

Rozia glanced around her. As usual the street was crowded with walkers and talkers, but no shoppers, for on the Sabbath in the Jewish area no shops were open. Above the boarded-up shopfronts, there were neatly painted signs indicating the butcher, the baker, the tailor, the hardware stores – some embellished with little drawings, none as neatly as the umbrella sign. The street was a dead end, with just a little archway through which pedestrians could walk. On three sides, four floors of identical windows rose upwards, one on top of the other, each window open to the street, offering its sounds and its smells. It always depressed Rozia. She liked open spaces and trees.

'Something is wrong,' Shosha said again. 'Come, let's walk. Don't talk if you don't want to.'

'But I do want to talk,' Rozia said. 'Can we go back to your house?'

'Everyone is there.'

Rozia nodded. Shosha's parents had two rooms. She and two of her younger brothers shared one room. The youngest, an unexpected baby, slept with his parents in the main room. The boys shared a bed made of metal with intricate rolled edges and ornaments. Rozia always thought it looked odd against the bare white walls and the poverty. It was chocolate brown with rural landscapes in muted greens painted in oval shapes at both ends. For propriety Shosha had her own bed, also made of metal, but painted pink; since puberty it had been her right to sleep alone.

For a moment Rozia thought of her own family home with its four rooms and luxury of a bathroom – even the maid had her own room behind the kitchen. She took Shosha's arm and the girls walked together. Shosha said nothing, just kept in pace with Rozia. Occasionally she touched her arm, occasionally she looked at her friend, but she knew better than to ask anything. Rozia would talk when she was ready.

'It isn't as easy as I thought,' Rozia said suddenly.

Shosha said nothing, waiting for her to continue.

'I've met this boy, . . . I like him, I like him a lot.'

'He is a gentile?' Shosha tried to keep censure out of her voice.

'Yes. But it isn't just him, it is all my friends. Jan is a Jew, but non-practising, he says we can only survive in Poland if we assimilate; Robert and Alekander and Wanda and Joanna, they are just like us. Well, almost like us.'

'The boy, Stefan – is he like us too?'

Rozia stopped walking. She turned to look at Shosha, her

eyes dancing, her lips formed in a half smile. 'No, he's special – to me he is special.'

'Rozia, be careful.' Now Shosha could not hide her concern.

'It's too late. It's too wonderfully late and the very best thing of all is that I think he loves me too.'

Whilst Rozia walked with Shosha, Stefan drank beer with his uncle. Stefan's mother, Sonia Gordanska, had excused herself and left the two men alone. Stefan had seen the look that went between his uncle and his mother. He knew what to expect. He sat down on the red velvet couch in his mother's plush salon, with its embellished red wallpaper and highly polished wooden tables covered with little objects and flowers in every conceivable container.

'How are you enjoying yourself?' Karol Boguslawski said without preamble. He was a corpulent man in his early fifties, with a handlebar moustache and little hair.

'Very much, thank you sir,' Stefan answered.

'I saw Piotr. He and his friends seem to be having a high old time. They sail and fence and swim, and drink,' he dug Stefan in the ribs, 'and flirt . . .'

'Yes.'

'But he doesn't seem to have seen much of you.'

'No. I have a different group of friends.'

'Tell me about them,' Boguslawski said.

'I have a feeling you already know as much as you would like to know,' Stefan said easily. He drank his beer, the froth leaving a covering over his upper lip.

'Robert and Joanna of course I know. Robert's father is a fine man, a fine man.'

'A rich one,' Stefan added.

If Boguslawski noticed, he said nothing.

'Wanda we have met too, and Alek – not from families that we know, but we have met them, your mother and I.'

'You want to know about Jan Poznanski and Rozia Mezeur-

48

ska?' The last name was the most difficult to pronounce.

'They are Jews?'

'Yes, but as different from each other as we are different to them.'

'What do you mean?'

'Poznanski sees himself as a Pole of Jewish descent. Rozia sees herself as a Pole of the Jewish faith.'

'I don't understand you. They are both of that tribe.'

'No, you wouldn't understand,' Stefan said, now a little uneasy.

'Piotr and his friends are thinking of creating a students' fraternity for Poles. It would not just be a drinking club, it would pursue Polish dreams and make them a reality.'

Stefan stood up. He did not want to hear more. 'I wish them luck. I am going to a rehearsal now. Did Mother tell you, we will be performing *Romeo and Juliet* at the end of this term? I am playing the Duke, not bad for a first-year student. I hope you will come and see me perform.'

'You would be better off understanding the needs of Poland than acting on a stage,' the older man spluttered.

Stefan smiled, satisfied that he hadn't heard what he didn't want to hear, not wishing to be forced to make choices.

It was just a few days after that, on the eve of the Day of Atonement, the holiest day of the Jewish year, that Stefan invited Rozia to go to the theatre with him. They were sitting in their café, as they now called it.

'I'd like to take you out. I'd like to spend an evening with you. I will take good care of you. They are performing Henrik Ibsen's *A Doll's House* at the Teatr Ruduta. I can get tickets. We could go next Thursday, if that is all right with you.'

Rozia never stopped to think of the possible complications such an excursion might provoke. She couldn't think of anything more wonderful than to spend an evening with

Stefan. 'It would be lovely,' she told him. She looked at the watch she wore pinned to her blouse as a little brooch; it had been Booba's, she had given it her on the first day of university. Its little face was surrounded by tiny silver embellishments that had been fashionable when Booba was young.

'I must go,' Rozia said, but she didn't want to; it was painful, as if she were losing a layer of her skin, part of herself. She swallowed quickly and let Stefan walk her from the café. She didn't want him to know how she felt.

Later that night, after the sun had set and the crescent shaped silver moon made its claim over the night sky, the Mezeurski family attended their devotional prayers in the synagogue. They, together with Jews throughout the world, bowed their heads in supplication, for it was the time for 'the still small voice' to issue judgement on the Jewish people and the world in which they lived. It was the time for penitence, when their fate for the year was decreed. Rozia, dressed in deepest crimson which enhanced her red hair and creamy skin, listened as the rabbi intoned the centuries-old prayers asking for mercy.

Ever since she was a child, Rozia had never asked God for mercy. She asked for His help to achieve her ambitions. Some might have called that arrogance, but Rozia would have argued with them; she would have said: 'I do not ask for anything without being prepared to commit my whole being.'

The synagogue was jammed, the men seated in the front, swaying in their prayer shawls, and the women behind, some in the wigs befitting their matron's status. All of the worshippers around her, even the young, beat their chests as a sign of repentance, begged almost for a healthy and peaceful year. In antisemitic Poland, the passion took on an extra dimension.

But Rozia did not have the same needs as her fellows. The

year before she had asked God to let her go to the University. Now her prayers were for Stefan.

On the evening they were to visit the theatre, Rozia told her mother that she and Shosha had been invited to a friend of Shosha's, and she would spend the night with her. It didn't occur to her that it was the first time she had lied to her parents. Stefan had wanted to collect her. She didn't explain to him that it would be impossible for a gentile boy to escort an orthodox Jewish girl to an evening at the theatre; she merely said she would meet him there. Rozia was uneasy about going to a conspicuous place which she knew to be frequented by the elite of Warsaw society, but it didn't occur to her that it might be considered more inappropriate for a young lady to travel across the city by herself at night.

Shosha was unhappy about Rozia's deceptions. 'You are not even telling the boy the truth, Rozia. Be careful.' She was sitting on the floor whilst Rozia tried to arrange her hair into a more pleasing style.

'It'll be all right. You'll see. Everything will be fine and at least it will give you the opportunity to spend some time alone with Mordechai. After all, it's ridiculous to imagine two people who are in love not being able to spend some time together.'

'It's to prevent temptation,' Shosha replied.

'If you love someone, it's natural to want to be near them.'

Shosha was shocked, and Rozia realized that she had gone too far. She touched her friend's arm. 'I am not suggesting that you do anything other than talk, but wouldn't you like to talk to him without someone always in earshot?'

Shosha nodded.

'Be a woman and enjoy it,' Rozia said, remembering Mordechai's pleasure when she had kissed him on the cheek.

When the girls left the house together, it was Rozia who told Bashela where they were going – what was one more lie to the girl who had never lied? After bidding farewell to

Shosha, Rozia took the tram to the theatre; she was so nervous as she descended at her stop that she forgot her gloves. A man ran after her.

'Hey, you left these,' he said.

She snatched at them without even thanking him and walked quickly, her heels making a tip-tap sound over the cobbled road. She saw the people gathered outside the theatre, waiting for the signal that the play was about to start, when they would charge for the several doors which could never accommodate all of them at the same time; but form had to be observed and so they stayed where they were, hailing each other, gossiping, or just waiting and watching. Rozia was suddenly aware that she had only once before attended a theatre, and that had been a family outing to the Polish State Jewish Theatre. At the time she had enjoyed the entertainment – for that is what it had been, more a collection of songs and sketches than a play. Now the thought of watching *A Doll's House* with Stefan worried her. Rozia never wanted to look stupid; she wished she knew more about the theatre and about the play which she assumed to be an important work because of the almost reverential tone in Stefan's voice when he had spoken of it.

She found him just outside the main doors, where he had said he would be waiting.

'It is not proper that you should come here on your own,' he told her crossly as he escorted her into the theatre. 'I won't let you return home without my accompanying you.'

Rozia wanted to tell him that she was meeting Shosha, but the sight of the rows of plush seats, of the beautiful women and the stylish men froze any response. The door of her world had finally been prised wide open and there was no yawning abyss crammed with snarling animals ready to bite, perhaps even to devour, should she miss the precarious footholds. There was light and laughter and beautiful people.

She was one of them and she held on to Stefan's arm and she was so proud.

The play overwhelmed her – she identified with Nora and understood her decision to leave her husband. She told Stefan, her tone fierce, 'Helmer is stupid and unthinkable. He is unforgivable.'

'Do you see all women like Nora, wonderfully self-sacrificing, and are we men all stupid and domineering like Helmer?' He was smiling at her.

'I think you are patronizing me,' she told him.

'No. I just wondered what your father was like, that was all.'

Rozia was surprised at the question. 'Papa is wonderful. He is kind and understanding, nothing like Helmer at all.'

'Then he will be happy that I have escorted you home,' Stefan said.

'No, I mean . . . I have arranged to meet Shosha. I am staying the night with her.'

His gaze was too searching.

'It helps her, you see. She told her parents she was with me, otherwise she would never have been permitted to be alone with Mordechai. That is just the way it is, ridiculous isn't it?'

Another lie from the girl who never told lies.

By then they were sitting in their café. Rozia was enjoying a *rouki* with her tea, Stefan was drinking wine. It was strange being in the café without any of their friends. She was aware that those tables which they always pushed together were now separate. A man sat at one of them, reading a newspaper from a rolled pole.

'Stefan, hey Stefan!'

They both looked up together as Piotr and a girl with long blonde hair and fur around her neck and cuffs, came over to the table. Stefan stood up, perhaps a little reluctantly, Rozia thought.

'Veronika,' he said and kissed the girl on her cheek.

'Come and join us,' she said.

'Yes,' said Piotr, 'come on.'

'No, we are fine,' Stefan replied.

'But there are Jews round here,' Veronika pouted. 'They should not come into our cafés, they should stay in their own areas.'

The man with the newspaper made no movement; Rozia looked at him, wanting to take his hand, but instead she stood up from the table. Tears were coming but she held them back, angry at her weakness. She had been so happy – what right had they to take it away from her? But she said nothing, just turned and walked out of the café. As soon as she reached the door, she began to run, she didn't know where – just away, away from them all; she hated them, even Stefan.

'Rozia!'

She heard his voice, but she didn't stop. Let him go back to his own people – she would have to cope as best she could.

'Rozia, stop. I love you.'

What was that? What had he said? Little rivulets of water ran down her cheeks, a mouth was kissing them away, licking them.

'I love you,' he repeated, pulling her into a quiet court-yard.

He touched her forehead; his hands moved to her temples, caressing the skin, and his fingers slipped into her hair, twisting the locks. Rozia shut her eyes and let her lips open; his tongue slipped into her mouth and she felt her arms encircle his neck. Their bodies curled into each other and Rozia felt his hand on her breast. She pulled away.

'No,' she pleaded.

'I'm sorry,' he said, hot and flushed.

They walked a little. Their feet moved in tandem, their

arms around each other. They didn't speak, there was no need.

'It isn't going to be easy,' Stefan said finally.

'Do you want it to stop?' Rozia asked, her heart was beating wildly – could he hear it?

'No. We'll change them, all of them.'

Rozia touched his hair, her fingers enjoyed the sensation. She smiled at him, into him. 'And it will change us too,' she told him, feeling very much older.

Stefan nodded. Rozia offered him her mouth and he took it, biting, fondling, moving his hands over her slim body, and when his hand reached for her breast again, she arched up to him.

'I love you,' she whispered.

The air was soft; the stars seemed to twinkle extra brightly, and Rozia knew they shone for her and Stefan – it was a night for lovers.

They walked back to Marshalkowska and Rozia saw Shosha and Mordechai by the tram stop.

'They are waiting for me,' she said, pointing to where her two friends stood. Rozia put her hand on Stefan's shoulder, and he kissed her lightly.

'Remember we love each other,' he said.

As she ran towards Shosha and Mordechai, Rozia knew Stefan was watching her. She wondered how he felt actually seeing her for the first time with her own kind.

As Stefan watched her greet the young couple, he was shocked at the gap between his world and Rozia's. There was no touching point between him and the black-suited young man who put his head so close to hers. He had always disliked Jews like him; somehow they looked dirty. They kept their eyes to the ground, and mixed only with their own kind, calling themselves the chosen people. Chosen for what? After all, they did murder Christ. But now he, Stefan Gordanski, was in love with one of them, totally in love.

He walked back to his home off Marshalkowska, thinking about his mother. The widow of a colonel in the Polish army, Sonia Gordanska had once been beautiful, but now she was too round and a little faded. His uncle was with her as often as propriety would allow. Their relationship was well known, but no one judged them. They behaved respectably and neither offended nor excited anybody. As Stefan reached the courtyard of his house, typical of middle-class Warsaw with attractive fascias and a caretaker, he realized that his own relationship, because it was with a Jewish girl, would not be treated as leniently.

Chapter Three

$\blacklozenge$

The following morning Rozia arrived at the little fountain earlier than usual. She was nervous, wondering if Stefan would be there. The evening before, when she had turned to wave at him after crossing Marshalkowska, she had seen his face clearly visible in the white glare of the street-lamps. He looked like a ghost, she had thought, suddenly shivering.

Mordechai said, 'Is that him?' and she had nodded, proud of her beautiful young man, full of his love.

'Why doesn't he wave at you?' he asked, his voice soft, almost compassionate, and his tone had worried her.

'What do you mean?' She knew she sounded sharp.

'Even I wave at my Shosha,' Mordechai told her.

She had turned back to Stefan, who was walking away, his shoulders hunched. She could not avoid the unbidden fear that now he had seen her with her own kind he might not like her as much. She shrugged then, pushing the thought away – well, if he didn't, then she wouldn't like him. But later, during that night, as she lay in her part of Shosha's bed, hearing the deep, even breathing, she wished that Stefan didn't mean so much to her because she didn't know how she would survive if he could not accept her Jewishness. It was funny, she had always thought of herself as Rozia, a Polish girl who was Jewish; but when he had walked away without even waving at her she suddenly realized that perhaps he saw Rozia, a Jewish girl. She didn't like it. In the dark she looked at Shosha's curls lying so close to her; she touched them, feeling their surprising softness, and Rozia Mezeurska wanted to cry.

As she waited in the weak autumn sun, her stomach was taut with expectation. She put her hand in the fountain, but the water was cold so she made no ripples with her fingers. She glanced at the little watch pinned to her blouse and realized that Stefan should have been there by then. She walked a little, looking this way and that – still no Stefan. He must have been delayed, but then perhaps he had decided he wanted no more to do with her. There was a pain too intense for tears. She walked away from the fountain and across the square, neither looking out for the traffic nor caring if she stumbled. So he was like the others, just like the others. Blindly she pushed through a group of students, slowly registering that someone was calling her name.

'Rozia, Rozia, come here, over here, now.'

She turned on her heel and saw Joanna waving anxiously. She looked quizzically at her and then registered that her friend was distressed. Something had happened to Stefan, something bad – she suddenly felt very frightened, but she could no more run to Joanna than she could have flown, because her feet were rooted to the ground as if by nails.

'Rozia, there you are. Stefan has gone to the prison to try to see them. I told him it was foolish, but he said he must try.'

Robert was talking to her, holding her by her shoulder. Stefan was all right, he had gone to the prison, to see them. Who? Who had he gone to see?

'What has happened?' she said, her voice sounding normal, no longer hurting.

'Alekander and Wanda. They were arrested last night.'

'Alekander and Wanda?' Rozia heard herself repeat. She knew she sounded stupid and she shook her head, trying to make herself more coherent. 'Why were they arrested?'

'The big strike in Krakow – they're pulling people in, looking for agitators.'

'Wanda isn't an agitator,' Rozia snapped. She was very

angry. Suddenly she saw all the small kindnesses that Wanda had shown her, like photographs being flashed in front of her, one after the other.

'Yes, I'm afraid she is. Apparently her job was to recruit members for a terrorist group – at least that is what the police are saying,' Joanna interjected.

'And Alekander, he can't be involved. He is too interested in women.' Rozia's anger was stilled for a moment – whilst incredulity took over.

'Alekander was or rather is the group leader. The business of flirting, the way he was, it was all a façade to delude us. Wanda was the gullible one.'

Joanna put her arms around Rozia. 'It's such a shock to find out what someone is really like; to realize they have been lying about themselves.'

The photographs in Rozia's mind changed to Shosha and Mordechai – and to Stefan walking away.

She didn't see Stefan until the break; she was sitting in the refectory with Jan, Robert and Joanna. They were quiet; worried for their friends' safety, but mostly shocked at their own naivety. Communism was not a comfortable bedfellow in Warsaw in the twenties; world domination was the avowed aim of Moscow, and the Poles believed they had stopped the flow westward when they repelled the Russion invasion in 1920, but even the Socialists worried about subversion from within.

'We all know that in Poland two people meeting over a table can mean three different political views,' Robert said suddenly, breaking the silence.

'What is that supposed to mean?' Jan asked.

'Just that we all have different ideas as to how to solve our problems – sometimes I worry that the differences between us are too great.'

'When our friends are sent to prison for something they didn't do, I worry too,' Jan said.

'How do you know they didn't?' Rozia heard Joanna say, but she did not hear who answered, nor what was said, for Stefan was walking across the refectory. He was tired, she could see that, but his eyes meeting hers told her there was no rejection for her, just the joy of blessed love.

Piotr stopped him as he reached their table. 'Your uncle would not be happy at your involvement with these anarchists and Jews.'

'Alekander and Wanda are not Jews, nor, Piotr, are they anarchists. They are not even to be tried – they are leaving Poland to go to Russia.' Stefan's sarcasm was undisguised.

'Then certainly they will be comfortable there with all those Jews.' Piotr's voice was loud.

Stefan's voice was low, but it carried across the refectory. 'I think your disaste for Jews should be kept to yourself, if you wish to remain a friend of mine, It's insulting to my Jewish girlfriend.' He pushed Piotr out the way, and Rozia got up, almost falling over herself in her haste to reach her prince.

Rozia and Stefan were a couple, and even when they were apart they thought of themselves as a pair, sitting and dreaming, imagining the other, building their shape so it grew like a phoenix, overshadowing the loneliness of being separated.

Rozia told him that she now truly understood what Plato meant in *Symposium*, when he said that humans were male and female before the gods split them in two.

'I think,' she said, 'that we live in a half stage and that being in love is trying to get back to our half, so that we become whole again.'

'I am whole when I am with you,' Stefan said seriously. 'Without you, I am cut and bleeding.'

Even though the weather became cold, they would walk

in coats, gloves and boots, and would go to the Palace on the Island in the Lazienki Park and there, under the benign eyes of the trees, their fingers would take liberties beneath the protective outer garments.

Rozia was alive, Rozia was in love. She sparkled, sprinkling happiness like drops of magic wherever she went. Robert, Jan and Joanna enjoyed their happiness, letting the magic rub off on them, making them joyful too. Her parents, Shosha and Booba, they all saw it, but they didn't see it; they didn't want to.

Professor Oberski seemed impressed with her. Often during his lectures she would feel his eyes on her, and when he came to the students' laboratories to examine their work, he gave her the odd encouragement and Rozia was flattered. She responded to him, not in her old little-girl cajoling way, but with pleasure. Rozia in love was a woman.

Once, when Rozia was sitting alone in the laboratory continuing with an experiment after the other students had already left, she was so absorbed in her little bottles, measuring and calculating, that she didn't hear Dr Oberski come into the room.

'Miss Mezeurska – you are still here. Why are you not going to your home?' he said.

'I am meeting a friend in an hour,' she told him, unaware that even her voice was in a lower key than it used to be. 'And so I decided to carry on with my work.'

'What are you doing?'

'A quantitative analysis of copper sulphate.'

'Ah, can I see your results?'

Dr Oberski assessed Rozia's neat handwriting.

'Excellent,' he said, 'excellent.'

He sat down in the seat opposite her, which was normally occupied by a fellow student who never spoke to her and always brought a piece of ham to eat whilst he worked.

'You want to be a chemist?'

'I want to do physical chemistry,' Rozia told him. 'When will I be able to combine that with my current studies?'

'In about two years' time – perhaps a little sooner, we shall see how you progress.'

He paused for a moment. 'Your parents must be very proud of you. It isn't usual for a girl from your background to go on to higher education.'

Rozia realized that the words 'from your background' were said without malice, and she did not take offence. 'I am ambitious,' she replied.

'And marriage?'

Rozia blushed. 'Why not?'

There was a small silence. Dr Oberski brushed some of the little pieces of that day's ham into his hand and dropped them into a wastepaper basket.

'Does your wife work?' Rozia asked, realizing that she was being forward; one did not normally engage one's professor in small talk.

'No, I am not married, so I have no impediments to my work. Really my only interest outside of chemistry is music, so I think it could be a little boring for a woman. I used to ride – when I was young – but not now.' He raised himself out of his seat. 'Well, I will excuse myself now.' He bowed and kissed the inside of her wrist. She was charmed by the gesture and as she watched him leave the room, wondered if he was lonely.

That evening when she got home, flushed from kissing and touching, hot from running because she knew she was late, her mother, barely managing to keep the irritation at Rozia's tardiness from her voice, informed her that her cousin Molka was getting married.

'He's marrying Leah Kleeman. Her father is a very rich man,' Hannah informed her daughter. 'The wedding is in three weeks' time. If you can manage to fit it in with your studies and your new life, perhaps you could manage not to disgrace your parents and not only be there, but be there on time. They have invited Leah's cousin from Switzerland especially for you.'

Rozia suppressed a smile. She wanted to put her arms around her mother, to share her happiness with her, but she knew that Hannah would never understand her loving a Christian boy – Papa was different, Papa would understand, but suddenly she wished her mother was more approachable, and she put her arm around Hannah's surprisingly slim waist.

'Of course I will be there, but I am not sure that I will like the Swiss man.'

'I understand that he is charming,' Hannah said, slightly mollified by her show of affection. She had sensed a change in Rozia since she had gone to the University and it worried her, but perhaps the thought of an introduction might just add a sparkle to her daughter's life. It must be hard, Hannah mused, not only to study, but to do so without her or Samuel's encouragement. She stroked Rozia's beautiful long hair; she was tenacious that daughter of hers – she could fight. Hannah wished she was like Rozia – is that what happens when we get older, she thought, we wish we were like our daughters? She felt great love for her at that moment.

Hannah's preparations for the family wedding were little short of those in Leah Kleeman's house. Clothes were washed and pressed, suits were brushed, and Jonathon had to have a new one. To their mother's horror and Rozia's great amusement, he had grown three inches since his bar mitzvah and no cajoling or stretching of material could coax more length from his trousers or jacket.

Rozia had a new dress, despite the fact that the crimson velvet she had worn for Yom Kippur was this season's. It was royal blue silk, cut in a modern style, reaching just to the ankle with long sleeves and a stitched panel at the waist, emphasized by a tiny belt and two flat bows. It was beautiful and Rozia knew it suited her. She took her hair up and folded it into a loose chignon; as she pinned it in place she didn't envy Joanna's short modern haircut. She swirled in front of the mirror and wished that Stefan could see her, wished that she was dressed for him. There had been talk that week of the New Year's Eve ball to be held at the Town Hall; most of the students were going, but Stefan had said nothing. Rozia allowed herself to hope that she might wear her dress for him at New Year's Eve; she told herself that this occasion was just a dress rehearsal for paradise.

It snowed on the day of the wedding. The Mezeurski women in their finery clicked their tongues and waited whilst Jonathon was despatched to find a droshki.

By the time they arrived at the Kleeman flat, located in a pleasant building near Grzybow Place, the snow had formed a carpet of white. Rozia pulled her coat closer and worried about her kid shoes, especially purchased for the wedding. She should have put on something more sensible for the journey, but vanity hadn't allowed for sense.

The bridal canopy dominated the salon which had been cleared of furniture for the occasion. Its rich velvet hangings were carefully embroidered in gold thread. The family group divided, as custom dictated, the men to one side, the women to the other. Some of the guests were dressed in the ritual clothes of the Chassidim, for Leah's father, as well as being a banker of some repute, was a rabbinical scholar and traditionalist. Others were dressed as their non-Jewish compatriots might have been, but all of them were united in the celebration of the happiest of events. Molka was dragged to his place under the canopy; it was form that he should protest and shout and cry because it was considered befitting for a bridegroom to appear unwilling. After a moment the bride was led in by her mother and her mother-in-law.

Rozia looked at her simple white dress and tumbling

black curls. Would they be cut as ritual decreed after the ceremony? Looking at Mrs Kleeman's absurd wig, Rozia was sure that Leah would be shorn.

The mother and mother-in-law carried long candles and walked the bride around her groom seven times, as if offering her for view. Rozia had seen it all before, but now she viewed it differently; by loving a boy who wasn't Jewish, she could no longer appreciate such rituals, for they would have no part in her future. She thought of Stefan and her cheeks burned, her breasts felt heavy with wanting. She looked at the bride and wondered if she had allowed her groom to even kiss her cheek. Rozia knew that after the ceremony the couple would be escorted to a room where they would consummate the marriage, accompanied by jokes and music and laughter from the assembled guests who would await behind the closed doors for the bloodstained sheet that would tell them the bride was a virgin. Did Leah long for that moment as Rozia now longed for Stefan? Half fearful and half wanton she filled her mind with visions of his lips on her breasts, of his hand between her legs, touching her, rubbing her.

'It's beautiful, isn't it?' Shosha's voice sounded unnaturally loud in her ears. She turned to her friend and saw that her eyes were shining.

'It will be you and Mordechai next,' Rozia said almost sadly.

After the ceremony the ritual chaffing began.

'Rozia, how are you? Still studying at the University? Filling your head with such things – a Jewish girl only needs to know how to make a home, to look after her man – isn't that right, Samuel?'

Rozia felt her father's hand in her hair, and for the first time Papa's princess squirmed at such a touch in public.

'My Rozia – she is doing magnificently. Her professor thinks she is the best pupil.'

'Papa, we have not yet had our assessments. I don't know what Dr Oberski feels.'

'Nonsense, the professor himself told me . . .'

Rozia listened to the words, and for the first time realized he was lying, for she knew that her father had never come to the University. But his friends could not know that, so they listened, as she had once done. Now she understood the implications of her love for Stefan: she was a stranger, she was the outsider. She picked up her small handbag, searched for her coat, buttoning it securely at the neck. She wouldn't have bothered to tell anyone she was leaving, but Jonathon saw her.

'Where are you going?' he asked.

'Tell them I have to finish an experiment,' she mumbled.

'You can't. You are about to be introduced to that one,' he said, pointing to a smiling boy, thickset with a full beard and the side curls of an orthodox Jew; Rozia noticed that his silk coat fitted as if it had been made for him and his full hat was thick with luscious fur, and then she remembered that he was the rich one from Switzerland. She thought he looked ridiculous in his clothes from another era, with his obvious religious taboos – he nauseated her. She could not bear to even look at him. She shook her head, shuddered and ran from the celebrations out into the cold. The streets were blanketed in a white embrace that softened harsh angles but froze gentle waters.

'I won't be able to make little waves any more,' she said to herself as she ran along, thinking of the fountain and her moments there with Stefan.

She found Stefan at their café. He was with Jan and Robert. She didn't speak, smiled at them all, and offered Stefan her hand. He excused them both and they went to their little Palace. There, protected from prying eyes by the trees and the cold, Rozia opened herself to him. As Stefan came into her she winced a little, but then lost herself in the

66

sheer joy of feeling him inside her. They rode together, clinging and touching and whispering and crying, holding on to the love they wanted to give each other.

Afterwards Rozia cried a little as Stefan held her close.

'If only we didn't have to be separated at Christmas,' he whispered into her hair, trying to warm her body with his.

'What happens at Christmas?' she asked, feeling strange at even saying the name.

'We don't eat the day before, on Christmas Eve. As a child I used to get very hungry, but in the evening we have a buffet of at least twelve dishes. After the meal we sing Christmas carols and open our presents and then we go to Mass, at midnight. I will light a candle to the Virgin Mary and thank her for bringing you to me. After all she was a Jewess – wasn't Christ born a Jew? So we are not so different after all.'

Rozia pulled Stefan closer, she felt him touch her there, between her legs.

As he came back into her, he said, 'After the holiday I shall come and see your father, and I will tell him that I love you, and if he feels for you even half as much as I do, he will help us; he will understand.'

And Rozia was completely happy, because she knew how much her father loved her.

Later, before they parted she asked, 'New Year's Eve, where will you be?'

'Krakow with my uncle's family. We always spend Christmas with them.' He didn't tell her of the threats, of the coercion when he had said that he didn't want to leave Warsaw, or more particularly Rozia over the holiday.

'This Jewish girl is no good for you. The Jews are different, her father will never accept you,' his uncle had said, barely concealing a fury born of self-interest. Piotr's father had expressed such displeasure at Stefan's choice of a girl-friend that it worried the lawyer.

Rozia said nothing, but Stefan could see the dismay, and he remembered the talk of the dance.

'But I will come back, if you want me to,' he said.

'I want you to,' Rozia admitted quietly, wondering how she would manage to excuse herself for the whole evening.

Chapter Four

———— ◆ ————

The Christmas vacation seemed eternal to Rozia. Her mother would scarcely speak to her. Her absence from the wedding had 'caused a small fracas' according to Jonathon who had recounted every moment with enormous pleasure. Rozia had giggled at the thought of the overstuffed boy in the silk coat, waiting for the sacrificial lamb to be presented for his inspection, but the sacrificial lamb was nowhere to be seen. The tongues clicked, Hannah cried, Booba tried not to laugh and even Samuel had seemed embarrassed.

Rozia managed to placate him. 'How could I meet someone like that, Papa? I felt like an animal about to be bought.'

'Marriage is not conducted like that,' he said.

'For me it seemed as if I was to be perused and then bought.'

'You would have perused too.'

Samuel was gentle then, understanding his Rozia's fears. She was too young for marriage – just a child – he couldn't understand Hannah's haste; he must caution her not to judge Rozia from the way she looked – which he had to admit was like a mature young lady – for of course she was still a child, as she had proved by her unseemly exit from the wedding.

Rozia agonized over New Year's Eve; how should she approach her parents? At first she thought she would ask them directly, but after her behaviour at the wedding, they would hardly countenance her going to a Christian ball. Shosha had to be the answer.

At first Shosha hadn't wanted to be involved in yet another deception, so Rozia had confided her magnificent secret.

'Oh Rozia, how can you be so immodest, and with a Christian boy?' she had said.

'If you love your Mordechai, how can you ask that question?' Rozia answered her softly.

They had been friends since they were small children, sharing their innermost feelings only with each other and, sensing Shosha's deep anxiety, Rozia leaned over and smoothed the undisciplined, wiry curls back from her forehead. Suddenly she felt years older. 'If you love someone, then no rules or barriers can stop what you feel,' she said.

'I am so afraid for you,' Shosha whispered, holding Rozia tightly in her arms.

'Why? Nothing can hurt me. I have Stefan.'

Confronted by such a confident love, Shosha agreed that Rozia could stay the night on New Year's Eve.

'It is fortunate that we are not on the telephone,' she shouted to Rozia's retreating, dancing figure, almost flying down the street with happiness that she had solved her difficulty.

'Shosha has asked me to stay the night again,' she said airily that evening. Her mother, still piqued at her behaviour but a little calmed now that her husband had spoken to her, merely nodded. Rozia sighed with relief, but when she raised her eyes from her sewing – a button had come off her white blouse – she smiled to herself and then averted her eyes very quickly from her grandmother's penetrating glance.

She smuggled her blue dress out of the apartment the day before New Year's Eve; the shoes would be hidden in her nightclothes.

At last the waiting was nearly over – tomorrow night she would be with Stefan. She knew that she would not sleep – her mind was playing such delicious tricks. She curled up under the covers, feeling their weight on her, and she hugged herself, remembering his touch, his smell. She turned her head into the pillow, burying herself in its softness, imagining all kinds of pleasures; but then she sighed and flung herself on her back, her arms covering her face. She could hear Booba's snores and they didn't allow any room for fantasy.

Finally it was daybreak and she could get out of bed and go into the bathroom. She pulled off her nightgown and looked down at her body. She thought her nipples looked a little pinker, bigger too; she touched them and they were sore, but they tingled. They seemed to be asking for Stefan's mouth and his fingers. She ran her hands down over her flat stomach and cupped herself between her legs. The thought of him made her flex her thighs.

She fulfilled as few of the morning pleasantries as possible, ignoring the breakfast table and the murmurs of concern when she refused to eat. She couldn't have digested any food anyway, because her stomach felt as if it was in her mouth. The delightful anticipation of seeing her lover was playing havoc with her normal functions. She went to the toilet three times before she finally managed to extradite herself from her mother's protestations.

She left the apartment at lunchtime.

'Be careful, Rozia, the Christians are celebrating their New Year. It is an excuse for drink, so do not be alone on the streets,' her father had warned her before he left for his work.

'Don't worry,' she told him, 'I will be absolutely safe.'

It had been arranged that Shosha would walk her to Joanna's home where Rozia would change for the evening. Stefan and Robert would collect the two girls later. Shosha would go to Mordechai.

'What will you do?' Rozia asked.

'Talk and . . .' Shosha stopped, embarrassed.

'So I am changing you too!' she said gaily.

'Yes. I am not sure if it is a good thing.' Shosha's voice was sharp.

71

Rozia glanced at her, suddenly nervous – her friend had never been so assertive.

'I will return home and tell my parents you have a headache and are staying with Deborah,' Shosha continued, but her voice still had an edge. 'Fortunately for you, Deborah doesn't have a telephone either. This is the last time, Rozia, that I will do this for you.'

Rozia nodded, she felt the chastisement and it hurt her. By now they had reached Joanna's home.

'Will you come in?' she asked Shosha, noticing the scarf drawn tightly over the white face, the black curls popping here and there from under the wool, the brown coat a little small over the many sweaters that she wore to insulate her against the cold. Shosha shook her head, and Rozia reached over and kissed her cheek.

'I don't mind about the boy, Rozia,' her friend said softly. 'I mind about the lying.'

Shosha's face stayed with Rozia until Stefan, cold from the night air, took her in his arms, kissing her and holding her, even creasing her dress. She wriggled a little, not wanting it spoilt before she made her entrance to the ball.

'I've missed you,' he said.

'I've longed for you,' she said, unashamed of her passion.

In the dark of Joanna's hall he touched her breast lightly, his fingers tracing patterns over her nipples. She bit her lip; they felt so sore, as they always did before her period, but she didn't want him to know, she didn't want him to stop. She could have pressed closer but this time she was mindful of the blue dress.

Joanna wore green. She looked pretty – Robert told her so, with generous compliments. Rozia felt the colour was a little hard, but she would never have told her so. She had hugged her after she zipped up Joanna's dress, and said that it was the happiest night of her life.

Rozia sparkled, like the icicles that hung from the roofs

– pointed and sharp; they were dangerous, but Rozia wasn't dangerous, she was in love. She danced in the snow, not caring that her pretty shoes were stained and torn.

'Wait until we get there,' Stefan said, twirling her around and around, overjoyed to be with her.

There had been no objection to him leaving Krakow early for the New Year's Eve ball.

His mother had said, 'The Jews won't let one of their girls go out alone with a Christian boy, so why shouldn't he go? Maybe he will meet someone else.' She had fluttered her eyelids in the way his uncle liked. Stefan would have hugged her if he hadn't seen a fat arm around her shoulders.

The music flooded Rozia's senses, she who had learned to dance only as a child floated with her prince, feeling him close, leaning on him, loving him.

'Let's walk,' he said, 'for a while.'

'To the Island,' Rozia whispered.

'No, we won't be able to get into the park – it will be closed,' he whispered back. 'But we will find somewhere.'

He grabbed a bottle of wine and put it into his coat pocket and together they weaved through the crowds, their hips barely touching yet moving in perfect symmetry, as if they were one.

Outside in the crisp cold air, they saw Piotr and his friends. There was a Jew, an old Jew. Piotr had pushed him up against a tree; he was laughing at him, pulling his beard.

'No!' Whose voice was that? Was it Rozia's?

She saw a group of Zionists – she knew it was them because they didn't creep like the apologetic Jew of the Diaspora; they swaggered, proud and powerful. One of them pulled Piotr off the old man. Piotr's friends stopped their catcalling – a fight, good, a fight, blood – Jewish blood would feel good on New Year's Eve.

Rozia felt Stefan go from her; she tried to hold him back, her hands sticky with sweat clawed at his arm. 'I've got to try and stop them,' he said, and then he was gone. She saw it all. She saw one of the Jews hit him, she saw the bottle smash as he fell to the ground, the wine run red. Piotr took a piece of glass and advanced like a prowling, vicious animal; a Jew, blond like Stefan, picked up another piece. Piotr hit the Jew – he fell on top of Stefan – his fist aiming straight for the nearest Polish flesh. In the bright lights of Warsaw's New Year's Eve, Rozia saw the diamond-shaped piece of glass clasped in the Jewish boy's hand, she saw rich red blood as it spurted up like a fountain. Was it blood-red wine? She saw the fighting stop, the protagonists, like puppets with their strings hanging loose – all of them were still, except for the one who lay on the white snow – blood, the wine of his life, draining from him.

'No!' Whose voice was that? Was it Rozia's?

She ran then, pushing, shoving them out of her way for the one who lay on the snow; reaching him, feeling him, cradling him.

'My God!' someone said.

She felt his blood drench her, pouring over her thighs as she gently held his poor broken body on her lap, his life ebbing away.

'I love you, Stefan,' she whispered. 'Stay still – someone will get a doctor.'

His mouth moved, but there was no sound. His hand raised, his fingers touched her lips and then he was gone. She held him, pulling his face into her breasts, waiting to feel his lips against her nipples, but there was nothing.

She felt someone reaching for her, saying, 'Rozia, Rozia.'

'Nooooo.' Whose voice was that? Was it Rozia's?

Someone was taking him away from her, she could feel them lifting his head out of her arms.

'Nooooo.' Whose voice was that? Was it hers?

Where was the joy? It had gone and now there was only pain, no more gossamer wings, just black shrouds of despair.

'Stefan!'

Rozia's voice cried out into the air, but there was no sound; there was nothing but the feeling of utter devastation. Blinded by tears that wouldn't come, she held out her hand in front of her. She could count the fingers, she could cut them, but she would feel nothing.

'Stefan . . .'

Now the sound came, terrible in its anguish. Someone tried to hold her but she pushed them away, fighting them off, clawing their skin as if they were attacking her.

She ran to a square, to a tree that might have witnessed their love and clung to its bark, holding on to it as if it were Stefan. She sobbed into it, scratching her face on its surface. She slipped down on to the hard-packed snow and cried for her Stefan, wanting to suffocate in her tears. She didn't understand the reality of his death; she couldn't absorb the finality, but she knew she didn't fly any more. She dug her hands into the white mass not even feeling the pain of the cold. She was demented in her grief, torn by her sorrow.

'The Virgin Mary was a Jewess . . .' She heard the voice, Stefan's voice. 'I will light a candle to her . . .'

Rozia suddenly knew what she must do. She must light a candle too, she would pray for help. The enormity of her feelings swamped her. Gasping for air she got up, ran her tear- and bloodstained hands over her face and her ears to stop the sound of the bells chiming to a New Year, and went as quickly as she could to the nearest church. She pushed open the door, feeling slightly apprehensive – she had never been to the Christians' place before.

She diverted her eyes from the big gold cross and the twisted body that hung from it and searched only for the Lady who was a Jewess. Unaware that eyes watched her, she walked over to a statue of the Virgin. There were candles burning underneath it. Rozia took one and, unsure of what to do, placed it in an empty container. She looked for a taper, but there wasn't one, so she took the candle out again and lit it from one of the others. Her mother always held her hands over the candles when she blessed them for the Sabbath, should she do the same? She didn't know. She began to cry, realizing that she would never feel Stefan's warmth again. The boy who had danced with her – holding, teasing, loving – had been crushed in the snow. The pain washed over her again, bringing with it almost a nausea.

A hand was on her shoulder, but she didn't even jump.

'My child, what has happened?'

'Oh, I am sorry, shouldn't I . . .?' She was confused. It was wrong for her to be in a church, but somehow she had to be, for Stefan's sake.

'It is all right. If you want to talk to God, you can and then – if I can help . . .'

Rozia didn't see the priest's eyes as they took in the horror of the blood that stained her.

'The Lady – she was a Jewess too. I thought she would help me.'

'Help you?'

'Yes. You see my friend is . . . my friend is . . .' She couldn't say the word.

And suddenly there was another voice, inexplicably familiar.

'It's all right, Father, I will take care of her. She is one of my students, her friend has been killed.'

'May God have mercy,' the priest said quietly.

'Killed . . . dead . . . gone . . .' Rozia spoke the words slowly, savouring them, finally understanding their irrevocability.

'Nooooo . . .' The wall of a keening woman, the anguish of mourning. She fainted.

When Rozia regained consciousness, she found that she was sitting on the floor with her head between her legs and a strong sickly smell eeking through her nostrils. She pulled away from the hands that held her. She didn't know where she was, her head was turning – there was black and then there were lights, golden lights like a thousand candles dancing in front of her eyes. She didn't want to look at them, the lights blinded her. She heard the sound of a small thing falling to the ground and her eyes centred on the noise. She focused. She saw that it was a small pot of incense. Then she saw the cross and remembered. There was horrible pain where once there had been happiness. She squeezed her hands together and wrung them as if she were drying out an old piece of fabric.

'Rozia, are you all right?'

She heard Dr Oberski's voice but she didn't look at him. She wanted her Papa. She wanted to tell him; he would understand.

'Can I go home, please?' she asked.

'Of course.'

Dr Oberski helped her into his car and drove her back to her parents' apartment. She burst in through the door and ran straight to her father. He held her tight without speaking, just caressing the long auburn hair over and over again. After a little while he took her arms from his neck and pushed her away a little.

'Come, calm yourself. Go to Mama. I will speak with your professor. Everything will be all right.'

He passed her to Hannah who cuddled and cradled her and took her to a warm bed with a hot drink of milk, honey and egg. She sipped it, feeling the warmth go through her – but it couldn't touch the stone inside where her heart should have been. She slept then, fitfully . . . she was running, looking for Stefan and he was there, just ahead of her, but always out of reach.

She woke exhausted. She sat up in her bed and buried her head in her hands.

'You are awake.' Her mother was sitting on the other side

of the bedroom. Rozia nodded and looked at her mother. She expected to be held and comforted, but Hannah did not make a move; she stayed where she was on the other side of the room.

'Dr Oberski has told us of your friendship with this boy. A Christian, I understand. Rozia, how could you do this to us? When we saw you we thought you had been hurt in the riot. Instead, you have been so deceitful. Papa has cried.'

'My love is dead . . . he is dead . . . do you understand?' Rozia shouted. She was demented, hysterical. How could her mother speak of her being deceitful when her love was dead?

'I have told Papa that there is no question of your going back to the University, and he agrees with me. You will go to stay with your cousins in Germany and whilst you are away, we will arrange a match. The sooner you are married the better.'

'Arrange a marriage?' Rozia could not believe what she was hearing. How could her mother imagine that she could contemplate a marriage after Stefan had bled to death in her arms, his blood running out of him, over her – a marriage was unthinkable! She knew Papa would never agree to this; he would understand. She pulled herself out of her bed and ran on trembling legs down the corridor, shouting for her Papa. She found him, sitting in near darkness in the salon.

'You see, my Rozia, what your deceptions have done?' he said as she came into the room. 'I couldn't even go into the office.'

'But Papa,' she said, coming to sit at his feet, her little white face the colour of her nightgown, looking up at his. 'What about my pain, my hurt? I have lost the one person I loved.' She held on to his feet, staring into the precious face.

'After he had tried to kill a Jew?'

'No!' Rozia cried. 'No, he was trying to stop the fight.

The man jumped on him when he was down – cut him.' Her tears came again; the pain was too much. 'The blood spurted from him and he died in my arms – Papa, they killed him.'

'An accident, the authorities agree, an accident. Rozia, Rozia, you will get over it, it is a passion – nothing else.'

'No. I will not get over it, because I love him and he loves me. You cannot make me get married. I am his and his alone. I belong to Stefan.'

Mr Mezeurski looked at his daughter slowly, his face contorted into a grimace. The features that Rozia loved so much, the soft brown eyes, the crinkled skin, the neat beard, the trimmed moustache, assumed a mask-like quality.

'Do I understand you?' he said, standing up, towering over her in a rage of distress and disbelief.

Rozia pulled her shoulders tight. 'You understand me,' she said quietly.

'Do you know what you are saying?' the half-strangled voice said.

'Yes,' replied the girl who once found it difficult to lie.

'Then you have shamed me and you are dead to me. Go to the Christians . . . Go . . . that is what you want.'

'Papa!' Rozia pleaded, unable to recognize the man who stood in front of her, his arm half raised as if he were going to strike her. 'Papa, please, I hurt.' She held her arms out, begging.

'You are dead.'

And the eyes that had looked upon her with so much love clouded over, and the light went out of them. They were steel; no warmth, no softness, no love – love was dead.

'Go!' he said, pointing to the door.

As Rozia got up from the floor, she saw her weeping mother.

'Mama!' she said, putting her arm on her mother's

shoulder. She saw the woman who once was Mama physically shudder.

She went to her room and dragged out a bag. Numb, unable to feel, she threw her clothes and her books into it. She pulled off her dressing gown and put on some clean outdoor clothes. She brushed her hair automatically.

'Rozia, what's happening?'

Jonathon was in her room, holding her close, whispering to her: 'I love you, don't go, I love you.'

'Jonathon, Jonathon,' Rozia whispered back, holding her brother.

'Go, Jonathon — back to your room, now.'

Booba, Booba, iron Booba was standing in the doorway. But Booba was not iron, she was crying. Booba did not recoil, she held her.

'You would have no life here, my child. You have set the die, now follow it. Go to Dr Oberski. Here, here is money — all the money I have. He will take care of you. I will pray for you.'

'I don't know where he lives.'

'I asked for his address; I knew what would happen.'

'Booba, I'm frightened.'

'I know, and so am I; we are dead without you. You were the spark, Rozia, you were the joy, the love, and without you there is nothing . . .'

'Jonathon!' Rozia said wildly. 'I must see Jonathon.'

'No, it will not be possible.'

Booba was kissing her, and pushing her to the door at the same time. Rozia could taste the salt from her tears.

'Jonathon,' she screamed.

'Rozia, Rozia, I want Rozia,' the boy shouted from behind the door that was held shut by his mother.

'Please,' Rozia cried. 'My brother, let me —'

'You have no brother,' the mother replied.

'She does, she does,' Jonathon screamed.

'Go, Rozia,' Booba said, holding her tight. 'What can you accomplish by staying? You will break his heart if you try to see him. Go. Go.'

And then the door was shut. The man who had been Papa was saying the prayer for the dead, and the woman who had been Mama was screaming. Rozia leaned against the door, listening for Booba and Jonathon – but there was no sound. Wearily she picked up her bag and carried it down the stairs. She walked to Dr Oberski's apartment. Her pains were so great that, when he opened the door, she just looked at him mutely. He nodded as he pulled his door wide open to let her in.

Dr Oberski made her some tea, English style with milk, and he offered her a few cakes set out neatly on a plate. She declined the cakes, but she did drink the tea. She noticed that he had been listening to some records on a gramophone. Another day she might have been interested, because she didn't know anyone who had a gramophone, but today, on the day of deaths, she could only register the title of a book which seemed to stand out from the many stacked untidily on his bookshelves: *Tristan and Isult* . . . doomed lovers. She felt the tears start again. Stefan was dead . . . she would never touch him again. And Papa, her Papa . . . that hurt was beyond tolerability. Her mind closed in on itself; she could not, perhaps would not, absorb the pain.

She was alone, totally alone in the world.

That was the reality she had to accept. Booba had given her money, but where would she go, what would she do? She would have to ask Dr Oberski to help her. Perhaps he would know of some rooms . . . somehow she had to go on, to survive. She tried not to think of Stefan, it was too painful. But his memory surrounded her; how he had held her when they had last been together . . . she relived their lovemaking, recreating every last detail in her mind, allowing her hands to touch the places he had touched, opening her mouth as if to receive his kisses. Her body cried out for him – but he was not there, he would never be there again. She saw him again and again lying on the road. She saw the boy on top of him, the glass in his hand – a Jew – a Jew had killed her Stefan, and she knew with a sudden terrible clarity that she hated them. A small part of Rozia rationally tried to remind her that all of them, Piotr and his friends, had really been responsible – they had attacked an innocent old man – but her grief and pain told her that Stefan was dead – dead because of the Jews. She thought of her father and his implacable rage, and with no other outlet for her furious sorrow, she consciously rejected her Judaism. She told herself that it was the separateness imposed by the Jews that had annihilated her life. It marked their tribe as 'chosen' – different from others, and those outside resented that distinction. Rozia understood them, for now she too was an outsider.

And so, in her loneliness and grief she used her faith as the scapegoat, that poor creature on which to vent her anger, to heap her sins and the sins of those around her. Like others before her, she loaded it with guilts and sorrows and drove it into the desert where it would die from lack of nourishment. Its flesh would be sucked from its bones which, stripped clean, would be left to rot in the hot sun until the winds, shamed by their nakedness, summoned up the sands to cover them so that at least they were hidden from view. Rozia could not understand the implications of her reactions, nor would she; but she resolved to push her Jewishness into a place somewhere far beyond her mind, so that it could never again come out and damage her.

She must have fallen asleep in the chair because when she awoke it was dark, she was covered by a blanket, and she was alone. Unperturbed, she got out of the chair – for what had she left to fear? Death would be preferable to the anguish that rotted within her, but she knew she would not die.

She could hear someone banging on the door. Was that what had woken her?

'Rozia, Rozia, open up. It's us, Shosha and Mordechai.'

She heard her friends' voices; they had come, they had not turned their backs on her. She raced to the front door and wrestled with the strange lock, pulled it open and threw herself into four welcoming arms that held and caressed her.

'Come in, I –'

But then all the words stopped as she stared, open-mouthed, at Mordechai. He was no longer wearing his hat or his skull cap, his hair was cut short, his face shaved, smooth like a baby's, and the black suit had vanished. Shosha was holding on to his arm and on the third finger of her left hand, she wore a bright gold wedding ring.

'What is this?' Rozia asked, touching the shiny thing.

'We are married,' Shosha said excitedly.

'And this?' she queried, touching Mordechai's face.

'I am done with it all,' he said tersely. 'If God can allow your family to pronounce you dead, then I have no faith in Him or His laws.'

'Maybe it isn't God,' Rozia said, shaken. 'Just the Jews.'

'We are Jews, and we are marked, Rozia. Look what happened to your Stefan, even he gave in to Jew-baiting –'

'He didn't give in to Jew-baiting – he was just killed by them . . .' she said bitterly.

'I know what happened,' Mordechai said, 'Jonathon told me.'

Rozia curled back on to the chair. Suddenly the thought of not seeing her young brother hurt her badly.

'Oh Rozia,' Shosha whispered, knowing that she could not possibly understand what her friend was experiencing, but feeling her pain. 'We've come for you. We want you to come to Palestine with us, for there it will not matter that you are a Jew and that you loved a Christian. No one will care.'

'How did you know where I was?' Rozia asked.

'Booba told us, she wants you to go.'

'I'd like to see Booba.'

'She will come and see us off on the train and she will bring Jonathon with her,' Shosha said.

'A bribe –' Rozia snapped bitterly.

'No bribe. It is the only thing for you. For us.' Mordechai scowled.

Rozia looked at him; defiance suited him, she decided. His shoulders were straight, he'd lost that pasty look.

'You still have not explained why you married, and who married you.'

'Rabbi Rosen. The young one,' Mordechai replied, and Rozia identified without difficulty another young Zionist.

'Surely he has not got over God,' she said dryly.

'Of course not. But funnily enough, Rozia, he did not approve of the way you were treated. He is coming with us to Palestine to make a place where Jews are not frightened by contact with gentiles.'

'And you think you can change generations of hatred?'

'Not here. Not in Europe where the legacy of pogroms and fear eats into the soul. But in our land it will be different. You must come with us. It is the only future –'

'No,' Rozia said. 'No. I love you both and I am sad to lose you, but my place is here in Europe. I am going to be a chemist.'

'But this place can only mean hurt. In Palestine you will be among Jews who won't –'

'No, I do not want to be among Jews. It is the Jews who have cut my heart out.' As she spoke, Rozia could almost feel Stefan's warm blood on her face, on her hands again. She stood up, turned to look at her friends, and saw their shocked, uncomprehending faces. She leaned towards each of them, one hand on one face and then on the other, like a blind person learning their features, etching them indelibly into her memory.

'Whichever way you look at it, Stefan was killed by a Jewish mob.' Shosha drew in her breath sharply whilst Rozia continued, 'And Papa expelled me because his Jewishness could not tolerate my belonging to Stefan. There is no compassion or love; it is a vengeful faith. Remember, "I am the Lord thy God, and I am a jealous God . . ."'

Shosha spoke quietly from where she stood beside Mordechai. 'You are wrong, Rozia. There is never any justification for hatred. And now you are as guilty as the others. Listen to me, your father is as trapped by his beliefs as a Catholic might be by his. Man-made religions deny humanity, I give you that point. But God, and you should listen to Mordechai, is above that.'

Rozia started to interrupt, but Shosha stopped her with her hand. 'I know you did not deny your belief in God; but you are a Jewess, and you learnt your identity from your mother's womb.

'Judaism does not mean your damnation, Rozia. We, the Jews, don't believe in Hell. The Christians do. Remember that.'

'And what is this?' Rozia said. She was crying now. 'This is Hell. And my father, my Jewish father turned me out — forgetting that I am his daughter, caring only for his Jewishness; if that is more important to him than me and my pain, then I want nothing to do with him or his faith.'

'It's not your father who is responsible, nor is it the Jews,' Shosha said. 'It is the hatred from the Christians to the Jews, and the Jews to the Christians which has done this to you.'

'Maybe,' Rozia said, quieter now. 'But I cannot undo what has been done.'

'You can,' Mordechai interrupted her. 'You can come with us.'

'No. I stay . . .'

'And become a Christian?' Shosha asked.

'Perhaps. I don't know.'

85

'Remember, Rozia, if you want to worship a God, one way is as bad as the other,' Mordechai said. He took her shoulders. 'We are leaving tomorrow from the railway station. We will wait for you until the last minute.'

He kissed her on both cheeks, his lips hard and firm. Rozia nodded her head and hugged him. She clung to Shosha. 'I love you, my little friend,' she said.

When Dr Oberski returned he did not come alone. He came with Joanna and Robert and Jan.

Her friends, her new friends, held her. Joanna asked her to come and live at her house.

'No,' Rozia said, stroking Joanna's hair. 'No.'

She could feel Joanna's tears on her shoulder as the Polish girl held her. She patted Joanna's back, the comforter, not the comforted. She told them, as they sat with her – awkward and unable to help staunch her pain or their own – that Shosha and Mordechai had tried to persuade her to go to Palestine.

'I can't. You see, going there is not possible for me. They were the ones who did it, don't you see?'

She looked into Jan's face, into Robert's face, into Joanna's face. She knew she was shouting but she couldn't help herself.

'They did it, they killed Stefan! They did it, they did it!' Rozia was screaming now, and she could feel her face contorting; she was hitting something, something soft, but she didn't know what.

Dr Oberski came back into the room as soon as he heard Rozia's screams. He had excused himself, hoping her friends could help her, but when he saw their tightly drawn faces just watching a demented animal clawing at his couch, punching his pillows, unable even to touch her, he pushed them away and told them to go. He took the girl into his arms, holding her, wiping her tears, comforting her, and in her pain he could feel the beginnings of his love.

Chapter Five

———— ♦ ————

Days merged into days for Rozia. She studied diligently, avoiding all the places she had gone to with Stefan. Robert, Jan, and mostly Joanna tried to entice her into spending time with them, but she rejected them, even spurning their affections. She felt they were blemished somehow by Stefan's death, as if a paintbrush had tinged their lives with grey, dulling their bright colours, and she could not bear to be with them. She preferred her solitude to their efforts at comfort.

After almost two weeks Joanna accosted her on her way to the laboratory.

'Rozia, why are you avoiding us?' she asked.

'I can't see you,' Rozia whispered. 'It hurts too much.'

'We are your friends.'

Joanna tried to touch her, but Rozia stepped back quickly; she couldn't cope with kindness.

'It's just that I cannot yet deal with the fact that I will never see him again.'

'I understand, and I do want to help you. Perhaps it might comfort you if you saw Stefan's mother?'

'Stefan's mother?' Rozia repeated.

'Yes. Oh Rozia, she is in a terrible state. Like you she can't come to terms with what has happened. She cries all the time, she can't even get out of her bed. Actually she has asked to see you, rather more than that, she has begged you to come to her.'

'Is that why you have come to see me? On a mission of mercy for Stefan's mother?'

'Rozia,' Joanna said, genuinely shocked, 'I came to see you for you. We are friends.'

'Were. Stefan is dead now,' Rozia screamed, pushing past Joanna, not wanting to see her alive, when her Stefan was dead, drained of his blood, under the cold earth.

She fulfilled her promise to herself to neglect her Jewishness from the moment she had made it. She ate ham, pushing it down her throat without tasting it. She ladled sour cream on to meat dishes. She ate unclean meat. She consciously and deliberately broke the Sabbath.

As soon as she was able, Rozia counted Booba's money. It was indeed everything the old lady had in the world – enough for her granddaughter to rent a room and continue with her studies. She told Dr Oberski that was what she intended to do.

'Are you sure?' he asked.

'I have no choice, there is nothing else for me to do. I started here with just my work.'

'But you had your parents then.'

She shut her eyes, feeling the tears spurt like Stefan's blood; they were so sore from her weeping they felt like his wound.

'No, I mean, I lived with them, but I didn't have their support. They never wanted me to go to the University. They wanted me to be a wife, a Jewish wife.'

'Your parents will get over this, Rozia – you will be able to go home.'

'They may, but I will not.' The venom in her voice surprised even her.

Dr Oberski arranged for her to lodge with his parents – an elderly, courtly couple who were aware that by taking in this young Jewish girl, they were performing their Christian charity. Madame Oberska particularly subscribed to the precepts of her faith. The priest came to visit her often and she was never to be found wanting in the performance of the rituals. They bound her to her God. And Rozia understood her needs and envied her the security and comfort it furnished.

Most of the time when she was not at the University she would stay in the little white-painted bedroom that had been allocated to her. It contained a bed, a wardrobe, a side table. Above her bed there was a simple black cross. She would gaze at it for hours, conjecturing about its symbolism. Once she had taken it down from the wall and held it between her thumb and fingers. What was its magic? What was the spell it had woven over men throughout the centuries, giving them a comfort and a belief in its power? Gingerly she put it back on the wall. Stefan had said Jesus was a Jew. The Virgin Mary was a Jewess. They were no different from her. They just offered another path to God. An easier one perhaps. There was no separateness.

At night, she would lie on her bed and think of Stefan. She tried to hold on to his memory, but even in the short time he seemed to have diminished a little in her mind. She could not summon up precious details, her images of him were blurred. She realized that she had never spent a night with him, never woken with him. When she herself slept, which was little enough, she would dream the same dream. He was just ahead of her, laughing, dancing, whirling around, but she could not touch him. And as she ran after him, her hurt increased. She longed for him, but still there was the distance between them. And then he was gone behind a cloud, hidden from her by a greyness that held no beauty.

Every evening Rozia would leave the little room to dine with the Oberskis. Fortunately for her, Dr Oberski had taken to joining them; a habit he had long since neglected except on Sundays. At forty-four years of age, he had no need of childhood ties. And the times he spent with his parents and Rozia were expensive. He was writing a book

89

with an English associate, Professor Lascelles – it was a medical research book offering theories on genetics that was far in advance of its years. It was primarily Jouk Obserki's work, but it no longer occupied his thinking; his time was now spent in selecting the right tie, in brushing his unruly hair or practising his charm in front of the mirror.

The reward for his efforts came quickly for just a few days after Rozia had moved in with his parents, he succeeded in making her laugh. He was charming and considerate; despite herself, she responded to his gentle teasing and once or twice she had to remind herself that for her, a widow in mourning, flirting was unseemly; but as she had to admit to herself, he was very nice. It wasn't that she was attracted to him, it was just that he was so very kind to her. She found his maturity very comforting – he had such nice brown eyes – but she was shocked to realize that she had also noticed he had a nice mouth beneath his thin moustache; that although he was a tall, rather thin man, Jouk Oberski did not hunch his shoulders, he stood straight.

Madame Oberska did not fail to notice that Rozia was beginning to respond to her son's attentions, and it worried her. She could see his affection for the young Jewish girl who, even if she converted to Catholicism, could never be her son's bride – Jouk, she knew, must never marry.

On Sunday mornings Mr Oberski would escort his wife to Mass. Rozia would watch them make their departure, carrying their missals, their beads and their devotions. On the third Sunday Madame Oberska forgot her missal. Rozia, anxious to help her, rushed to look for it, and found it in the salon. Almost unwillingly she opened it and scanned the pages. The prayers had a similar quality to those she had learnt as a child. They were offered to the mercy of an unseen God, but they turned for help to real people. They used the Mother Mary, and saints far too numerous to number to intercede for them. Rozia longed to feel the balm of God's love. She felt alone, beyond healing without it. She felt the tears well up again.

Madame Oberska, who had come into the salon, silently observed Rozia. 'Would you like to come with us?' she asked after a few moments.

'Yes.'

The majesty of the service comforted Rozia. She found peace in the sonorous words of the priest and the gentle hymns. She watched in awe as those who had confessed partook in communion, unifying themselves with the actual body and blood of Christ.

It was enough to know that God was present as he was in the synagogue, but it demanded different disciplines and Rozia felt drawn to those differences.

'Would you like to learn more?' Madame Oberska asked.

'Yes, please,' Rozia replied.

When he heard, Dr Oberski tried to prevent her.

'It is too early for you to think properly, Rozia. You are still coming to terms with the changes in your life. Catholicism cannot replace your Jewishness. It has to be a slow process.'

'No, I want to learn,' she said. 'It is the only way to find out whether it is right for me or not.'

One morning, early, Rozia was racked by a bout of sickness that made her feel as if her stomach was coming away. The nausea stayed with her, but by lunchtime it had eased. The next morning, at the same hour, the unpleasant symptom was repeated. After she had washed out her mouth and thrown water on to her moist forehead, she realized that in the anguish of her loss, she had overlooked the absence of her monthly period. The possibility of pregnancy loomed at her from the recesses of her mind, but its implications were shelved in a moment of clear-thinking practicality. She had to find a doctor. There was no question of her visiting old Dr Schmann who had handed out whatever had been required to cure childish ailments. Where to go? What to do? She couldn't ask Madame Oberska.

She decided upon a hospital. She dressed quickly, excused herself from breakfast – her stomach would not accept food or drink anyway – and made her way to Warsaw's main infirmary.

She sat waiting on a long bench, averting her face from the sick who surrounded her, the coughs of the tubercular, the blood of the hurt.

After an hour her name was called. A starched white impersonal nurse took her to an office. A bored young doctor sat writing notes. He ignored her whilst he completed his task. She waited, summoning all her courage. She had to face the ordeal, there were no choices.

'Yes?' he said.

'I think I'm pregnant.'

'Name?'

'Rozia Furswerk!' she said; conscious of the lie, she fiddled with her fingers.

The doctor stared at her, and didn't write anything down on his sheet. 'Real name?' he said coldly.

'Mezeurska,' Rozia whispered.

'Go over to the bed. I will have to examine you.'

The nurse helped her remove her clothes; she was allowed to keep her petticoat on. The doctor washed his hands, covered them with gloves which he lubricated with a grease, and then inserted his finger – a cold unwelcome intrusion that prodded and probed.

'The cervix is softening,' he said.

Rozia sighed. She didn't need an explanation – now that she knew the reality, the nightmare could take over. She touched her stomach, aware of the seed within her. She wanted to feel joy; to have Stefan's baby should be the most wonderful thing – and if he had been alive . . . but he wasn't. And all she could feel was panic.

Who could she go to? Joanna, yes, Joanna was her friend. She would help her; in her need and desperation Rozia had forgotten her last meeting with the Polish girl.

She found her in the café, holding hands with a boy – Rozia had seen him around, but she couldn't put a name to his face. As soon as she saw her, Rozia blushed: she could see that Joanna had no intention of welcoming her. She told herself she must not notice, she must overcome Joanna's reserve. She walked over to the table where they were sitting. Finally, after what seemed like a very long time, Joanna looked up.

'How are you?' Rozia asked.

'Very well,' came the reply; there was no hostility in the voice. 'And you?'

Rozia shrugged.

'Stefan's mother has been quite ill. You remember I told you she was very distressed? We were all quite shocked that you couldn't spare her any time, not even a note. You may remember I told you that she so wanted to see you. After all, it was her son who died – you had only known him for four months.'

As soon as she had finished talking, Joanna turned her back on her. Smarting, Rozia stumbled from the café. A man called her name but she ignored him, intent only on herself and her pain.

From the other side of the street Robert swore to himself. He wanted to help Rozia, but if she wouldn't let anyone even talk to her, then what could he do?

Rozia forced herself to think of the baby. She would not be able to stay on at the Oberskis. She had to find somewhere and some way to live. She would need money, more than she had. A baby would need clothes and she would have to find someone to look after it while she was at the University. She would have to find a part-time job. She couldn't allow herself to think of the emotional implications of her state;

she had to be practical – if she were not, she would quite simply have arranged to die.

After her rebuff from Joanna, she went straight to Dr Oberski. There was no question as to whether she should or not. He was her friend, her only friend in a bleak and empty world.

'Do you really intend to bring up the child alone?' he asked kindly, after she had blurted everything out – unable to stop the torrent of words.

'What else can I do?'

'Marry.'

'Marry? How can I marry? Stefan is dead!'

Jouk put out his hand to touch her hair, and then stopped himself, pulling his hand back, and stuffing it down the side of his chair, almost as if to wedge it so that it could not escape free and offer a caress.

'Rozia, I am older than you. I cannot offer you youth or passion. But I can offer you love, security and a name for your child. But there is something you must know about me. Something intimate and most painful for me.'

He paused, swallowed, and turned to look out of the window. Rozia, sitting slightly to the side of him, could see him staring ahead, almost aimlessly, except that his stance conveyed the tension of anguish. For a brief moment Rozia forgot herself, and she wanted to touch him, to help him. She suddenly realized how fond she was of him, but at the same time she was embarrassed, because it was dawning on her that he was about to offer marriage. She couldn't consider that. She would never allow someone else to father Stefan's child, and there was no question of giving herself to another man. Rozia belonged to Stefan. She would fight for herself and her child alone. She had to stop Dr Oberski from compromising himself any further.

'I think I know what you are going to suggest and I –'

Oberski whirled from the window. 'You cannot possibly know,' he said.

Rozia was shocked at his tone. It was almost violent. She drew back on her chair, holding her knees, her eyes fixed on his face.

He swallowed again. 'I am sorry, I should not have spoken like that.' His voice was quieter now. 'But you must let me continue. You see I cannot love – that is to say I am physically incapable of the act of love. It has not always been so. When I was in my twenties I was engaged to a young girl, a fine young girl, and we had many hopes for the future. We too, like all lovers, believed that only we understood the intensity of passion.' He glanced at Rozia, his face sad. 'So I understand about you and your Stefan, more than you perhaps realize. Irene liked to ride. I not so much; even then I preferred the more academic pursuits. But because it was her pleasure, we would go, every Saturday, into the woods with our horses. We had many happy hours there. One particular Saturday, her horse bolted. Irene was very frightened. She screamed. I raced after her, driving my poor animal beyond his endurance. But I couldn't help it, I had to get to Irene. She fell off her horse. I hit my mount and the whip caught his eye. I blinded him, and in his terrible pain he threw me. He could not see where I was lying. He brought his hoof down on me. And now I am incapacitated.'

'Oh my God,' Rozia whispered.

Dr Oberski came towards her. 'It is all right, Rozia. I am well, I have no problems. I have my work and my pleasures, I am not distressed. I have come to terms with my disability, although, of course, there has never been any question of a family; but now someone I love very much is wounded and lost, as I was, and perhaps we can help each other – all the same, I know it is a great deal to ask a young woman to marry a man in my situation.'

Rozia got out of her chair. She was near to tears, but

she held them back, knowing that it would be wrong to cry. Instead she said, 'Do you still love her very much?'

'No, not now. I love you, Rozia.'

Rozia put her hands over her eyes. She cared deeply for Dr Oberski, but she knew she did not love him. 'Please, it is not your – incapacity that bothers me. I could never think of having anyone else in that way . . .'

'That is your youth, Rozia. The fire of your love. But when the memory is dimmed by the years, your body will awaken, and you will have needs.'

Embarrassed, she drew away from Dr Oberski.

'But I will try to help you. There are other ways . . .'

Colour flooded into her cheeks. 'No, no,' she said quickly. 'I am trying to explain, it isn't that. If I could love again, I pray that it would be you, but I cannot marry unless I love. It is impossible.' She swallowed, wringing her hands, rubbing the palms with her thumbs and then, realizing what she was doing, pressing one on top of the other on her leg, pushing into her flesh until she could feel the bones. 'It is very hard for me to reject your proposal,' she continued. 'Not only because it would make my life easier, but because you see I am fond of you,' she bit her lip. 'Very fond. And because of that I cannot live a lie.'

Dr Oberski just nodded and Rozia could see his distress; his eyes were dry, he made no sound, but his face was creased like an old map.

Timidly, she touched his arm. 'But we can still help each other. We can still be friends.'

He nodded again. 'Of course, yes, but you will need more than friends now. Perhaps your family might feel differently?'

Rozia didn't dare look at him. She felt a sudden jump in her throat. Perhaps the child could bring about a reconciliation. The possibility was too painful to contemplate and she told herself not to hope for too much. But she would write to her grandmother. Yes, she would tell Booba.

She smiled at Dr Oberski. 'I will try to contact them,' she said.

'Good,' he replied.

He tried to be pleasant, but Rozia knew he did not want her to stay with him.

Sensitive to his feelings and careful of them, she said, 'I thank you. I will go now.'

'Yes,' he said, his eyes fixed on a point above her head.

She went straight to her desk and wrote a careful note to Booba, asking if they could meet. She suggested a place, outside the University, and a time – four-thirty – and a day – Thursday. Today was Wednesday, so she would not have to endure too many hours of trepidation. She hugged herself and permitted a small realization of how much she missed her family. She knew, of course, that nothing could be the same, but perhaps if Papa would just see her, there might be a chance of something.

Despite the bitter cold of the Polish winter which caused ice to hang on the breath and bite into the skin, the old lady, dressed in clothes of another century, was waiting for her when she came out of the University.

Rozia wanted to run to her, to bury herself in a remembered scent, but she hung back, unsure of her welcome. But Booba, the tears licking her thick lashes that had held on to their youth despite the wrinkled face, extended her arms and Rozia almost fell into her embrace.

'You are pregant,' said the wise old lady.

'How did you know?'

'I know.'

'Dr Oberski said he would marry me.'

'Yes?'

'Yes.'

'Marry him.'

'No, I will bring up Stefan's child on my own. I can do it, I know I can. I'll find somewhere to live until I qualify and I'll get some work which I can do whilst I study.'

'And you can fly as well, Rozia . . .' the old lady said quietly.

'I don't understand.' Rozia drew back a little from the tight embrace.

'It is not possible for you to raise a child alone. You will be shamed, the child will be shamed. And the difficulties. It is not easy to look after children when you have a husband, but when you don't . . .' Booba caressed her hair. '. . . I know you loved your Stefan, but he would not want his child to grow up without a father. If Dr Oberski is prepared to take on an illegitimate child, then you must accept the offer of respectability.'

'Booba –' Rozia started to say.

'No, for once listen to me. I know you have turned your back on your Jewishness. You don't have to admit or deny it, but don't lose your God, Rozia.'

'That is what Shosha told me.'

'I wanted you to go with them,' Booba said quietly.

'I know.'

'It would have been best.'

Rozia shook her head wearily.

'Listen to me,' Booba entreated her. 'Marry Dr Oberski . . . whatever the price. Give your firstborn a name, a home, security, a father. You have no right to deny it that. Your thoughtlessness has denied it its proper heritage, now stop being selfish and be sensible.'

Rozia swallowed hard. 'I don't love him in that way. Perhaps if Papa and Mama –' Booba held up her hand, but Rozia ignored the gesture. 'I know they cannot accept me in their home, but if I could see them, and Jonathon, just . . .'

'Rozia, they are trapped by their own beliefs. They are in terrible pain. They miss you. They love you.'

'Then if they love me, why will they not see me?'

'You have broken their code.'

'But you came to see me,' Rozia said bitterly.

Booba said nothing, just stroked the long hair again and again.

'I cannot promise success,' she said, 'and it does not alter my mind that marriage to Dr Oberski is the only answer.'

'I understand, but please try,' Rozia entreated. She touched her grandmother's arm. 'A new life, Booba, it's a new life inside me. Surely that must mean something?'

Booba kissed her hard. They walked together to the corner, their arms linked. And then Rozia had to let go. Booba waved and gingerly picked her way over the hard-packed snow that was an accepted reality of winter. She stumbled and Rozia saw her frailty; she wanted to run after her, to help her, but she didn't, she just watched until the little figure rounded another corner and was lost from sight.

That evening Rozia went for her first instruction in Catholicism and she learned of Original Sin, and that baptism was the only sacrament which could cleanse her and allow her to achieve total unity with Christ. She tried not to wonder how Booba's efforts were progressing, but despite all her attempts at self-discipline, she hoped.

Rozia was working on experiments in the laboratory when, some four days later, she was asked to go to the Head of the University. She tried not to be concerned – she knew she was doing well in her studies, but such a summons was unheard of amongst the students, unless a question of discipline was to be discussed. Rozia was not aware that she had done anything wrong, except of course, the baby. Perhaps Dr Oberski had told them. What would they do? Would they want her to leave, or could she stay? Trying to ignore her anxieties, she walked swiftly down the passage and up the stairs to the office. Someone was waiting for her outside the door, someone she longed for – Jonathon. She flung herself at her brother, sobbing her delight at seeing him. Booba had worked the miracle – they wanted to see her, it was going to be all right. Jonathon was pulling himself away from her.

'Booba's dead,' he said.

Rozia saw his tear-stained face, his white skin, the black shadows under his eyes. And then the ravens came and they plucked out what was left of hope and love . . .

'How?' she whispered.

'A tram, it knocked her down.'

'When?'

'Four days ago. She was badly hurt, but conscious. She died early at three o'clock this morning. I can't stay, the funeral is later.'

'I must come with you.'

'No, Rozia, you cannot. She tried to ask them to see you, but they wouldn't. They said that the only way they could survive was to think of you as dead, that you had to find your own direction. I brought you this. It's in my own handwriting, she dictated it to me yesterday. I think she stayed alive in order to do this last thing for you. She loved you. She loved us both.'

'Jonathon, I must come.'

'No.' He was already moving away from her. 'I love you, Rozia, and I will never forget you,' he said, and then he was gone.

Rozia opened the note. It said: *Marry Dr Oberski. Make a life with him, there is no other way.* She thought of her grandmother – hurt and broken on a cobbled road – Booba, who had come out into the biting winds because of her.

She showed the note to Dr Oberski as soon as she got back to the laboratory. She was dry-eyed. There were no tears left to cry. The ravens had taken them too.

After the other students had left the class he came over to her.

'I will make you happy, Rozia, I know I can. Just give me a chance.'

Mutely she nodded.

'We will marry, go to England – Rozia, you will have a new life. You can continue your studies.'

'Why England?'

'I'm working with a professor from London University – we are writing a book together, so it would be feasible for me to go there – my English is good enough. You can apply for a place in a chemistry faculty to start next year which will give you time to master the language.'

'And I will become a Catholic,' she said.

'No. You are a Jewess, even if you don't practise your faith. I don't need you to be a Catholic.'

'I need to be. My child must be baptized,' she said quietly into Oberski's horrified face, 'otherwise it will never see the Kingdom of Heaven.'

'Rozia, what are you talking about?' he said.

'I believe. That is what I am saying.'

'No, you don't, you are looking for an escape route.'

'I am not. I believe. And who are you to doubt me?'

Rozia completed her instruction and was baptized and received into the Catholic faith some three days before her marriage to Jouk.

During that time she had applied to the universities of London, Oxford, Cambridge and Edinburgh and she received her final rejection, from Edinburgh University, on the morning of her marriage. They had all told her the same thing, that they had enough women applicants from England for their quota and that, in any event, without a perfect command of the English language, further study would be impossible.

After she had read the letter, Rozia sat very still. She felt her dreams evaporate, her ambitions disappear; the belief that anything could be achieved was all a farce. There was nothing left for her. She was sitting at her dressing table, and the reflection that stared back from the mirror was flat, puffy with grief, the face no longer pretty, the eyes dead, the flat cheekbones without colour; all that was left was the rich long hair.

On the afternoon of the previous day, Rozia had gone to her father's office. Ignoring the thudding of her heart, she had climbed the wooden staircase to what had once been her little place of dreams above the leather shop. She had taken a tram to the corner of Grzybow Place and walked quickly down the familiar streets as if she were a stranger. Once she felt as if someone recognized her, but she made no attempt at contact.

She noticed that her father's door, which he had always left open before, was shut. She knocked.

'Yes?' she heard him say. At the sound of his voice, her knees buckled and she had to hold on to the door handle.

'Come in.'

She prised open the door, for it felt as if it were heavier than a ton of steel.

'Papa,' she whispered.

An old man stood up, for that was what he had become.

'A dybbuk, that spirit of the dead, a dybbuk of my dead daughter come to haunt me.' He covered his eyes as if fearful to look at her.

'Papa?' There were tears of blood now, Stefan's blood, Booba's blood, Rozia's tears . . . 'Papa, I am going to have a baby.'

'Dybbuk,' the man who had become old screamed, 'dybbuk, get thee gone.'

She stumbled down the stairs, behind her the old man shouting and screaming and praying, reciting the Kaddish – the prayer for the dead. As she heard it, Rozia put her hands over her ears, trying to blot out the terrible sound of her father's entreaties to a jealous God that his daughter's evil spirit be gone from him, forever.

As she remembered the sound of his voice and the dreadful prayer, she reached for her little ivory-handled nail scissors. Papa and Mama had given them to her on the day before her thirteenth birthday.

'Now you are a young lady,' her Mama had said, 'you must take care of your hands and your nails, be proud of them. They are a delight, and please God they should never know hardship.'

Rozia glanced up at the pale blue dress she had chosen for her wedding, its front panel loose to conceal her burgeoning waistline and the cloche hat which Madame Oberska's dressmaker had assured her was the height of fashion – 'You must push your hair up, out of the way, such long locks aren't the thing at all now.'

But Rozia did not think of the fashion, only of the wedding she might have had, had she never wanted to be different, had she never wanted more than just a husband and children. Would she have married Leah Kleeman's cousin? If she had, they would have cut her hair, and she would have protested, she knew that. But now, now that she wasn't going to marry a Jew, she would, as a gesture to all that she had lost, fulfil the rite which she so despised.

She picked up a single strand and slowly cut it short, just above the ears, and then with increasing haste, continued until the rich auburn locks lay like a carpet at her feet. Hurriedly she pulled on the cloche hat, not wanting to look at her head. She opened a lipstick, a bright vermilion colour, and applied it to her lips. Her face looked stark and white – the lipstick making the pain of loss more obvious. Satisfied, she stood up and stepped over her hair, pulled on her dress, picked up a small clutch handbag and walked out of the little white room.

Later that night, when they had prepared for bed, Jouk touched her shorn head.

'Why did you do that?' he asked.

'It's childish to wear hair so long,' she told him, shying away from his touch.

Rozia wanted no part of the arrangements to leave Poland. She understood that she was responsible for their self-imposed banishment, but reconciled herself by saying that once they reached England she would take over a housewife's responsibilities. As it was, she concerned herself only with her grief, realizing, of course, that she was turning in on herself but unable to do anything about it. It was as if a burden of intolerable weight had positioned itself around her shoulders, like a cape she couldn't throw off. In England, she thought, it would be better and she told Jouk, 'When we get to England, I will feel fine.'

And Jouk told her, 'When we get to England, you will feel fine.'

He had arranged the purchase of a house through his friend Professor Martin Lascelles, who had also eagerly obtained the position for him within the chemistry faculty of London University. Jouk was a famous man in his field, and his expertise would be welcome; Professor Lascelles was not an ambitious man, and he was content to bow to Jouk's obvious seniority. Not so Mrs Lascelles, who awaited the arrival of the Oberskis with less pleasure than her husband.

Rozia made no effort to see her family, not even Jonathon. Jouk suggested that she might like to invite Jan, Robert and Joanna for a small farewell, but she declined – remembering her last meeting with Joanna. He himself attended various functions, but without Rozia; he knew that he could not subject her to the curiosity that was prevalent amongst his colleagues.

On the morning of their departure, Jouk excused himself

from his small apartment which had been their temporary home and went to say goodbye to his parents. He never told Rozia of the tears and the hurt of such an unexpected separation; he had no wish to inflict his sorrows on his young wife. And he was so aware of her youth, of her pain, of her vulnerability. He would lie in their bed, separated from her by no more than a few inches of mattress, and he would listen for the signs of even breathing which would announce her asleep. Sometimes they came quickly, sometimes not at all. On those nights he would lie still and worry for her; when she finally slept he would silently move out of the bed and on to the little ornate couch, for he could not rest whilst the bruised, but to his eyes still vibrant, young beauty lay so close to him.

Rozia tried hard to conceal her anxiety from Jouk. She was so aware of his kindnesses to her; she wanted to be worthy of them, but in Poland she could not. She knew he slept badly – she saw his red eyes, and wondered and worried. One night she had awoken, dreaming of Stefan, of Booba, of evil spirits – of herself in a coffin with the earth being piled up on the lid, unable to reach air, buried but not dead. She had wanted to cry out, but then realized that Jouk was not beside her. She sat up and saw him sleeping on the little couch, his large frame awkward and bent. She got out of the bed, repositioned his cushion and allowed herself to kiss his forehead and stroke his hair. He stirred and she scampered back to her side of the bed, in case he should want to hold her.

After his farewell to his parents, Jouk returned to his home – now stripped bare of his personal effects: his books, his records already sent ahead; the furniture sold – Rozia wanted new things in England. She was dressed in a cream coat with a heavy beaver collar, and a small cloche hat, with cream gloves, shoes, and bag to match; her hair, now coiffed, shone in the sun coming through the windows, and though her skin was pale, Jouk noticed with relief that she looked more composed.

'How are you feeling?' he asked, with his usual concern.

'I don't know,' Rozia answered truthfully.

She took his arm and walked out of his apartment. On the journey to the station in his father's car, she looked neither to the right nor to the left, not savouring, as Jouk did, the final moments of Warsaw. At the station he bought her flowers, rich red roses. The colour matched her lipstick, and, her skin merging with her cream coat, the effect was terrifying – like blood, he thought, and had to look away.

Rozia glanced at the deep red, velvet-like flowers in her arms, and she too thought of blood, Stefan's blood as it drenched her thighs on the night they had both died. She thought of his child inside her, and momentarily wondered what she would feel for that child – she had no idea what emotions to expect, but she knew, despite everything, that she wanted to feel love – she hoped she would.

As they walked down the platform, she heard her name being called out loudly, 'Rozia, Rozia, stop!'

Was it Jonathon? It wasn't Papa. Who was it? She turned her head quickly, just in case . . . And she saw Robert running after her, carrying a bunch of spring flowers, hastily arranged by a rushed florist; its colours – blues, pinks, yellows – soft and welcoming.

'Rozia, you are a fool,' he said, 'you didn't give us a chance.'

She stopped, drew in her breath, tried to say something.

'Take care of yourself.' He gave her the bouquet, offering it clumsily.

She took it, unaware that the roses had slipped to the ground. Jouk saw and bent to pick them up, but at that moment the porter walked past with their luggage and squashed the velvet heads, crushing them – making them look like spilled blood.

'Give you a chance for what?' Rozia was saying to Robert, anxious that he should not go.

'To be your friend. We love you.'

'Loved' Rozia thought, but she said nothing.

'We knew you were so hurt, but you wouldn't let us get close to you.'

'I couldn't let you,' she said. 'You were all alive.'

'And Stefan was dead,' he finished softly.

Rozia nodded. She could feel the tears closing up her throat.

'Good luck,' Robert whispered – and he was gone, running down the platform, taking her youth with him.

And she allowed Jouk to help her up the steep steps into the train.

Jouk saw that Rozia was holding her spring flowers, smelling them, breathing in their scent. Spring is a time for birth, he thought, and turned away from the red roses.

—PART 2—

The Life of an Exile

Chapter Six

———————— ◆ ————————

To Rozia's young eyes, the English seemed to thrive on inconsistency. It seemed to her to be the national sport. There was the glamour in Regent Street and Bond Street, crammed with their shoppers and strollers and more cars than the whole of Warsaw. But unlike Marshalkowska there were no roadside cafés to sit and drink and talk at, no smell of *rouki* cooking over open fires, no sound of violins; Rozia never got over the pain of suddenly hearing Chopin on one of those crystal sets that Jouk bought her soon after they had arrived. Oh, there were nightclubs – she'd heard about them – and there were places where one might go for a tea dance, but the people of Rozia's acquaintance never seemed to go there. They talked about Sir William Joyson Hicks, the Home Secretary, who prosecuted people who ran the nightclubs, people who had fun. And there was the other side of England, the side of inequality, of poverty, of malnutrition – Rozia learnt about that England from her maid and through the newspapers. Her middle-class life kept scrupulously clear of the smell of deprivation.

As soon as she arrived in England, Rozia decided with a return of her customary zeal that she would learn English. Father O'Flynn, the parish priest of their local Catholic church, found a Miss Dent – a retired schoolteacher in a neat grey dress and a bun – to help her. Rozia received her in the ornate salon which she had furnished with the frills and tassels of her childhood. Side lights sat on lace-covered tables. The couch and chairs were 1920's chinois in black and gold, upholstered in burgundy. The carpet was a patterned Axminster, incorporating the burgundy of the suite. The curtains were heavy gold brocade, the walls papered in a dark red floral design. She herself was dressed stylishly. The loose dresses of the period, which she now wore, concealed any bulges that might be considered unseemly, but Rozia was being very careful about what she ate. She had no intention of losing her figure.

She was teaching her maid, Mary, how to cook. The good plain food of the English table offended Rozia's delicate palate, and puddings and overcooked bland cabbage were rejected in favour of cheesecakes and cabbage in sour cream. She made the cream sour herself by mixing it with lemon juice.

Rozia's first English lesson was unintelligible, what with trying to cope with rules of 'i' before 'e' except after 'c', except of course for the several hundred exceptions. After eight such lessons, she appealed to Father O'Flynn who had never allowed her lack of words to isolate her. He used his hands, an extraordinary conglomeration of pidgin English, a Polish dictionary and a lot of understanding. He was the first person she laughed with in England, and would be the first person she cried with in England. He had taken to visiting her often for he admitted to himself that, had he not reached his fifty years with a considerable amount of satisfaction from his vocation, he might well have found Rozia Oberska just a little too pleasing. He spoke with Miss Dent and from then on the lessons revolved around newspapers and the radio and shopping lists.

As soon as she was able, Rozia devoured those newspapers – at least they kept her in touch with a life that never seemed to touch her own. There was a Prince of Wales, a handsome young man who would one day be King. Rozia thought him quite beautiful – but not as beautiful as her Stefan, who still dominated her nights, dancing just ahead of her, whirling in time to forgotten music, smiling, beckoning to her, but when she caught up with him, just a lifeless body on a white carpet of snow. And she would wake up crying, aching for the feel of him.

Jouk tried to help her, to be as supportive as possible. He scrupulously protected her, shielding her from contact with even his colleagues and their wives, waiting until she had had the baby.

'You will feel better, when you have had the baby,' he would tell her whilst she wept.

And she would say, 'I will feel better, when I have had the baby,' whilst she dried her eyes.

Sybil Lascelles, however, had other ideas. Mindful of doing the right thing, she invited Rozia for tea.

'A pregnant woman gets so tired,' she told her husband, 'so dinner is out of the question.'

But Rozia declined; Sybil Lascelles, to whom Jouk referred with increasing servility, seemed too great an event to be faced before she felt at her best. However, Sybil was not that easily put off.

'We will come to you,' she said, with an impoliteness that surprised even Jouk.

A statuesque woman, the stalwart of the tennis club, with a 'bright young thing' as a daughter, Sybil seemed to Rozia to personify England in all her majesty. Sybil lost no time in examining Rozia's salon. Nor did she waste moments before revealing that, '. . . of course Martin is not as inventive as your husband.' She turned to Jouk who was translating for Rozia. 'Inventive?' Rozia said, brightening at the thought of a subject she could excel at. 'Chemistry is not about being inventive. It is a specific science. You see –' Jouk interpreted her words exactly.

'Yes, well, your husband did say you were a student of his. Quite a romance I hear. But tell me, you are so very young, your parents must be distraught at your decision.'

'Decision?' Rozia repeated. She felt numb, and her cheeks blazed.

'To come to England, of course. And tell me,' Sybil leaned nearer and Rozia could see the line where her powder ended quite clearly on her neck, 'how did they feel about you marrying a man so much older than yourself?'

'I am sure they were happy that Rozia would be taken care of,' Martin Lascelles interjected so speedily that Rozia almost wondered . . . She liked him enormously. He had Jouk's kindness, but he treated her as a father might, cosseting her, admiring her.

'You know, you should go to the Wembley Exhibition, my dear,' he said, fidgeting with his small cucumber sandwich, that Miss Dent had said should be on the menu.

'Don't be ridiculous, Martin. The girl's pregnant.'

'Oh, tell me about it,' Rozia interrupted, using her heavily accented English for the first time, 'anyway . . .' She dropped her eyelids in a way she had almost forgotten.

'It's wonderful,' Martin Lascelles continued. 'There are fifteen miles of streets, a Palace of Engineering, the largest concrete building in the world.'

'Oh Martin, really, we don't need to know all of that,' Sybil cried, fanning her face with a handkerchief.

'I am fascinated,' Rozia murmured quietly.

'Do you know, they have models of the Prince of Wales and Jack Hobbs – he's a cricketer, you know about cricket of course . . .'

Rozia nodded. She didn't know anything about cricket, but she had no intention of saying anything which would encourage Sybil in her dreadful erosion of her husband's interests.

'. . . done entirely in butter, Canadian and Australian,' Martin finished triumphantly.

'How amazing,' Jouk said.

'It'll be a wonderful day out.'

'The girl is pregnant,' Sybil repeated darkly.

Rozia looked up at Jouk. 'I would love to go – just for a few hours.'

'I wouldn't risk it, Joseph.' Sybil's voice ended on a downward note.

'We call my husband Jouk.' She blushed.

'I don't use derivatives.'

'It isn't a derivative, that is his name.'

'It is a derivative, my dear. My name is Joseph.'

Rozia was very angry. She didn't know exactly what derivative meant, and now Jouk had shown her up and she didn't like it. She pursed her lips like a small girl.

'And of course Sybil is right. You cannot possibly wander around an exhibition like that in your condition.'

It seemed to Rozia that Jouk had imprisoned her in the small house which looked exactly like its counterparts in the suburban English road. It had a neat front garden and in the summer, shortly after they had first arrived, rosebushes crowded the sides of the red-tiled path which led from the little gate to the front door. There were bay windows on the ground floor, but instead of the usual flimsy net curtains a heavy lace, fringed at the ends, concealed the interior from prying eyes . . . Neither Jouk nor Rozia knew their neighbours, beyond the polite lifting of a hat when Oberski went to work, or perhaps a nod as Rozia stepped from the gate to the pavement. But as she discovered, that was the way it was in England.

Rozia tried not to show her resentment. She applied herself diligently to her English lessons; she concentrated on teaching her maid to cook. But Jouk could see that his once bright flower was now pale and languid. She spent a lot of her time in bed. He was not a doctor, but Joseph Oberski knew enough of the physical body to realize that this was not good for Rozia.

As if reading his thoughts, Father O'Flynn accosted him on his way home from church. 'That wife of yours, she has never been out since you brought her here, apart from the odd trip to look at Regent Street and gawp at the Palace. Take her out, dear man, take her to the theatre.'

Jouk was surprised. 'Mrs Lascelles did not think –'

'Whoever Mrs Lascelles is, she has never been alone in a strange country. Nor is she nineteen. A bit of fun, that's what the girl needs.'

So Jouk made inquiries. A musical, he was told, would be the thing. London's big show was *No No Nanette* at the Palace Theatre. Two tickets for the dress circle were procured and Jouk even borrowed Martin Lascelles' car for the evening. Rozia was thrilled – an outing at last, despite the rain. It seemed to have rained continuously since she had arrived in England. She had a dress especially made for the occasion in palest grey with silver embroidery.

They arrived at Cambridge Circus just fifteen minutes before the curtain was due to go up. The lights dazzled Rozia. She couldn't help but compare it all with the last time she had been to the theatre, just a few months before, when she had been so proud and passionate, so in love, so committed.

'Your enjoyment will not be affected by your lack of English,' Jouk told her.

They still spoke Polish then, quietly, unobtrusively.

In the bar, people crowded against each other; the florid walls and excessive use of ormolu seemed vulgar to Rozia. Jouk offered her an orange juice, although she would have preferred one of those cocktails. Suddenly she needed the lavatory. She found herself asking a lady in Polish, and never quite forgot the astonished look on the matron's face, to imagine that anyone couldn't speak English. She resolved then to use her English.

'I find myself the way!' she said to an amused Jouk, as he

escorted her down the gently sloping corridors filled with people moving towards the auditorium.

The bright lights, the sophistication, the music, the bathing belles, were a long way from the art of Ibsen, but they had their magic too and Rozia lost herself in the world of make-believe.

Later Jouk took her to the Embassy Club. He bought her a gardenia from the one-legged man at the entrance and walked her down a sort of tunnel. The Embassy was a restaurant with a small square in the centre which was used as a dance floor. Jouk and Rozia had a table at the back, but the waiter made sure to point out the Prince of Wales' sofa table.

'He always comes on a Thursday,' he confided, 'and we know when he is about to arrive because his equerry comes in first.'

Rozia stared at the empty table throughout dinner. She would have loved to have seen the future King, as she thought of him. Jouk invited her on to the dance floor. As he held her, she realized that it was the first time he had put his arms around her. As he manoeuvred her around the dance floor, she tried not to think of Stefan.

On September 2nd, 1924, just a year after Rozia Mezeurska had entered the University of Warsaw in the faculty of chemistry, Rozia Oberska began to feel the pains of child-birth. A doctor came and a little after him, a nurse arrived with a suitcase. She would stay because there was to be a child in the family.

Upstairs, heavy blue velvet curtains were drawn over the windows of the main bedroom, filtering the light, obscuring the freshness of daytime. The atmosphere was heavy, sticky, even oppressive. Gold filigree wall lights, the bulbs naked without their dainty blue shades, shone down on a sweaty, dishevelled woman lying on her matrimonial bed, legs raised and pressed against the large thighs of a midwife who stood, poised, ready to help the newcomer into the world.

A tank of ether stood in the corner of the room, unused. It made Rozia sick.

'Mama!' she screamed, her voice hoarse, despairing.

'Come on dear, you're going to be a mother soon yourself. Be brave, I can see the head.'

Rozia pushed down, wanting to be rid of the cause of her pain, feeling the pressure on her bowels.

The doctor spoke from the other side of the room, where he was washing his hands in a white tin basin. 'You're being very good. I know it's been hard. But soon, soon it will be over.' His tone was bland and impersonal in its encouragement.

Rozia clutched at the midwife's left hand. 'Please,' she said to no one in particular, 'let it be finished.'

Downstairs Jouk Oberski listened, and laying his head against a wall, prayed to the Holy Mother.

In the bedroom the doctor prodded under the sheets. Rozia writhed. The midwife grabbed both her hands, holding them tight.

'Push now,' the doctor instructed.

Rozia strained and heaved. '*O moi Boze, pomoz mi!*' she shouted.

And then the screaming stopped. The sudden silence frightened Jouk. A maid stood awkwardly by the door.

'Dr Oberski?' she asked nervously.

'I don't know,' he said as he ran up the stairs. He paused outside the bedroom door, and after a moment pushed it open.

'Good, the head is through. Now, wait,' the doctor instructed Rozia.

'No,' she snapped.

'It's better for the baby. Give it a chance, wait,' repeated the doctor, shocked out of his cocoon of dissociation.

118

'Get it out,' Rozia wailed and using all her strength, she bore down and dislodged the baby's body. The doctor and the midwife were surprised that such a small frame could be capable of such a massive thrust . . . and then the small blue mass was there, covered in the white film of birth. It was slapped rudely and it cried. Jouk sighed with pleasure. He went deeper into the room and watched as the midwife cleaned the newborn's nose and eyes.

The doctor cut the cord and pushed hard on Rozia's stomach, forcing the afterbirth from her. The midwife finished wiping the child's face, wrapping it in its swaddling clothes and offered it to Rozia.

'You have a daughter, Mrs Oberska.'

Rozia turned her head away. 'She hurt me,' she whimpered.

Jolted, the midwife backed off.

'Give her to me,' Jouk whispered and he took the child and held her close.

No one moved, no one spoke, and then Rozia reached up for her baby. As Jouk passed her over, the child yelled loudly. Rozia didn't even bring her to her body, she just handed the bundle back to the midwife, avoiding Jouk.

'I'm tired,' she said. 'Leave me alone.'

After the birth Rozia lay in her bed, content to let the nanny, hired at the advice of Sybil Lascelles, deal with the baby who seemed to have no part of her. She relived Stefan's death, feeling the pain again, as if it were her own – wishing it were. She saw her parents, and Booba, and Jonathon as clearly as if they were by her bed; she talked with them, pleaded with them, 'Forgive me. Love her.'

On the third night, despairing, she got out of her bed and went to the nursery. She stood by the crib, its white bows and flounces a tribute to her handiwork, and called out to her father: 'Papa, come here, come and look. She is your grandchild. Speak to her, see her.'

Jouk heard her, but kept himself hidden by the door, watching his young wife weep out her pain in angry, bitter tears; he knew he was unable to help her and cursed his impotence, wanting to scream himself.

Nanny Morgan had no such inhibitions. 'Mrs Oberska, what are you doing? You'll disturb the child – get back to your bed,' she cried, anxious for the woman, anxious for the child, and angry at the unnecessary disturbance in a night when sleep was precious. Rozia allowed herself to be taken back to bed, and a warm cup of tea was brewed for her from the thermos of hot water which was always available by Nanny's bed.

'Now,' said the woman paid to care, 'go back to sleep. Whatever it is that you have left behind in that country of yours, it has no place here. Cover it over and concentrate on getting your strength back so that you can enjoy all your young years.'

Rozia heard her words, and she heeded them. Papa, Mama, Booba and Jonathon – they were gone, just like Stefan. But, to her surprise, she resolved that there must be one more tribute to what had been, and with that decision she turned on her back and fell asleep.

In the morning when Jouk came to inquire after her night's rest, pretending all had been peaceful, she told him. 'I have decided on the child's name. She will be called Hannah.'

The question of baptism was raised by Father O'Flynn. Rozia sighed. It seemed to her that there were decisions to be taken every day, every hour. She felt weighed down by it all, and now the biggest decision of all – who would be the godparents?

'I'd be happy to be a godfather,' the priest offered. Rozia took his hand, and held it tight; her way of saying thank you.

'But who could be the godmother?' she asked, feeling panicked and alone, 'I couldn't face Sybil Lascelles.'

'No,' said Father O'Flynn, never having met Mrs Lascelles, he shouldn't really have formed an opinion, but the name seemed symbolic enough. 'Have you met Mrs Wheeler? My Mrs Wheeler?' he asked.

Rozia looked quizzical.

Father O'Flynn had called just two weeks after Hannah's birth and they were sitting in her favourite salon. She was wearing a loose afternoon gown, but the work on restoring her figure had already begun. Immediately after the birth she had insisted on being bound in great white bandages, like a corset. She wouldn't allow the thought of sagging flesh to even enter her mind.

'She is rather special, is Mrs Wheeler. Her husband died in the war, and she never remarried; it was a love match.'

Rozia shut her eyes briefly; she liked the sound of Mrs Wheeler.

'She looks after me now,' Father O'Flynn was telling her – and his voice seemed to come from a long way down.

'Can I meet her?' Rozia asked.

'Of course, whenever you like.'

'Next week? I will arrange a special tea.'

'Fine.' Father O'Flynn smiled. 'Now, where is your little girl?'

Rozia led the way to the nursery where the baby Hannah lay in her beautiful white cot. O'Flynn picked her up and thrust her at her mother. 'Kiss her,' he said.

Rozia looked at him.

'Kiss,' he repeated and smacked a large moist mouth on Hannah's forehead.

'Kiss,' Rozia said slowly.

'Yes.'

'Yes,' she repeated.

She took her child, and looking into the deep blue eyes that were Stefan's, she felt the stirrings of her love.

That evening when Jouk returned from his work, he went immediately to the nursery – it had quickly become a ritual for him to coo over Hannah, enjoying her, and Rozia found herself relegated to the role of observer. During the first weeks she hadn't minded very much. She hadn't expected great outpourings of maternal love, but she had been surprised and worried at her own initial reaction of coldness. Rozia didn't know why she didn't feel about the baby the way Jouk obviously did. After all, she was the mother. But after being with Father O'Flynn in the nursery that afternoon, she suddenly didn't like Jouk's appropriation of the child.

Rozia moved over to the fireplace, she wanted to light a cigarette, but she wouldn't smoke in the nursery; she had begun to smoke soon after their arrival in England – Jouk hated the habit.

'Father O'Flynn has spoken to me about the baptism. He has offered to be the godfather.'

'I will be the godfather.'

Rozia turned, stunned by Jouk's voice. It had a hardness she had never heard before. He was leaning over Hannah's crib, tickling her face, kissing her cheek.

'How can you be?' Rozia's voice was hard too, but it was loud as well. 'You are her father here, remember? If you are not her father, there is no point in me being in England at all.'

She flounced from the nursery, trying not to hear her daughter's cries, or Jouk's voice as he petted and cajoled; trying not to dislike Nanny Morgan's obvious capability as she took the distressed child and comforted and soothed her in the way that a mother should.

'If you are going to argue, Dr Oberski,' she heard the

nanny say, 'kindly do so out of earshot of the little one.'

On the threshold of her bedroom, Rozia felt the rebuke as if it were a slap.

England, Rozia had discovered, was a land of gentlemen and players. Mrs Wheeler was a player, but Rozia didn't care for such distinctions.

The tiny birdlike lady – with her long, blonde hair combed into a coil on top of her head, her neat hands and her deep set, blue eyes – was a delight to Rozia. At last she felt her shoulders relax as she offered small square pieces of *mazurek kroleski*, the chocolate cake her mother had offered in her own home. She hadn't made it since she had come to England, but she so wanted to please Father O'Flynn.

Mrs Wheeler savoured it, her nice mouth chewing carefully, her little feet put together as if she had placed them deliberately in one line. 'How lovely, Mrs Oberska,' she said. 'Can I see the little girl?' she asked as soon as politeness allowed.

'Of course.' Rozia leapt out of her chair, leading the way.

Nanny Morgan, who belonged to the breed of English nannies who raised their children and offered them for inspection to the parents between the hours of five and six, and who cared for their broods until they were despatched to the confines of a good prep school at the unholy age of seven years, was appalled at the choice of godmother, but Rozia registered none of the disapproval in her nanny's eyes. All she saw was a tenderness that had gone from her life, and hands that softened and held, hands that she did not resent cuddling her baby.

Later, when Father O'Flynn was temporarily out of earshot, Rozia put her soft hand over Mrs Wheeler's thin bony wrist. 'I am sorry about your husband,' she said softly.

The little bird-woman suddenly seemed to change. Rozia

saw the breasts beneath her neat white blouse and the lines of her legs under the black skirt.

'England is now a land of women without men, Mrs Oberska; we lost our husbands, our sons and our fathers. None of them were spared, even if they did live. It was bad you see, in the trenches.'

Rozia wanted to put her arms around her, to comfort her, but suddenly the breasts were gone again, the skirt revealed no legs and the little woman, who had shown such want, became a housekeeper again.

'I would consider it a great honour to be Hannah's god-mother,' she continued as if she had never revealed herself. 'A great honour.'

'And I would consider it a great honour if you will be my friend,' Rozia said, not feeling quite so alone.

When Hannah was seven and a half months old, she turned herself over. At last she could do something, and Rozia found it amusing to watch her. One particular evening Jouk was not at home and she was alone with her child. She touched the small, still plump legs, and kissed the little knees. The baby gurgled in delight. Rozia smiled back. It was pleasant. She hadn't touched human flesh for so long like that, and she cradled Hannah in her arms, kissing the hair line, and felt the baby wriggle in her arms. She found herself rocking her, singing an old lullaby, a long-forgotten memory of a childhood that at that moment did not hurt. Hannah fell asleep and Rozia let her voice drift off, and she contented herself with just looking and occasionally letting her fingers stray over a cheek or an eye. She didn't hear the door open, or Jouk tiptoe into the room. She just became aware of his presence, almost like an acknow-ledgement rather than a greeting. She smiled at him, re-membering how much she cared for Jouk. Jouk watched the expression in his wife's eyes and he understood it. He did not attempt to take the baby from her, or to touch her, but contented himself with being a part of the tableau.

Later that night, when they were in bed, Jouk reached for her. Expecting his customary affectionate embrace, Rozia turned into him, but his hands held her down and she felt his fingers reach for her and begin to touch her, caress her sensuously. At first she tried to push him away, but then her body gave in to the pleasures of his fingers. She arched her back, wanting to guide him into her – reaching for him, but her fingers found no response.

'Oh God,' she whispered, suddenly remembering.

'It's all right. It's all right. I want it for you. I love you,' he whispered back.

And as he brought her to orgasm she sobbed out in relief, but when she turned into her pillow, after kissing him good night, she realized to her horror that it would never be enough.

Chapter Seven

———◆———

In the summer after Hannah's birth, Rozia and Jouk were invited to stay with the Lascelles' at Sybil's former family home which she still used at the weekends. It was situated by the sea near Bognor.

The invitation had been delivered about a month before. Rozia was appalled to discover from Jouk, confirmed by Nanny Morgan and re-confirmed by an amused Mrs Wheeler, that she would be expected to leave Hannah behind. She was not pleased. She viewed the whole thing with distaste, supposing that all they would do was play tennis, play tennis . . . and that was the moment Rozia decided to learn tennis!

She contacted a Polish acquaintance, Dr Przenicki, a correct and precise Pole who wore a monocle in one eye. He was attached to the Polish Embassy. Rozia never did find out what he did exactly, apart from attend all the shooting parties, the opera, theatre and the latest nighteries. But he could play tennis.

'Learn in a month?' he said, amazed.

'Yes,' Rozia said defiantly.

When he realized that it was a matter of honour, the Pole said nothing more. It was understood that Rozia must be ready. They played every day for four hours, except Sundays. At first Rozia could barely lift the racket, but she had natural ball-sense, and within two weeks she could play a game. Two weeks after that, Rozia was passable.

'You must join a club now,' Dr Przenicki told her, 'the Westmoreland, it's nearby and you will make friends.'

Rozia had a test to see if she was good enough. An elegant man, Mr Adams, a local lawyer, threw balls at her over the net.

'Jolly good,' he said, admiring her form.

'Yes, you are good,' said Mrs Adams, who recognized Rozia from her frequent attendance at Mass. She noticed that she talked a lot to Mrs Wheeler; obviously the young foreign girl did not know the ways of England; she resolved to teach her.

Bernice Adams was very aware that her family had been English Catholics forever. So had her husband's; it comforted her to know exactly who she was. She was a small, if slightly plump woman who was very proud of the fact that an ancestor had been burnt at the stake. Actually the ancestor was more closely connected to the Yorkshire branch of the family, but Bernice never told anyone that part. She and Leo had no children. It pained her, so she never talked of it. Instead she played a lot of tennis . . . well, Leo liked it and what else was there for her to do? She had never contemplated a life without children – it had been such a shock when the doctor told her she had to have everything out. That kind of thing happened to other people, never to oneself, she admitted to Leo. For a while it had drawn them together – they indulged in little romps, calling each other lion and mouse, even changing roles when the mood suited. But there was less of that now. Bernice told herself she didn't mind. Leo was a good lawyer and she enjoyed her little comforts, so if she ate too many chocolates or guzzled a few too many of the little fairy cakes that her maid provided with a regularity that palled a little, no one said anything.

At last the weekend arrived. Rozia prepared herself carefully and Sybil Lascelles was surprised when she joined her and the other guests in white, the women in their Suzanne Lenglen look-alikes, the men in tight white flannel trousers.

'I didn't know you played, Rozia, you never said,' she offered a little too politely.

At first Rozia contented herself with the talkative tennis, enriched with plenty of 'Oops', and 'Yours partner'. Her partner, Simon Eastwell, was a young foppish Englishman with a smooth baby face and long blond hair that hung around his neck. He was a friend of the Lascelles' daughter Rosemary, who didn't like the idea of him playing tennis.

'Just too boring, darling,' she cried petulantly, curling up her legs under her dress.

But the young Englishman liked the exotic foreign flower who was his partner, and he flashed smooth charm encompassing Rozia. She responded, remembering how much she had liked to flirt. At first she dallied on the court, this way and that, and then suddenly she wanted to win and the foppish Englishman, with his overabundance of charm, began to irritate her. She played, going for the shots, working her body, unashamed of the sweat. Jouk watched her, enjoying her movements as she reached and crouched, as she ran and hovered. They won.

'Well done,' said the Englishman, unsure of the success of their victory.

'Extraordinary,' Sybil said over a beautiful tea of strawberries and cream and Scribban's Dundee Cake.

Later, before dinner, as she stood with her hand on the drawing-room door, about to make her entrance in her pretty silver dress now re-made since the birth of Hannah, Rozia heard her hostess remark: 'Well, she's foreign of course, they don't understand that it is how you play the game, not who wins that matters. Goodness, she even took poor Gilbert's shots, appallingly bad taste, my dear . . . What is England coming to? These people are taking over everywhere.'

'The husband isn't so bad,' said the woman she was speaking to.

'No, he's delightful, but it is in the breeding you see. He comes from an old Polish family and it shows.'

'What's her background?'

'No idea, but she looks Jewish!'

If she could, Rozia would have run then, run to her bed, run to soft warm covers that would conceal and hide her shame. But Rozia Mezeurska Oberska couldn't run anywhere. The Polish girl who didn't know how to play the game swallowed and walked into the pre-dinner drinks and tried to pretend that she didn't hurt inside.

Rozia Oberska had been living in England for twelve years when Adolf Hitler left the Olympic arena in Berlin rather than acknowledge the prowess of Jesse Owens and his American Negro team mates over the Aryan heroes of the Master Race.

'Bad form,' Martin Lascelles had observed. 'Doesn't he realize it is not who wins, but how you play that is important?'

Listening to him, Rozia wondered how Mr Hitler might feel if he knew that he was bracketed in behaviour with a Polish, once Jewish, immigrant who played tennis to win.

Rozia had established a life for herself – its power points were the Church, Jouk's work and the tennis club. She was a good if slightly distant mother, trying to do her best for Hannah. Jouk was her friend, and now that she had settled down to a life in England she was grateful to him for rescuing her, as she saw it. They never discussed the past; it was as if life had begun in England, and that was the way Rozia wanted it. She centred her social life on monthly dinner parties: an adept cook and a charmer, she was a popular hostess – with the men; the women found her too rich for their taste, like an over-embellished dessert, perhaps . . . at least that was what Rozia felt.

She had established a relationship with Bernice Adams,

who taught her that one did not associate with 'players' like the priest's housekeeper – although Mrs Wheeler's name was never actually mentioned – when one was a 'gentleman' like Rozia. Rozia spent many hours with her one great friend, Father O'Flynn, trying to work out how she, so obviously a woman, could possibly be a 'gentleman'. The Irish priest had laughed till the tears flowed as a Rozia of the past inquired whether she should wear trousers and perhaps carry a cane, or maybe a monocle and a small cigar would be more suitable. However, despite the laughter, Rozia had heeded Bernice's advice, even though she assured Father O'Flynn that she wouldn't. The priest hadn't commented, because he knew Rozia's life was difficult enough.

And so Bernice had become a sort of confidante, the kind you talked to, just to share gossip, the tittle-tattle of the day – harmless enough, but in a rare moment of honesty Rozia told Jouk, 'It is stultifying, sometimes I feel as if I am choking to death with politeness.'

To Rozia's surprise Sybil Lascelles, who appeared to be the caricature of the quintessential English woman, had very little time for Bernice's little chats.

'It's very sad that she can't have a child,' she told Rozia firmly. 'But that is no excuse for indolence – she does nothing with herself . . .'

Sybil worked on a committee for the Red Cross, and she was a member of the Women's Voluntary Service. It was because of her efforts in community work that she and Martin were invited to a garden party at Buckingham Palace.

'We didn't have an exclusive invitation,' she explained to Rozia and Bernice at one of Rozia's little teas the following week. 'There were two thousand of us, but I did see "him".'

Rozia didn't need to ask who 'he' was; she had been in England long enough to know that it wasn't necessary to give the handsome young King a name. She remembered how entranced she had been by the idea of a prince when she had first come to England – at the memory, an image came into her mind of her own long-gone fairy prince, and she stiffened and pushed it away, forcing her attention back to Sybil.

'There is gossip,' Sybil was saying, 'that he is in love with an American divorcee.'

'How thrilling,' Rozia said.

'How appalling,' Bernice said. 'Where is his sense of duty?'

'He is in love,' Sybil said, allying herself with a surprised Rozia.

It was just three days after the tea that Rozia heard that Sybil's daughter Rosemary had drowned on a sunny Sunday afternoon, just a few yards out of her depth – opposite the Lascelles' weekend house. She had drunk too much, and eaten too much, at lunch, and had ignored her concerned father and rushed into the sea to 'cool off'. They'd found her, some hours later, when the tide turned and brought her body back to the shore, laying it gently on the shingle beach like a much-loved rag doll.

Jouk told Rozia that the postmortem revealed that Rosemary had been pregnant. Apparently she had been having a relationship with a married man in London. It had been going on for some time which was why she had never married. The man had three children – as a doctor, he had told Rosemary, he could never face the scandal of a divorce. Sybil had read it all in Rosemary's diary.

Sybil had done terribly well at the funeral. It was Martin who gave way to what might be considered an unseemly display of grief. Sybil had been aware that she wanted to help him, to share his pain, but she couldn't. Quite simply, had she allowed herself to comfort Martin, she would have collapsed. It wasn't a question of propriety – it was a matter of her own survival – she wasn't quite sure how to cope with the agony.

However, it had not gone unnoticed to her that Martin did have a comforter – one who simply stood and held his arm, who touched his hair, who allowed him to cry. Rozia Oberska, uncaring of boundaries and form, had sneaked her way through the mourners to be at Martin's side. She had even reached out to Sybil at that dreadful moment when her child's remains encased in oak thudded against the dry, unwelcoming earth. The English woman had let her hand be held, taking strength in the firm dry warm grip, and would have held on if Rozia had not withdrawn herself.

Therefore it had come as no surprise to either woman that when Sybil came to sell her weekend house – she had to, she knew she would not be able to cope with looking at the sea, knowing that Rosemary had died there – it was Rozia whom she invited to share the last few days. Sybil had not gone back to the place of memories out of choice – but the house had to be cleared of its furniture, of its things, and that had to be done by Sybil herself. She knew her responsibilities; there was no question of asking anyone else to take on that chore.

When Rozia arrived, she welcomed her cordially enough but there was a formality, not of behaviour but of unease. After some hours Rozia, sure of her role, understood that she could not allow the pattern to be set. 'You have to mourn,' she said. 'I know it hurts, but you have to.'

Safe in her family house, without even Martin's eyes to pursue her, Sybil took her daughter's favourite ballgown and walked along the beach and wept bitter, angry tears. In her rage she shredded the flimsy pretty dress, threw it on the ground and heaped sand and shingles on it, burying it as she had buried her child. But this time, alone in the dark, she allowed herself to rage against Rosemary, against the doctor – why hadn't she noticed her daughter's unhappiness? – and then she grieved. She thought of Martin, how she had never thought him quite 'good enough'; but he was, it was she who had failed, and the little Polish woman of whom she knew so little had shown her that – and Sybil Lascelles knew in her deepest misery that in order to go on she had to change. She was so sad for all she had lost but she knew she would go on.

Rozia waited; she brewed tea and sat on a couch, clasping her knees close to her. If she shared in a kind of mourning of her own she did not reveal it, but when the English woman returned to the house in the early hours, without the ballgown, Rozia held her, not just to comfort, but to take comfort too. If Sybil recognized Rozia's need she too said nothing, but comforted and was comforted.

Shortly after their return to London, Rozia insisted that Sybil join her tennis club; at the same time she raised what was for her a delicate matter.

'I know it is very late, but I made a wrong choice when I selected Hannah's godmother,' Rozia said, knowing that she was speaking a little too quickly.

'I would be delighted,' Sybil told her, speaking a little too quickly herself, 'but I can't take part in the formalization of such an act. I am not a Catholic and I can't see myself holding a twelve-year-old girl at the font.' There was a wry smile that made Rozia catch her breath.

Chapter Eight

———— ◆ ————

On a crowded Platform Four of Victoria Railway Station, during the summer of the year 1938, Hannah Oberska, aged thirteen, was making patterns in the dirt of the station platform with her shiny new shoes. Around her people jostled each other in their impatience to begin or end their journeys. Drivers and stokers strode purposefully to and from their great black engines; coal dust had impregnated the crevices of their skin, their overalls had no colour, and soot tinged everything they wore.

The business of the railways whirled around Hannah: the sounds of whistles, the cranking of machines, the screeching of brakes, the passengers spilling from carriages like herds of cattle anxious to be freed from their pens. Clipped inanimate voices handed out travel information over loudspeakers that distorted and newspaper vendors shouted out their wares.

Ignoring the mêlée, she concentrated on the movement of her feet as they formed circles and squares with straight or squiggly lines. Hannah had grown into a fine-boned girl with small hands and slender feet. She had a perfectly proportioned face which was nevertheless dominated by her deep blue eyes.

She was travelling to Poland with her parents, who were making a last attempt to persuade her grandparents to come to England because of the talk of war. That possibility meant nothing to Hannah, but the expedition was another matter. She was thrilled with the thought of a different country, a different language, the strangeness of it all. She knew of course that her parents were Polish, foreign really. But she was English – she couldn't even think of herself as anything else, she knew no other way.

She glanced up at the grubby canopy which covered the railway station. Smoke and grime had smeared it with a film of muck, but she could still see the sun shining through as if screened by a curtain. She found the effect quite beautiful.

'Hannah, what are you doing to your clean shoes?' her mother's voice penetrated the crowd.

'Nothing, I was waiting for you,' Hannah replied.

'They're dusty,' Rozia said.

'Everything's dusty here, can we get on the train?'

'No, we must wait for Papa.'

'Where is he?'

'He's gone to collect our reservations.'

Her mother was elegantly dressed except for a ridiculous hat, which covered her upswept shoulder-length auburn hair – Rozia's hairstyles were totally dictated by fashion. The smart suit and white crêpe de chine blouse might have seemed inappropriate for a journey across four countries, but she had no intention of travelling in discomfort. Her well-made-up face could have been the model for her daughter's, except for the fact that her eyes were brown. She was nervous, her red nails pulling anxiously at Hannah's long blonde hair.

'Mummy, don't,' Hannah said, irritated.

'Sorry, but you look so pretty.'

'I don't feel it.'

'It doesn't matter what you feel. You look nice.'

Rozia wondered why Jouk was taking so long to collect the tickets. She was trying very hard to appear calm in front of Hannah, but her heart was thumping. It had been hard, the decision to go to Poland, but Rozia felt she had no choice. Everyone knew there was going to be a war and that Germany would try to invade Poland. She had read the carefully censored reports of antisemitism in Germany with increasing horror and worry. Matters had been brought to a climax when at one of Sybil Lascelles' dinner parties, she heard a German professor of chemistry, recently exiled from Vienna, speak of Adolf Hitler's maniacal dreams for a 'Jew-free Europe'.

'What will he do with the Jews?' Rozia found herself asking, and even she could hear that her voice was trembling.

The German put his head in his hands, rubbing the bridge of his nose with his fine fingers with obviously manicured nails. His neat receding hair was ruffled a little as he turned back to Rozia. 'God knows, Mrs Oberska, but I fear for them.'

Rozia had glanced at Jouk, but said nothing.

On the way home in their little Wolsley car, she had shivered despite the early summer sun and said, 'I should go.'

'We should all go,' Jouk replied.

And he booked the tickets before she had time to change her mind. At first Rozia insisted that Hannah shouldn't go with them, but Jouk said, 'She is the one weapon you have against your parents' prejudices. I don't think we can afford to leave her at home.'

She prayed that the bribe – Rozia accepted Jouk's reasoning that Hannah was the bribe – would work.

Rozia looked down at Hannah and noted, without reaction this time, that the child was covering her shoes in dirt again and she suddenly realized that she had no idea if her parents were still alive. Her brother, Jonathon, had been just a year older than Hannah when she had last seen him.

'Here we are. I have the tickets.'

Jouk broke into Rozia's thoughts and she was grateful. She wanted to take his arm, but he lifted Hannah up, his arms around her waist. The child's face was turned towards him as if she were a lover.

'Let us board,' he said.

Pushing away from him, Hannah ran to the train. She had waited so long and now, at last, she could mount those steep steps. She stumbled, blackening her white socks. A uniformed attendant steadied her and ushered her into a plush first-class carriage. Hannah marvelled at its opulence, at the little light over every seat, at the rich red fabric. She loved it and wished they were travelling in it all the way to Warsaw, not just to Dover where they would take the boat. Nothing, she decided, could be as special as this.

Moving over to the window she blew little patterns on the glass, watching the small area mist over. She touched the window with her finger, wiping it clean, wanting to start again, to recreate another pattern which she could eliminate when she wanted.

'Hannah, help your mother.'

Her father's vaguely rebuking voice made her turn to the exasperated Rozia, who said, 'You know we have a lot of things to organize, you might help me instead of standing daydreaming.'

She watched her mother explain to a porter that the trunk was to be stored in the luggage area for Warsaw whilst the small baggage would travel with them. Hannah couldn't understand what she could have done to help. Everything was already done. She sat on a seat and swung her legs absently.

'Please try to sit like a lady,' Rozia snapped.

The child shrugged and leaned back in the seat, crossing her legs as she had seen her mother do.

'Don't do that.' Rozia looked as if she were going to explode.

'Do what?' Hannah asked.

'Sit like that.'

'You told me . . .' Hannah didn't bother to continue the sentence; she realized that her mother was in one of her moods.

137

'Excuse me, I believe I travel with you.'

Rozia, Jouk and Hannah turned to the intruder – an elderly man. His coat was a little big and it was shiny – it had been worn too often – but his shoes were well polished.

Hannah was interested in the prospect of someone sharing their carriage – she thought of it as theirs. She was curious about other people, wondering how their lives might differ from her own.

'I'm sorry to intrude,' the man said, smiling apologetically.

Rozia was shocked. He was a Jew, she was sure of that, a Polish Jew. It was the coat, they all wore coats like that. Suddenly there were so many memories; she was not sure that she could cope. Sensing Rozia's reaction, Jouk was embarrassed. He extended his hand, introduced himself, adding his wife and daughter's names almost as an afterthought. Taking Jouk's proffered hand the intruder announced himself as 'Dr Weinstein'.

Hannah thought the man looked sad. 'Are you going on holiday?' she asked him.

The train jerked, and with a lurching movement edged its way from the station.

'We're going, we're going!' she shouted.

She waved to some of the railway workers, but as the speed increased the faces of the onlookers blurred, and then they were gone, still standing in the same spot whilst those in the coaches were transported away. 'It's wonderful, don't you think? You don't know what it is going to be like at the other end,' Hannah said to Dr Weinstein.

Jouk spoke in Polish, suddenly changing the atmosphere, making it personal. 'Dr Weinstein, excuse me, but you're a surgeon, I believe. You operated on a friend of mine in Warsaw.'

'I was. I was lucky to come to England, but my family . . . they are still there. You know how it is.' He shrugged.

138

'But it is dangerous for you to go back,' Rozia interrupted. 'The train goes through Germany.'

'I am not a German, Madame. I am a Pole.'

Dr Weinstein opened a battered briefcase, took out a document and studied it. Hannah peeped at him from the corner of her eye.

'This is my entrance visa for England. This means I can come back. These documents are for my wife and for my unmarried daughter.'

'Oh, you have a daughter,' Hannah said.

'I have five daughters . . .'

'Five daughters! Gosh. Any sons?'

'No, no sons, just sons-in-law.'

'Five daughters,' Hannah repeated, musing.

Five girls. She wondered briefly if she would have liked four sisters, but then she decided that she would not. It would mean sharing Papa, and she couldn't bear to share Papa with anyone.

'We've missed something, you and I, Hannah,' Jouk said fondly.

'What do you mean?' she asked.

'You and I are only children. I an only boy, and you are an only girl.'

'I haven't missed anything . . . I have you, Papa.'

'You wouldn't have lost me, if you'd had brothers and sisters.' He dug into his pocket. 'I think I might have something here.'

'Papa, bon bons!' Hannah shrieked, clapping her hands.

'Really Jouk, she's growing up now. Stop treating her like a child,' Rozia said somewhat sharply.

'Let me see what colours I have here for my little princess. Pink for a girl, pink bon bons for a girl, Papa's favourite girl . . .'

Hannah opened her mouth and in an obviously well-rehearsed ritual, Jouk unwrapped a pink sweet and put it in her mouth. She sucked it carefully and flung her arms around his neck.

'Don't sprawl over your father, you'll crease your dress,' Rozia said sharply.

'Oh, Mummy.'

'Don't be rude, Hannah.'

'I wasn't –'

'Enough, Hannah. Remember we have a companion. He doesn't want to hear you being insolent.'

Stung, Hannah sunk back on the seat. She glanced at Papa for help, but he seemed engrossed in the countryside. He never came to her aid when Mummy picked on her. It was so unfair.

Rozia fidgeted. She wondered what Dr Weinstein was doing in a first-class compartment, he looked poor. She stared at him – did she know him? No, but he looked like all of them; he had the same calm eyes. She grabbed the door handle and levered herself up.

'What is it?' Jouk asked.

'Nothing, nothing at all. My head – I need some air,' she said.

As the carriage door shut behind Rozia, Hannah turned to Jouk. 'What's the matter with Mummy?' she asked.

'Nothing, she has a headache – she said so.'

After a few moments Jouk joined Rozia in the corridor. She was leaning towards an open window, enjoying the small breeze, her eyes shut.

'Rozia, can I help you?' he asked.

'Help me? No, you can't help me.'

'Why don't we talk about it?'

'Talk about what? A headache?'

Jouk sighed and went back inside the carriage. Hannah was playing with her dress. He sat by her and took her hand. He wondered if he ought to offer an explanation, but Dr Weinstein seemed engrossed in some documents. He glanced at Hannah. He loved her so much; she was like Rozia in so many ways. This journey would be traumatic for her. She would discover that her mother had parents and that they were Jewish. He wondered how she would feel.

Rozia was aware only of her stress, of the taut feeling in her stomach. She tried to breathe deeply, to overcome the sensations that were building up within her. She had to control the irrational feelings she had against Dr Weinstein. Dimly, almost objectively, she noticed a child painstakingly making its way down the narrow corridor. It must have been five or six, but there was something strange about its face – the little eyes painted around black holes, white skin highlighted by little pink spots on the cheeks. A red mouth insisting on recognition, and yet it had no character – it was devoid of lines. The train jolted unexpectedly and the child slipped, tumbling to the ground. There was the sound of something shattering on to the floor and Rozia saw to her horror and disbelief a fallen mask – pieces of a caricature – destroyed. The child screamed, its real face revealed: little round eyes, little pink cheeks and a rosebud mouth open in terror.

Rozia went over, put a hand awkwardly on its arm and with the other, tried to scoop together the pieces on the floor. Someone came, grabbed the child, telling it off for wandering out of the carriage. The voice changed tone slightly and thanked Rozia for her help. The child was jostled, still crying, down the corridor. Rozia stayed where she was. She began to reassemble the pieces of the mask. The eyes, the cheeks, the mouth . . . but it was disfigured by a great gap, which, like a gash in the surface of the skin, exposed its fallibility. She tried to juxtapose the pieces in order to eradicate the ragged edges, but she couldn't fit them together. Intent on her work, she didn't hear the carriage door slide open, nor did she see Dr Weinstein kneel down beside her, but she was immediately aware of the hand that pulled her little pieces of papier-mâché apart.

'It's only a mask and now it is destroyed. It doesn't matter as long as there is something underneath,' he said.

'Underneath there is nothing. Look, there's just a dirty floor,' Rozia replied, her hand skimming the area where she had tried to reconstruct the mask. She stood up quickly, feeling tired and somehow damaged. She ignored Dr Weinstein as he straightened his knees and stood beside her at the window.

After some moments he said, 'It is very hard to go back, and it is even harder to forgive.'

'Forgive – what a funny thing to say,' Rozia snapped.

'Is it? You see, Mrs Oberska, I must forgive myself for resenting my birth – my Jewishness. It is very hard to be a Jew. You are not accepted. You are told you are different and yet you feel no difference. Sometimes, I would like not to be Jewish.'

'Well, you don't have to be,' Rozia retorted. 'You just have to make the decision.'

'You cannot do that,' the old man said gently. 'You are what you are. You can pretend, but inside . . .' He pointed to Rozia's heart.

'It is up to the individual,' Rozia said curtly.

Inside the railway carriage Hannah was fidgeting, feeling uneasy. 'Mummy is upset. There is something wrong,' she said to her father.

Jouk clenched his fists. He wondered if he had been right to agree to making the journey. It seemed right at the time, but Rozia was obviously and understandably overwrought, and Hannah wanted to know why. He swallowed hard, a habit of his when he was upset. He had not discussed with Rozia who should tell Hannah about her parents. It had been an unspoken agreement between them that nothing would be said unless Mr and Mrs Mezeurski agreed to see Rozia, but Jouk realized that perhaps it was not possible to ignore the reality, which could so easily be hidden in England, where it had played no role.

'Hannah, your maternal grandparents are alive. They live in Warsaw together with your mother's brother. I am sorry not to have told you the truth before, but we do not have contact with them, because they were very sad when your mother and I married.'

'How could they possibly be sad?'

'Because we are Catholics. Your grandparents are Jewish.'

'Jewish? I don't understand. I didn't know Mummy had any parents – she once said they were dead.' Hannah looked at him intently. 'Why don't they see you and Mummy?' she paused for a moment and pulled at her fingers, 'and me?'

'It is against their religious beliefs for your mother not to be Jewish and they were very upset when she became a Catholic.'

'Does it make it all right if they don't see her?'

'It's complicated.' Her father sighed.

'What can be complicated about parents not seeing children . . . they must be awful.'

'No, it isn't as simple as that. I will try and explain, but you must be very patient.' Jouk paused, trying to compose himself.

He found the prospect of recounting his marriage to Rozia quite painful. He was suddenly very aware, for the first time since her birth, of Hannah's real parentage, and he was angry at the need to fabricate the story. He loved Hannah – she was his, he had raised her.

'I was forty-four years old when I met your mother. She was one of my students. A clever, pretty girl – just like you. She was studying chemistry. Your mother could have practised if she had been able to qualify in England.' He drew a breath and continued: 'We fell in love. Your grandparents were worried about the age difference. Your mother was only eighteen, just a few years older than you are now.'

'She fell in love with you when she was eighteen. Oh Papa, that's wonderful, it's so romantic.'

'Your mother was beautiful. She had very long hair – she was very proud of her hair,' Jouk said, remembering Rozia as she had sat in his classroom.

He enjoyed the pleasure of those times. He remembered how he had looked forward to his work, to the anticipation of seeing the young Jewish girl.

'Was Mummy Jewish when you knew her?'

'Yes, she was.'

'I have a Jewish friend, Esther,' Hannah said.

Jouk nodded.

'But Papa,' she continued, 'I still don't understand why they don't see us. It can't be because you married Mummy.'

'You're right. It is stupid, but there you are. It is just that they cannot accept Mummy being a Catholic so they er . . .'

'But why, Papa? Why?'

'I can't answer you. I can't explain prejudice. It isn't a rational thing.' His voice was clipped, discouraging further comment.

Hannah wanted to discuss the situation properly and she didn't understand why Papa seemed to be preventing it. She would have carried on with her questions, but at that moment the carriage door slid open and her mother came in looking very pale. Dr Weinstein stood silently behind her.

'I believe we are at Dover,' Rozia announced.

The old man collected his things and turning to Jouk, said, 'I will no longer disturb you. We will not be travelling any further together. The second-class compartments were full until now.'

'Oh, but you are going on the boat?' Hannah inquired.

'Yes, but we travel separately – I have a second-class reservation.'

'What does that mean – we're on the same boat aren't we?'

'We're travelling first class,' Rozia said sharply, gathering her furs around her shoulders.

'We'll see you on board,' Jouk said warmly.

The surgeon inclined his head and smiling at Hannah, said, 'Goodbye, enjoy the trip. I think you will find it even more exciting from now on.'

Giving her mother a challenging look, Hannah said stubbornly, 'I'll definitely see you on the boat.'

The train came to a halt and Hannah watched her mother's slim legs enveloped in silk stockings, the seams straight, as she climbed from the train, and she tried to imagine how she would have appeared to her father when they first met. Maybe all the pain of leaving her parents had hurt. She grabbed her father's arm as he helped her off the train and they walked down the platform together.

Rozia was standing with the cases, her face drawn. Jouk left Hannah and went to her, whispered in her ear, touched her cheek, comforting her. Hating to see their occasional intimacy, Hannah turned from them and ran towards the boat.

'Hannah, wait. What are you doing? Stop this instant.' Jouk had raised his voice and Hannah, realizing that he was irritated, stayed where she was, bouncing on first one foot and then the other in a little jogging motion. When Jouk reached her he grabbed her hand and walked her, without speaking, towards the boat. It was crowded with travellers, the wealthy shielded by their furs, the tourists eagerly studying maps or brandishing language books . . . and then there were those with less to look forward to, who carried their fears as an extra piece of baggage.

Hannah didn't register their differences – to her they were all the same: just like her, explorers in new territory.

It was Rozia who recognized those in dread – they were her brothers and sisters and they loomed at her, in spite of her lush protections. 'Come, Jouk, I want to get down to our cabin,' she said.

Hannah was upset, she had wanted to stay on deck and

watch the boat leave. To placate her Rozia retired alone, but immediately the vessel had manoeuvred itself from the shore, Jouk propelled her, despite her vehement protests, down a steep staircase. The small cabin contained just four bunks, two up, two down – Rozia was already lying on one, stretched out, a slim hand covering her eyes. Hannah was told to sit down, whilst Jouk fussed around his wife. She had never seen her father behave in this fashion. For as long as she could remember, she had been the centre of his attention. When he came home from his work at the laboratory, it was Hannah who would always run to him. Her mother would receive them in the lounge and then they would all dine together. In the morning, Hannah breakfasted with her father alone. She treasured the moments when, over the weekend, she would sit curled up at his feet whilst he worked over his books.

She endured school in the company of just one friend, Esther Levene, with whom she had formed an alliance in the first week. Esther was Jewish and she was Catholic with foreign parents. It was an unspoken fact that as neither of them had been invited to join the cliques that dominated their particular year, so necessity had sponsored their union. The Jewish girl and the Catholic girl were the outsiders, the ones who were different. They had to be friends.

Hannah thought about Esther as she lay back on her bunk and watched the sea through the porthole. Esther would have been as fascinated by its movements as she was. At one moment it would cover the entire space, and the next it would disappear completely. She turned to tell her father, but she saw him cuddling her mother, who seemed to be crying.

Rozia felt comforted by Jouk's arms. She was suddenly so scared. Suppose her parents wouldn't see her – then this whole awful journey, which brought back so much hurt, would have been for nothing. She glanced at Hannah. She felt so sad that she couldn't talk to her own daughter. Perhaps if it all worked out, things would be different between them.

'Hannah is watching us,' she whispered to Jouk.

'I know. It is good she should see her parents together.'

Hannah was uncomfortable. She didn't like her parents being in one bed. They slept apart at home, in twin beds. Feeling bold, she said, 'I'd like to go up on deck.'

'Yes,' Jouk answered, 'why not? Put your coat on. Stay near the cabin area.'

Hannah rushed up to the air. Immediately thoughts of her parents were banished. She relished the sea, the swirl of the water, the little white racers on top of the waves. She was fascinated by the thought of actually being on top of the water. Suddenly she noticed Dr Weinstein leaning over the railings. She sidled up to him.

'Hello,' she said.

'Hello, Hannah. You like to watch the waves too?'

'Yes, the sea is beautiful.'

'It is said that after every seventh wave there is always a big one.'

'I know that game. You count the waves. Shall we do it?' she said in a tone which, if she had been an adult, might have been construed as flirtatious.

'Why not?' Dr Weinstein began to count, and Hannah joined in, 'One, two, three,' and then they started to laugh and lost track of the waves.

'Do we include the little ones?' Hannah asked.

'Of course, how could you leave them out? Just because they are little waves, not yet grown up. How would you like it if they said we won't include you because you are not big enough?'

'They do say that,' Hannah said, her eyes bright.

'Yes . . . well . . . er, you don't like it,' Weinstein muttered, not knowing quite how to answer. Hannah linked her arm with his and they stood at the rails counting waves.

Rozia and Jouk lay quietly together. There was no sexual contact btween them. Rozia had actively discouraged it in the early years of their marriage, finding no pleasure in an unshared experience. She suppressed any desire to touch herself. She didn't want to awaken her longings.

'Rozia,' Jouk said quietly, 'I have told Hannah.'

'Told Hannah what?' she said, leaning away from him.

'That your parents are Jewish, and that they are still alive.'

Rozia tensed, she was angry. 'Don't you think that was my prerogative?'

'Yes, but the circumstances were such that –'

'It appears to me that the circumstances are always such that you have to take over everything to do with Hannah. It would have been better if I had explained. It was up to me, Jouk.'

'I realize that, and I am sorry.' He was genuinely upset. 'Why don't you go and talk to her now?' he said, knowing that even if she did, there was nothing left for her to say. 'And,' he coughed. 'There is something else.'

'What?'

'I am sorry to bring this up, but, you see, my father . . . he does not know about my accident. He will assume that Hannah is . . .' He couldn't go on. He had an intolerable pain between his chest and throat.

'That Hannah is your child?' Rozia prompted gently.

'Yes.'

'But she is, you raised her. And she loves you more than anyone else in this world . . .'

Jouk turned over on his back. He heard the hurt in her voice. 'Rozia, I –'

'No,' she said, putting her hands over her eyes. 'Please, I don't want to talk about it.'

'But we must. You have never reached out to her, Rozia, she . . .'

'Perhaps you and Hannah were too engrossed in your love affair to notice whether I did or not.'

At eight o'clock that evening, Belgium welcomed Hannah with a promise of the unknown and the babble of a strange language. The huge Moscow Express dwarfed her. In what seemed moments, she was crawling, gratefully, into crisp white sheets on a bunk bed in a carriage not dissimilar to the one she had left a few hours before. She fell asleep immediately.

So as not to disturb her, Rozia spoke quietly to Jouk. 'They check our papers at Arken – the Belgian border – and then it will be the Germans.'

'I don't know why you are worried. We are British. There is no reason for this panic.'

'I wonder,' she said absently, 'about Dr Weinstein.'

'Yes. He has a lot to worry about. Perhaps I will ask him to join us.'

'No!' Rozia's voice went hard. 'He is travelling second class. There would be an investigation.'

'You are really frightened,' Jouk said.

'Yes, I'm really frightened,' she replied.

The train started with a jolt. Rozia smoothed her skirt, and reaching into her handbag, brought out an elegant silver cigarette case. She carefully removed a cigarette and inserted it with almost loving care into a long cigarette holder, ignoring Jouk's eyes.

'You know I don't like you to smoke,' he said.

She drew deeply on the lighted cigarette, savouring it – enjoying the inhalation.

Hannah dreamt she was at sea, the waves pounding around the ship. Dr Weinstein, or was it her father, was counting. 'Don't worry,' he kept saying, 'you don't want them to be little, do you?'

The sea grew bigger, beating on the boat. The boat itself got smaller and smaller until she was surrounded by waves that seemed to engulf her.

He kept repeating, 'You don't want them to be little, do you?'

She felt the spray, and began to scream. Dr Weinstein put his arms around her.

'Stay.'

'No, I want to go!' she shouted.

'Hannah, Hannah, wake up. You've had a nightmare.'

Dimly she became aware of her father sitting anxiously on her bunk. She reached for him. He put his arms around her, comforting her by rubbing her back.

'It's all right, you've just had a bad dream, that is all.'

Hannah felt the warm, good hands soothing, calming. She snuggled against her father. 'There were waves. I was frightened. Dr Weinstein was there. I like him, Papa. It's just that in my dream, I think he tried to be you.'

Rozia leant over and touched Hannah's hair, but Hannah ignored her gesture. She walked out of the compartment and stood smoking in the gangway. Glancing at her watch, she saw that it was fifteen minutes to eleven. The train heaved. It was coming to a halt. The lights showed Arken, the Belgian border town with Germany. They seemed to Rozia to be enticing her to jump off the train, to run away. She wanted to make that jump, but it would mean going back into the carriage, collecting her coat and her bag. That would minimize the gesture. It wouldn't be impulsive, it would be commitment and she couldn't do it. She heard some noises and then the attendant came into the gangway.

'Madame, we are very sorry, but you must vacate the train and cross the border by foot,' he said.

'By foot?' she echoed. 'Vacate the carriage, in the middle of the night? I've a child.'

'We know, madame. The train company is most upset to have to disturb you in this way.'

Two Belgian immigration officers walked into the gangway. 'Your passport, madame?' one said.

'It is in the compartment. My husband has our documents,' Rozia replied.

'It is late,' smiled the young officer.

'Yes, it is. And we must get off the train.'

'It is not the Government of Belgium who insists on these regulations, madame,' said the other immigration officer.

'I know. I know,' Rozia said impatiently. She pushed open the compartment door. 'Jouk, they want our papers.'

Jouk reached into his briefcase and removed the three blue passports, their gilt inscriptions carrying an authority that should inspire. It did. They were examined very briefly, stamped, and then the officers left. The attendant, ant-like in his fineness of limbs and twittering appearance, found Hannah's coat.

The child was confused. 'Why do I need that?' she asked.

'We must get off the train, Jouk, and cross the border by foot to have our papers stamped by the Germans,' Rozia said, glaring at her husband. 'Come, let us dress the child.'

Hannah found herself hauled out of bed. Four hands dressed her, two cold and thin, but fevered as they pushed and pulled her into warm clothing, but two were quiet as they held her upright.

Hannah shocked herself into waking up. 'Let go. I can do it.' She pushed her parents away and stumbled into a jumper and skirt. Although she was only thirteen, she was already aware of her body and didn't like anyone touching it. There were small mounds on her chest that embarrassed her and little touches of hair between her legs. She had preferred her body when it was smooth and straight.

Jouk got off the train first. It was very cold and Hannah dragged her coat tighter. She noticed all the passengers standing in a line near a post which she supposed to be the frontier. On the other side of the barrier there was a table at which three men sat. They were erect and uncreased, unlike the Belgians who had a comfortable, worn appearance.

Hannah popped out of line for a closer look. 'There's Dr Weinstein! In front of us,' Hannah cried. 'Let him come with us.'

Jouk nodded. 'Dr Weinstein,' he called, 'join us. It is nicer to stand and talk than to wait alone.'

The doctor, just a few passengers in front, didn't turn around.

'Dr Weinstein, join us,' Jouk called again.

'It is better for you,' the doctor waved his hand and continued, 'if I go alone. The child –' he pointed to Hannah – 'there may be trouble.'

'There won't be,' Jouk shouted. 'You have papers.'

The barrier rose. One by one the travellers walked through and up to the desk. Passports were perused, stamped and handed back. Those who had passed through quickly returned to the train. Then it was Dr Weinstein's turn. He stood still for a moment and then walked over to the desk. Jouk pulled Hannah and Rozia with him and tried to follow.

The policeman at the pole put out a hand. 'Wait!' he barked in German.

Hannah strained to see what was happening. She saw Dr Weinstein standing very straight. She heard laughter and the three men pulled at his papers. She could see another man coming over.

Rozia's nervous nails reached for Jouk's arm. 'I want to go home,' she said.

The German policeman heard her. 'Please madame, don't worry. That man, he's a Jew. We don't like Jews. None of us like Jews, do we?'

Rozia stared at him. 'No, we don't. They killed Christ,' she said.

'*Ja*, they killed Christ,' the guard agreed.

Rozia didn't hear him. She heard her own voice over and over inside herself. 'They killed Christ . . . I killed Christ. I didn't know Him.'

She saw candles, her mother's face, screaming. 'I didn't know Christ, how could I have killed Him?' Her mother being kicked, hurt – her mother spitting back, and the spit running off her face – thick, like drops of blood.

Dr Weinstein stood very straight in front of the German immigration officials. 'I am a Polish citizen with re-entry visas for myself and my family to England,' he told them.

'Why should we let you into Germany? You are a traitor.'

'I am not a traitor to Poland,' the old man replied.

'You are nothing. You are a Jew,' one of them said.

'Repeat it,' said another.

'I am nothing. I am a Jew,' replied the doctor in a voice filled with humiliation. This was all they wanted. They stamped his passport and pushed him towards the train.

The Oberski family walked up to the desk. Jouk held the blue and gold documents tightly in his hand. He hated these hollow men whose lines appeared to be carved neatly by needles and not by character.

One of the officials smiled at Hannah. 'It's late, I'm sorry. Little girls should be in bed,' he said in English.

'I'm not little, I'm thirteen and no one should be out of bed at this hour,' Hannah said pompously.

The men laughed, but they laughed with the little girl, not against her. Rozia held her tightly. Jouk handed them his papers without speaking. He could see they were interested that his place of birth was Warsaw, but Hannah's was England. That seemed enough. The documents were stamped.

They were handed back with a polite smile. Rozia found she couldn't move. Her legs had stuck into the ground.

'Come on,' Jouk said in English.

She dragged at her feet. They moved, but it seemed to her as if she were on stilts, propelling herself through the air with no contact with the ground. They reached the train. She clambered in, ignoring her child, her husband. Dr Weinstein stood in the gangway.

'I told them we killed Christ,' she whimpered.

'I know, I know,' the old man whispered.

He put an arm around her shoulders and took her into the compartment. She began to weep. Great gasping, shocking sounds from deep inside her. Jouk and Hannah stood behind her, neither knowing what to do, whilst the old man cuddled her as if she were a child.

'I understand,' he whispered.

At that moment, there was confusion behind them. Some men came on the train. Their uniforms were black, emblazoned with silver stripes.

'Dr Weinstein, your papers. They are not correct. You come with us, please.'

'No!' Rozia shouted. 'He has entry papers back to Britain.'

'He is a Jew. His entry papers mean nothing. Jews are nothing, madame.'

Rozia had a moment, a small moment, when she could have aligned herself with Dr Weinstein. Jouk held his breath. Although he knew it would have meant dreadful danger for them all, he wanted her to do it. He willed her, but even as he wished it, she turned her back.

'Nothing, just nothing,' she said, turning her face to the window.

Hannah couldn't understand what was happening. She was confused . . . she had heard her mother crying. She heard bad things about Jews, and yet her father had told her – was it only yesterday? – that her mother was Jewish! Nothing made sense. She wanted to talk to her mother. How could she not help poor Dr Weinstein? The three men were almost carrying him from the train. Hannah threw herself away from her father and with the bravery of the young, she ran after him.

'Stop!' she cried. 'Leave that man alone. He can come back to Britain. He doesn't want to stay in your beastly country, anyway.'

Dr Weinstein tried to wave her away, but Hannah

wouldn't go. Every time the Germans moved forward she danced in front of them. Jouk ran after her. He reached her, but she ignored him – just carrying on her little dance with the Germans. Like a set piece the three figures moved forward, almost carrying the old man, and the little girl danced in front, carrying on her tirade.

'Leave him alone.' She was so sure, so intense, so furious, as if someone had stolen something that belonged to her. The German senior officer turned to his companion. They spoke. Hannah couldn't understand them, but she stood on tiptoe and kissed the old man on his cheek. They let the old man's arms go. He seemed to disintegrate. Hannah tried to pull him up, but she was too small to gather the bundle together. Jouk took her arms away from the man.

'I will help him, you go back to Mummy. You are very brave,' he said, kissing her on the cheek. She felt herself swell like a bloom in the spring. She smiled at Dr Weinstein. And then she became aware of the smell of fear, that had made him foul himself. She didn't like it. She ran back to the train – to her clean Mummy. Jouk helped the old man to his feet. He realized that Dr Weinstein was trembling. There were tears in his eyes.

'I am ashamed,' he said quietly.

The Germans laughed.

'You want the company of this shit-bag?' one said. 'If you like the smell, he's yours.'

Jouk didn't offer Dr Weinstein his arm. He wanted the old man to make the journey back to the train himself. He escorted him to the washroom and waited outside until the door opened and Dr Weinstein emerged, and then they walked back to the carriage together. Jouk saw the attendant.

'Dr Weinstein will be travelling with us.' His authoritative voice didn't brook any argument from the little man.

Rozia and Hannah were curled up together, arms and legs intertwined. Jouk didn't realize that they were both awake.

Hannah woke first. It was early, seven-thirty a.m. by her mother's little watch. Gently disentangling herself from the disordered mess that was her mother, she was aware of breasts, of a slightly open mouth, of the sounds of breathing. Her father slept on his back. Gentle snores came from his open mouth. She went over to him and placed a kiss on his brow. He was the only one who had not disappointed her. She turned to Dr Weinstein and was disconcerted to find him awake. He smiled at her, but she looked away. He had expected that. He stood up and took his battered case off the shelf.

'Where are you going? Papa wants you to stay,' she said.

'I am going to wash . . . for the day. I see my family today,' Dr Weinstein said. He paused, and then continued, 'Hannah, you are a brave little girl. I don't think you understand how brave. Perhaps if you knew, you would not have behaved as you did.'

He didn't wait for a reaction from Hannah, just took his case and went to the bathroom. He did not return to the carriage – no one mentioned his absence.

In the early afternoon, Rozia began to prepare her daughter for the arrival at Warsaw. Her heart was beating furiously – she could feel the blood racing around her body. She channelled herself into coaxing Hannah to be beautiful. The child's hair was brushed into ringlets; clean socks gleamed white against the polished shoes, the neat coat cramped her shoulders. She even had to wear gloves, just like in church! Was it going to be that boring? she wondered. She didn't like anyone at that moment, even Papa.

Rozia stood by the mirror, her hair pushed into small waves, the little black hat perched on one side of her head, the veil concealing her set face. The train shunted and shuddered. Suddenly Jouk was standing by her, his hand on her arm.

'We're here,' he said quietly, in English.

She looked up at him. 'Yes,' she said.

Chapter Nine

Rozia had come back, Rozia had come home . . . Despite herself this was Warsaw, this was her life. She glanced through the carriage window at the people, at the station; it seemed so much cleaner than Victoria – there appeared to be no dust or grime, but perhaps it was just her imagination.

Clasping her daughter by the shoulder, the woman who had been a girl when she was last here gingerly climbed down on to the station platform. Suddenly, with dreadful clarity, she saw Robert's spring flowers and she remembered that she had dropped Jouk's red roses. She pulled Hannah closer to her, wanting, needing her, as so many memories came back to greet her.

Jouk wanted to be by Rozia's side, with her, with Hannah – but he heard someone calling him, a man, a tall elderly man, with cropped white hair and a small moustache, a loved man, a loved face, his father. He ran to him, embracing him, kissing him on both cheeks.

Rozia held back, almost clinging to the train. Neither she nor her father-in-law knew how to greet each other. She offered the side of her face. His kiss merely grazed the surface of the skin. Jouk was impatient for their charade to be completed – he wanted to present Hannah.

'Papa, my child.'

He pushed her forward. Rozia had done an excellent job. Hannah gleamed from the top of the painfully curled hair to her tee-strap shoes. Mr Oberski's eyes feasted on the granddaughter. His great arms lifted her from the ground –

hugging her, surrounding her with his body. She noticed the trace of a tear.

'Welcome,' he said in Polish.

'Thank you,' Hannah whispered in English.

His enthusiasm stultified her. She shrank from him, unconsciously copying her mother. She had understood him: Jouk had spoken to her in Polish since she was a baby, but she never liked speaking the language. If anything, she thought her pronunciation might be too English and she had no intention of changing that.

As they went through the railway station, Jouk noticed Hannah and Rozia walking together, clinging on to each other almost. He noticed the flower stall, the same flower stall, and he ran over to it, dodging orderly commuters as if they were puddles on a pitted road. Rozia watched him purchase three bunches: pink roses, yellow carnations, and yellow roses. He presented the yellow carnations, their leaves tinged with red, solemnly to Hannah. She handled them awkwardly – at thirteen, not knowing what to do with them. To Rozia he presented the yellow roses, and she smelt them, grateful that they were not red ones, enjoying their strong scent.

Hannah's first view of Warsaw was of a wide street, cobbles and trams, crowded pavements and gracious buildings; there were trees, and even roadside cafés, but not many cars. It seemed a long way from England and she felt a momentary wave of homesickness. She glanced at her parents; both seemed preoccupied, looking this way and that, but not, she noticed, at the same landmarks. They were not sharing their homecoming. She glanced at her grandfather; he was manipulating his shining Ford V8 as if it were a heavily burdened pram, gripping the steering wheel firmly, aiming directly ahead of him. The car bumped over tram lines and the cobbled surfaces, avoiding irreverent pedestrians who seemed to have no respect for the right of the motor vehicle.

Hannah noticed horses and carriages neatly lined up, waiting for customers. The horses pawed the ground impatiently. She couldn't quite make out what the drivers wore, but she could see bright, flashing colours and little hats – she thought they looked as if they were in fancy dress. She'd never seen anything like that before, not even at Bognor, the seaside town where they went every summer, following the English custom of staying in the same boarding house year after year.

'What are those, Papa?' Hannah cried out to Jouk, pointing at them with a finger.

'Droshkis. I would like to take you in one, we could drive around the city.'

'There won't be time. We are going to the country. We want Hannah to see Tatra,' Mr Oberski said, turning to smile at his granddaughter.

Rozia smelt smells she had forgotten and for a moment she remembered other times. She wanted to know what reply there had been to her mother-in-law's letter to her own parents, she had to assume there was nothing, otherwise surely Mr Oberski would have told her. She glanced at her father-in-law, but his face showed nothing, just the same impassive concentration on his driving. Rozia could feel a pain in her chest that seemed to travel up to her throat.

She listened to Jouk as he told Hannah, 'You are in one of the world's great cities. Look, Teatr Weilki – the largest theatre ever built,' he said proudly.

Rozia's heart stopped. She remembered a young girl at Teatr Ruduta, on an evening when the stars had shone for lovers, and the pain was too much. Finally the car stopped in front of a big, grey stone building topped with a red roof. A tall, majestic figure, wearing a long black dress with a diamond cross sparkling at the neck, stood in a carved stone doorway. She cried when she saw her son, when he presented her with the flowers, bowing as he made the offering – it had been a long separation from her only child.

Joyfully, Jouk swept into his parents' home. He couldn't wait to show everything to Hannah.

'This is where I grew up,' he said.

He pulled her over to two long windows, outlined in black lead. Pushing one of them open, he indicated a tiny balcony.

'When I was a child, I used to climb out of this window and stand on the balcony for hours, gazing at my city. I imagined that I could see into every house – and that I could know how the people lived. And then my dreams would be interrupted by my mother, who used to be very angry – didn't you, Mama?'

He was playful, but at the same time there was a seriousness that Hannah had never seen before. His mother smiled at him, with him – almost into him.

'Ju, Ju . . . I was anxious only that you were standing on the balcony – it is dangerous, and if you tell your child these stories she will copy you. Then you will share the worries I had, when you were young.'

They both spoke in Polish. To Hannah, the words seemed to merge in a never-ending stream, but she was glad that Jouk had prepared her for this other culture by speaking Polish to her. And it was another culture to her; the furniture was heavier than in England, the rooms more formal – there seemed to be less clutter even than in her own home.

Rozia and Hannah were shown Hannah's bedroom and Rozia saw that her daughter was to sleep in the little room that once had been her sanctuary. Briefly she touched the bed. Her head began to ache.

'Come,' she said quickly to Hannah, 'let us go and see where Papa and I are to sleep.'

Jouk managed a quick word to his mother. 'Have you heard from the Mezeurskis?' he asked.

'No, I have not. But I did tell them in my letter that we were going directly to the Tatra Mountains – let us hope,' she said.

Jouk relayed the information to Rozia. He did not look at her – he could not.

The doorbell rang incessantly. Friends and family came in ever increasing numbers. Hannah found herself thrust into a strange environment, where people were kissing and crying, and behaving in an altogether disturbing manner. The noise was engulfing. She was constantly given cakes, and some kind of sticky cordial which she hated. Her normally docile father had become red-cheeked with drinking something he called 'porto' from a glass decanter topped with silver. All she wanted was sleep, but there was dinner to go through first. She was aware that her mother seemed strange too: she held a drink, but she sat at the side and not in the centre of the group. The woman who was her grandmother kept coming over and pinching her cheek and telling her how much she loved her. How could you love someone you've never met before? Hannah wondered.

Rozia could feel the muscles in her jaw aching. They always ached when she was tense. She watched Jouk greet his family and his friends. The embraces, the warmth, they were all for him.

'Madame Oberska – welcome home,' said a small man.

'Thank you . . . I, er . . .' she said, feeling awkward, searching for a name, ungrateful almost.

'Professor Katz. I taught you.'

'Oh yes, of course.' How marvellous – someone knew her. She clasped his hand, pumped it up and down, up and down.

'You have a daughter, I understand,' he said, trying to release his cramped fingers.

She dropped the hand and tittered nervously. 'Excuse

me,' she said, pointing to his hand. 'Please come and meet her.' She marched the little man over to Hannah.

'This is Dr Katz, he was one of my professors,' she said, proud of the connection.

Hannah wasn't very impressed; she didn't like teachers, but she was curious. 'Was my mother a good student?'

'Very good and very pretty too.'

'Papa said that.'

'It's true, you could have even lectured, you were excellent.'

'My life took a different course. Marriage . . . Hannah . . . this is my work,' Rozia told Dr Katz.

People were coming and going. Hannah and Rozia walked over to a couch and sat down, like two neat dolls, standing up, sitting down, shaking hands, smiling, nodding. Rozia glanced at Hannah – the child looked exhausted. At least she could be excused from dinner. She envied her.

Suddenly she wondered what had happened to Jan, and Joanna, and Robert. Really it was only Robert she cared about, and then she remembered Alekander and Wanda – what had happened to them? The tension made her flutter inside now she was home – but it wasn't her home. Tomorrow she would go and find her family. She couldn't bear the pain of being in the same city and not being with them.

She got up and went over to Jouk. He was in the centre of a group.

'. . . and then you fell in love with the lovely Rozia,' Dr Katz was saying.

'Yes, I did,' Jouk said and put his arm around Rozia's waist. 'And here she is. We are reminiscing, my darling.' Jouk had been drinking; he was mellow, he wanted her to feel as he did.

'I'd like to put Hannah to bed. She's very tired,' Rozia told him.

'Of course, the little one must be tired. Such a long journey,' Dr Katz said.

Rozia went back to Hannah. She didn't say anything, merely held out her hand. Hannah stood up and took hold of the fingers. She was manipulated into a large bed and as on the previous night, someone helped her – she thought it was her mother – but it could have been anyone. The lights were turned out. A kiss . . . was it Papa? And then sleep.

Rozia went back into the salon. Her head was splitting. A set of glass doors was opened into the dining room. Garlands of flowers were strewn over a heavy lace cloth; cut glass and bright silver set off the green foliage. Murmurs of compliments were whispered through the air.

She was seated next to her father-in-law. Soup was offered from a heavy tureen, a deep pink beetroot borscht, its sweet and sour flavour enhanced with thick cream – Rozia only took a little. She was feeling hot and a little nauseous.

'Rozia, your mother-in-law has cooked this especially for Jouk – it's his favourite,' her father-in-law said and he ladled more into her plate.

'I'm sure it's delicious,' she said.

'Is it difficult to find beetroot in England?' Madame Oberska inquired politely, looking for conversation.

'No, it is quite easy. Often – when I'm in the kitchen that is – I make a borscht.'

'Do you have a cook?'

'Yes, but she makes English dishes. I like them,' she said.

'But it is important for Hannah to learn about our cuisine. She must learn to be a good Polish wife,' Mr Oberski interjected.

'She's still a child,' Jouk said, pouring himself some more wine.

Rozia watched as the deep ruby-red liquid slid into the glass. She heard her father-in-law comment that Hannah was not so much of a child. She was thirteen. And that she, Rozia, had married Jouk when she was eighteen.

'Rozia.' Her name sounded strange on her mother-in-law's lips.

She turned towards the matriarch sitting at the head of the table. She smiled – she hoped encouragingly. 'Yes?'

'Do you like England?'

'Yes, thank you,' she said.

Madame Oberska tried again. 'How do you make your beetroot borscht?' she asked.

Rozia was irritated. 'I make a stock from the beetroot, add acid, sugar and lemon and then I thicken it with egg yolks.'

'Don't you make stock from a ham bone? It is the best way.' The old lady sounded surprised.

'No, I don't.' Feeling quite sick, she put the soup spoon down and it made a small splash. The pink liquid jetted out of the soup bowl, staining the beautiful tablecloth.

'Oh, now look what you have done,' Madame Oberska said.

'I'm sorry,' Rozia said. 'I'm just tired . . . I'm . . . I'm sorry.'

Mr Oberski poured salt on to the stain and began to dab it with water from a jug. Rozia glanced at Jouk, but he seemed deliberately to be looking away from her. No one spoke to her. She felt abandoned. The soup plate was removed. The pink stain was obvious – like an accusation.

She looked at her watch; it was nine o'clock. Somewhere in this city her mother would be sitting in a chair, a light behind her. She would be doing embroidery . . . her father would be seated in his chair, perhaps listening to music. A lemon tea and some fruit would be at his side, a book on his knee. She stood up, wanting to excuse herself. Jouk noticed and he immediately got to his feet.

'Rozia,' his voice sounded metallic to her, 'let us drink a toast.'

She automatically picked up her glass. She was frightened she would spill some of that on to the tablecloth, and tried to hold it steady.

'To our parents,' Jouk said.

'To our parents,' Rozia repeated slowly. Her head was heavy and she coud feel her hand losing its grip on the stem of the glass; she heard the tinkle as it smashed on the table, voices raised in confusion . . . There was a roaring in her ears – then a nothingness; she had fainted.

Chapter Ten

———— ◆ ————

The following morning Hannah woke early. She felt strange, and she didn't know what time it was. She got out of bed, drew back rich red curtains and looked at the still silent streets. The sky was grey, but there was a heaviness about the atmosphere which permeated, even to her. She pushed open the door of the bedroom and walked down the hall, looking for Jouk. Hearing voices, she rushed through a door and then stopped – still. She saw her father, on his knees, helping her grandfather into his boots. It seemed incredible to Hannah that her father should kneel to anyone. She couldn't comprehend what she was seeing. She knelt to her father at night when she brought him his slippers, at the end of his long day, and now he was kneeling to someone else. She didn't think of that someone else as a father – he was a stranger.

Jouk was deeply disturbed at how his parents had aged. He was determined to try and make them come to England but he knew, inside, that it was a hopeless task. He pushed at his father's boot and eased the bulky man into the soft leather.

Mr Oberski stood up. 'Thank you, Jouk. It is a long time since you have done that, my son.'

Jouk found it sad that his parents expected him to slip back into the role of a child. How easy it is for parents never to accept their children as adults – he thought the hardest aspect of child-raising must be the moment when the parents have to accept that the child is no longer an extension of themselves, but an individual. He thought of Hannah, of the pain he would experience at facing that situation, but he dismissed the thought – she was still a child. She knew nothing of his worries . . . to her he must seem as this man, his own father, had once seemed to him: indestructible. It was so hard to accept frailty in parents; and then, once having acknowledged it, harder still to pretend it didn't exist.

He stood up and saw Hannah. She looked so small, and he smiled at her, extending his arms. She remained at the door for a moment and then, clasping the clumps of voluminous material that made up her nightgown, she ran to him.

Later, after a family breakfast of rolls and milky coffee for the adults and milk for Hannah, Rozia announced that she and Hannah were going out.

'But where, Mummy?' Hannah asked. 'And why isn't Papa coming?'

'My dear, where are you going?' Jouk cut through Hannah's questions, overriding the child.

'I would have thought it would be obvious that I want to go and find my family,' Rozia snapped.

'Oh, I –' Hannah started to say, but Jouk put his hand on her shoulder. 'Wouldn't you prefer me to accompany you and let Hannah stay here?'

'No.' Her short answer made it quite obvious that there was to be no explanation.

'I'd like Papa to come.' There was no mistaking the whine in Hannah's voice.

'Your place is with me,' Rozia said, looking coldly at Hannah.

'How long do you think you will be, Rozia? We have a long journey; perhaps we should travel tomorrow.' Mrs Oberska spoke very quietly.

Rozia jerked her head in a nervous movement, clearing her throat. 'I shouldn't think we would be more than a few hours. I don't want to disturb your arrangements, but I cannot leave Warsaw without making an attempt to find my family.'

'Of course,' Jouk said. 'No one would disagree with you, but it is just the wisdom of Hannah going with you.'

'Hannah is my child.' The challenge was there, unmistakably, and Jouk acknowledged it with a slight nod.

'I will be waiting here for you when you return.'

Rozia did not excuse herself from the table, she merely slipped off her chair and walked from the room. Her palms felt wet, her heart seemed to have lost its place in her chest – jumping from her throat to her stomach – her head ached, and her mouth was dry.

That morning, she had lain in bed yearning for her family. Jonathon, how would he be? A man now – of twenty-nine. Was he married? Did he have children? And how would he settle down in England? Because, of course, now she had made her decision, there was no question that they would not come to England. They could not stay here in Poland.

She found a droshki and ushered Hannah in before she mounted the little steps herself. The sound of the horses' hooves had an unpleasant familiarity; she felt as if she were trotting to her own funeral – the decaying corpse of her childhood was waiting for internment. Would it be a dignified affair? Or would the body be thrown on to a rubbish heap of rejections? She grabbed Hannah's hand, wanting to feel the child's warm flesh, wanting to touch love. Instead she felt fingers that were straight and ungiving, and turning to her daughter she saw worry and, more shockingly, fear. She was about to speak, when the droshki turned into a side street that Rozia knew well, and she drew her breath sharply. Poverty, hunger and despair was her welcome home.

She saw that some of the Jewish shops were now boarded up, or had been taken over by gentiles. There were more beggars where once there had been more pedlars. There was a scent of hunger and death.

The streets were still crowded and noisy and the droshki drove through as if it were giving a sightseeing tour. Rozia knew that he was taking a ridiculous route, but she didn't argue. Eventually they arrived in Elektoralna. Ignoring the luxury of memory, Rozia rushed through the courtyard where the rail for beating carpets was now unused. Oblivious of the overflowing garbage and the people watching her, she raced up the stairs, dragging Hannah behind her. But the name on the door was changed, the Mezeurski family no longer lived there.

Rozia banged on the door, and a maid came, shuffling on worn shoes.

'Yes?' she said through a crack, suspicious of the well-dressed foreigners.

'Mezeurski – this apartment was owned by the Mezeurski family – where are they now?'

'They left. Now who knows?' The maid shut the door.

Rozia stood for a moment, her eyes shut.

Hannah touched her hand. 'Is there a priest we can ask?' She was timorous, she had never seen her mother like this before.

'There aren't priests, there are rabbis,' Rozia snapped, instantly deciding to visit Rabbi Gurr. She was unaware of time or physical motion, her feet felt like lead and she ran, pulling her daughter along, pitter-patter, pitter-patter.

The rabbi was studying with his students. Here time had stood still – there were the same pale faces, the same curly heads of hair, the same intense scurrying eyes that couldn't look at a woman. Rozia drew her shoulders back. She was suddenly conscious of her high heels and sheer stockings – her sleeveless suit in grey and black worn with a silk blouse of which she had been so proud in England.

She approached the rabbi, speaking quietly and respectfully. 'I am Samuel Mezeurski's daughter, Rozia. Where is he?'

The rabbi wouldn't look at her. The sexton answered, 'Samuel Mezeurski's daughter is dead.'

'I am not dead, I am alive. Where are my father and mother and my brother?'

There was no response save the dull tuneless chanting from the ritual books. Rozia groaned from the inside, the sound animal-like.

Hannah moved forward. 'Excuse me, please,' she said in English, 'all we want to do is find my grandparents. Could someone just give us an address?'

A boy, who couldn't have been more than fifteen, looked at Hannah, curious about her. His neighbour, an older man, pulled his head away.

Hannah tried to speak again.

'It's no good,' Rozia told her, 'they won't answer us. We don't exist, we are just figments of someone's imagination.'

'Is there no one else we can ask?'

'I'll try one other person,' Rozia said.

They went deep into the little streets; Hannah was confused and troubled by the smell, the poverty and the despair that surrounded her. She saw little children, some peeping out of doorways, others playing in the alleys, their tiny faces and slender limbs less disconcerting than their huge, dark eyes. Rozia stretched her twisted back, trying to get relief from a tension that she knew would be her bedfellow now. She was anxious to reach their destination – at least if she could find Shosha's mother, Bashela, she might be able to help her.

As they hurried through the streets, there was a sound of someone shouting: 'Rozia, Rozia Mezeurska – I'd have known that hair anywhere.'

Hannah couldn't understand the language, to her it was a babble. But Rozia did, she knew it was Yiddish. For a moment she was shocked, unable to recognize the little old woman who carried her bag of shopping so carefully. And then she knew who it was – Bashela. She reached out a hand to the old woman, but it was ignored.

'Come,' was all Bashela said, leading the way. There were no niceties.

Rozia followed, pulling Hannah along with her. She hadn't remembered the flat being so small or dishevelled. The conditions shocked her.

'Well?' Bashela said, looking at Hannah.

'I want to find my parents. I went home, but they're not there any more.' Rozia shouted in Polish.

'Yes,' Bashela replied in Yiddish.

'Why?'

'Your father's business collapsed. There was a boycott against the Jews.'

'Are they all right, where are they?' Memories now of soft silks, of Friday nights, and of gentle warm hands.

'They are as you can expect.'

'Is my father working?'

'For Simcha, the shoemaker,' Bashela answered.

'But he used to buy leather from us. What is he doing with him?'

'Repairing, a little.' Bashela was not willing to say much more, but Rozia had to know everything.

'How are they living?'

'Not well.'

'And Jonathon?'

'Hum, such *muzel* from their children. Jonathon is a Communist. He is in Russia.'

'I see,' Rozia said quietly. She would have liked to sit down, but the invitation to do so wasn't forthcoming. Disappointment grabbed at her. 'Bashela, please, where are they?'

'They are not in Warsaw at this moment.'

'Please, Bashela?' She was begging, but she didn't care.

'I will try for you. There has been so much pain, and your father is an old man now, don't shock him. Be patient.'

'How can I be patient? If my father is old then I must see him. Supposing something happens to him, it would be terrible for me.'

'Rozia, think of them, and how they must feel.' Bashela's rebuke hurt as sharply as if it had been delivered with a slap.

'And me – what they did to me?' Rozia could feel the tears now.

'You betrayed them.'

'I fell in love.'

Bashela moved to her sink, her little shoulders shaking as she began to clean a saucepan. Rozia was white; her eyes unnaturally bright and her skin stretched taut, she looked almost like a caricature of herself. She was pulling at her fingers in that nervous gesture which Hannah found so disturbing.

'Mummy, you fell in love with Daddy. You don't have to feel sad about that. And if your parents can't understand then just leave them, don't see them.'

She could not understand what was being said, but she could almost touch the animosity between the two women. Rozia bent over and grabbed Hannah in a fierce embrace. The material of her suit scratched at Hannah's face; the tight breasts in their hard brassiere were unyielding and she wanted to fight her way free, but she submitted, even putting her arms around her mother's neck, hugging her; how dare this woman criticize her mother for falling in love with Papa? She wanted to leave. She tugged at Rozia's arm, and signalled to the door with her head. Rozia nodded. But she had to ask one more time. 'Will you help me?'

Bashela nodded. Rozia opened her handbag and took out a pen and a piece of paper, writing her address in Warsaw and in the Tatra, and then adding her address in England. She gave it to Bashela; there was nothing else for her to do

– the wall was unbreachable – she just had to hope. Her writing was clear and bold.

'How is Shosha?' she asked, as she handed the address to Bashela. 'See here,' she pointed, 'I've put my address in England. Ask her to write to me.'

Bashela took the note without a word, putting it into a side pocket of her overall that doubled as a dress.

'Please give my love to Shosha,' Rozia said, and her voice sounded so troubled. Bashela touched her cheek; the gnarled hands with their broken dirty finger nails were a shock to Hannah, but the play was not yet finished. Rozia covered the hand with her own and bent forward and kissed Bashela on the cheek. Hannah was amazed, she had never seen her mother embrace another woman, ever.

Immediately upon Rozia and Hannah's return from their unsuccessful mission, the Oberski family, grandparents, parents and daughter left Warsaw to spend the summer holiday at the Oberski family house in the Tatra Mountains.

It was unusual, Rozia explained to Hannah, to have a house so far away. '. . . most people have apartments in holiday places near Warsaw.'

'But this house has been in my family for two generations,' Jouk interrupted her.

They were to travel in two cars, Mr Oberski's car driven by a chauffeur, whilst he and Jouk travelled in a less commodious vehicle. It took two days and it was hot and sticky. They stayed overnight in a little inn, which Hannah hated, because the noise of the farm kept her awake and it smelt.

During the drive Hannah was squashed in the back between her grandmother and her mother. She was bored, and the hide upholstery made her feel sick. When her grandmother pointed to places of interest, she couldn't look, the movement outside the window made her feel even worse.

When they finally reached the summer house Hannah was very tired. It seemed as if she had been travelling for weeks.

'Look,' her grandmother said, speaking English, 'your father is here already waiting for you.'

The car door opened and Hannah felt Jouk scoop her into his arms.

'Tomorrow we will go and see if my old treehouse is still here.'

'Your treehouse is over forty-five years old, I would think it is rotten by now,' Madame Oberska commented.

Hannah stared at her father's face. Forty-five years, that was a lifetime. She couldn't understand the time span.

In the evening light she could see her grandmother's face. It had a crêpe-like texture, and she wouldn't like to touch it. She couldn't work out how old her grandmother was, but she was sure she must be ancient, but Papa wasn't ancient . . . he wasn't even old. Her grandmother leaned heavily on a stick.

'Come child, you must go to bed. I will arrange for some sour milk to be sent up to you.'

Hannah had never drunk sour milk. She wondered what it was. She was sure she wouldn't like it, and certainly didn't want to be taken over by this rather austere woman.

'Papa, you will come up and kiss me good night?' she said plaintively.

'Of course,' Jouk replied.

'She's lovely,' his mother said.

'Come to England and you will be able to watch her grow up,' Jouk replied.

'We are too old – we will stay,' his mother said quietly.

No one had taken any notice of Rozia, who still sat in the car. She slid out across the seat and got out of the oppressively hot vehicle on the opposite side from the house, and walked down the road towards the outskirts of the village. She had her back to the big house, to Jouk, even to her daughter. The air was soft – clear, mountain air, she realized – and she stared ahead.

She took in the tiny village, dominated by the church whose ornate steeple, pointed turrets and two onion domes betrayed the Russian influence in Tatra. Rozia remembered Jouk had once told her that the church had been built in the seventeenth century, though not the gate which was just simple, slatted wood. She noticed two small village children picking their way through the dry mud and stones that was the footpath.

The village seemed to be one main street of wooden houses with the same pointed roofs as the church, heavy front doors situated at the side, and tiny windows poking out between the blocks of tree trunks that had been used to make the walls. Rozia wondered if they were all as crude, but she noticed that the windows were carefully fashioned with simple lattice work. Flowers were massed around the front doors and paths everywhere.

There were larger buildings further up on the hills, farmhouses she realized when she saw their outbuildings. The largest and most prosperous house was the Oberski summer residence – built in the same style as the rest of the village by Jouk's great-grandfather, whose years as a medical student in Moscow allowed for good relations with the Russians. He had been a doctor, a good one, and Jouk's father, augmented by money and land from a good marriage, had never worked. The house had two storeys, split by a veranda like jam between two slices of cake. Rozia wondered how many times an Oberska wife had stood, dreaming and looking out towards the mountain slopes. She lit a cigarette, and huddled her shoulders slightly in the evening air.

Hannah walked into the house, trying to keep pace with her grandmother. She was taken to a bedroom on the first floor, which she was told was next to the one in which her parents would sleep. There was a small bed, with a striped print brown and white coverlet, and a crucifix hanging on the wall near a small icon. She noticed that a pitcher and basin had been placed on a small round table near the window. Was she supposed to use this for washing? She put her finger in the water – she was surprised to find it was warm. She felt awkward. Her grandmother was sitting on the bed, watching her. She didn't want to get undressed in front of the old lady with grey hair piled up on top of her head in plaits, who assumed an intimacy with her. Hannah didn't dislike her, she just didn't know her. As she removed her dress she watched Papa's mother in the mirror. It was strange, she loved Papa so much she would have thought that she could love his parents on sight, but she didn't – and it worried her. She found it difficult to lift the pitcher, and anyway she would have preferred a bath.

Rozia finished her cigarette and walked back to the house. Jouk was sitting on a bench outside the front door, smoking a pipe. She felt, rather than noticed, her daughter's absence.

'Where's Hannah?' she asked, her voice staccato, demanding an answer.

'My mother took her up to bed.' Jouk pulled easily on his pipe, a habit of his which Rozia abhorred. Her nerves were stretched, she was impatient and irritable.

'Where will I find her?'

'Oh, I suppose she will use my old room. Up the stairs – the last door on the left.'

Whilst his tone was lazy, she realized that the words were deliberate, spaced, inviting comment. She gave none. She swept into the house, ignoring the dark splendour of the Oberski summer residence with its carved staircase and heavy wooden stairs. She found a door open.

Hannah was standing in her vest, folding her petticoat.

'You must have a bath,' Rozia said in English.

'I would like one, Mummy, but she – I mean Papa's mother – had this put in here,' she pointed to the pitcher, 'but I don't think I can lift it.'

Rozia turned to her mother-in-law. 'She must have a bath.'

Madame Oberska tapped her stick on the floor. 'If you insist.'

'I insist,' Rozia said.

Hannah was taken down a long corridor – she saw white walls, heavily patterned rugs over the solid wooden floor disappearing under her feet – to the bathroom, which was a tiny room, dominated by an enormous bath perched on four little legs. High above it was an antiquated water heater – all its pipes gleaming, polished chrome. Rozia turned on the taps and, ignoring Hannah's protests, almost hurled her into the swirling water.

'Wash,' she said in English. Hannah took the proffered bar of soap and self-consciously began to lather herself. She wanted to lie back and enjoy the warm wetness, but she was pulled out, towelled and dried. The white flannelette nightgown with its neat buttons was slipped over her head, and even the top button done up. Hannah was uncomfortable. The neck was too tight, but she knew she couldn't say anything to her mother when she was in this mood. She would undo it later in bed. Meekly, she held out her arms and was put into her dressing gown. Then there was the trip back down the corridor. The bedroom door was flung open, the bed pulled back.

'In,' Rozia ordered.

'Her prayers, she must say her prayers,' Madame Oberska's authoritative voice pierced the close atmosphere of the bedroom. 'Surely you don't expect her to go to bed without saying her "Hail Mary" at least?'

'Not normally,' she said, 'but the child is exhausted.'

Rozia realized that Hannah hadn't said her devotions for the last two nights. She wondered why she had forgotten – she was normally so pedantic about observance. She shrugged her shoulders.

'Rozia,' her mother-in-law spoke again, 'she must say her prayers.'

Hannah didn't particularly enjoy the nightly ritual, but it really didn't make much difference to her. She got out of bed and knelt by the side of the icon. She recited her 'Our Father . . .', then rattled off 'Hail Mary full of Grace'. She forgot 'I believe in God' and rushed into 'I confess to Almighty God'. She looked through her spread fingers at her grandmother's implacable face and noticed that her mother was looking out of the window. Hannah knew she was supposed to be working out what sins she had committed during the day, and then to say the act of contrition . . . but her sins were always the same. Yet again, she apologized to God for her lack of care about her mother, and promised to do better tomorrow. She wondered what punishment God might have in store for her.

She thought about her other sins. She felt it was ridiculous that she ought to confess that she didn't love her grandmother. God ought to understand that she didn't know her. She rushed through the rest of her prayers, the act of contrition, the meomare – asking the Virgin Mary to intercede on her behalf – and then the de Profundis. 'Jesus, Mary, Joseph, may I breathe forth my soul in peace with you'. She finished, got up from her knees, crossed herself, and looked up at the little icon. She thought Mary's face must be nicer than the one painted on the piece of wood. She knew the two women were watching her. She didn't like that.

Hannah burrowed into the little bed piled high with blankets. She pretended she was a dormouse, hiding from the cats, waiting for them to leave so she could carry on with her games. She felt her mother's cool lips, her grandmother's warm ones. Then Papa came in and she raised her arms from the blankets, hugged him. She could feel him holding her hand, but she felt drowsy, and surprisingly comfortable.

She shut her eyes, and felt the weight of the bedclothes. She thought of the two babes in the wood being covered by leaves – keeping them warm whilst they were shielded from the night air.

Chapter Eleven

———————◆———————

It was very hot – a dry stinging heat that made Hannah want to take off her clothes – but despite the holiday atmosphere her mother insisted that, in matters of dress, formality must be observed. Although the materials were lighter, Hannah was still forced into perfectly cut little dresses and pristine white ankle socks. The only concession was that she might wear sandals instead of constricting black patent shoes.

Despite the discomfort, it never occurred to Hannah to question her mother – she was already conditioned as to the variations that could be allowed. New clothes were worn on Sundays, older ones during the week, and holiday clothes meant the prettiest dresses in her wardrobe. She, like her mother, never dressed for convenience.

On the second day of their holiday, the village priest came to pay his respects. Hannah found him sitting in the salon with her grandfather. She had been looking for her father and prised open the door gingerly, not wanting to be seen. But her grandfather summoned her. She approached with discretion, holding her hands behind her back. She didn't particularly want to stay in the still room, with its shutters closed against the heat of the sun.

'My granddaughter, Hannah. Her Polish is not as good as her English yet,' Mr Oberski told the priest.

The priest's eyes flickered over her. He took both her hands. 'Hello Hannah,' he said.

'Hello,' she replied.

'Pass Father Dubsink some cakes, Hannah,' her father's father instructed.

She reached over to the small side table in front of the priest, and offered him a dish of the sticky cakes she had eaten on her first night in Warsaw.

'Do you like our country?' the priest asked.

'Yes, thank you. It's very nice.' She was ill at ease in Polish.

The door of the salon opened again, lighting up a long triangle of the apple-green carpet which had faded almost to white. Rozia stood there, framed in the shaft of sunlight which streamed in through the door. The priest stood up.

'Father, please – sit.' She came over, extending her hand.

Rozia looked into his eyes. She thought how nice they were, soft, limpid – a rather beautiful brown. She sat down in an overstuffed brocade armchair with almost a sigh. Hannah wanted to be excused. She bobbed out of her chair and sidled over to her mother.

'Mummy, may I go into the garden?'

'No, Father Dubsink has come to visit us,' Rozia hissed.

'But Papa will be wondering where I am – we were going to look at the treehouse.'

Rozia ignored her and motioned with her hand towards a small chair by her side. Hannah walked back and sat by her grandfather. The gesture was noticed by the priest.

She listened to the conversation . . . some farmers had been unlucky with their crops; Mr Oberski had lent some money to a church fund in order that the peasants might have enough to eat until the next harvest. The priest was grateful. Hannah heard her grandfather described as a good man.

'Charity is man's responsibility to his fellow man . . . Our Lord taught us that,' Mr Oberski said gruffly.

'You will be rewarded in heaven,' the priest said.

Hannah thought that her grandfather might have been better pleased if he was rewarded on earth.

'And it was good of you to employ Danuta as a cook – she

is a good girl, and it helps her father. It is hard to bring up sons and a daughter without a mother,' Father Dubsink added.

Mr Oberski raised himself out of his chair with difficulty. It looked as if even his bones hurt him. He walked over to the ornate serving table and reached inside one of the carved doors, searching for a bottle. He produced a dusty white mixture.

'We will take some advocaat,' he said to the priest.

Hannah thought that Father Dubsink looked as if he had received his reward for being good on earth. Madame Oberska swept into the room, regal, demanding.

The priest greeted her warmly. 'Ah, madame, you are always so gracious. You are a pleasure to my country eyes.'

'You are a flatterer, Father Dubsink,' Madame Oberska replied, obviously relishing the compliment.

Rozia sat in perfect symmetry. Her ankles crossed and placed at the side – hands resting in her lap. She would have liked to pick up her tapestry, but she felt it would be disrespectful. The priest asked her if she liked England and, as usual, she was effusive in her replies.

Jouk joined them. He had been running, and the effort and the heat had turned his lightly tanned face red; his light silk shirt clung to his body revealing its lithe lines . . . his head was protected by a straw hat and as a concession to the holiday, he carried his jacket. Father Dubsink immediately stood up. The two men embraced.

'You've met my family . . .' Jouk said.

'Yes, I have – your charming wife, your lovely daughter. You're a lucky man.'

'I am,' Jouk commented, looking at Hannah.

Rozia couldn't take her eyes away from her husband. He had a youth, a vitality about him that was not usual. She loved the way his shirt clung. She watched him remove his hat and sink into a chair. He wore light trousers, and she was fascinated by the way his legs were flung apart carelessly. Unable to control herself, she looked into the centre of the V of his legs. She could see, to one side, the outline of his penis as it hung, unrestricted. Her body began to stir – she remembered a desire that had long been dormant. She felt hot. Looking up, she found that the priest was staring at her. She returned his gaze – blatant, defiant, letting him think what he wanted.

That night as Rozia prepared for bed, combing her hair, creaming her face free of its coating of make-up, she gave into the feeling between her legs and she touched herself, but it gave her no respite. She slid into the bed; when Jouk came in from the bathroom he blew out the candle, said good night and turned on one side ready for sleep. She lay there, burning, and then she turned her head too, but she didn't sleep – the ache was a sweet pain that was almost too much to bear. She wanted . . . furtively she ran her hands over her breasts, feeling her nipples sharpen under her nightgown, and she cried silently into her pillow.

When Rozia awoke the next morning, it was five o'clock by the little clock on her bedside table. She could hear the birds twittering outside. She turned over and touched Jouk's body, remembering how he had looked to her yesterday. She felt the desire again – it had been so long. The ache bit into her. She turned over on her front, burying herself into the pillow, trying not to think of her burning body. Of what had made it move out of its sleep. She wanted it to quieten, to go back to its state of numbness. Anything was better than this torment.

'Are you all right?' Jouk said quietly, aware that she was awake.

'Yes, it's just that I . . .'

'What?'

'Nothing . . .'

'I've spoken to my parents about coming to England.

183

They don't seem to understand that there is going to be a war. I feel so impotent.'

Rozia smiled to herself, aware of the full irony of Jouk's words. She ran her hands across her breasts, feeling her nipples again. Jouk saw her. He reached for her, touching her. She turned towards him, pushing her body against his, her mouth searching for his mouth. He turned her on her back and began to kiss her, using his tongue as he had not done for years. Wildly she reached out for him. He pushed her away.

'No, Rozia, no.'

She heard the desperation in his voice and she pulled her hand away immediately. Neither of them spoke. They lay on their respective pillows, unable to comfort each other.

Rozia waited for news of her parents. None came. The days passed in endless monotony for her.

Jouk and Hannah would spend hours walking in the country, searching for birds. When they found a new species, they would note it in a lined exercise book. Jouk would write its description and then Hannah would try to draw it. Rozia thought that Hannah's birds all looked the same, but she had to admit that at least they did look like birds.

Whilst her husband and daughter were out on their excursions, Rozia would be left with her parents-in-law. Starched politeness was the keynote. To escape she would go to church, liking the little place of worship in the centre of the village. Father Dubsink would watch her come in, light her candle, say her prayers and leave.

On Saturday, she went to confession. The priest retreated into the little cell box, the darkness camouflaging him. He placed his surplice around his neck and his head made strange shadows on the wall in the dim light.

Rozia sat quietly and then began: 'Father, forgive me for I have sinned.'

Her voice was softer than he'd remembered, gentler. For

a moment he felt protective towards this new child of Christ. She spoke of her sins . . . her unease with her parents-in-law, her discomfort in their house. He understood and spoke with compassion of the difficulty of adapting.

'But if the heart is pure, then there is no sin. It is only if you lie in your heart.'

There was a sharp intake of breath, and then she said, 'I did lie. I renounced my faith.'

'You blasphemed?'

'I said we killed Christ.'

'We?' The voice drew in on her anonymously.

She did not answer, and then she said again, 'I blasphemed.'

'It depends on the reason. God forgives if He knows what is in the heart.'

Something seemed to snap inside her head, an actual physical jolt. God knew what was inside her head, God knew she had never confessed to being with Stefan's child before her first Communion.

'My child, God loves you. He has given you the Sacrament of Confession so that you may pour out your heart, examine your conscience and be at peace with Him.'

'Oh, Father, I want to be at peace, I have lived so long without it.'

'God wants you to be happy, my child.'

'Father, Father, when I first went to confession before my first Communion, I omitted . . .' her voice closed, she couldn't go on.

'Go on, my child . . . did you actually lie?'

'No, I just omitted to tell my confession.'

'But God knew that you were not being honest with Him.'

'Yes,' she whispered.

'You have been guilty of the grave sin of sacrilege.'

'Yes, but Father, I am contrite. I beg you. I have suffered so much.'

'I am listening, my child.' The priest's voice was gentle.

'I was young, just eighteen. I . . . er . . . I lay with a boy at the University – we were going to marry, but he died.'

'So you did not deliberately take steps to stop the birth of the child?'

'Oh no, never, we loved each other, we wanted . . .' she couldn't go on. Her hurt would not allow it.

'Did you conceal this from your husband?'

'No, he knew everything. He gave me a future, when I was alone and abandoned.'

'Is that why you converted to the Faith?'

'Yes . . . no, no, it isn't, Father. I can truthfully say that is not the reason. Once I left my family, I knew that Judaism could not help me.'

'You wanted to answer yes.'

'For a moment, I thought it might have been true, but it wasn't the only reason.' She spoke quietly, almost to herself.

The priest sighed. 'My child, Christ suffered on the Cross. He suffered great pain for the sins of mankind.'

'Must I suffer for my sins?'

'God does not ask you to suffer, but I feel – that if it brings you closer to Him . . . Remember He is the vine and all who cling to Him are the branches. God allows His children to take pleasure in the act of sex as an inducement to childbearing – not to enjoy the act itself.'

'Oh Father, forgive me . . .' Rozia pleaded. She was desperate. 'I will do anything.'

'My child, if you are truly penitent, you know that God will never deny you.'

'Oh Father, I am . . .'

'My child, cleanse yourself . . .'

Her mind was a confused montage of naked bodies, intertwining lovers – disfigurement. She felt disgusted – she wanted to purify herself, to scourge her body – she wondered what she must do to free herself of these thoughts.

The priest offered her no more comfort. He granted her absolution, provided that she truly repent not only for the sin of omission, but also for the original act itself. Rozia remembered that act, the passion – and she remembered that it was the only time she had ever received anyone into her body – was that her punishment? If only she could quieten the ache of longing that was within her again.

Walking down the village street, Rozia noticed some baby lambs walled into a small pen. They were surrounded by straw, and the neat little heads were beginning to lose the lamb-like features, assuming the ugliness of sheep. She watched them play for a while, leaning over the edge of the pen. She picked up some of the straw and began to tickle one of the lambs. It blinked, and shook its head – almost pet-like in its reactions. She wanted to hold it. She reached over and scooped it up. It bleated, and the other lambs were crying at the human intrusion – the noise surrounded her, but she ignored their pleas. She loved the feel of the lamb's warmth against her, and she began to caress it, running her fingers through its wool. She would have liked to take it home. She cooed in its ear, almost as if it were a baby. She nuzzled it to her breast, tempted to push her blouse open, to lay its head against the naked flesh for it to suckle.

She didn't hear the barking of the dogs, only the beating of her heart . . . and then she saw them, two – one large and black, one grey – menacing, snapping at her legs, jumping for the lamb. She screamed, her voice mixing with the baaing of the sheep, the howling of the dogs; men shouted, they approached her, lashing the air with their sticks. She thought they were going to attack her too, and she backed towards the pen, feeling the frail fence behind her. She hoped it would take her weight. She held the lamb tightly – 'We are both to be sacrificed for the good of God,' she whispered in its ear. 'The lamb of God – this is how I will expiate my sins . . .'

The men beat at the dogs, but it made no difference, they seemed immune to the blows, intent on reaching Rozia and her lamb. They jumped closer, almost reaching the animal, their claws catching her stockings, wrenching the fine silk to shreds – a paw caught her arm which held the lamb.

Rozia's terror prevented sound escaping her half-open mouth, and her eyes were glazed. She felt a stick, heard a curse and thought, 'The men will get me too.'

And then the dogs were gone, dragged off, barking, growling. Rozia's voice found its sound . . . the scream was terrifying, and the men retreated, frightened. The lamb, sensing the danger was over, began to struggle for freedom. Rozia felt tears pricking her eyelids. She fought them off. Shaking, she handed the lamb back to one of the men. He said nothing, but a woman pushed at her, shouted at her for being stupid. She turned and ran away from the village – back to the solitude of the house.

When she got into the safety of the sombre hall, she sat on one of the chairs, trembling. She heard Jouk come into the house.

'I just had a horrible experience,' she said.

'What happened?' he asked – his back to her as he hung his hat up on one of the pegs.

'I – I picked up a lamb and fondled it. Then there were some dogs and they started barking,' she added lamely, realizing as she said it that her pain could not be explained in words.

'Are you all right?' he asked, noticing her white face, her smeared make-up, her torn stockings.

'Yes, yes, I'm fine.' She paused. 'But I was so frightened.'

'I'm sure you were. It was very stupid of you to remove the lamb from its pen.' He touched her head lightly. 'Have some tea with lemon, it will refresh you.'

'Yes, and I'll take a bath,' she said sadly.

'Good idea.' He smiled at her and watched as she walked to the kitchen.

Jouk went to find Hannah. He wanted to show her his collection of butterflies. He found his daughter in her bedroom. She was lying on her bed, her hands clasped behind her head.

'Are you all right?' he asked.

'Yes, I'm fine, just a little tired from the sun.'

She didn't want him to know she was bored and that she wanted to go back to England. When she had first seen the village, it had seemed a land of fables with its spinning wheels and wooden houses, but there were no children of her age for her to play with. The nine to fourteen year olds had gone to a summer camp higher in the mountains, where they ran and swam and rode; Hannah wished she was with them.

'Would you like to come and see my collection of butterflies?' Jouk asked.

'Butterflies?'

'Yes, I collected them when I was a boy.'

He pulled her off her bed and awkwardly tried to push a brush through her hair. She pulled it away from him and did her hair herself, shaking her long tresses when she had finished. He took her hand and led her down the corridor past the bathroom to an arch. Hannah was curious, she had never been through the arch, thinking it led to the servants' quarters. In a sense she was right. This area had been the nursery wing. Jouk pushed at the nearest door; when it stuck, he put his shoulder against it and thrust it open. The room beyond was large, with polished floorboards, white walls, high windows . . . even a window seat. Hannah was delighted. She saw toys, boys' toys – even a rocking horse. In the corner stood a cot shrouded by a christening shawl. She looked questioningly at Jouk.

He smiled and nodded. 'Yes – that was mine.'

She went over to the cot and touched the shawl, almost reverently. She felt close to her grandmother as she fingered the fine lace.

'And this was my nursery. I spent most of my time here with my nurse.'

Jouk bent down and picked up a soldier from a low shelf. His hand lingering over it. He thought about the woman who had reared him. He spoke quietly, forgetting Hannah for a moment. 'I loved her very much. She was my wet nurse.'

'What's a wet nurse?' Hannah asked.

Jarred, Jouk said, 'It's a sort of nurse.'

'It's the woman who takes over the mother's job and breastfeeds the child.' Rozia's voice bit into the conversation.

She had come into the room unbidden. Hannah dropped the shawl she was holding. She felt dreadfully embarrassed at the thought of a woman's breasts in a child's mouth – and to think that child might have been – was – Papa. She felt sick.

Jouk ignored Rozia. He went over to a cupboard and began to pull out glass cases.

'Hannah, come and help me,' he said.

She put the shawl back on to the cot and went over to him. Rozia felt excluded; she knew they didn't want her with them at that moment – and they were right – she was upset with herself, she hadn't meant to say what she did. She left the room quietly. Jouk carefully placed his cases on the floor, one after another – in a long line. Hannah stood, held in gruesome fascination as her father explained each imprisoned wing. She felt sorry for the beautiful insects, pinned to their felt for eternity.

The heat was beginning to affect Rozia. She never felt cool – even at night. Madame Oberska made every effort to be pleasant, but they had little in common, except perhaps for Hannah and the Church. Once Rozia asked Madame

Oberska directly if there had been any communication from her parents.

'There has been nothing for you,' the old lady said, looking down sharply at her crocheting.

Rozia wanted to scream, but she kept the feeling down, hurling the scream itself back deep inside. She tried to concentrate on her tapestry, but her eyes wouldn't focus properly. Her head was beating.

She liked the afternoons best. The whole household, including the staff, would sleep after the heavy midday meal. Jouk would lie in the big double bed in their room, and when he was asleep Rozia would slip out of the room, down the stairs and out of the house. She would sit under one of the large trees in the garden, and watch the remorseless sun filtering through the leaves. She would feel protected by its enormity; sometimes she would even cling to its bark, enjoying its roughness against her. When would she hear something? She couldn't doubt that she would.

The afternoon after she had been to confession, she had lain on the ground and picked up a twig. The priest had spoken of suffering – she understood it to be mortification. It frightened her, but she took the twig and drew its sharp end over her arm. It hurt, but she quite liked it. Rozia pushed harder until the spike penetrated the skin and she could see bubbles of blood popping up from her arm. She was fascinated. She felt she could cope with this physical pain, she could understand its throbbing . . . there were no battles to be fought inside her head. This penance was easy.

On the Sunday morning, during Mass – whilst the choir transformed the little church with its pale pink and pale blue and orange carved woodwork into a haven for God – Rozia stood and waited to partake of the body and blood of Christ. As she knelt before the priest he noticed the welts on her arm. She looked up and he smiled – his beautiful eyes compassionate. She raised her own eyes above his head and was confronted by a painting of one of the blessed martyrs – St Sebastian . . . his body pierced by arrows, as he lay dying, ready to be unified with his Maker – and she cried with joy, for she would be worthy. As the priest blessed her, she entered into her commitment with God – promising to honour Him all the days of her life, and beyond.

Chapter Twelve

———— ◆ ————

One night, during the second week, Hannah woke – she was thirsty. There was no noise – everything was still in the house. She sat up and lit her candle, still shocked that her grandparents had no electricity. Throwing back the bedclothes, she went downstairs to get a glass of water. She padded silently into the kitchen. It was cool and comfortable, but strange. She hadn't been there very often. She knew there was a cook, and a maid – village people – but she had had no contact with them. She sipped the water, feeling it slip down the back of her throat. She imagined it making its way through to her stomach.

'Who's that?' a rasping voice asked in Polish.

Hannah could make out a figure, holding a candle.

'It's me, Hannah,' she replied, but in English. She held on to the side of the sink, feeling frightened.

'Oh, Miss Hannah.' The figure moved forward. 'I thought it was an intruder.'

'Who are you?' Hannah said, her nerve ends still feeling tight. She used Polish unconsciously.

'I am Danuta, the cook.'

'Oh!' Hannah's relief was obvious and then she added crossly, 'You frightened me.'

'You frightened me. I didn't know who it was,' the cook replied.

Hannah was curious about Danuta. She didn't seem much older than herself, and she had a round comfortable face, blonde curly hair, large hands.

'Do you live here?' Hannah asked. She moved nimbly

over to the table and heaved herself up – her legs flapping in the air.

'Yes, when Mr and Mrs Oberski are here,' Danuta replied.

Hannah kicked at a chair with her foot. 'Sit down,' she said.

Danuta took one of the wooden kitchen chairs and gingerly sat on the edge of it. 'I am not sure if I should be here with you.'

'Why?'

'It's almost five o'clock. You should be in bed.'

'So should you.' Hannah pulled the candle over and looked hard at Danuta. 'How old are you?'

'Eighteen,' Danuta replied.

'How long have you worked for my grandparents?'

'Only this year. My mother used to work for them.'

'Why doesn't your mother work for them now?'

'She died.'

Hannah didn't know what to say. Death worried her. She knew people died, but the thought of it made her nervous. She worried about being put into a coffin and then sunk into the earth.

'It must be awful, not having a mother,' she said.

'It's hard, but there are seven of us. It's bad for my younger brother, he misses her.'

'How old is he?'

'He is fourteen, like you.'

'How did you know how old I was?' Hannah asked.

'We know everything about you,' Danuta said. She was fascinated by the little girl, her hair hanging to her shoulders, her neat, white nightgown with its tucks and its buttons.

'Did he go with the other children to the summer camp?'

'No, we don't have the money for those things and anyway he must help my father on the farm. What is it like in England?' the Polish girl added quickly, wanting to change the subject, not wanting sympathy.

'England. It's like being here, really – except it's different. We have a porridge for breakfast.'

'Porridge, what is that?'

'It's sort of white and creamy. You have it with sugar on top. Can I have an apple? I'm awfully hungry.' Hannah was speaking in English now.

'I don't understand you,' Danuta said.

'Don't you speak any English?'

'No. Why should I speak English? I live in this village. I work here, and one day,' she paused and blushed a little, 'I will marry.'

'Do you have a beau?' Hannah used the word 'beau' in the French fashion.

'Beau?' Danuta said the word again, inquiringly.

'Boyfriend, only more so.'

'Yes, I do,' Danuta replied, going over to the larder. She opened the heavy door and disappeared inside. Hannah got off the table and followed her. Inside the door there was a small room stacked with flour, fruit and preserves. Large pieces of meat hung from hooks, some already cooked – hams, legs of lamb – others still raw hunks of flesh, geese, chickens – and there were piles of eggs in the corner. Hannah had never seen so much food.

'Here you are,' Danuta said, handing her an apple. 'Now you must go to bed.'

'All right,' Hannah said, and then she added, 'Can I meet your brother? I haven't met anyone from Poland except my grandparents.'

Danuta spoke slowly. 'Madame wouldn't like it.'

'Why? I get very bored sometimes. Not with Papa, of course. But when he's off somewhere, I get stuck with my grandparents.'

Danuta felt sorry for Hannah. She knew the girl must be lonely. She was either with her father or she sat alone with her colouring book. Her brother Stash drew too. The teachers said he could have studied in Krakow, but it was out of the question. He would have to stay on the land like their father and brothers. He resembled their mother: he was slim and dark, unlike the rest of her brood of brothers and Danuta herself, who resembled their father. They didn't understand Stash as her mother had. Danuta sighed. Hannah had a mother, but she didn't seem to spend very much time with her. Why couldn't she meet Stash? What harm could it do? And they might have a nice time. He might never have a chance to meet an English person again.

'I will get a message to my brother,' Danuta said. 'Go and draw by the old treehouse. He'll meet you there after he has helped my father on the farm. His name is Stash.'

Hannah grinned and impulsively she hugged Danuta. 'Thank you. I know we'll have a lovely day.' She scampered to the door. 'Oh, here – my apple core.'

She gave Danuta the remains of her eaten apple and the Polish girl took it in her hand. Neither of them questioned Hannah's right to pass on her leftovers for Danuta to dispose of.

After a sleepless few hours in bed, Hannah got up. She chose her favourite dress, of white muslin, with neat mother-of-pearl buttons, a small collar, and a large sash which tied at the back. She took pleasure in her appearance, examining her nose for any redness that might have resulted from too much sun. She brushed her long blonde hair and let it hang down her back. She grabbed her colouring pad and pencils and went down for breakfast. Opening the dining room door, she discovered the four adults seated around the table.

'Hannah,' Papa said, 'you look lovely – doesn't she, Rozia?'

'Yes, you do . . . you have even brushed your hair the way I like it,' Rozia said.

Hannah was annoyed. She didn't do her hair the way her

mother liked it – she did it the way she liked it. She sat at
the table and drank the milk which was set in front of her.

'Hannah,' Jouk said, 'I am going to Krakow today.'

'Oh . . . are you?' Hannah tried not to show that she was
pleased. She didn't know what she would have said if he
had wanted to spend the day with her.

'Are you going, Mummy?' she asked.

'No,' was the sharp reply from Rozia.

'Rozia, I've asked you – please come, it would be nice for
me . . . I could show you –'

'I've told you, Jouk, no.'

'Why for God's sake?' Jouk exploded in English.

'I don't want to go there,' Rozia replied in the same tone.

Hannah hated to see her parents argue, especially now
when her grandparents sat with them, saying nothing, just
smiling politely, eating their black bread and drinking their
sweet tea.

'Mummy – stop, go with Papa,' she said.

'Hannah, remember your place, don't involve yourself in
things that do not concern you,' Rozia snapped.

Hannah reached for some bread and began to butter it.
Rozia drank her coffee. Jouk just sat at the table, hoping
she would change her mind.

He tried again. 'Rozia, I know it must be difficult for you,
but perhaps if you came . . . it might . . .'

'It would not, Jouk. I don't wish to visit that town. Do
you understand? Why don't you invite your father?'

'I wish you would tell me why.'

Rozia set her coffee down. She drew up her shoulders,
not wanting to show her feelings, remembering another
voice, *We will go to Krakow for Christmas*.

How long ago had all that been . . .

'Hannah, you must have more than bread for breakfast,'
she snapped at her daughter.

'I don't like radishes or eggs.'

'Do as you are told,' Rozia ordered.

Hannah pulled her mouth down. She didn't see why she should be shouted at just because her parents had a row. Her grandmother reached for a plate and placed some hard-boiled eggs on it, handing it to Hannah and smiling encouragingly. She took it, and for the first time responded to her grandmother. The old lady motioned to the plate with her head. Hannah knew what she meant . . . eat . . . it's better for all of us.

Anxious to get away from the conflicting atmosphere, Jouk said almost too quickly, 'Father, would you like to join me?'

'That would be pleasant,' the elder Oberski replied. He was grateful for the chance to spend a day with his son. 'Yes, I will come with you.'

After breakfast was finished, Jouk and his father drove to Krakow. Rozia and Hannah stood on the terrace and waved them off. Hannah was impatient to get to the tree for her meeting with Stash.

Rozia wanted Hannah; suddenly she wanted to be with her. 'Come, let us sit together,' she said.

'I was going to draw,' Hannah answered.

'Fine, you draw. I'll do my tapestry.' She linked her arm in Hannah's, apparently unaware of a slight withdrawal. 'We can talk. We don't often spend time together, do we?'

'Well, er, no.'

'What are you going to draw?' she asked. That day she wore an apple-green linen dress with a big white collar that framed her face. If Hannah had looked at her mother she would have noticed deep shadows under her eyes, but Hannah didn't look, she was too intent on negotiating her escape.

'Look, if you don't mind, I would really like to be on my own,' she mumbled.

Rozia withdrew her arm from Hannah's, too quickly. She

picked at a loose cotton on her sleeve. 'No, of course not. I just thought you might have liked to be with me, but it doesn't matter. You go off, I'll sit inside away from the heat. Don't get any sun on your face.'

'I'll be back soon . . . it's a surprise,' Hannah said in a rush.

'Don't get grass stains on your dress,' Rozia called to her, retreating as she ran towards the old treehouse. She thought Hannah looked like a young deer, suddenly freed from a cage as she watched her lopping movements, her hair flying behind her. She walked back into the house and tried not to mind.

It was cool inside. Automatically, she picked up her tapestry from the couch where she had left it the night before. She noticed a small section, a rose, which displeased her – the stitches were not neat enough. She decided to unpick it. She went straight to Madame Oberska's small sewing box to look for a pair of scissors. There were some papers inside – it was almost as if they were being hidden. Rozia ignored them, but her hand flickered over an envelope in case the little silver scissors had slipped inside. Something made her take the envelope out and look at it. She saw the postmark first – the letter had come from Warsaw – and then she saw the handwriting, the narrow letters, the flourish – it was from her mother. Shaking, she opened the envelope. The letter was brief:

Dear Madame Oberska,
Thank you for your letter advising us of your son's visit to Warsaw. We have also heard from a friend of ours that your daughter-in-law visited her, trying to find us. I'm sure you will have great pleasure in seeing your son again. The visit would have no personal meaning for us. We have no daughter. She is dead and we mourn her.
Yours sincerely . . .

We have no daughter. She is dead . . . The letter flickered in Rozia's hand, dropping to the floor. She tried to hold herself together – she felt numb, but into the numbness came a creeping agony. She bent down to pick up the envelope and saw her mother-in-law standing in the doorway, watching, her face expressionless.

'I was looking for the sewing scissors,' Rozia heard herself say.

Madame Oberska had a deep sympathy for her daughter-in-law, but she could never voice her feelings, for that would promote an intimacy which Madame Oberska considered impolite. So she ignored the desperate fumblings of a distraught, despairing Rozia. She excused herself quickly, shutting the door behind her so she could not hear the crying that she was sure would start. But Rozia didn't cry; she just stayed still, holding her stomach, wanting her own child.

Hannah was out of breath when she reached the treehouse. She sat down under the big tree. No one was there. Disappointed, she took out her pad and began to draw. She imagined the treehouse before its decay – when Papa was young. She sketched fast, in easy strokes, enjoying her small skills. Occasionally she would stop and admire her work. The sun was high. She felt its rays discovering the crown of her head, and shifted into the shade.

'The perspective is wrong,' a boy's voice said.

Hannah looked up and saw a small white face, finely sculptured, white skin crowned with dark hair. 'Are you Stash?' she said.

'Yes.'

'You're very rude. I didn't ask your opinion about my drawing and you're late.'

'I couldn't come before midday. I have to help my father on the farm. If we don't have a harvest, we don't eat.' His voice was brisk. Hannah didn't know why, but she flushed.

He sat down beside her, taking her pencil out of her hand.

'Look,' he said, 'your tree, it's nice, but it isn't right.' He held the pencil towards the tree, eyed it over the straight surface, and then began to correct her lines with brutal strokes. 'My school teacher taught me about perspective,' he said proudly. 'She told me I could have studied in Krakow.'

'Aren't you going to?'

'How can I? We don't have the money.' He paused. 'I've left school.'

Hannah didn't know what to say. She looked closely at the boy. He was tight-lipped.

'I'm sorry about your mother,' she said awkwardly.

'My mother?' he said.

'Danuta told me – last night.'

The boy didn't respond. Hannah thought he had a fierce face. She felt embarrassed.

'My father had a treehouse up there.' She pointed up to the branches.

'I know. I go up there,' he said.

Hanna was surprised. 'I thought it had perished.'

'I rebuilt part of it – just the base, further up.' Stash stood up. 'Do you want to see it? I'll let you.'

'Let me? It is I who should advise you that this is my father's tree. You are . . .' Hannah couldn't find the word for trespass in Polish, but Stash understood her meaning.

'Trees don't belong to people, they are part of nature, like the land – it should belong to everyone,' he said hotly.

Hannah was amazed. She had never heard anyone speak like that before.

'Come on then.' Stash lifted a satchel-type arrangement on to his shoulders and shinned up the tree. Hannah watched him. He knew all of Papa's footholds. He moved stealthily until he was obscured by the foliage, and then called out again: 'Are you coming?'

It was funny. She had been so upset when Papa hadn't

let her climb the tree, but now she was frightened. She wasn't going to let this Polish boy know. She squared her shoulders, hitched her muslin dress and placed her foot in the first hold. Stash appeared and took her hand and pulled her. She snagged her dress on a twig, caught her blonde hair on a branch. Stash had to untangle it. Hannah just held on to the trunk, terrified. She couldn't look down, she was sure she would fall. She felt the strength of the boy's hand as he dragged her up the bark and she responded to his voice, but she didn't hear what he was saying. Her palms were sweating and it was difficult to get a hold. She slipped and he seemed to drop from somewhere above her head. His feet found spaces hers couldn't. She scrambled and clung whilst he swung and glided. He pushed her, climbing behind her until they reached the remains of the first platform. The wood had rotted and Stash had removed a lot of it, but there was still a small ledge. She stood on it. Her eyes were shut.

'I'll help you – you can do it.' He spoke quietly without antagonism.

She whimpered something.

He said, 'It's just above – look.'

'No, I can't.'

'You can – it's beautiful. You can see everything from there and no one can find us.'

He put his hands around her waist and propelled her legs forward, kicking first one and then the other. She obeyed his movements; both were unaware of the perfect linking of their bodies.

The branches cleared, the sky was blue – unprotected even by small clouds. It was open, welcoming, almost embracing. Hannah felt the platform under her feet. She sat down, scared because of its vibration. She felt Stash by her side.

'You have nothing for your head. You will suffer from the sun.'

'I didn't think I was going to sit in the sun,' she said.

He took out a large handkerchief from his pocket. She noticed that he wore short trousers supported by braces. He knotted the sides of the handkerchief and put it on her head.

'There, the crowned princess of the tree.'

The disciplines of time vanished. Safe in the branches, Hannah obliterated the outside world. She had never been able to do that before. Stash looked at her. She grinned and made rolling movements with her eyes, rubbing her stomach with her hand, sticking her tongue out. He laughed at her, handed her some ham and took some for himself. She noticed that he carried a bottle of sour milk. He took a gulp and passed it to her. She had never drunk from a bottle before, but neither had she climbed trees, even though she had wanted to. She took the bottle and placed it on her lips and tipped her head back. She felt the liquid go into her mouth, and she swallowed, but some of it came out of the side and rolled down her face on to her dress. She rubbed her face clean with the back of her hand and handed it back to Stash. She noticed that his apples were not as green as the ones they had at the house. The wind blew softly. Stash lay back, gazing up at the sky; he didn't talk. Hannah sat for a moment, and then she too lay back. She looked up and imagined she was a cloud racing across the sky. There would be no restrictions: she could go where she wanted – foreign countries . . . she imagined China with its yellow people, its mysteries, Persia, India – she sighed with pleasure. Stash looked over at her, disturbed by her small noise. He sat up and began to sketch her. She lay still, fascinated by the speed of his strokes. When she moved a little he said, 'Don't. I can't do it if you change position.'

She lay still until he'd finished. He handed the drawing to her. She was delighted, but she didn't know if she looked like that.

'Come on. I want to show you something else,' he said.

He gathered the remains of the food together and knotted

it into the handkerchief which he took off Hannah's head. He took her hand and guided her back down the tree. She was sad to leave it. He jumped the last few feet and then held up his arms to Hannah. She jumped too and he caught her.

'Why don't you get some flowers for your mother?' he said.

'Yes, I would like that.'

They ran through the woods until they reached a stream. The water flowed, clean and pure. Hannah stopped. She was fascinated by the ripples, the stones at the bottom, the little fish weaving their way around them. Stash watched her for a moment, then took her hand again. They made their way to small stepping stones over the stream. He went first and Hannah followed, holding her dress high above her knees, forgetting her femininity. He waited for her and then they walked swiftly up a bank.

Hannah drew in her breath. Ahead lay a field full of red flowers – the most beautiful she had ever seen. They were wild poppies. She ran into the middle, sucking in their lushness. Stash stood at the side of the field, and she wondered if perhaps he didn't want to disturb the flowers. She lay down on the parched ground and looked at the poppies rising around her. Timidly she took one, breaking it off by its stem. She sat up and stuck it in her hair. She spread out her hands and began to collect more flowers until she had an armful. Going back to Stash, she offered him a poppy. He took it and put it behind his ear.

'We're twins,' he said.

Hannah grinned. She was sure her mother would love the flowers. Her mother, the time. Suddenly she was scared.

'What time is it?' she asked.

'I don't know, about two o'clock,' Stash said.

'No, it can't be – I've missed lunch.'

'No you didn't, you had some with me.'

'No, you don't understand. I've missed it at the house.'

'Were you expected at home?'

'Yes.'

'Then you shouldn't have come,' he said comfortably.

'I have to get back.'

They ran back over the little stream, through the wood, past the treehouse. They reached the gate at the back of the white stucco house. Stash opened it and Hannah preceded him. She turned, offering her hand.

'Hannah!' Her mother's strident voice exploded the silence. A fraught, hysterical Rozia marched towards the children. Her skirt extended as she lengthened her stride to reach Hannah. She could no longer control herself.

'Where have you been?' she demanded.

'At the treehouse.'

'You were not, I looked for you. What have you been doing?'

'Doing? I met Stash. Mummy, this is Stash.' The boy held out his hand.

'Get out!' Rozia said.

'What . . . why are you saying that?' Hannah cried.

'Get out,' Rozia said again. She pushed Stash. The boy looked at her and then at Hannah. The tears had come, unbidden, into Hannah's eyes. 'Don't go, my mother doesn't –'

'Your mother knows exactly what she is doing. I said get out. You'll find your sister at the end of the road waiting for you. Her employment is terminated!' she screamed.

'Danuta . . . why?'

'Because she arranged for you to meet him, behind my back. God alone knows what could have happened.'

Rozia wouldn't have been able to explain why – she didn't know herself – but she just wanted Hannah back with her, by her. She had waited for Hannah with increasing impatience as the hands of the clock moved on. Finally, at twelve-thirty almost hysterical by then, she had asked if anyone knew where she might be – it was then that Danuta admitted that Hannah was with her brother. Quite suddenly, Rozia had exploded with a rage prompted by intolerable jealousy that her child was away with someone else, without her knowledge, when she needed her so desperately.

'I asked her to,' Hannah said.

'She had no right . . . Go!' she ordered Stash.

'But why – what was wrong with me meeting someone of my own age?' Hannah asked her mother.

Rozia didn't answer her. 'Go now. Get out,' she said again.

'You have no right to dismiss my sister.' The boy's voice had a dignity which contrasted with Rozia's raucous screaming.

'And you have no right to tell me what I may or may not do! Now go before I set the dogs on you.'

Hannah was frightened and upset that Danuta had been sent away. She wanted to stop Stash going, she wanted him to stay with her. Stash moved slowly. He had no intention of letting the mad, hysterical woman push him out – he would go at his own pace. He shut the gate behind him and did not look back.

Hannah was still holding the flowers, the tears coming freely now, streaking down her slightly dirty face, making neat little rivulets of water. Rozia snatched her arm and shoved her towards the house and into the salon. Neither of them spoke. Jouk was there, seated in a chair.

Hannah went to him. 'Papa, I'm sorry, but we have had such a lovely day.'

Before Jouk could answer, Hannah turned back and held out the flowers. 'I gathered these for you,' she said to Rozia.

The light was behind her, and it cast almost a halo around her hair. The white dress shone, the blood-red poppies were offered again. The eyes were full of tears.

Rozia's face was cold, the mouth curled in distaste; somehow she was nauseated by the sight of the dishevelled girl in white offering her stained flowers, stained red . . . red with blood. She was distorted with rage.

'Whore!' she screamed, giving in to her hysteria.

Hannah backed away from her, and Jouk stood up and put his hands on the girl's arms.

'Stop it, Rozia,' he said.

'She's a slut!' Rozia couldn't stop the words, her heart was thumping so hard. 'She's a slut, she's been with that boy. Look at her! Her dress is torn, her hair – look at her.'

She pointed a finger and watched Hannah back into Jouk's arms. Rozia was revolted. She couldn't understand how Jouk could touch such a defiled creature.

Jouk thought Hannah looked beautiful – a Pre-Raphaelite angel in white with red flowers.

'Rozia, calm yourself. You were worried about her, but you can see she's safe.'

Rozia couldn't believe Jouk's blindness. How could he hold Hannah? She was dirty. She could see the white stains on her dress . . . 'Don't you understand, Jouk? She's been with that boy.'

'Rozia.' Jouk's voice was cautious. He thought his wife was going mad.

'Slut, cuddling Jouk, just like you cuddled that boy. What did you let him do? What did you do?'

Hannah's face was etched in surprise and then shock. She was beginning to understand her mother. She tensed away from her father. Jouk realized too and he was very angry.

'Stop this! It has gone too far. And let us talk in English.'

'I agree,' Rozia said in Polish. 'I don't want the entire household to know she's a tart who sleeps with village boys.'

'You've shouted that several times already,' Jouk said in English, 'and it's ludicrous to imagine that Hannah has slept with the boy. It is your lurid imagination that has –'

'Shut up!' Rozia shouted back, at last in English. 'My

imagination! I am clean – I have no bad thoughts. I am at one with my God.'

'At one with your God . . . you don't know who He is!' Jouk shouted back.

'Blasphemy . . . blasphemous,' she cried, holding her stomach, doubled over.

Hannah had never seen her mother like this – demented, wild, her normally neat hair ravaged by her hands, her eyes glaring.

'I'm sorry,' Hannah said. 'I didn't mean to worry you. We climbed the tree . . . and found your treehouse, Papa. Stash had built another further up. It was so beautiful. We lay back and we watched the sky.'

'Is that enough, Jouk?' said Rozia, her voice quiet now.

'Is what enough? She climbed a tree, that's how her dress got damaged. Her hair –' Jouk went over to Hannah – 'was presumably dishevelled by the branches. I told you not to climb the tree, Hannah.'

'I know, Papa, and I am truly sorry.'

'And you didn't think about the time. That was discourteous to your mother, and you have caused her deep distress . . .'

'I know, but I wanted to bring her these flowers that we found in a field.'

'I don't believe this.' Rozia's voice was slurred, and she was consumed with a sudden vile loathing for her daughter. She recalled another time, another white dress, and she remembered the loving. She imagined Hannah lying there in the field, her dress awry, the boy moving into her, and Hannah answering his thrust.

'Don't you realize what has happened? Look at her face.'

'Nothing's happened,' Jouk said shortly. 'She went off and forgot the time. She's only a child. You're making too much of it.'

'Am I?' Rozia's voice was dangerous. 'She's just a child

is she?' Her hand shot out, the muslin tore like paper, in the sun the small breasts rose to the air, the pink nipples tiny, untouched, inviting. 'There's the child, but she's not your child is she?'

'Rozia, what are you doing?' Jouk half-whispered. His chest constricted.

'Look at her,' Rozia said.

Despite himself Jouk stared. He saw a young woman – embarrassed he turned his back.

Rozia stood with her arms by her side – she was triumphant. She watched Hannah look down at herself, cover her breasts with her hands, dropping the red flowers to the floor. She heard her say, 'Papa, Papa, please . . .'

'Don't call him Papa. I've told you he's not your father. Your father is dead. Tell her, Jouk.'

Jouk stood with his back to the room. 'She is my child. I held her when she was born, and I love her. She's mine.'

He half-turned back to the women, but then, in a moment, he realized he could not face them and he went from the room.

Rozia's voice was harsh. 'Listen to me, Hannah, your real father is dead. His name was Stefan and I loved him. He died, and I married Jouk so that you could have a name and a home.'

Hannah's face was ashen.

'Slut, do you understand what you are?' Rozia said, kicking the flowers.

'No, you're the slut. You – you are.'

'No!' Rozia's arm rose with a will of its own, and she slapped Hannah's face again and again, and when Hannah bent over to avoid the blows, she continued to hit her on her back – on her legs. Finally she stopped and left the room.

Hannah lay curled up on the floor. She didn't move, she didn't cry. She didn't notice her drawing lying next to her, crumpled and dirty, distorting the once pretty face that had adorned the paper just half an hour before.

Chapter Thirteen

———— ◆ ————

It was just three days later, on August 18th, that Jouk together with Rozia and Hannah embarked on their journey home, the entire family having returned from the summer house the day before. It was a restrained but mournful farewell, as if the participants appreciated that this was the real ending. Each in their own way nursed their hurt, making them oblivious to the need of the others.

Jouk embraced his mother at the door of the apartment house, touching her face, her arms, like a blind man learning the outlines of another human being so that he might keep it in his brain forever. Hannah choked back tears as she watched the man she had assumed to be her father bend over and formally kiss his mother's wrist, taking leave of her quite simply forever.

The old lady caressed Hannah's hair. 'Goodbye,' she said in English.

'Goodbye,' Hannah replied and impulsively, perhaps out of keeping with the formality of the occasion, she hugged her and the old lady hugged her back.

Rozia merely offered her hand, her face set as a sculptor might if he wanted to portray grief.

Mrs Oberska offered comfort. 'Take care of yourself, Rozia, come to terms with your new life. You have opportunities. Do not look back.'

There was no rancour in the speech. At another time, Rozia would have cared for its sparseness, but on that day she just wondered how much of the argument the old lady had heard.

Mr Oberski drove them to the railway station himself. He cried, but that was easier to deal with, for embarrassment can be an acceptable panacea against pain.

In the eventual sanctuary of the railway carriage, Jouk looked at his women, for he still thought of them as his. Politeness had been stretched like violin strings, producing the right notes when the bow was drawn carefully, but now it had been used rashly and the discordant sounds had destroyed all that he, the composer, had tried to achieve. He surveyed the wreckage without remorse, sorrow or pity, and being without bitterness he was ready to reconstruct and to salvage what he could.

He waited until they had been travelling for several hours before he began his work. Hannah was curled up in the corner, her feet drawn under her, her tongue firmly clenched between her teeth. She was reading Angela Brazil, brandishing the exploits of the English public school girls as if it were a badge of acceptance, laughing a little too loudly, making sure that the title was hidden from no one. She was English, she was accepted, she was part of the club. The fellow travellers, an elderly Polish woman and her middle-aged daughter, were treated with complete disinterest; even the fresh-faced German soldier who joined the carriage after they had crossed the border, this time conducted with little of the extraordinary, save the rather intimidating militarism, warranted not the slightest reaction.

Rozia herself, the perpetrator of this latest anguish, sat quietly and apparently composed in the other corner of the carriage, opposite her daughter. Her legs were crossed, the neat black suit and veiled hat presented an elegant woman. But the red nails drummed on the seat and pulled at each other when they were without the respite of a cigarette, that was smoked without apology.

'Soon we will be home again,' Jouk said to them both.

Neither answered. He sighed, but quietly. He did not expect anything else, but his resolve was undiminished.

After the return to England, it seemed that all was as it had always been in the Oberski family. Jouk returned to his work at London University, Hannah quickly re-formed her alliance with Esther and Rozia re-established her lifestyle, caring for her house, arranging the flowers in the church, an activity she had taken on just a few years previously. When Sybil asked, a little too pointedly, how the holiday had gone she had been sharp, but not unpleasant, making it clear she wanted no discussions. She played her tennis, even more aggressively than before. None of the other members of the club liked it – except for Simon Eastwell, who had once been Rosemary Lascelles' boyfriend. He had grown to like playing with Rozia – he liked winning and he liked watching the sweat as it formed on Rozia's skin.

The most upsetting part of Rozia's return, however, was when she discovered that her beloved Father O'Flynn had died of a sudden heart attack. Mrs Wheeler told her. She had never forced the relationship she had intended with the housekeeper; Rozia had learnt from Bernice Adams not to associate with players.

It was as if all her stability was being swept away, for the priest had meant some kind of family to her and now he too was gone. The new priest was a Father Gately. Rozia knew he didn't have Father O'Flynn's humanity; he was young but he had thin lips and she would never be able to talk to him in the same way, he would never be her friend.

Rozia and Hannah communicated very little, but Jouk re-established his relationship with his daughter. Immediately upon their return, he had taken her on to his lap, as if she was still a little girl, had cuddled her and spoken quietly and reassuringly:

'What your mother told you was true. Your real father

was killed long before he even knew you were to be born. I was lucky enough to hold you within minutes of your arrival into this world and then I staked my claim to be your father, therefore, I am your father.'

Hannah was grateful; she disliked change and distress and above all else she loved Jouk. Father and daughter took an extra delight in each other, spending their evening hours in almost conspiratorial pleasures.

Rozia tried very hard to understand her actions. She examined and re-examined the events of the day itself, excusing, even justifying her motives. She disliked self-pity, but found herself indulging in it which made her even more uncomfortable with herself. She deliberately blocked any news from Europe – not wanting to hear about 'the gathering storm' her English friends, the Lascelles, the Adams' and Simon Eastwell, talked of so endlessly in hushed tones – and immersed herself in the pleasures of life.

She was just beginning to come to terms with herself, when at eight o'clock on the evening of September 1st, 1939, Jouk returned from the University pale and strained. He didn't greet Hannah, but went straight to Rozia, his hands gently touching her shoulders.

'It has begun,' he said quietly, 'Germany has invaded Poland.'

Rozia's throat worked as if she wanted to speak, but no words came out.

Later, she and Jouk did talk. Jouk went to the kitchen and made some tea. She followed him.

'Will the British help us?' she asked.

'Chamberlain will resist, but in honour there is little else they can do. If it were Churchill . . .'

The following day, Rozia met Bernice at the butcher's shop. 'We are at war,' she told her.

'No we are not, Chamberlain will find a way out.'

Suddenly the pain at Father O'Flynn's death bit hard.

He would never have said such a thing, he would have understood.

Rozia walked away from her friend then. She had no wish to continue her shopping. Her head was aching, she kept seeing German soldiers like the fresh-faced youth in the railway carriage, but this time he was firing a gun, he was killing – and the corpses, Warsaw corpses, littered the streets and she wept.

'Don't forget the doubles this afternoon,' she heard Bernice calling, but she didn't answer her – tennis balls and cannon balls crossed over one another, exploding in the streets. Her eyes became red and sore, but still the visions haunted her. She saw an old man being dragged across the ground and, remembering Dr Weinstein, she saw herself avert her eyes, she saw the man's face, she saw his terror – he was her father.

She managed to get home. She tried to concentrate on the preparation of the food for dinner, but there was a sinking feeling inside her stomach, her palms were damp from perspiration, and she couldn't hold the knife to peel the potatoes. If she had to explain to anyone how she felt, she would have said it was as if small animals were crunching their way through her intestines, crawling into her vital organs, suffocating her. And Rozia couldn't cope any more – she needed Hannah, she had to have Hannah. She got to the bottom of the staircase; it seemed enormous, the prospect of negotiating each step gargantuan. Her head felt as if it were exploding. Was she ill? she thought with a dreadful clarity.

Hannah was in her bedroom, curled up on her bed. Esther sat at the other end, listening enthralled as Hannah explained, worldly-wise about such matters, about her love.

'Stash was so wonderful . . .' Rozia heard her say as she opened the door . . . 'If you could see him confronting that screaming harridan who has the nerve to call herself my mother.'

The gnawing started then. Rozia found it difficult to breathe – her veins seemed to have opened, bleeding anguish.

She could see Hannah loom up off the bed. Funny, the child looked anxious. Why should she be anxious? The eyes seemed to swallow the face: no cheeks, no nose, no mouth, just eyes. Hannah's eyes, Stefan's eyes. Where was Stefan? How could he leave her, where was he . . . dead from a Jewish hand or a German tank?

'Mummy, Mummy, I'm sorry. I didn't know you were outside the door. I'm so sorry. Are you all right? Here, let me help you. I'll never hurt you again. I swear I'll never do it again, Mummy.'

Rozia could hear the sorrow in the voice; it was so real that she could almost touch it. She was sad for Hannah, but she couldn't help her. Hannah tried to hold her – Rozia could feel her arms around her – but she didn't want anyone to hold her, holding might hurt her.

'I'm all right,' she said, grabbing the bed, wanting to get up, but the room was spinning like some sort of merry-go-round. How could she stop it? Where was the switch?

She heard Hannah telling Esther to telephone Papa. The sound echoed around the room, bouncing off the walls . . .

'Papa, Papa . . .'

But whose Papa was Esther calling? Hers wouldn't come, and she wanted him so much . . . Why wouldn't he come?

'Papa, Papa!' Was she shouting for him, or was it for Jonathon or Stefan, her beloved Stefan? She didn't know . . . but no one was listening, no one could hear her. They were dead – or was she the one who was dead? She wept for the corpse, not knowing whose it was.

Rozia lay in her bed, neither talking nor eating. She would drink when a worried Jouk or Hannah offered a glass or a cup, but she declined any food. At first she slept a great deal, taking comfort in the oblivion. On the third morning she sat up. There weren't any thoughts in her head, just the desire to sleep forever. She knew it would be a problem to get out of the bed. Her legs felt heavy, they wouldn't move; her body wouldn't obey her brain. For a moment she wondered if she were paralysed. She could hear voices, but she wished they'd be quiet. She knew it was Jouk and Mary, their old maid. She didn't mind Mary. She enjoyed watching her perform normal tasks, and it pleased her to see the shelves dusted – the floor cleaned. There was a beauty in her activities. Rozia wanted to tell her, but she couldn't remember any English. She didn't like speaking English anyway.

She decided to blackmail her body into behaving.

'You can sleep forever if you will just take me to the bathroom and the medicine cupboard this one last time,' she told it.

She pushed the blankets off. Her body was bathed in perspiration. She knew that if she could put one foot in front of the other, she could manage to reach the door, and from the door she would be able to get across the corridor and from there to the bathroom. Rozia dragged at her feet, clinging to the wall, unaware of the damp hand marks that stained the wallpaper. She pulled herself into the bathroom, but she couldn't stand up any more. She lowered herself, stomach first on to the cold floor, and slithered across the lino, squeezing her breasts together between her arms, propelling herself by her elbows. She clutched at a chair and then at the bath. Reaching the basin, she hauled herself up. She opened the medicine cupboard, looking for her sleeping pills, but she knocked some bottles out of the cupboard. They crashed into the basin, splintering it. Crying in rage, she pulled out all the contents of the cupboard, throwing them on to the floor, screaming unintelligibly because she couldn't find her little bottle. And then she laughed. It was suddenly so funny – where were her pills? Who had hidden them? It was such a little bottle – no one would want to hide it. She laughed and laughed. Someone held her.

'Don't do that,' she shouted, her English fluent again. She fought off the hands. She knew they were Jouk's. It was him, he was the enemy.

Get away – away from them all – back, back to Stefan. She felt the needle in her arm. There was a roaring in her ears – and then nothing.

The bedroom looked exactly as it always did. The mahogany dressing table, the ormolu lights, the delicately patterned pink wallpaper with its little shepherdesses seated demurely, whilst lambs and puppies frolicked at their feet. As Rozia gazed absently at the walls, it seemed as if the patterned wallpaper disengaged itself and moved to the centre of the room. The little figures, which had looked so attractive, assumed another dimension. They writhed on the floor – the little shepherdesses, the lambs, the puppies – who had all been so charming whilst imprisoned within the wallpaper. Now that they were free, their prettiness dissolved. They were ageing whores with over-rouged lips, pursed for kissing, smudged eyes which mocked Rozia as she lay in her bed. Their mouths opened, one after the other. She could see that they had no teeth – just rotten, bleeding stumps. The shepherdesses unlaced their bodices and brought out heavy swollen breasts and suckled the lambs.

Rozia remembered that once she had cuddled a lamb, feeling its warmth. She reached for one of the sheep, but as it came to her she saw the black and pink orifice that served as its mouth. Its breath was hot on her hand. She felt sick, pushing at the head, trying to get it away. The dogs turned on her, yapping and bounding around the bed. She didn't want to be part of the game so she heaved herself from the bed, determined to get rid of her guests. She knew that if she could turn the handle on the door, she would be able to shut them out. She couldn't hold on . . . everything felt sticky . . . blood, her blood – no, it was sweat, she knew that, her sweat.

The women laughed; their animals brushed close to Rozia's skin, making her flesh crawl up her bones. Desperately she pulled at the door – it opened, smoothly. The sheep and the dogs left first – two by two, like the creatures leaving the Ark, then the shepherdesses, their clothes awry, their curls dishevelled. They looked back at Rozia, as if to warn her they could be back. She slammed the door behind them, thrashing her body against the firm piece of wood, sighing and gasping for breath.

'Mummy, Mummy, it's all right – Papa will be here soon.'

Rozia opened her eyes. She was in bed, the blankets and sheets were in a pile on the floor. Hannah was trying to stroke her hand.

'It's all right, darling. I'm all right. I've had a bad dream – that's all,' Rozia said.

She was tired, but quite clear-headed. She glanced at the wallpaper – the little shepherdesses played innocently, but Rozia knew better. She would re-cover the walls and obscure them forever.

That evening Rozia got up from her bed. She knew that the doctor would be coming to visit her, and she was determined to receive him in her clothes. She carefully selected a becoming black dress. She bathed, made up, styled her hair and having located her tapestry, went downstairs.

Jouk was sitting in his favourite chair, smoking his pipe. Hannah sat at his feet. Rozia thought that they made an exquisite tableau – their faces licked by the orange and blonde tongues of light from the blazing fire. They were not talking, but Jouk's hand rested on Hannah's head in a proprietary gesture. Rozia cleared her throat.

'Mummy, are you all right?' Hannah got to her feet.

'I'm fine, darling. Jouk, my love – a chair – by yours, I think.'

The other armchair was pulled out of the shadows, and she eased herself into it. She picked up her tapestry, smiled at her husband and then at her daughter. Jouk sat back in his chair. Hannah fidgeted a little and then took a book and sat at the back of the room.

'Darling, don't stay away from the fire. You'll be cold. Come here.' Rozia patted the cushion that Hannah had been sitting on.

'No, it's all right, I want to read,' Hannah answered, and put on a standard lamp positioned behind her hard-backed chair as if to emphasize her point. Rozia, smiling again, began to count her stitches out loud.

It seemed to Jouk and Hannah that Rozia had come out of her 'crisis', as they called it, remarkably well, but Rozia knew differently. Just beyond the borders of her mind was a hell that beckoned in the small hours of the night. The war helped; somehow external fear was much easier to deal with than internal terror, a descent into an indefinable, and thus a much more frightening horror.

When the Phoney War ended in May 1940, Rozia Oberska embraced the conflict, using it as a solace against her own pain. She had managed to vote, along with the other members, to turn the Westmoreland Tennis Club into a vegetable garden. Hannah was never evacuated – not that she wanted to go. London had been as silent as a graveyard in the beginning, during the Phoney War, but now that the conflict was starting, Londoners were staying at home, to live or die with their city.

Jouk had been seconded from the University into some special war work. Rozia never inquired about his activities – it wasn't a time for asking questions.

As soon as she was able, Rozia re-planted her garden with vegetables, but she kept her rose trees – she was insistent about that. She joined the Women's Voluntary Service, wanting to do something, trying to find a way to channel her energies. She seemed to sit on interminable committees – Sybil Lascelles and Bernice Adams relished their lives as organizers, but Rozia grew to despise the talking – she wanted to be active. After Dunkirk, England had become a refuge with French, Dutch, Belgians, and more importantly for Rozia Oberska, Poles – at least some of them – arriving.

Wanting now to be part of their own war effort, she offered her services via Dr Przenicki to the Polish section of the BBC. She was told to go to Broadcasting House and report to the European Section.

She had been nervous on that first day, standing outside the vast door of Broadcasting House for quite some moments before plucking up enough courage to go through the mighty portals. The journey in the lift seemed the longest she'd ever taken, but once through the doors of the Polish and Czech sections, there was no time for nervous indulgence. Rozia was at work. The head of the section, a charming, courteous Pole who reminded her of Robert, immediately assigned her as a researcher to the 'Agony Column', whose job was to report on the whereabouts of Polish refugees.

'Get in touch with the Polish Air Force Liaison Officer, Jerzy Lukaszawicz,' he said, 'he'll be very helpful.'

She didn't have to call him, he had already called her with names and addresses and messages. The lack of time didn't allow for caution. So they barked at each other down the phone. At the end of the day, a tiring day, Rozia knew that the shepherdesses were gone forever.

After several weeks, Rozia invited Jerzy for lunch. 'Bring some friends,' she said.

'Would two be all right?' asked Jerzy, and she could hear the pleasure in his voice.

'Yes of course. Come on Sunday,'

And she became, almost miraculously, the girl she had

once been, and her body moved as if waking from some dreadful sleep.

Hannah found the change in Rozia unnerving. She was used to a sharp, almost bitter woman and suddenly there was someone else, a stranger who bubbled and laughed, who turned the radio on and once, when she thought no one was watching, danced and held herself, touching her own arms with her long slender fingers, almost caressing herself.

Hannah knew of course that three Polish airforce officers were coming for lunch – no one in the household could have ignored that fact. Expeditions had been undertaken for the right kind of food; despite rationing, Rozia had acquired what she needed. When Hannah got home from school, the smell of baking filled the house, the tablecloth was already laid out in the dining room, the white napkins folded into little hats; the greenery that had been selected to embellish the table in true Polish style had been gathered from the garden and placed in buckets of cold water. The house gleamed: every table had been polished, every window shined, every floor waxed, every carpet brushed and hoovered. She herself had been told to wash her hair, and her dress was to be starched and ironed. Rozia had decided upon a pale blue dress with a neat collar and cuff sleeves, but Hannah told her she didn't like it.

'Don't be silly,' her mother replied, 'you are a young girl and the dress is very becoming. The colour particularly is wonderful for your hair.'

'You didn't think I was a young girl in Poland.'

The words were out before she could stop herself. Hannah bit her top lip. She hadn't meant to talk about that incident ever again, but now she was glad, she didn't want that day to be forgotten – lost and overlooked. Her mother had no right to laugh and dance; she had hurt her and she hated her for it.

'I am very, very sorry about that day,' Rozia said quietly. 'I had no right to speak to you as I did, and do the things I did. I will regret that all my life, believe me, Hannah.'

Hannah looked at her mother standing in front of her. Even she could see that Rozia was beautiful, but she didn't register the sad, but calm woman who faced her, she saw only the demented hell-cat who had screamed and ranted and stolen her childhood, and unable to forgive, Hannah answered that woman: 'But you did do those things, didn't you?' and she walked out of the kitchen, slamming the door behind her, before Rozia could stop her. She went up to her room and locked the door.

She remembered Papa's face when he had seen her breasts: he had been surprised and shocked. What was so shocking about them? Hannah took off her school tie, undid the buttons on her Vyella school blouse; in the mirror she saw her breasts cupped by the sensible pink brassiere, chosen, of course, by her mother with the help of a fitter at the local department store. Hannah pulled it down, looking at the swelling mounds with their pale pink tips. She was curious, she wanted to touch them, but somehow that was something she could not do. She heard Rozia's angry footsteps.

'Hannah, please open this door, let me talk to you.'

Hastily, Hannah pulled up her vest, buttoned her shirt and put on her tie. As she did the knot, she called out, 'Leave me alone, I have homework to do.'

On the other side of the door, Rozia Oberska cried soundlessly.

At work someone remarked that Rozia looked tired.

'I'm all right,' she said, 'quite all right.'

Sunday was one of those soft summer days that happen only in England. It was July, the air was clean and a small breeze licked the grass and the trees so that they rustled and swayed gently, almost as if they were enjoying the movements.

Hannah got up early; she went into the kitchen, buttered some bread, and deliberately left the crumbs on the work surface. She opened the pantry and took out the strawberry jam, and didn't shut the door. She spread her bread liberally with the jam, knowing there was rationing and she was being selfish, but she didn't care. She decided to take her breakfast out into the garden. For a moment she was tempted to put the jam on the white tablecloth that lay on the dining-room table awaiting its adornments of green leaves, shining cutlery, and sparkling glasses, but Hannah knew that would be considered childish, even in her own eyes.

She opened the little door off the hall that led into the garden. Although it was only eight-thirty there was a warmth in the sun. She sat down, enjoying the feel of the air. She heard footsteps, identifying them as Jouk's even before he appeared.

'You left the kitchen in a disgusting state,' he said in a mild voice.

'Yes.'

'Why?'

She shrugged. 'A protest against the new order of light and joy, I suppose.'

'Hannah, you shock and sadden me.'

Hannah hated to upset Jouk, and she put her arms around him, unaware that she now thought of him as Jouk, rather than Papa.

'I'm sorry, it's just that she is so different all of a sudden, and she expects me to be different.'

Jouk caressed his daughter's hair, for he still thought of her as his daughter.

'She isn't different, Hannah, she is returning to what she was when I first met her. The fire is coming back.'

When Rozia had told him that she was returning to work, he had been delighted, telling himself that maybe – just

223

maybe – the old Rozia might return, but now as he held Rozia's daughter he felt the first tremor of unease.

The three Polish officers were handsome and charming. They brought flowers and kissed Rozia's hand on the inside of her wrist and then offered the same greeting to Hannah; despite herself, she had to admit she liked .them, and she couldn't wait to tell Esther. Physically they were very different: Jerzy Lukaszawicz was dark-haired with the brown eyes of a gypsy, his skin stretched taut over high cheekbones, and he presented the other two – Stanislaw Zagorski had curly brown hair and the look of a naughty schoolboy, and Piotr Holzman was blond and blue-eyed. For a moment, Hannah thought she saw a shocked look of recognition on Rozia's face. It disturbed her and she excused herself, taking the flowers from her mother's arms, offering to arrange them, unaware that she too was blonde and blue-eyed and that, at that moment, Rozia was looking at her with painful longing.

The lunch was an enormous success. By common consent they spoke English, but indulged in Polish delicacies like *pierogi* – triangular dumplings stuffed with cheese – pea soup, ham and new potatoes in soured milk, dishes of tomatoes and radishes and cucumber and, to finish, a wonderful cream cake.

'I did it,' Rozia said without modesty, and the men drank her health, saluting her charms, and she loved them all.

Rozia continued to work at the BBC, coping with the terror of the Blitz with the fortitude of a Londoner – for that is how she saw herself (not English, she reasoned, for she was not that, but a Londoner was something different, something to be proud of) – even on October 15th, 1940, when a five-hundred-pound bomb was dropped on a sandbagged Broadcasting House, killing seven people. But when, just two months later, a land mine exploded in Portland

Place, Jouk remarked that Rozia's exposure to such dangers might not be in Hannah's best interests.

Rozia transferred her services to the Polish Air Force itself, taking on part of Jerzy's job, acting as a liaison officer between the Poles and the Polish section of the BBC. He, to Rozia's surprised distress, had reported back to an operational unit. She had hoped that at thirty-one he would be too old for such duties, but the Battle of Britain was taking its toll and those who could fly flew.

Chapter Fourteen

———— ◆ ————

In late October 1941, the Second World War had been raging for two years. The people of Britain had altered their pattern of living to cope with the difficulties of an existence virtually under siege. Cities, towns, and even villages were battered by messengers of death. Travel, even by foot, was hazardous. The recurring blast of the air-raid warning would mean a scramble to find a shelter. Craters punctured every road, skeletons of burnt-out houses marred the skylines. Charred remains of vehicles littered the streets. Above all there was the eerie silence of a land without bells.

Schools did try to function. During the worst days of the bombing, classes were conducted in the air-raid shelters below ground. Rows of children would sit on bunk beds, using their satchels to prop up their school books.

Hannah Oberska, now aged seventeen, was amongst those who had not been removed to the safer climate of the countryside. Her school in Maida Vale had amalgamated with two others in the neighbourhood. The main complaint would not have been the overcrowding, nor the decampment to the cellars, but that school food had plunged further into the depths of culinary disaster – carrot puddings and dried eggs could do little to stimulate the palate. It was the great age of the nut rissole. But Hannah and her peers studied for their exams with the same dread as their predecessors had done in the days of peace. Hannah needed good results. She wanted to be a teacher – a wish nurtured by her father. It was not only a continuance of his own chosen career but also, he felt, a suitable profession for a girl who would one day be a mother.

Rozia was now very active with the Polish community, and Jouk's work kept him away from home quite a lot so Hannah, as a convenience, grew closer to Esther and her family. She didn't particularly enjoy being seventeen. She felt awkward about her femininity, not knowing what to do with it. A few of her friends went out with boys, but she hid behind her lack of self-confidence. Neither Jouk nor Rozia forced her into the social stream.

Hannah received an invitation from Esther to attend the party following her brother's bar mitzvah.

'I don't think I can come,' Hannah told Esther as the two girls were walking home from school, their satchels bulging with homework, gas masks dangling from their sides. Hannah's uniform was slightly small for her; the skirt clung to her hips and the purple sweater did not curl over in a flat roll as it should, but she looked tidy – she always looked tidy.

'Of course you will, I won't take no for an answer. I can't take it on my own without you anyway.'

Esther was a mess; even at the start of the day she would be in a disordered state. She wasn't particularly comfortable at home, where her parents' affluence embarrassed her. She preferred their life in Stoke Newington, where they had lived before moving to the plushier surroundings of St John's Wood. The arrival of riches in her family at a time of war worried her, but she never inquired how her father managed to accrue, rather than lose, like most of his neighbours.

'And you can meet my brother Ben, he'll love you, and you'll love him.'

Hannah and Esther had their rituals. They would walk to the corner of Hannah's road and stand and gossip about the day's events until they bade each other farewell as if they wouldn't be meeting the next day, or ever again. Esther would take the bus and Hannah would walk up the sloping road which led to her house.

So Hannah went to David Levene's bar mitzvah party. The Dorchester Rooms in Kilburn stood out like a beacon of luxury in an otherwise gaunt location. But its phoney grandeur bore little resemblance to its namesake in Park Lane, W1. Hannah stood in the corner of the room, her dress of pink slipper satin made by Rozia out of one of her own simpler war creations. She looked wonderful – blonde and shining – and Rozia had cried when she had seen her, brushed a hand over her cheek and whispered, 'I wish your father could have seen you today.'

'What time will Papa be home?' Hannah had asked as she went out of the front door. She thought Rozia looked perplexed, almost as if she hadn't understood the question.

She watched the extravagance of emotion as families greeted families, friends greeted friends.

'Esther darling, you look lovely. Doesn't she look lovely?'

'Such a nice girl, and clever I hear.'

'How much do you think all this cost?'

'What about rationing – how did he deal with that, our host, Harry Levene?'

'You know Harry!'

'Awful isn't it?' said Esther's voice.

'Awful? No, it's interesting.'

'It's interesting if you've got nothing to do with it. They're all so pushy.'

'They're funny.'

'Yeah - maybe. Come on, meet my brother.'

Esther was ruched from neckline to hemline in apricot chiffon. Hannah could have cried for her – she looked like a pudding – but then she realized that Esther wasn't aware of the dreadful creation. She held her head up and her face glowed with a pleasure that belied all her disparaging comments.

She plunged Hannah into the sea of talking, moving bodies. Cigars and heavy perfume mingled in the atmosphere, fanned by the heat. A soldier whom she now knew to be Esther's brother, with his creased khaki uniform, was a beacon in the mass of opulence. Esther dragged her over to him.

'Ben, this is my friend Hannah . . . the one I told you about.'

'Hello, Hannah.'

'Hello.'

Did his hand hold hers a moment longer than necessary? She felt sick.

'Ben, you haven't seen Aunty Beck – Oh, hello Hannah, don't you look pretty? Isn't she pretty, Ben, Esther's little friend?'

Mrs Levene's long fingers chucked her under the cheek and Hannah felt herself colour. 'It's a lovely party, Mrs Levene. You must be very happy,' she said.

'To tell you the truth, I'll be glad when they're all sitting down, having a good time.'

'Ladies and gentlemen, dinner is served,' shouted a puffy-faced flunkey in a red jacket.

'That's Uncle Arnold. I can't think why my mother got him into a red jacket. I think she thinks she's at Buckingham Palace,' Esther whispered.

If Hannah had been asked to recount her impressions of the following hour and forty minutes, she would have uttered but one word: food. In wartorn Britain, she had never seen so many chickens, chocolate – and even fruit. The guests devoured the feast with a speed that amazed her. She was sure that they would all be very sick when they got home. She and Esther sat at a table surrounded by Esther's cousins. She leaned back and looked around for Ben, and was disconcerted to find him staring at her. Hannah felt her face freeze – she couldn't even smile.

After a seemingly endless number of courses, the meal ended in a flourish of ice cream. Prayers were chanted to thank God for the sustenance. Most people ignored the little rabbi who sat at the top table, recounting the blessing. They were too busy trying to conjecture where Harry Levene had managed to acquire such a banquet – God didn't seem to come into the reckoning at all. The lights went out – a funny little band made up primarily of violins and accordions played, 'For he's a jolly good fellow' and a big cake was wheeled into the room with candles blazing. A blushing bar mitzvah boy cut through the hard icing to much applause. Speeches were delivered extolling the family's virtues, the boy's obvious brilliance and his occasional idiocies.

Finally, the guests rose as one – with the exception of a confused Hannah who struggled to her feet a little after the others – and applauded as an awkward thirteen year old propelled his mother around the dance floor to the violinist's version of 'Mammy'.

'I didn't have to go through all of this – they didn't have any money when I was bar mitzvahed,' Ben said quietly to Hannah.

She hadn't noticed him come over.

'It's really nice.'

'Yes, in a way it is.'

Not many people were dancing, but Hannah couldn't resist the offer of the outstretched arm. She had never danced before with a boy – only Papa, or the ballroom teacher at school. She stumbled a little, but he pulled her up and closer. She tried to relax, but she was too aware of the tall boy, of her sweaty palms. The music stopped, and in a way she was relieved. The violinists took off their jackets and the accordion player moved to the front of the stage. Folk music replaced unhappily rendered ballads. People got up from their chairs, and formed circles. Ben thrust her into a group with the women – he joined the men. Everyone linked arms and they began to weave their way around the floor, going in opposite directions, turning and coming together and then separating. Laughing people joined in, broke away and joined again. The music throbbed, there was no time to be shy – Hannah took off her shoes and she and Esther linked hands in the centre, leaning back until they fell over. Hands pulled her up – Ben's. Most of the people had left the little square dance floor – just the young and the children continued their whirling. Ben held Hannah tightly around the waist. In the speed of the music – the pleasure – he kissed her lightly on the lips.

In the midst of the gaiety, a long moaning sound intruded, its level fluctuating like a wave, rolling, high – low – high again . . . the air-raid siren. The band stopped playing. The guests gathered their coats, bags and the occasional chicken piece, which had been carefully hidden under a plate for transport home to a member of the family who had not been invited to the celebration – after all there was rationing. They collected by the doors, ready to file out – they knew the procedure.

They trekked to the nearest underground station, strutting like peacocks, flaunting their flamboyance against the bleak surroundings like splashes of colour on a newly acquired artist's palette. But the queuing, until they could descend to the platform and safety, was orderly.

'Go on down, I won't be a minute,' Ben said to the girls.

'Where are you going?' Hannah asked.

'I'm going to wait and make sure they all get into the shelter. Some of them are stupid enough to try and make it home.'

'Come on, Ben. Don't get involved.'

'I won't be long. Save me a place,' he said, and then he was gone, pushing his way through the crowd, angling his body like a fish's fin cutting its way through water.

'He won't find us again in this mass of people,' Esther said crossly.

When they got into the station, the girls hitched their skirts high above their ankles and started to clamber down the stairs. Their heels were constantly being caught in the little iron grids which made up the surface. Hannah saw that the young bar mitzvah boy, surrounded by his doting parents and friends, had chosen to carry his own cake. Obviously it had been decided to bring the precious delicacy with them, rather than leave it to the possible maulings by greedy little fingers and mouths not invited to the bar mitzvah. David was having a problem balancing it.

'Be careful!' shrilled Mrs Levene.

'I'm trying,' he snapped. He shifted his weight. The cake teetered. Mrs Levene's red-tipped fingernails hovered over it anxiously.

'I don't know why you don't let your father carry it,' she said.

'It's my cake,' David answered rudely. A few of the onlookers tittered.

Esther turned to Hannah. 'I could die with embarrassment. But at least no one knows that they're anything to do with me.'

'Esther, what are you and Hannah doing over there, walking down in front of us? Come over here so that we can all be together,' shrilled Mrs Levene.

Esther's shoulders rose, her head crept into her body like a snail retreating into its shell.

'It's all right. We'll keep up with you,' Hannah called back.

Esther made her hold back as the main branch of the Levene family made their way on to the left-hand platform – northbound. The girls turned right – southbound. Bunk beds were stacked along the walls, three high. It looked like a giant, rather dirty dormitory. They found an empty one to sit on.

'Why didn't you want to go with your parents?' Hannah asked.

'You have no idea what it would be like – more cake, less cake, no cake,' Esther replied.

Children ran around playing – a few babies cried. Most of the adults sat around talking, eating or playing cards. The atmosphere was congenial, like that of a club almost. It would have been hard to realize that these people were sheltering from a bombing raid which might destroy their homes or even kill a few of them.

'Do you think we'll have to stay all night?' Hannah asked a man nearby. 'My parents will be worried.'

'Don't fret yourself, love, it's only five o'clock. I expect there'll be an all clear and then there'll be time enough for you to get home before the heavy stuff starts.'

'Thank you,' she said.

'You both all right then, sitting on that bunk? Want anything to eat?' he asked.

The girls couldn't resist a small giggle at the thought of more food.

'No thanks,' Esther said.

The man nodded and went off – ambling down the platform, looking for companionship. Hannah didn't want to talk. She wanted to think about Ben . . . to savour him. She felt strangely excited. It was as if her stomach had become her centre. A great bubble of joy seemed to have grown inside her and it sent little shivers of happiness throughout her body. She'd never experienced such a feeling before. Occasionally she glanced around, searching for Ben, but she knew she would never be able to find him in the mass of people. She wondered when she might spend time with him again. She liked him so much.

Esther, bored with Hannah's lack of conversation, had fallen asleep. Time passed. Then there was movement; the all clear had been sounded.

'I wonder where Ben is?' Hannah said, trying to sound unconcerned.

'I suppose he squatted down somewhere and thought about Karl Marx.'

It took a long time to get out of the underground station. Patient waiting was rewarded only by intermittent shuffles forward until they finally reached the exit.

'We're like moles coming up for air,' Hannah commented.

'Moles prefer the underground life. I prefer fresh air,' Esther replied.

It was the sight of the ambulance that first caught Hannah's attention. And then she saw Mrs Levene bowed over, like a broken doll. The girls ran together, searching for each other's hands.

'Mummy . . .' Esther's voice was fearful.

Mrs Levene didn't answer; she seemed to be awash with tears which streaked her mascara into angry black lines. There was just a bubbling noise, and then she reached for Esther – pulling her away from Hannah, holding her close.

'Esther, my baby. It's Ben – shrapnel. It killed him.'

She motioned inside the ambulance. A white sheet covered a body; an army sleeve hung loose, its hand limp. Someone picked up the hand and laid it back under the sheet.

'Bastards!' Esther shouted. 'Bloody fucking bastards.'

When the killing finally stopped, there was the euphoria of victory – and the accounting of the dead. Into the mire of distress stepped Rozia Oberska. With the revelations of Auschwitz Birkenau, Treblinka, Maidenek, Dora and Plaschau, together with all the other camps in Germany and the other occupied European countries, she mourned her parents, her brother and her past.

She locked the door of her bedroom, resisting Jouk's requests for entry, not hearing Hannah's guarded words of comfort, and wept for the man she had called Papa, for her mother and her brother. The worst pain was that she had no idea where they had died – no place to identify on a map of Europe, nowhere to mourn. She wrote a careful letter to Shosha, but then she tore it up, for she had no way of knowing where her friend might be.

Jerzy Lukaszawicz came to share her pain. After his sight no longer allowed him to fly, he had survived the war in a desk-bound job. Frustrated and angry, it was Rozia who had seen him through those final years, who had held him when he wept for his dead wife and children, who made him lemon tea and baked him cakes, and now it was his turn.

He had gone straight to her room, and he was admitted. He was shocked by her grief. She told him then, quietly and without emotion, about Rozia Mezeurska, about Stefan Gordanski, about Booba and Papa – she left nothing out. He sat and listened and touched her forehead, offering an intimacy for the first time.

He returned ten days later with a letter. It was from the Red Cross, informing Rozia that Samuel and Hannah Mezeurski were transported to Auschwitz concentration camp in June 1942. They were selected for extermination on arrival at the camp, and they met their deaths in the gas chambers within eight hours of their arrival.

It was Jerzy who took her to the synagogue. She sat at the back of the ladies' gallery, a scarf on her head, and said the prayer for the dead in a long-forgotten language and on that Saturday in August 1945, Rozia Oberska forgave. She left the synagogue immediately the service was over and went to her church. There, quietly and without prayer, she lit candles for the souls of her parents, her brother, and all those who had died.

She told Jouk what she had done, when she returned. He said nothing, for he knew that there was nothing for him to say.

Hannah told Esther that her grandparents had died in Auschwitz.

'Bastards, fucking bastards,' Esther said and Hannah remembered back to the other time when her friend had said those words, and she felt a sadness that she could not share Esther's passion.

By 1947, the euphoria was over. On January 19th of that year the Lublin Committee became the legal government of Poland, thus sentencing the Poles in exile to a life in exile.

Diplomats and aristocrats became doormen and boot cleaners; those with youth or a skill fought for a new life, while others, bewildered and betrayed, turned on their allies, living in their midst but shunning their company. In 1947 Rozia Oberska, a Polish exile among Poles, opened her home to her fellow exiles.

Jouk took refuge in his work. This new Rozia, this Rozia with a cause, was lost to him as surely as Rozia Mezeurska had been lost to him, all those years before in Warsaw. If he was a sad man, for he loved that Rozia, he kept his sadness to himself – for at least he had Hannah.

Hannah's Story

—PART 1—

To Have and to Hold

Chapter One

———— ◆ ————

There was a moment of rejoicing in the bleak aftermath of war for the Oberski women – the tennis club was re-opening. Not a matter of national importance but a return to the way things were, or at least an attempt at it.

The grass courts had been re-sown in 1946 and in the spring of 1947 the reinauguration of the Westmoreland Tennis Club took place. It was decided that four members would play a show match. Bernice Adams and her husband Leo were of course one pair, and it was decided by unanimous decision that Rozia should oppose them, but Simon Eastwell was one of the young men who had been a victim of Hitler's war and Rozia, out of respect for his memory, had refused the offer of a replacement. Some at the club, like Cicily Woolcote who had never liked Rozia, muttered that it was typical of her sheer egotism. Others, new members and a few older ones, were touched. They thought it a fitting tribute. Rozia wore white trousers – she felt that at the age of forty-two they would be more seemly than shorts – and her hair was pulled back in a white chiffon scarf. Hannah, no bad player herself, sat at the side of the court watching her mother, unaware that she herself was attracting attention from a blond, handsome young man who had just joined the club.

Hannah always loved to watch Rozia play tennis; she admired her mother's natural grace and fluid movements and she enjoyed her style, wishing sometimes that she could play as well. Had Rozia started earlier there was little doubt that she would have been a champion, and at one time, briefly fortunately, she had wanted that for Hannah. A sharp word from the tennis mistress had stopped her carrying out her ideals with a single-mindedness that would have brought about success, but little happiness for the small girl. There were times when Rozia wondered if she had been right in her decision not to pursue for excellence – there was nothing wrong with that, surely – but Jouk had shared the school's view.

'Why push her? She is happy as she is, she plays and she enjoys it.'

So Hannah was good, but not good enough.

After the first three games Rozia was tired; she realized she hadn't the strength she had had before the war, and running against two opponents who might be said to have been stretching her, was too much.

She called to Hannah. 'Come on now, it's your turn.'

Hannah walked on to the court gingerly, her long legs underneath her smart white shorts and blouse looking very appealing. She wore her hair long, like Veronica Lake, but she had clipped it back in white slides. She served using her whole body, she ran using her whole body and the young man watching her wondered, when she loved, did she use her whole body, too?

Hannah was working as a teacher; the fact that it was her parents who had persuaded her that it would be a suitable career didn't prevent her from enjoying what she did. Her special subject was history and she taught girls from the age of twelve to eighteen; younger children bored her. She didn't use her textbooks as much as she should, because she thought them far too narrow in their attitudes.

'It is as if all civilized existence ends at the borders of the British Empire. It's no wonder we are such a chauvinist nation – we don't know about any other countries,' she told Esther over a cup of tea in Esther's parents' kitchen, whilst she tucked into a savoury fish ball. She was particularly partial to Mrs Levene's fish balls; they were sweet and peppery, sometimes boiled, sometimes fried – she liked them both ways. 'Anyway I try to widen the scope, have a bit of argument and discussion. It's good for them.'

'It would be better for them if they weren't segregated in a private school.'

Esther, who worked for a small publishing house, was now a Communist. '. . . a natural result of the horrors of war and the excesses of my parents,' she claimed.

Hannah sighed; she knew she and Esther were in for one of their favourite arguments. Hannah agreed that selection was inequitable, that elitism was wrong, but neither was it right to level down.

'But you don't have to,' Esther argued. 'It's a presumption of the better off that they make better students.'

'I didn't say that,' Hannah protested. 'I merely think there has to be another way. There must be a system where children can find their own level. Not every child is good at maths, not every child is good at history. The schools should be devised in such a way that the children can find their standard in each particular subject. We must stop stereotyping, we must be more creative.'

'More indulgent you mean.'

'Your system would be as rigid as the one we've got now. Communism would mean just as much structure.'

'Nonsense,' Esther snapped. 'The trouble with you, Hannah, is that you are a hypocrite. You speak of changing the world and yet you teach privileged children in a private school.'

Hannah blushed and Esther saw it. 'You've got the right thinking, Hannah,' she said. 'You are just woolly-headed.'

Hannah smiled. 'What you really mean is that, with just a bit of persuasion, I'll be converted to the real faith and discover that all those pictures of God with a white beard and a halo of hair are right – it's just the name that's wrong. He is really Karl Marx.'

Esther had the grace to laugh.

Hannah saw a lot of Esther. Mostly they met in each other's homes; occasionally they might go to the cinema and when they could afford it, the theatre. They talked a lot, swapping ideas and even dreams. Hannah wanted to be a famous, revolutionary educationalist. Esther just wanted the revolution; but what they both longed for was the mate, the man to share their lives – the knight on his white charger. In the times they weren't together, Hannah played tennis and Esther attended political meetings.

Hannah had noticed a blond man who also played at the tennis club. She thought he had a marvellous face – in fact she liked the look of him 'all over' as she put it to Esther. She'd even asked Sybil Lascelles about him. She was fond of Sybil, who had become a sort of confidante to her, particularly over Rozia's illness and now about this man. She found the English woman's no-nonsense approach so much easier to deal with than Rozia's sense of the dramatic.

Sybil's relationship with Hannah was important to her, but she never saw her as a surrogate daughter, even though she sometimes noticed that Hannah saw her as a surrogate mother.

'Don't know much about him, darling – just know he's called Anthony Simpson. However I'll engineer a little do. Leave it to me.'

And a little do was organized, '. . . for the younger members,' Sybil said.

Hannah wore a white organdie blouse and a straight black skirt. She insisted that Esther come with her.

'What am I going to say to a bunch of tennis players?' asked Esther, who was far more interested in Alan, the shock-haired secretary of the local branch of the Communist Party.

The party had started when they arrived. Glen Miller blared out from the gramophone. Beer flowed and gin and tonic. Some couples were smooching, others talked; a lot of the guests stood around on their own. Cigarette smoke clung to the atmosphere. Hannah looked around for Margery, the club vamp – every club had a vamp and she was theirs – and there she was, sitting on the couch, flamboyant in a red dress, her hair black and long, its texture seeming to invite fingers. She was talking to a man whom Hannah had never seen before. She saw him light two cigarettes, holding them both on his lower lip so that they hung in a strange kind of invitation. He took one out of his mouth, played with it for a moment and then placed it between Margery's lips. She watched while Margery sucked on the smoke, allowing her hand to rest on the man's knee. It seemed to Hannah as if they were becoming an extension of each other, intertwining, mingling, overt, and she was strangely excited by it.

Esther was standing in a corner. She was quite slim now, and wore a tailored black suit with a white blouse, the same colour scheme as Hannah's but a stark, almost masculine outfit.

'God, what a crew,' she said to Hannah. 'I was right, I shouldn't have come.'

'They look as if they are enjoying themselves,' Hannah replied, not a little ruefully.

'They are welcome,' Esther snapped. 'None of these people have any comprehension of life.'

'On the contrary, most of them, the men that is, have actually faced death either for themselves, or vicariously through their friends,' a blond young man said.

Hannah stared – it was *the* young man, and she was thrilled.

'Don't talk to me about facing death. I know all about it.' Esther's voice was clipped in anger. 'Excuse me,' she said pointedly, and walked away.

'What did I say?' the young man asked.

Hannah shrugged. 'Her brother was killed in a bombing raid in London. It's just her way.' She glanced at the young man. He was rather nice-looking, she thought, very nice-looking.

'I am sorry,' he said.

Hannah shrugged, smiling at him; there was nothing else to say.

'Would you like to dance?' he asked. 'I am Anthony Simpson, and I noticed you on the first day I came to the club – I've been hoping to meet you.'

'Have you?' Hannah replied, hoping she didn't sound coy.

Anthony had been an officer in the army, and now he was in pupillage, the English euphemism for the kind of apprenticeship which would eventually allow him to become a barrister. He was thirty years of age, a little old to begin a career, but the war had ensured that there were a lot of men in his position. He talked easily and Hannah felt surprisingly comfortable in his company. Her European parents had done little to help her cope with the vagaries of English life, so she didn't always find a common meeting point with her fellow countrymen, or women. It was a revelation, therefore, to discover that her dancing partner was as disassociated from society as she was. Anthony was angry at the years lost fighting the war, and the barriers that had to be crossed without the help of money. He told Hannah he shared her sympathy for socialism.

'Let's have a drink one night,' he suggested, 'and salute the new egalitarianism.'

'Will you be at the club next weekend?' Hannah asked, hoping she sounded casual.

'Yes, why don't we have a game and then a drink?' he said, and she noticed that he did sound casual. It was only then that Hannah realized she hadn't seen Esther, and she wondered, feeling horribly guilty, whether she was still at the party.

She telephoned Esther the next morning – early. She woke Mr Levene.

'She's out,' he said, 'on a march or something. She said you would ring. She said to tell you: "Sorry I flounced out – see you Tuesday".'

For most of that week, Hannah thought about Anthony. She found herself conjecturing about him in the most intimate of ways, and her thoughts thrilled and frightened her. Her thighs tightened at the fantasy of his mouth on her mouth. In the privacy of her bedroom she caressed her breasts and watched, amazed, as the nipples hardened. How would they feel to a man? she wondered. How would they feel to Anthony?

She waited on the veranda of the tennis club – she tried to be easy and relaxed, and not to seem as if she was waiting for him. Uncle Leo gave her a big kiss and hug.

Margery, looking wonderful in her latest mink, walked past. 'Saw you lost no time in grabbing the newest hunk,' she muttered.

'We just talked,' Hannah said in her own defence.

'He was eating you up with his eyes.'

'Was he?' Hannah said, really pleased.

She glanced at her watch – where was he? Should she go and get another game . . . perhaps he wasn't coming.

'Hannah! Hi,' she heard and he was there.

She could see that he had a deep indentation in his brow, and she wanted to touch it. They played on their own – both of them enjoying the other's movements. Anthony stretched and ran. Hannah reached and crouched – both tried to play and not to win.

After their match they had a drink, and then another. By then it was eight o'clock. Hannah wore a pale yellow dress. The skirt caught her legs when she moved – she had left the petticoat in the dressing room. Anthony bought her supper of fish and chips with bread and butter and a cup of tea. They giggled at the cross waitress and a leaky bottle of vinegar. Hannah made faces at an intense young man in a beret and he made faces back. Anthony leaned over, tapped his shoulder.

'She's mine,' he said. 'Go and find one of your own.'

And Hannah laughed – she was happy.

'Next Saturday,' he said, and there was no question in his voice.

'At the club?' she asked.

'No.'

'Oh,' she said.

'Don't let's make that a habit – I want to take you out.'

When she finally got home she found Jouk in the kitchen, washing up a lot of cups and saucers; the remains of Rozia's special cakes littered a few plates, ashtrays were full – waiting to be emptied.

'You have had a lot of people here.'

'Yes, we have, it was very pleasant. Your mother is setting up an advice centre for people who need help settling down in England. She and Jerzy invited several people who have agreed to act as consultants: our priest, a lawyer, a doctor, oh and Mr Soames, our bank manager. It's a good idea.'

Hannah noticed that Jouk looked tired. Where was Rozia? Why wasn't she washing up? Hannah was suddenly very irritated.

'Go to bed, Papa,' she said. 'You look exhausted, I'll do this.'

'Mama is seeing the guests out,' he said, offering an explanation as if he had heard her unspoken questions.

Hannah gently pushed him away from the sink. He smiled at her, and without attempting further argument went out of the kitchen. That worried Hannah, it was so unlike him to be acquiescent. She heard a voice in the hall, Rozia's voice.

'Jouk darling, I am glad you are going upstairs now. I shall bring you some tea.'

Hannah saw her young mother sweep into the kitchen.

'Darling, hello. Did you have a nice time?'

'Yes, thank you.'

'It's special, isn't it, being with a boy you like?'

Embarrassed, Hannah turned away; she had no wish to share any intimacy with her mother.

Rozia tried to concentrate on brewing Jouk's tea and not think about Jerzy Lukaszawicz. Rozia was a moral woman, a married woman, and she was five years his senior. They were friends, good friends, but that was all. She had put her arms around him once, when he had heard that his wife and two sons were dead. Yes, it was true that they had both experienced grief and pain and now they both wanted to live. She must find a nice girl, someone to take care of him; she looked at Hannah . . . perhaps? No, no, she couldn't bear that.

On the following Friday, Rozia met Jerzy in the street. She told him they must not see each other any more.

'I love you, Rozia,' he said.

'You mustn't,' she said, walking away.

Chapter Two

———— ◆ ————

For Hannah the days leading up to Saturday sped by. Rozia had been difficult and tense, more like she used to be before the war. Hannah tried to ignore her, concentrating on her work, allowing herself to daydream about Anthony. She thought he was so handsome with his fine, blond hair and his sculptured features.

'He's beautiful,' she told Esther.

'Is he beautiful inside?' Esther asked. 'I know that Alan is.'

'I don't know,' Hannah giggled. 'I haven't looked.'

'Well I have.'

'Have you?' Hannah asked, sitting up straight. Tell me, have you?'

'No,' Esther said too quickly. 'Not because I wouldn't, but because the opportunity hasn't been there.'

She turned away from Hannah in case she noticed bright red cheeks – because Esther had and she had loved it.

Hannah played tennis during the day; she'd looked for Anthony, but he wasn't there so she went home and prepared himself for the evening. She bathed and washed her hair. She let it hang down loose over her eyes, hoping she looked like a Hollywood film star.

'Sweep your hair back, Hannah. It looks untidy the way you have done it,' Rozia said from the doorway.

Hannah tensed. She never liked her mother to watch her dress.

'I want it like this,' she answered shortly.

'Do you really like this young man?' her mother asked, sitting on the bed without invitation.

'Yes, very much.'

'He's a Catholic, of course?'

'No.'

'But Hannah . . .' Rozia swallowed. 'Well, be careful. You mustn't get too serious.'

'Why not?'

'Because you couldn't marry. You just told me he isn't Catholic.'

'Nor am I.'

'Don't be ridiculous, Hannah.'

'It's not ridiculous. I don't believe in a God.'

'Hannah!'

'Look Mother, I realize it is different for you. You are, but I find the rituals empty.'

'How can you be so blasphemous?'

'Oh, Mother, it's only blasphemy to you.'

Hannah got up from the dressing table and went over to Rozia.

'I am not trying to upset you. It is just that as I don't believe in God, there's no reason for me to adhere to any symbolistic religion. I don't see how it is possible to observe an empty shell if you don't think there is anything inside. Surely that would be far more sacrilegious?' She couldn't stop what she was saying – the words came too quickly, too easily. 'It's a substitution, all this observance, and the emphasis on the Church only masks any deficiencies within the individual. It's very comforting, you don't have to worry about the living, you can concentrate all your efforts on the deity . . . it's easy, you're off the hook. If you light your candles and say your prayers you'll be in with God and Jesus.'

'Hannah, please don't say such things. Perhaps if you talk to Father Gately . . .?'

'Father Gately! That bigoted old man. His devotion to the Holy Mother worries me. I sometimes think he sees her as a substitute mistress, wife and mother . . .'

Rozia stood up, her face white. 'That is enough, Hannah,' she said, turning and walking towards the door.

'I am sorry, that was unforgivable of me,' Hannah said, and involuntarily reached out her hand towards Rozia. She could almost touch her mother's distress and she was sorry for that, really sorry. 'I'm going to wear the dress you made me, the blue one,' she said.

After a moment, Rozia replied, 'Yes, yes, you will look lovely in that.'

When Hannah had left the house, Rozia went to Jouk – her daughter's lack of faith mattered to her. Jouk said nothing for a moment, just drew on his pipe, and then he took his wife's hand.

'There is nothing you can do, Rozia. Hannah is no longer a child, she is entitled to her own views.'

Whilst Rozia agonized over Hannah's lack of belief, Hannah herself feasted on Anthony. She thought him particularly wonderful that evening. He wore white trousers, a white shirt and a white cricketing sweater.

'It's a bit old,' he said, indicating the sweater. 'I had it when I played for my school. And that was a long time ago.'

'Were you a batsman or a bowler?' she asked.

They were in a boat on the Serpentine; Anthony was rowing, Hannah had let her hand drop into the water, feeling it run through her fingers like silk.

'I am impressed by your technical knowledge.'

'Hardly technical – wait till you try me on silly mid-on – and silly mid-off.'

From the way he looked at her, Hannah realized that Anthony was falling in love with her. She was ecstatic. It was wonderful.

He manoeuvred the boat to the side – he was quite expert, there was no fluffing – nor did he fluff when he put his arms around her and gently kissed her on her mouth.

'I don't want to be with anyone else,' he said, 'just you, I want to see you every day.'

But they couldn't manage that – there just wasn't enough money and Anthony did have to study sometimes. The days in between passed in a mixture of pleasure and some discomfort. Work no longer held the same importance for Hannah. She still enjoyed it, but sometimes she would find herself drifting – she would see Anthony in her mind and would savour some moment they had shared, and its pleasure would diminish whatever else she was doing. The weather was hot and so debilitating – they didn't want to play tennis. So much of their time was spent in trying to avoid crowds and seeking cool, isolated places. They walked on the heath in Hampstead; they liked it there because they could find little hollows to curl into, and in a sort of privacy they could kiss and touch. Hannah loved the feel of Anthony's hands on her skin, she enjoyed his tongue in her mouth, but most of all she loved the closeness of a male body. She was aware that he was aroused. Sometimes she wanted to reach out to him, but inexperience and fear held her back. For the moment she was content to let him do the roaming. His fingers strayed over her breasts and he would kiss her neck, her shoulders, and when the intensity of their feelings allowed them to get carried away, he would slide his fingers under her bra and curl them around her breasts. Hannah felt as if she could die from the pleasure of it and the ache between her legs would make her arch to him, wanting more.

Anthony had had just three sexual experiences prior to his entanglement with Hannah. Two had been with prostitutes and one, a wonderful brief interlude with Carole, the wife of a fellow officer. When the officer had gone missing, presumed killed, Carole, out of guilt, had ended their relationship. Anthony still missed her, but he did love Hannah, there was something so appealing about her femininity.

Hannah still saw a lot of Esther. She valued her friendship more than ever now that she had a boyfriend. Esther too was deliriously happy; her secretary of the local Communist Party was every bit as enjoyable to her as Anthony was to Hannah.

Just two months after they had first met, Anthony decided to ask Hannah to marry him. He planned it all carefully, wanting it to be just right. Hannah was so special to him. She seemed like some beautiful exotic creature with her lush lips and her large eyes. He had known she wasn't English the first time he had seen her. It was the flat cheekbones and flaring nostrils. Sometimes when he was trying to work she flitted across his mind, distracting him so that he had to hold and touch himself. He thought of her as a siren who had come to bewitch him.

He couldn't afford to take Hannah to dinner at the Savoy, but they would go there after they had eaten – just for a drink, he would tell her – and then, very simply and without any preamble, he would ask her to marry him.

Hannah herself knew that this was to be a special night – it was the way Anthony had said, 'Meet me at my chambers, we'll eat first and then a surprise.'

She wore a black dress with a very full skirt. They ate at a small café – she noticed Anthony picking at his food, and she put her hand on top of his. 'Are you all right?'

'Just not hungry,' he said. 'Let's go to the Savoy.'

So determined was he that the proposal should take place in the right surroundings, that he overlooked the fact that she hadn't finished her chicken.

Hannah had never been to the Savoy before, and its gloomy splendour didn't impress her. She grabbed his arm, and they walked over to where the sailing lists were posted in the hall.

'I love the idea of those big ships cutting through angry, swirling seas.'

'Shall we go now?' he whispered, his mouth close to her ear.

She nodded. He pushed her towards the bar and ordered a bottle of champagne – and then they sat down at one of the tables.

'Will you marry me?' he said.

There was roaring in her ears, a pounding in her chest – was it happiness? 'Yes,' she whispered.

And they drunk the entire bottle – giggling, whispering and dreaming.

Anthony had borrowed his father's battered old Alvis and they sat close together on the front seat. He had driven into a lay-by near Hampstead Heath. There were no street lights, no one was around. He manipulated himself so that he faced Hannah. He put his arms around her shoulders.

'Now,' he said, 'let me see you.'

'You've seen me,' she said.

'Not the parts I want to see.'

He touched her hair. He liked the way it curled into her neck. He kissed her and undid the zip at the back of her dress. She was arching towards him as she always did. He felt quite dizzy. The neckline of the dress gaped. He pulled it down, searching, his fingers found the top of her bra and he pulled it down, grasping her nipples. Hannah gasped as his mouth closed around the pink tip of her breast. She felt the surge of pleasure between her legs as he sucked and pulled the skin. She put her hand on his head.

'Anthony, I want to make you happy . . . what do I do?'

He stopped sucking and looked at her. He thought she looked quite lovely in the night light: the blonde hair, the white skin, the naked breast. He loved her.

'Nothing, I'll do everything. You don't have to do anything. I'll show you.'

He went back to sucking, noisy and wet; and then Hannah

felt his hand crawl to the top of her stocking. She felt paralysed. Was he going to touch her there? Yes, she could feel the fingers edging their way past the suspenders, inside her knickers. She couldn't breathe. She felt his fingers push between her thighs, forcing them to open. She felt wet even to herself, and she was embarrassed.

'Lovely, juicy,' she heard him say, and then suddenly there was something else happening. The fingers were inside her, up her, clawing, scratching a little. She felt nothing.

'You're nervous. Don't worry,' Anthony said.

He removed his fingers – pulled her skirt back into place. She tried to straighten her top, but he pulled her hands away.

'No, I want to look at you like that. You look so wonderful,' he said.

Then he seemed to be fiddling with himself, buttons opened, a flash of white and then there was a long hard piece of flesh which quivered in the night light. Hannah pulled back, but he took her hand in his and guided it down on to the flesh.

'Rub it,' he said.

Terrified, she complied, feeling the skin pull and push. He laid his head back, moaning. Hannah was horrified, not knowing what was going to happen, and then she heard a groan and a spurt of white liquid shot out over her hand. She looked at it, feeling its stickiness. She continued to pull hard on the piece of flesh, but it seemed to have lost its rigidity.

'Steady, you'll do me some damage,' Anthony said.

He pushed her hand away and tidied himself, putting the buttons back into place. Hannah looked down at her hand, and wiped it on her dress. She was confused, wishing she knew more about sex. She hadn't enjoyed what had happened. She felt quite sick, but she didn't want to.

Anthony drove her home; they didn't speak until he drew

up outside her house and leaned over and kissed her gently on the lips.

'I am so very happy, Hannah. I'll do my best to be a good husband to you. I ought to speak to your parents.'

'Yes, I suppose so. Come tomorrow. For dinner,' she added, without thinking.

Rozia and Jouk were already in their bedroom when Hannah let herself into the house. The cream-painted hall, dominated by the heavily gilded chandelier which to Hannah's taste was far too overburdened with bunches of grapes, suddenly looked a little grubby. She turned out the standard lamp which was positioned in the corner near the fireplace – it was always left on until she came in. She glanced into the gilded wall mirror that was so obviously bought to match the chandelier, and noticed that her lips were bruised and swollen. Seeing a shade of light under her parents' door, she quickly applied some red lipstick and smoothing her hands on the side of her dress, she walked over the polished floorboards, avoiding Rozia's prized Persian carpet. She wanted them to hear the tip-tap her high heels made as she climbed the stairs.

'Hannah, is that you?' Rozia called out.

Satisfied, she knocked on the door. Jouk was in bed reading, Rozia was sitting at her dressing table, rubbing cold cream into her face. Her hair was pulled back by a blue chiffon scarf which Hannah noticed matched her blue night-gown.

She could see both her parents looking at her expectantly, for she never entered their bedroom normally, calling good night if the light was still on or else creeping past, avoiding the squeaky parts of the floor.

'I've got something to tell you,' she said awkwardly.

She would have liked to sit down, but the one chair, a small cane armchair with black lacquered arms and legs, was just too far away from where she was standing.

'Anthony has asked me to marry him and I have said yes and he is coming to dinner tomorrow night to ask your permission.' The words flooded out, one after the other, and she knew she could have said it better.

Rozia had stopped creaming her face and was looking at Hannah through the mirror of her dressing table.

'If that is what you want. We would just like you to be happy.'

Hannah noticed that her mother looked sad.

'Hannah, sit down,' Jouk said, patting his bed. She perched on the edge, aware of her parents' unease. Rozia swirled round on her stool.

'I will forget that he is not a Catholic, that does hurt, but you have made your position clear. All I want to know is, do you love him?'

'Yes, I do.'

And Rozia saw the softness in her daughter's face. She got up and came to her daughter, touched her shoulder and kissed her awkwardly. 'Be happy,' she said.

Jouk smiled at her. 'I shall reserve my judgement until tomorrow,' he said.

Hannah had expected that. She kissed him and hugged him, loving him so much.

When Hannah Oberska returned from school the next evening, the house was awash with the smells of her mother's cooking. Rozia greeted her in the hall.

'Dress yourself, Hannah. I don't need help. It is all done.'

'Thank you very much. You must have worked very hard,' Hannah said formally. She didn't know quite what else to say, so she fled upstairs, grateful for some moments of privacy before Anthony arrived. She would have liked to telephone Sybil Lascelles and Esther, but she knew there wasn't any time; Anthony would be punctual, and at six-thirty precisely the doorbell rang. She grabbed her perfume spray, squirted herself liberally and ran to open the door.

'You look lovely,' he whispered, 'and you smell of spring.'

The dinner was a strain. Anthony didn't speak much to Rozia . . . he found it easier to talk to Jouk. They discussed politics with the safe observer's eye, commitment to a policy would have meant involvement and possible disagreement. Disassociation allowed polite dinner table chitchat.

Hannah glanced at her parents. Suddenly she found them bizarre, exiles from another culture: Rozia in a plain dark dress with a ruffled white collar, with her heavily accented voice, her excessive hand movements, and Jouk, so obviously a European from his bow tie and the cut of his clothes. Anthony, casual in a tweed suit, was so alluring. His blond English looks, the slightly curling hair, and fine almost delicate features beckoned her, and she felt a surge of desire for him. She felt Rozia's eyes on her and she returned her mother's stare blatantly. Rozia smiled at her.

At that moment, Anthony formally asked Jouk for his daughter's hand in marriage, and Jouk gave it.

Hannah made her telephone calls the next evening. Esther was quiet – the secretary of the local Communist Party had resigned. He was going to America – to live. Apparently there was this girl there, a girl he liked a lot. Hannah felt awful – she was so happy and Esther sounded so sad.

Sybil Lascelles was another matter.

'I am thrilled for you,' she told Hannah. 'I want you to come to dinner, Monday week, all right? Martin will be so glad.'

Dinner with the Lascelles was comfortable and fun. It wasn't just the four of them – there was also a young cousin of Martin's, Bob Duncan and his American wife, Annie. Bob was a barrister.

'Useful, I would have thought,' Martin said quietly to Hannah and Anthony in the hall.

He'd aged since Rosemary's death. Hannah hugged him

– she was so fond of him. Anthony liked Bob. Hannah liked Annie.

'The whole thing went off terribly well!' Sybil told Martin, after they'd shut the front door on their departing guests. She touched Martin's face and he put his hand over hers – there was no need for words.

Chapter Three

———◆———

Hannah Oberska's wedding day was clear and bright. The weather had finally broken after the long hot summer, but there was no rain on that day. It was as if there had been a great springclean, in preparation for the long winter. Fresh little white clouds played catch with the sun, racing over a blue sky; a breeze rustled the leaves and lifted skirts, but it was a playful, cheeky wind and when it dared to dance around Hannah's lilac dress with its fitted bodice and new-style longer skirt, she just laughed and held on to her matching lilac hat.

There were just five people in the bare registry office apart from Hannah and Anthony – the registrar who married them, Colonel and Mrs Simpson, Rozia and Jouk. They were to meet the other guests at the small church hall that Rozia had hired for the reception. Hannah had no recollection of the legalities that had just taken place. She had watched Anthony sign the marriage certificate and then she had put her own name almost automatically on the document. That apparently was all that was necessary. She was now Mrs Anthony Simpson.

'If only you could have had a blessing,' Rozia said, and for a moment Hannah agreed with her. The room was so bleak, the official hadn't even congratulated her. Suddenly she wanted all the pomp and pageantry of a church wedding. The Mass, with its pure beauty, would have signified a birth, a proper start for a marriage. She understood why the symbols she insisted that she so despised were so important, for without them the important times were very bare. There were no flowers in the registry office, she hadn't even had time to remove her glove before Anthony was trying to place the wedding ring on her hand.

The reception provided a happy antidote. The cacophony merged inside Hannah's head – corks popped, voices rose and fell in different decibels in a mixture of languages, there was a lot of laughter and even a few songs, loudly supported by a piano player who thumped out his wartime memories on an untuned instrument in the corner of the room. Rozia had done well: there was luxurious food, including even sausage rolls – a gesture, she said, to the English – and there was champagne.

Hannah noticed Esther on the other side of the room. She negotiated her way over to her, avoiding little groups of people as one might pools of water on a pitted tarmac after the rain.

'You look gorgeous and the affair is a roaring success,' Esther crooned.

'The dress is not bad for Harrods, is it?' Hannah said and spun around, showing it off.

'Flagrant disregard of thrift, you'll never wear it again,' Esther said, laughing.

'I don't care – it is my wedding day!'

Rozia was looking her very best in a navy blue suit, like Hannah's dress with a longer skirt – she was aware that they were the only two to be wearing that new indulgent fashion, and it rather pleased her. She saw Jerzy, she knew he was watching her. She resolved to be very kind and motherly, but her heart was beating in an anything but motherly way.

'We are really glad you came, how are you?' she said.

'I am well, and you look beautiful.'

'Hannah would have looked wonderful in white, don't you think?'

'Rozia, you cannot make life the way you want it to be. It is the way it is,' Jerzy told her.

She moved away quickly, she didn't want to cry.

Anthony's best man, a brother officer George Brown, banged on the table. He had been badly injured in France. He had an artificial arm with a clumsy claw, Hannah was embarrassed whenever she saw it, and careful not to show her disquiet, but she always felt as if it were a steel spider and she worried in case it crawled over her.

'Ladies and gentlemen, it is my solemn duty to propose the toast to our beautiful bride and her not so beautiful husband.'

The obligatory smirks and occasional laughter punctured an awful speech from George that was heavy with innuendo and old army jokes. Hannah glanced across at Rozia and Jouk, standing with Bernice and Leo and Sybil and Martin. The expatriates . . . looked as if they were stranded on a boat in the middle of an unfathomable sea, but she saw that Jerzy was with them; almost immediately she realized that she hadn't seen him for a long time – she wondered about that.

'And if I may close by welcoming Hannah into the ranks of the married, although I am not married, and wish her luck – and to Anthony who flies with her.'

George raised his glass with his one good arm and the guests applauded.

Hannah was aware that Anthony was squeezing her hand, and then he moved forward to answer George's toast. He spoke quietly.

'Hannah and I would like to thank you all for coming. It has been a super day for us. We'd also like to thank my parents-in-law, that sounds strange, and especially Rozia for this wonderful spread. I don't know how you managed to organize it all. To my own parents I would just like to say thank you for the guidance and the help you have shown me, and to you, my beautiful bride,' he turned to look at me, 'I am very lucky and I will do my best to make you happy.'

Hannah stood on her tiptoes and kissed her husband, she heard the laughter and the cheers, but she didn't do it for that – she did it because she really loved him.

'Can we leave?' she whispered.

'Whether we can or not, we are going to,' he whispered back.

They bade their farewells. Rozia and Jouk looked as if they both might cry.

'Don't you dare,' Hannah hissed, but she wasn't angry. At that moment she even loved her mother.

'Welcome to the family,' said her new father-in-law as he kissed her cheek. Hannah thought him the most courtly of men. She felt shy of her mother-in-law – she knew Anthony was in awe of her – but Mrs Simpson hugged her. As Hannah looked into the clear eyes and saw the fine features, she knew who Anthony favoured, and it made her feel easier.

The honeymoon could only last a few days and Anthony had chosen the venue with special care. The small town of Filey, not far from Scarborough on the east coast of England, was untouched by the scars of war. Its neat Regency terraces overlooked cliffs which led down to a vast expanse of white sand. Anthony had been there before, but he didn't tell Hannah. He felt a little embarrassed and he hoped that the landlady of the boarding house wouldn't recognize him, but he was sure that there had been so many young officers passing through her doors that he would be only one of a mixture of faces. He had been happy there, briefly, with Carole and he wanted to recreate the joy. He should have felt guilty, but in wartime one didn't – one just took comfort when one could. There had been a feeling of live for today – they could all have been dead tomorrow.

Anthony drove fast, or as fast as the Alvis would allow. He enjoyed the sensation of speed. Occasionally he would look at Hannah and she would return the glance. They didn't speak.

The hotel had been taken over by another family – no connection with a wartime romance would mar his honeymoon. Discreetly, he had left Hannah to change after the car journey. He didn't even go up to the room but went straight to the bar, telling himself that it was for Hannah, but actually he was nervous and he needed a drink. Anthony knew he would be Hannah's first lover and he wasn't experienced enough himself to know how to cope.

He had tried the night before to read through a book on sex, but he had found it vulgar, titillating – not the kind of sex that he intended to enjoy with his wife. He looked at his watch. He had been in the bar for twenty minutes. Long enough, he thought. He would go up to the room. He found it strange that the stair carpet hadn't changed.

Hannah was sitting on the bed when he entered the room. She was still wearing her going-away outfit. For a moment he was disappointed. He thought she might have changed into a negligee or something like that, but he noticed that the cases were unpacked.

'Are you all right?' he asked.

'Yes, fine . . .' Hannah fidgeted. 'I unpacked.'

'Er . . . yes, thanks.'

Anthony sat down on the bed next to her. He could feel her tension. He looked at his watch. An hour before dinner.

'Would you like a walk?' he said.

'Yes, that would be nice,' she answered, a little eagerly he thought. 'Is it far to the sea?'

Anthony stood up and walked over to the small window. He noticed a man on his bicycle pedalling up the small road. He looked old.

'No,' he answered Hannah. 'Come here, I'll point it out for you.'

She got up and joined him, craning her neck. He bent his head, touched it with his lips. She turned into him naturally, and put her arms around his neck. He kissed her.

They moved to the bed, each responding to the other. He undressed her, and then removed his own clothes, quickly, to hide his awkwardness. And then he felt comfortable. They were both naked, unhindered. He liked that. He saw Hannah reach up for him, her arms outstretched. He felt intense gratitude. And then, without deliberation he caressed her, enjoying her softness. He found her centre and using his penis, carefully in case he hurt her, he entered her. She felt wonderful, warm, yielding. He stopped for a moment and looked into her eyes. They were open and unperturbed. Suddenly he wasn't aware of her any more, just of this great hole that he wanted to fill, and fill again. He felt himself swell and then explode. He sunk on to her grateful – happy.

Hannah felt the bed under her back. The mattress was lumpy and Anthony was heavy now. She felt engulfed with tenderness. Gingerly she touched his hair, and he responded by moving against her breast. His mouth found her nipple and he touched it with his tongue. But she didn't mind now. She loved him. He hadn't hurt her. She loved the way he used his hands, rubbing her back. And she hadn't even minded when he had come into her. She had felt a throbbing, and then a sort of pain, but it wasn't really a pain. She had wanted it to go on – to come to some kind of conclusion, but Anthony had shuddered and she had felt him grow and grow – and then it had been over.

The sound of the dinner gong intruded into the peace. Anthony was startled. He'd been asleep. They looked at each other and giggled.

'Quick,' he said, 'get dressed. I'm starving.'

'So am I. I hope the food is good,' she said.

He almost said it used to be, but remembered in time and didn't. He rushed into his clothes and waited impatiently while she selected a dress. She combed her hair and applied lipstick. He didn't think it necessary. She looked beautiful without it, but he said nothing, just touched her breast, not

266

in intimacy but in pleasure. She responded by pressing her hand close.

They didn't care that they looked newly married. They were happy.

The weather was good, the food fuel, little else, but they learnt to know each other's bodies, not to be embarrassed at watching one or other brush their teeth. Baths were shared, water trickling over bodies, sex was exploratory – wonderful for Anthony, but Hannah felt as if something more would come from it. She didn't know that she wasn't having an orgasm. And her lack of knowledge was her protection.

On the third day of their married life, they reluctantly gathered their clothes, put them into their cases and stowed them into the car. Anthony paid the bill and Hannah happily contemplated her married status.

Hannah made Anthony stop on the way back to London. She wanted flowers, she told him.

'We can't really afford such luxuries,' he said.

'Oh, come on Anthony, we've just married,' she cajoled, rubbing her cheek against his.

'Right.'

He noticed the flower barrow before she did. The colours of the massed flowers shimmered in the drizzle of an English autumn day. Hannah watched as he ran over to the old man. As he made his purchase she thought him very beautiful. She loved the way his hair hung over his forehead.

'Flowers for my wife,' he said as he got back into the car.

Hannah saw that they were red roses. 'Oh Anthony, how lovely,' she said, wishing that he had bought her a bunch of chrysanthemums – their muted oranges, ambers and golds appealed to her far more than the blood red of the autumn roses.

When they arrived at number 54 Milton Park, in Highgate, where their three-roomed flat formed the top part of an

Edwardian terraced house, Anthony reached over and kissed Hannah. His tongue strayed over hers, tempting her. She arched her back, pressed her breasts against his chest.

'Come on,' he said, swinging his legs out of the car. Hannah waited for him to open the door. She half wanted him to carry her over the doorpost but, whilst another part of her brain told her she was being silly, Anthony pulled her into his arms.

'You're a weight,' he grumbled, as he fumbled for the front door key.

'That's romantic, I must say,' she whispered, nuzzling his ear with her teeth. But before Anthony could turn the key, the door swung open and they saw Rozia, Jouk and Colonel and Mrs Simpson standing on the stairs. Inwardly she sighed . . . Rozia had organized a homecoming.

'It was Mrs Oberska's idea,' Colonel Simpson warbled, obviously embarrassed as Anthony hastily put Hannah down.

It was Jouk who stage-managed the departure. Ever sensitive to mood, he poured sherries for everyone, insisted on a quick toast and shuffled the relatives out before Rozia could say anything.

'But all the food . . .' she started to say.

'For Hannah and Anthony,' Jouk said firmly.

'Thank God for my father,' Hannah said, flopping into one of the overstuffed armchairs which were arranged on either side of the gas fire.

'I second that,' Anthony said, bending down to the blazing fire and turning it off. 'Who put this on?' He turned to Hannah. 'Your mother I expect.'

'I expect,' she agreed.

Anthony reached out his hand and Hannah took it. She pulled his fingers up, one by one, licking them, swallowing them, coating them with her saliva. She slipped to the floor, wanting caresses, but Anthony was impatient for her, he pulled up her skirt, pulled off her pants and slipped inside her.

'You're ready,' he whispered.

She felt him moving backwards and forwards. She wanted to be a part of his pleasure but she wasn't.

Chapter Four

———— ◆ ————

Jouk Oberski died in his sleep in January 1948 – just four months after Hannah's wedding.

Hannah learnt of her father's death in the early hours of the morning. She and Anthony did not have a telephone in their part of the house but the landlord, Mr Owen, did.

'It's only to be used in emergencies,' he had told them when they first moved in, but being a kind man he would waylay Hannah on her way to the cold telephone box on the corner of the street and invite her into the warmth of the front room where his sister always lay dozing in the chair by the fire – a cup of tea and a plate of biscuits always close to hand.

'You can make that call here,' he would say, 'just leave the money by the telephone.' And Hannah would do so, stacking her coppers neatly in a pile. Sometimes she would have preferred to go to the box on the corner – at least she would have had some privacy and she could have spoken for longer, but Mr Owen was always so kind, so insistent.

No one used Mr Owen's number to telephone either Hannah or Anthony so when his loud knocking awoke them, and his voice said, 'Telephone, it's urgent I would say,' Hannah knew that something terrible had happened. She wondered, hoping the call would be for Anthony, but when Mr Owen added, 'It's for you, Mrs Simpson,' she knew Jouk was dead.

The pain did not come until she saw him lying in his bed. He was so peaceful, so still. For a moment she wanted to laugh; you've made a mistake, she wanted to tell Rozia, he is just resting, but then she touched him, and his flesh chilled her and the cold of death scared her.

Rozia was dry-eyed but the grief was obvious, her face looked as if it had been just slightly re-arranged so that the features were no longer ordered – the eyes were too big, the nostrils too flared, the cheekbones too pronounced. She kept re-arranging the coverlet, plucking at it and smoothing it.

Hannah was surprised, she had never realized how important Jouk was to Rozia, but then nor perhaps had Rozia.

Anthony was appalled when he heard about the rituals necessary for a Catholic burial. Used to what he considered the more proper dignity of a Church of England funeral, he contemplated the prospect of the public farewell with the top off the coffin with distaste. Once his father-in-law had been consigned to what Anthony considered to be the proper resting place for a dead body, namely a sealed coffin, he discovered that there would be a funeral Mass in church the night before the actual event.

Anthony assumed that his mother-in-law would give way to a tasteless display of public mourning so he cautioned Hannah, but as gently as he could because he did know how much she had loved Jouk.

'I know it's difficult, but please try not to be too emotional. I understand there may be quite a number of people present and you wouldn't want to embarrass them, would you?'

Hannah was too tired, and too numb, to question his expectations of her behaviour.

The actual funeral service was simple, stark almost, as Jouk himself would have wished. Rozia did not hide her tears; she wept for the man who had cared for her, recalling him as he had been all those years before in Warsaw. She remembered his kindness and his patience and she blamed herself for her lack of kindness and patience.

'Goodbye best friend,' she whispered, as they shouldered the coffin towards the hearse. She faltered as they placed it inside, and reached for Hannah's hand, grasping it tightly, feeling the fingers curl around hers. She looked up at her daughter, for Hannah was now taller than she was, and she was impressed and saddened by her daughter's composure.

Hannah tightened her back, feeling the fingers of tension creep through her shoulder blades and spine. She concentrated on that physical condition rather than think of her father, alone in that small box, going to oblivion. But at the graveside, as the clods of earth thudded down on to it, she realized she would never see the man again, never hear him again, never touch him again – and then she cried.

Anthony watched the women, unified in their grief as they had never been before. He felt awkward and excluded. He noticed that they even seemed to walk in unison, like chorus girls, he thought irreverently. He just wished they would stop weeping.

Later, Hannah watched the dozens of cups of tea, and the occasional drink consumed by those who came to comfort, and those who felt obliged to do so. Sybil and Bernice had organized everything. She was very grateful to them – and then she realized she had not seen Rozia for a while.

'Where's my mother?' she asked Esther, who stood quietly, her back against a wall, waiting for the opportunity to spend some time with her.

'Probably quite sensibly wailing her heart out,' Esther replied. 'This civilized chitchat that you have indulged in during the last hour has amazed me. You've just buried your father for God's sake, and I know how much you loved him. Stop being so bloody polite and do what your mother's done.'

'If people have been nice enough –' Hannah started to say, but Esther interrupted her.

'Those who love you won't care whether you cry, disappear or just sit in the corner, those who don't shouldn't be here.'

Anthony appeared and Esther moved to one side. 'Hannah, my parents are leaving, where is Rozia? They'd like to pay their compliments to her.'

Esther couldn't help tutting.

'I expect she needs to be on her own,' Hannah said a little too loudly.

'Quite,' said Colonel Simpson. 'Well, my dear, take care of yourself, we'll see you both soon.' Awkwardly he kissed her on the cheek, his grey moustache tickling, and Hannah suddenly realized she was rather fond of him.

'Come on, Hannah – you need a good sob,' Esther said, taking her hand.

'There are still people here,' Anthony said.

Hannah looked at them both, her friend on one side, her husband on the other – there was no question as to what she should do.

Gently she took Esther's hand from hers. 'I'll have time enough for the sobbing later,' she said as kindly as she could.

Esther left shortly afterwards, but she was careful to make the proper farewells.

Anthony put his hand around Hannah's waist. 'Why don't I drop the parents off and I'll make a lot of noise about doing so. Hopefully they will give the hint to everyone else and then you can have some time with your mother, have a private cry perhaps.'

Hannah kissed his cheek. 'Thank you for being so thoughtful,' she whispered.

'I am not unfeeling, I know how much you loved him.'

Hannah felt the tears come; Anthony kissed each eyelid and for him she swallowed quickly and held them back.

The English, even Bernice and Leo, left but the rest, mostly Poles but also some Rumanians and a French professor and his wife, and Sybil and Martin, still sat on, quietly talking.

'Why don't you go to your mother?' Jerzy said. 'We are

273

not here to be entertained, we are here to remember too.'

Hannah registered him as if for the first time – she recognized that he was a young man, but for a moment he seemed to her to be very like Jouk.

She went straight to her parents' bedroom, assuming Rozia would be there, but it was empty. Surprised, she walked back into the hall, and it was then that she noticed the dull red glow from what had been her own bedroom. She pushed the door open and saw her mother lying prone on her bed. The gas fire was on but otherwise there was no light – in the gloom Rozia's face was white and still, making her seem as if she were the corpse.

Hannah sat on the bed, she took her mother's hand – it felt warm and clammy – Jouk's hand had been so cold.

'I am so sorry you are in such pain,' she said. 'I had always assumed that you didn't love him.'

Rozia lay with her face towards the fire; she made no movement towards her daughter, simply to let her hold her hand.

'He was so good to me. I was completely alone, and he took me in and cared for me. Oh Hannah,' she turned herself and raising her head, making her eyes roll slightly because of the angle, 'I loved your father so much.'

Hannah jumped, jolted by a shock that hurt. The murky figure of whom she knew nothing suddenly seemed so near, so tantalizingly near, that she wanted to reach out to him.

'Will you tell me about my father?' Hannah asked. 'If it isn't too painful.'

'I loved Jouk as well, but it was different,' Rozia whispered, 'and I didn't know how much until today.'

'I know and I do understand,' Hannah said, trying not to show her impatience. 'My father, my real father, what was he like?'

'He was my prince – and you,' she touched Hannah's hair, 'are so like him. Sometimes when I look at you I see

274

him as if he were here with me, and at those moments I want to hold you in my arms so tightly, but then I know you are not him and it hurts too much even to look at you.'

Hannah felt cold, not cold like Jouk had been, but an afflicting cold, a living cold.

'Tell me what he was like,' she said again, knowing she was insisting, perhaps being unfair, but she could do nothing about it.

'What was he like?' Rozia repeated. 'How can I know? I was eighteen, he was the same age. We knew each other for a little over four months, but I will tell you how he seemed to me then.' Her face lit with a strange glow, with a smile that touched her eyes and opened her lips. 'He was tall with blond hair – like you, you have the same eyes as him. He was very strong and very sure of himself. He was going to be a lawyer but he preferred to sail and to dance. He loved the theatre, I think if he had lived he would have become involved with that in some way – maybe a director, but I don't know. I can only tell you of our times together, and now that I think of it I realize that is the real tragedy. He was a passionate man and we both thought we could change the world. But my love for Stefan destroyed my old world before we had a chance to make a new one together.'

'It must have been very hard for you,' Hannah said gently.

Rozia nodded. Hannah could not bear to look at her mother and see the pain, so she moved closer to her and put her arms around her. Rozia's body felt so thin, almost angular, and Hannah found it not only unfamiliar but uncomfortable to hold her.

When Rozia awoke she was alone, the fire was still on but the house was quiet. She realized that, exhausted by the years of pain, she had fallen asleep. Her head throbbed and her mouth felt dry, and to her surprise she wanted a cup of tea – so she had become a little English after all. She eased herself off the bed and stood up. She wondered how Hannah was.

She went into her own bedroom and turned on the lilac bedside lamps. She was so used to going to bed after Jouk, to seeing his still form curled into sleep, that for a moment she thought he was there – and then she knew it had just been a reflection of what was now a memory.

The sadness clung to her and she accepted its embrace, welcoming it almost as she might a companion.

She heard a noise in the kitchen, someone washing up: it must be Hannah, of course she should have gone home to her husband but Rozia was incredibly grateful that she had not done so.

She knew Hannah wanted to hear about Stefan, but there was so little she could tell her. Quickly she went into the bathroom and washed her face, her mouth felt stale so she cleaned her teeth which made her feel better. She brushed her hair, leaving it loose. Usually she wore it up in combs which was the fashion – it wasn't the curtain of fire of her youth, but it was still extraordinary.

As she descended the staircase she could hear that the radio was on, albeit quietly, playing Chopin. She was surprised, she could not recall Hannah liking Chopin, it was Jerzy who loved the work of the Polish composer – so it was not Hannah who had stayed to comfort her. She felt the sharp edge of her disappointment.

Jerzy was at the sink, his white shirt rolled up to his elbows revealing his brown skin and fine brown hair.

'The kettle is on,' he said, 'we are really English now.'

'When I woke up and realized that I wanted a cup of tea I thought the same,' Rozia replied.

They were both uncomfortable but they didn't try to hide it.

'How are you?' Rozia asked. 'I don't even know what you are doing now. It has been so long since I have seen you.'

'I am beginning my career again. I shall be an architect, here in England,' he smiled, 'and later, when the time is right, I shall court you.'

'Impossible, I am older than you,' the widow Rozia said, ashamed because for that brief moment she felt neither a widow, nor the safety of her five extra years.

Hannah couldn't wait to talk to Rozia again. As soon as she had finished school the next day she went straight to her mother's house, using her key to let herself in.

'Who's that?' Rozia's voice sounded high-pitched and strained.

'It's only me,' Hannah called out as calmly as she could; she was worried, she didn't want Rozia to be ill again.

'Oh, I didn't expect you, you didn't telephone,' her mother said, coming into the hall from the salon. She looked tired, and white – but better.

'I thought I'd come and have tea with you,' Hannah said.

'Yes, I have just made some, you can come and join us.'

'Us?'

'Yes, Jerzy is here. I needed someone to talk to.'

'So do I.'

'Yes, of course.' Rozia paused for a moment and then she added, 'But you do have a husband who loves you.'

'I can't talk to my husband about my father.' Hannah knew she sounded petulant, but she felt hurt and rejected.

'Of course you can, it's important that you do.' Rozia walked over to Hannah and put her hand on her shoulder. 'You must always talk about Jouk, that way he will never die for you.'

'I am not talking about Jouk, I am talking about my father.'

Rozia shut her eyes briefly, and then flicked them open. 'There is nothing more to talk about, I have told you all I know. Now, do you want some tea?'

'No thank you.'

'Please do, I have told you it is in the pot.'

'I am not a guest, I don't need to be invited like one. I am your daughter,' Hannah told Rozia as she opened the front door; she shut it behind her without a further word. She walked along the cold streets, her head bent down, tears stinging her cheeks; she hated Rozia.

'Perhaps you were unkind, Rozia,' Jerzy said to her when she went back into the salon.

'Perhaps, but it is true, Jerzy – I loved him, but you see we only loved each other for four months – I didn't know anything about him.' And then she realized she had used the word love in the past tense.

Chapter Five

———◆———

In the late summer of 1952 Hannah Simpson, the wife of promising young barrister Anthony Simpson, conducted the business of being a housewife efficiently, but without much pleasure. Their daughter, Margaret, named after the Princess Margaret Rose, had been born in November 1949, and was nearly three years of age.

Hannah's passionate concern for the betterment of the populace had been forgotten. It wasn't that it didn't exist, it had just become suspended beneath the overall necessity of the care of her family. She didn't share her beliefs any more, they were private, divorced from the realities of her life.

Anthony's socialist leanings had long been buried beneath the worship of success. He no longer felt on the outside; he was now a member of the Club, so he didn't feel resentful of its rules – he supported them avidly. He had joined the night he became a barrister.

He had sat, surrounded by his fellow barristers, at a long, deep brown table adorned with crystal glasses, bone china and polished silver. There were always excellent wines in the Temple dining room, but even to Anthony's unadventurous palate the food was unappealing; however on that night he hadn't even tasted what he ate. He hadn't been aware of the liveried servants or of the table facing the room at which the learned judges dined. He had been intoxicated with the knowledge that he was on the first rung to achieving his ambition. He wanted to become a King's Counsel, to wear a silk gown instead of cotton, to plead in front of the bar at court and not behind it, even perhaps to become a judge. He knew that he had to work as a barrister for at least fifteen years before he could apply to the Lord Chancellor for the silk gown. If he were accepted to become a member of the elite coterie of barristers who walked in the procession at the beginning of each law term, he would receive a long envelope. If not, a short one would be dropped on to his desk. He longed, yearned even, for that long envelope.

He was still thrilled when he recalled how, on that night of nights, a sonorous voice had intoned: 'Mr Simpson.' He remembered that he had stood up, his throat dry, and walked up to the head table. Just in front of it, on a small desk, lay a book, and he could see the signature of those called before him. He had tears in his eyes as he signed, his hands unsteady. He shook hands with those above him, bowed to his pupil master, and walked back to his seat. He had become a barrister.

Hannah didn't like his easy conversion to the establishment, but she never discussed it with him. When she thought about it, it served to remind her of her separateness and she had no wish to bring that aspect of her life to the fore.

She spent a great deal of time on her own. Anthony would often work late, and would sometimes dine with colleagues or other lawyers. She was glad not to be included in business dinners. She found them difficult. Her upbringing had not prepared her for English middle-class life. Minor public school, or at least a good grammar were particularly pleasing to the neighbours especially if one had a long history and continuity of family, mother to daughter, father to son. Class definitions were alien to Hannah, she didn't understand them, and yet background was so important to the new society that she herself had craved. But now, uncomfortable within that group, she became fascinated by her Polish ancestry – she read a lot, and through Rozia and Jerzy she met a number of Poles, but Hannah wasn't totally at home with them either. With the Poles she was too English, and with the English she was too Polish.

Rozia no longer played tennis – it had happened quite suddenly, some nine months after Margaret was born. Rozia had been worried about her daughter, it seemed to her that Hannah never went out and so she persuaded her to meet at the club and play a quiet match. As she prepared herself in the ladies' dressing room Rozia couldn't really remember the last time she and Hannah had been opponents on a court, usually they played together or against people of their own age.

Hannah arrived, hot and flustered – it had taken longer to get Margaret ready than she had expected and then she had missed the bus.

'Are you sure it is worth it? I am going to play badly – it's so long since I have been on a court.'

'Don't play to win – let's just knock up,' Rozia replied as she strode to the base line.

But Hannah did play to win. As Rozia's daughter what else could she do?

The baby girl rocked herself in her pram whilst the two women fought out their private duel. The old champion, relying on skill and nerve, was determined not to give in to the younger, more powerful girl. At first Rozia outmanoeuvred her daughter easily, but as the match ground on Hannah began to feel her strength, and like an animal who senses his prey's weakness she smelt her mother's tiredness, and as she felt the flush of possible victory her strokes became smoother, her services more accurate, her speed faster.

By now Rozia was breathing hard, she was sweating so heavily she couldn't hold the racket properly and her legs were aching.

'Hannah, it's enough now, my legs are tired. Let's stop now.'

'No –' the reply was sharp – 'we play.'

And play they did until Hannah, the victor now, placed her shot and won the final point.

The women stood looking at each other.

'Thanks,' Hannah the daughter said, extending her hand. 'I needed that.'

'I am sure you did,' Rozia the mother replied.

It was shortly after that that Jerzy encouraged Rozia to open a little café. They had bought a house off the Finchley Road; Jerzy used the very top for his office, and they lived on the middle floor in a Polish-style apartment. Its windows were draped in white muslin, there were polished floors, and sparkling mirrors. Rozia's heavy furniture was now re-covered in velvet of a different colour, but the cut glass and profusion of plants were still the same as in the house on Exeter Road.

She opened the café from eleven till four-thirty only. Morning coffee, Polish-style lunches, tea and delicious cakes were her speciality. She had acquired a reputation and many came to drink her coffee and lemon tea, to gossip, play chess, and read newspapers.

With her closer involvement in the Polish community, Rozia saw less of Bernice and Leo Adams, unlike Sybil and Martin they were not comfortable with foreigners en masse. However Rozia did try to see them occasionally – 'They were very good to me when I first came to England,' she told Jerzy.

Hannah liked to visit the little café, but Anthony found little pleasure in these excursions. He thought it an odd habit to sit inside in what he considered to be an unhealthy atmosphere of smoke and stale air – he much preferred to walk on Hampstead Heath.

Jerzy and Rozia had married two years after Jouk's death. Hannah had long since accepted Rozia and Jerzy as a couple. At first it had been difficult for her to believe that her mother was in love, but once she understood the depth of Rozia's feelings, it was she who broke down her mother's intrinsic reserves and told her that she had a right to happiness.

'But he is younger than me,' Rozia protested.

'You love him.'

'Yes,' she admitted.

'Then marry him,' Hannah said.

'And you – what about you? Will you mind?'

'A little bit but not for the reasons you think.' She smiled and kissed her mother on the cheek. She had no intention of revealing that her reserves had little to do with Jouk, for she was captivated by the fragments of the man who was her father. With Jouk's death she had discovered a yearning for Stefan Gordanski that she could not assuage; even the birth of her own child did nothing to diminish its intensity, but she kept the longing private. Anthony did not even know that Jouk wasn't her real father.

Hannah no longer hated her mother, nor did she even resent her, she just felt separate from her. She liked Jerzy, and she particularly cared for the way he loved Rozia; only occasionally, in the bad moments, did she admit to a little envy.

She and Esther kept in touch, but they didn't see each other on a regular basis. Esther was very involved in her work. She was the editor of a small political publishing house . . . overtly Communist. She wasn't married, but she no longer lived at home. She joked about her parents having given up on her. Hannah wondered about her life, but Esther never seemed lonely. She always had a boyfriend.

They would talk on the telephone and very occasionally meet for lunch. After those meetings Hannah would feel charged and excited . . . but that euphoria would usually have evaporated by the day after.

Hannah and Anthony had moved into their house in 1950. The confined space in the flat with a small baby yelling long into the night wasn't conducive to cementing their relationship. At the time Hannah was constantly tired. Anthony did not involve himself with the baby, he found the business of a small child boring. He had tried in the beginning to make a contribution but soon, driven by the feelings of exclusion that can exist when a child comes along, even in the very best of marriages, he retreated to his office. His career blossomed by his own efforts and he was able to afford a house sooner than most of his colleagues. The necessity for more space was his overriding consideration. Hannah became the proud mistress of a detached residence with four bedrooms, two reception rooms and a separate garage in Hendon, a slightly more suburban area of London than the one she had been used to.

One particular day in early September, Hannah's kitchen was in a state of total disorder. Margaret and her toys added to the confusion. It looked as if every bowl, every saucepan and all the cooking utensils had been used. She looked dishevelled, her blouse half open, her face flushed from the oven. She was giving a dinner party. A few days before she had had an awful sore throat and had felt terribly tired.

She still didn't feel well, but when she had suggested that they cancel the evening Anthony had been most upset – it was very important for him, he had said, he had invited Tom Jackson and his wife Aileen. Tom was apparently an important solicitor – young and successful – Anthony's mentor? Hannah wondered. He gave Anthony a lot of work. It was the first time Hannah would have met him. To add to the party, she had invited Bob and Meg Marr, her neighbours. Their daughter, Cathy, went to the same school as Margaret.

She felt a bit better but now her head ached – she'd even been sick – and she was still irritable.

'Oh Margaret, move your toys,' Hannah snapped. Her

feet had almost gone from under her as she collided with a plastic cookery set, a present from Rozia.

'Mummy, my pastry,' the child wailed.

'You shouldn't play in the kitchen . . . anyway, it's time for your bath.' Hannah looked anxiously at the clock – a quarter to six. Just enough time to get her daughter ready for bed, make up and dress before Anthony arrived home. She had worked all day on the party preparations and the table looked wonderful, she thought, dressed with flowers, pretty plates, and of course the precious glasses of Polish crystal Rozia had given her that had once belonged to Jouk. Hannah hoped the food was all right, for she had experimented with a recipe that Rozia had given to her over the telephone. She had made small tarts piled with cheese and onions. There was chicken in wine, and a rich chocolate pudding for dessert. She had used up all of her and Anthony's sweet ration for the chocolate, but it didn't matter, they didn't like sweets much anyway.

She grabbed Margaret. 'Come on,' she said, pulling the child's arm.

Margaret's blonde hair was pulled back from her head by a blue band. She wore a blue and white check dress which Hannah noticed, almost irrelevantly, was too short for her.

'Wait Mummy, I haven't done my cake.'

'Come on, I've told you I am in a hurry,' Hannah snapped. She watched as her daughter set her mouth in a thin line.

'I've got to do my cake,' she protested.

'I am not in the mood for games, Margaret.' Hannah picked her up in both arms and marched up the stairs. She ignored the kicking feet, the yelling voice, the arched back. Her side was really uncomfortable now, and she decided she must go to the doctor about it. She dumped Margaret in the bathroom, shut the door to prevent the little girl from running out and ran the bath. She tried to undress her but the child stood still, uncooperatively rigid. Hannah glanced back at the tub and saw a flannel floating in the water. She reached over to lift it out, but her left leg seemed too heavy, she had difficulty in stretching over.

'Sorry, I should have waited until the cake was made, but I have got to do Daddy's party – are we still friends?' she asked, holding out her hands.

'Yes,' Margaret replied, and started to pull off her clothes.

'Can I help?' Hannah asked.

'Yes,' the child said, looking up at her. Her eyes were wide, like Anthony's – limpid grey.

'The table looks pretty,' Margaret said as she got into the bath.

'Do you think so? I hope Daddy likes it.'

After Hannah had put her daughter to bed, she lay down in her room. She still liked the sensation of sinking into her bed – enjoying its womb-like feel, the heaviness of the blankets, even in the heat of summer. She and Anthony had separate beds now, twins as they were called. Little white and gold headboards occupying spaces side by side on the wall, the occupants safely separated by the blankets tucked around them like bandages, enabling them to avoid contact . . . and infection. It was Anthony who had suggested that they sleep separately. He tossed at night. Hannah slept neatly, like a little squirrel, legs and arms entangled, almost tied up.

Hannah raised her head, listening . . . but there was no sound. Margaret was asleep so there was nothing to rob her of the precious moment of peace which had been offered to her. She noticed that the ceiling light, its little pink shade slightly askew, needed dusting. Her eyes skimmed over the fitted wardrobes nestling in opposite sides of the room; her white and gold dressing table conveniently placed under the window. The bedroom looked unused to her, as if the residents were away, and the thought made her smile a little.

She looked reluctantly at the small bedside clock – the

guardian of her day. Time to get up – time to go to sleep – just enough time for lovemaking, when it happened. And now it was time to get ready. She got up off the bed, smoothed the salmon-pink coverlet, not liking the slight indentation of her body on the surface. She shook her leg, rubbed it – it seemed numb – if it was no better tomorrow she would have to go and see the doctor.

She drew a bath and pinned her hair up, smoothed cream on to her face, and poured into the water generous amounts of a bath essence she couldn't really afford. She felt herself relax in the scented water. She normally enjoyed the ritual of the bath, but today she felt so numb. She resolved to ignore it, sponged her body without looking at it, for she was unaware of it as anything other than a machine for walking, talking, eating – all the functions of a human being. She let it be used in lovemaking, enjoying the small orgasm which she occasionally experienced, but afterwards always felt rather lonely and a little let down. Instinctively she felt there was more to the act of sex, but she didn't know what. She was sure that Anthony wasn't at fault. It was her – she seemed unable to give somehow, and it worried her. Hannah let her mind pass over the thought, sighing as she lay back in the bath.

She thought about Margaret. She was aware that they didn't have the closeness she had envisaged before the child's birth. She couldn't identify what was wrong, but she felt removed from her daughter. She had tried to be a good mother but the first year had been so difficult in the small flat, and then by the time they had got to the house the pattern had been set. She knew she snapped, but sometimes she felt so bored with the business of housekeeping. She had suggested to Anthony that she go back to work part-time but he had refused to even listen.

'Your place is with Margaret,' he told her.

She heard the sound of his car in the drive. Immediately

287

she let the water out of the bath, gathered up a white towel and draped it over her body. She walked quickly back to her bedroom. She had to get dressed. She didn't want to be late.

Later, Hannah's beautiful table looked as if debris had been spilled all over it: bits of bread littered the pretty cloth, there were overflowing ashtrays crammed with cigarette butts, and the flowers were wilting in the smoke-filled atmosphere. She thought it was very unpleasant. Strange that just a few short hours before it had looked so special, dressed for an occasion, almost like a bride on her way to the wedding.

Anthony was talking too much, and too loudly. He was describing a case he had recently handled. . . 'And would you believe the silly old woman didn't realize that the judge was awarding her costs . . . she wouldn't have to pay a penny. She just sat there and wept and wept.' They laughed, the Marrs, the Jacksons, Anthony.

'She'd been very frightened. She thought she was going to lose her home,' Hannah said quietly. She was feeling much worse now.

'Oh Hannah, don't be so pompous,' Anthony snapped. 'Come on everyone, let's have another drink.' He stood up awkwardly and looked around for the brandy.

'Where's the brandy, Hannah?' he asked.

'Oh sorry, it must be in the kitchen. I'll get it,' she said, but she didn't move from her seat.

'Don't worry, I'll do it.' Anthony went off to the kitchen as Aileen Jackson said, 'May I use your cloakroom?'

''Course, I'll show you,' Anthony said from the door. Hannah watched Aileen undulate towards him. There was no other way to describe the way she walked. It was overtly sexual, the movement of the hips encased in a tight skirt, black, and the scarlet blouse echoing the red of her lips. Her brown hair was cut in the latest style, which served to add to the coquetry of her personality. Hannah didn't like her much, she thought she was flippant. Still, she supposed Tom liked her that way. She turned back to her guests.

'Well, Hannah, I must say that was quite some meal you prepared,' Tom Jackson said. 'I propose a toast to our hostess, the hostess with the mostest,' his voice was slurred, 'and definitely the mostest here.'

For one moment she wanted to throw her drink straight in his face. She imagined what it would be like with the liquid running down it; she wondered if he would lick his lips, so as not to miss any of the precious stuff as it slipped past his mouth. He was a pig, and he ate like one, slurping his way through his food with little respect for those around him. But instead of throwing her drink, she inclined her head graciously.

'Tom, how kind.' Honeyed words.

Flattered, he said, 'I know a good one when I see one.'

'Meal . . .' Hannah said.

'Yes, meal.'

She tried to laugh suavely, but it came out like a giggle, rather innocent, totally opposed to the context of the words that had preceded it. Somehow it heightened the lewdness of it all.

'Shall we go into the lounge?' she said. 'On the way I'll collect Anthony and the brandy bottle.'

As she stood up Hannah realized her leg was very much worse, and she felt as if she couldn't arch her back. She managed to usher her guests out of the dining room. She seated them on her overstuffed chairs and sofa and went to look for Anthony, almost having to drag her leg behind her like a heavy bag of coal that couldn't be lifted. He wasn't in the kitchen and she wasn't quite sure what made her look in the scullery. The brandy bottle certainly wasn't in there.

She saw intertwined fingers, heard little mews of laughter. She didn't move, and for a ridiculous moment she was fascinated – then she realized it was Anthony and Aileen. They saw her. Her leg wouldn't move – for a moment everything went black. Her hand slammed back involuntarily. It caught a milk bottle which rolled to the ground, the noise deafening.

'Oh God!' Aileen said.

'Hannah!' Anthony shouted.

But she said nothing – she couldn't hear anything. Her heart was thumping, now she couldn't breathe, and she was very frightened.

'It was only a bit of fun,' she heard Anthony whisper. 'Don't make anything of it.' He sounded worried, but she didn't care what he felt.

'Anthony –' she gasped – 'I can't breathe – Anthony.'

She could feel him holding her. 'The ambulance is coming and Rozia . . .'

Hannah wanted to cry, she could feel the tears . . . she felt so hot, her leg, her leg – it should hurt, but there was nothing there and she couldn't breathe . . .

She wanted Rozia, but there were only two men with masks . . . She heard 'polio' and she fainted.

Chapter Six

———— ◆ ————

There was the sound of voices, soft murmuring voices that rose and fell like the tide on a shore . . . one, two, three, four – the seventh wave is the big one. 'You want to be big, don't you . . .'

Hands lifted Hannah, put her on a stretcher – even she could hear her rasping breath, and the panic was terrible. She tried to tell someone, clutched at someone, but no one seemed to be listening, or looking.

'Please . . .' she whispered between gasps, but no one heard.

Suddenly it was cooler, she was being taken outside. She could see the trees, why couldn't she get enough air? If she was outside, she should feel better . . . Polio, had she heard them say polio? My God – Margaret, what would happen to Margaret? Would she get it? *Margaret*, she wanted to scream out but she hadn't the energy, she hadn't enough breath.

Anthony was with her; he was holding her hand, sponging her face.

'It's all right, it's all right,' he whispered.

She grasped his hand, needing someone, needing help.

They rushed her in through doors, down long corridors, into a room, and then she saw it, the great black iron lung.

'Noooo . . .'

But someone else was there, someone whose hands calmed and helped, someone who said, 'It will help you breathe, it will help you. Don't fight it, go with it.' The voice was strong, so strong.

Hands took off her clothes, wrapped her in white, and put her in her coffin. Hannah could feel the sweat on her face, her hair felt wet. Her leg . . . she cried, but still she couldn't get her breath. She could feel something like a pressure, but it wasn't working and she didn't want to be in that thing, that dreadful thing.

'Help me!' she screamed. 'Help me.'

The strong, quiet voice – was it a man or a woman? – soothed her.

'Where's Anthony?'

'Outside with Jerzy,' the voice said. It was Rozia, her mother, Rozia.

'Mummy . . .'

'Calm yourself, calm yourself.'

She heard another voice. 'It's no good, she's fighting it, look at the pulse rate. We'll have to sedate her.'

'No . . . No . . .' Hannah tried to thrash them away but she couldn't move, and she still couldn't breathe. It was terrible – she wanted help, she needed help, why wouldn't someone help her? And then a needle in her thigh, in the thigh she could feel, a roaring in her ears and then white and nothing . . .

Rozia sat in the corner of the room, her head in her hands, the fingers reaching into her hair, the palms over her eyes. She watched her now quiet daughter, she watched the dials on the machine, and Rozia cried.

They let Anthony in. He was quite white, like Hannah Rozia thought irrelevantly, and suddenly she noticed he had a weak chin. Funny that she had never noticed it before.

'Who is with Margaret?' she asked.

'Jacksons, friends of mine – ours.'

'Does she know them?'

'No.'

'Then go home,' Rozia said, turning away from her son-in-law.

Anthony looked across to Hannah. He would have liked to touch her, to kiss her, or something, but he didn't know if he should. He backed out of the room, pulled his mask off. Jerzy was sitting outside.

'Rozia says I should go home to Margaret.'

'Of course you must,' Jerzy said. 'I will stay until Rozia decides what she wants to do.'

'I ought to be with my wife.'

'Your place, for the moment, is with your daughter. I am sure that is best. We can only wait and see,' Jerzy said kindly. He stood up; he would have liked to hug Anthony, but he knew enough of England to understand that this would be unacceptable.

They kept Hannah sedated for three days. And for three days Rozia watched her . . . oh, she slept a little, in a room they put at her disposal, she washed, changed her clothes, but mostly she watched. And then she remembered that once she had been a student of chemistry. On the morning of the fourth day she asked if she might use the hospital library. Rozia walked over to the medical school, and as she felt the air on her skin she realized that she had not been outside for three days. Her heels clip-clopped over the courtyard, she tripped and then she realized she was walking over cobbles, and she smiled slightly.

Rozia asked a young man, who she supposed was a student – she wouldn't have known him if she saw him again – for something on polio. He got out a large volume for her. 'Christie is the best,' he said.

And Rozia began to read, and as she read her fears grew. She shut the book quickly. She located a telephone box and rang the Lascelles, inserting the four pennies that she always kept in her coat pocket for emergencies.

'Martin?'

'Rozia, we knew you would ring. What can I do?'

293

'I want whatever textbooks you have on polio. Please bring them to me here – at the hospital.'

'Yes,' Martin said, 'I will, but in the meantime ask about Sister Kenny's theories.'

Rozia replaced the telephone and clip-clopped back to the library.

'Anything on Sister Kenny?' she asked.

'Kenny?' the student repeated.

'Yes, Kenny.'

'No,' he said.

Rozia went back to Hannah. She was not sedated now, she was calm.

'Mummy,' she said as Rozia came in, seeing her through a mirror that they had put above her face, angling it so she could watch something, anything, not just the ceiling.

'Mummy, the worst part is not being able to go to the toilet properly.'

'I know, darling, I know.' Rozia brushed her hair back out of her eyes.

'They open some sort of door, and hold up a bedpan, and I hate it,' she said, turning her head away, 'and I can't go, and I need to go.'

Sister bustled in, a small, buxom, dark-haired woman with thin lips and kind hands. She instructed a young nurse to push the bedpan into position. Then she poured a glass of water.

'I don't want a drink,' Hannah said tiredly.

'It's not for drinking,' the sister said. 'Put your fingers in the glass.'

'What?' Hannah said, doing as she was told.

'You'll go wee-wee in a minute. We used to do this at school, during the night, with the slouches. A bit unfair I suppose, but it was standard practice.'

Aghast, Hannah stared up at the sister's worn face, at her dark hair.

As if to prove her point they both heard the tinkling into the pan and Hannah had a marvellous feeling of relief.

'Now,' said the sister, after the bedpan had been removed. 'We are going to turn the machine off for a moment or two.'

'What?' Hannah was frightened.

'You are not as bad as you think, and I want you out of that big ugly thing. Mr Sinclair, the head of the ward, will be here. Be very brave, just breathe as deeply as you can. I'll let your mother stay.'

Rozia moved towards Hannah's head; she cupped her hands around her head and massaged her neck with her thumbs.

The physician, a burly, rather handsome man in his forties, strode in with several students. He looked surprised when he saw Rozia, but said nothing for he could tell by her manner that she might help. He grinned at Hannah impishly.

'You were very rude to me last time I saw you, young lady.'

Hannah half smiled.

He was surprised, pleased. Few of his patients even reacted to his little jokes. He resolved to be a little more attentive to Hannah Simpson.

'We are going to leave you in there, and Sister is going to turn it off.'

Rozia watched the dials; Rozia held her child, and she breathed loudly, slowly.

Hannah was sweating. She tried not to panic, but there it was again, the lack of air, the inability to bring anything in . . . She watched Rozia's face, and she tried, she tried.

'Good girl,' Mr Sinclair said, as she felt the machine again.

Hannah smiled at Rozia, Rozia smiled back and bent down and touched her daughter's lips with her own, feeling her tears.

'Shall we try again later?' Mr Sinclair asked.

Hannah looked at Rozia, and Rozia nodded, and Hannah nodded.

'Good lass.'

Three times that day they turned off the machine, and three times Hannah tried not to panic, tried to follow Rozia's breathing, tried to feel only her mother's hands.

Martin Lascelles was waiting outside Hannah's room when Rozia came out for a cup of tea.

He was shocked by her appearance: she had lost so much weight, but she seemed to have grown. Rozia was no longer little.

'I've found Sister Kenny's book,' he said. 'I rang the publisher.'

Rozia took the book from Martin's outstretched hand.

'What is your opinion?' she asked.

There was no need for niceties. 'I don't know, Rozia, she is unorthodox, but in the case of an incurable disease – and let us face realities, polio is incurable – one should try anything.'

Rozia took Martin to the cafeteria. She bought coffee and two greasy eggs that she amazed herself by eating. Martin talked as she ate, telling her that Kenny's treatment for the effects of polio was a form of heat treatment and manipulation. Rozia asked if there were any exponents in London. He wasn't sure. He would find out.

On the second day the machine was turned off six times. On the third day the machine was turned off twelve times. On the fourth day, it was left off during the day.

On the sixth day they took Hannah out.

She couldn't stand up, she couldn't do anything. Rozia saw that her pelvis was out of line – 'a secondary effect,' Mr Sinclair told her.

'Of what?' she asked.

'The leg,' he replied.

Rozia and he were standing in the corridor, the obligatory

group of medical students having been despatched to another ward.

'Are you saying to me that my daughter will be crippled?'

'You have to accept that she is alive, and she will, once she has regained her strength, be able to perform most of her tasks.'

'So your answer is yes,' Rozia said quietly and walked away.

She told Anthony that evening.

'At least she is alive,' he said, 'and she has all her faculties.'

'Not quite,' Rozia said, remembering the lithe, slim young woman who had beaten her on the tennis court.

That night she telephoned the Sister Kenny Institute in America; she had to wait for the call and when she did get through, the line was bad, but she spoke for long enough to understand what was required and who to contact.

The following day she contacted a practitioner of the Sister Kenny method, Nurse Lillian Calthorpe, a blonde pretty lady in her forties who looked as if she might be more at home in a nightclub than in a hospital.

When Rozia and Nurse Calthorpe arrived Hannah was lying with her back to the door, her shoulders curled over.

'What is it?' Rozia asked, and there was no softness in her voice.

'They've told me,' Hannah said, her voice quiet, without pity, but quiet.

'Told you what?'

'A leg brace.'

'No.'

'Mummy –'

'No.' Rozia marched to Hannah's bed, she turned her around by the shoulders roughly. 'I said no leg brace.'

'I . . .'

'No. This lady, this lady I've brought with me here, she

297

is going to manipulate you and help you unlock your muscles and you are going to fight, you are not going to give in.'

'Anthony –'

'This isn't between Anthony and you. This is between me and you. My child is not going to be crippled. Do you hear me?'

Hannah stared into her mother's face which was almost deformed with anger. 'They seem to think . . .'

'I don't care what they think. Start now, Nurse.'

Hannah looked on as the pretty nurse washed her hands, came over and bent down towards her.

'I don't think I can take much more distress,' Hannah said, biting her lip, trying to be strong. 'No false hopes – unlike my mother I am a realist.'

'Your mother isn't giving you false hope,' the nurse said, and she set about her task of correcting Hannah's pelvis. Rozia watched as first she fetched hot towels and applied the warmth that would relax the muscles, and then carefully manipulated the leg. Within minutes Hannah's pelvis was straight.

'Now will you fight?' Rozia asked.

'Yes,' Hannah said, and the pretty nurse smiled.

Mr Sinclair was stunned. At first the nursing staff and the medical team assumed he would be enraged at someone else interfering with one of his patients, but he said nothing, merely nodded and asked about the next phase. When they came to measure Hannah for the leg iron, they found her on her feet, the sweat streaming from her face as she tried to get across the room. Rozia sent them away.

When they came again, they found Rozia holding Hannah's hands as she exercised her leg, forcing it off the bed, both women willing that wasted muscle to work.

When they came again Hannah was in the swimming pool. After that they didn't bother to come any more.

The women waged their battle whilst the men watched,

298

Jerzy loving and caring, bringing flowers and chocolates, Anthony knowing he had no part in Hannah's recovery. She had never asked him how he felt about her dalliance with the Kenny treatment – for a dalliance was what he felt it was. He was angry at his exclusion – but then Hannah had excluded him for so long.

He felt so awkward, and so bad. Yes, bad about Hannah bursting in on him and Aileen. It had only been a bit of fun – nothing to take out of proportion, but he did feel so awful about it.

He had married Hannah full of hope . . . and ambition. That ambition was fuelled by having to support his family. Margaret came along early – oh, how he loved her. Sometimes he thought he loved her more than Hannah did. But as soon as she had been born, this gentle cooing extension of his flesh, with her little bud-like mouth, had demanded and taken. Hannah, her milk, and the breasts which he loved became the property of his daughter. He had wanted to suckle from them, they were his, but Hannah hadn't allowed that. They were for Margaret and Margaret had made them sore. He had felt strangely allied to Margaret, both wanting her, and receiving enough from her.

He had tried so hard to give Hannah what she wanted, but she made him feel inadequate. He knew that she had difficulty in achieving orgasm, and he felt bad about it. Women should have more pleasure than Hannah. But she wouldn't let him help her, she refused to allow her sexuality. She kept it tight inside herself, just like the passage which led to her womb, tight and dry. He shivered when he thought of his attempts to bring something out of her, the fondling, the touching, the caressing which left nipples flat, cunt dry. He felt sometimes as if he were being driven from his home. And the affairs – they meant nothing. He knew that, but he had to have some pleasure – and in the brief moments of coupling those women made him feel important, something that Hannah could never do. If only she would try and look at things from his point of view for once. He wanted to make her happy, and the fact that he didn't deeply distressed him. If he could, he would have cried. But men, grown men didn't cry.

He had taken to working late. There was a young typist, Penny, who didn't seem to object to putting in extra hours for him. He couldn't help but notice her luscious lips that half smiled so charmingly. She wore white blouses a lot, and sometimes when he looked at her he wondered how she would look in just a skirt and no blouse.

He went to see Hannah one Monday lunchtime. She was intent on her exercises. He had brought her flowers, even put them into one of the hospital vases himself.

'How are you feeling?' he asked.

'Fighting.'

'Yes, you most certainly are.'

'What do you mean?'

'You are even fighting me.'

'No Anthony, I am not fighting you, I am fighting myself. Can you imagine what I feel like?' The voice cracked – was she near to tears? If only she would let him hold her, touch her, involve him in some way.

'It meant nothing,' he said softly, trying to hold her hand.

'Is that all you can think about?' she asked, turning away from him.

Anthony stood up quickly. Hannah was wearing a new nightdress, part of Rozia's 'you must look nice campaign'. Her blonde hair hung down to her shoulders but it was lank, without health, and she looked tired and sad, but what worried him most was that she looked bitter.

When Anthony got back to chambers he asked Penny if there might be a possibility of her working late that night. He had an opinion which he needed typing urgently, he was so sorry, he hadn't realized that the client was coming to see him at eleven the next morning.

'Of course I'll do it for you, Mr Simpson.' Penny's voice was light, he thought, and quite pretty. She smiled alluringly, almost adoringly, his ego told him.

Anthony left the door of his room open so that he could hear the sounds of his fellow barristers leaving. At six-fifteen he checked for remaining occupants. There were none – they had all gone home. He took a half bottle of champagne out of the cupboard and opened it, enjoying the little pop the cork made. He poured two glasses and carried them to the cubbyhole which was called the typist's office.

'Penny, a small thank you,' he said, putting the glass down by her typewriter.

'Oh, thank you.' She was obviously surprised. She had nice brown eyes, he thought.

'How is it going?' he asked.

'I've finished.'

'Good girl. You bring the pages. I'll bring the drink and we'll both check it in my room.'

'Oh no, sir, you have work to do. I'll go through it myself.'

'You've done enough, and so have I. We'll drink the champagne and go over it together.'

He had never realized quite how boring his opinions could be. He listened to his voice droning out the details of the case Selwyn v. Court Properties. Mr Selwyn was suing the landlord for not doing the repairs required under the lease. Mr Selwyn could have afforded to do them himself, but it was the principle, he had told Anthony. Listening to himself, Anthony resolved to establish himself in a more flamboyant area of the law.

'God, to think you have to type these every day,' Anthony said, staring at Penny. He noticed that her blouse strained against its buttons, her skirt clung to her hips. He wanted to run his hands over her, undo those buttons. He came over and bent down as if to study her typing.

'Well done,' he said quietly.

'Thank you,' she said, and he noticed that she licked her lips. He let his hand brush her breast, and he felt her nipple against his fingers.

'Oh Penny,' he said, 'I've watched you every day. I've . . .' But he didn't finish the sentence, he couldn't. Penny had turned in her chair, she undid his fly buttons and buried herself into him. Anthony felt her lips nip and tease him into life and then she was sucking him and all too hastily he felt himself drain into her.

'Aaah . . .' he muttered. Suddenly he loved this girl, this wonderful girl who had given him so much pleasure and he wanted to do something good for her.

'Me too,' she said, and lifting her skirt she pulled her delightful white panties down. A little unsure, he knelt in front of her.

'Your first time? I don't believe it. I'll show you.'

Penny parted her legs and raised herself slightly in the chair. She pulled his head towards her and he put his tongue on her and shivered with delight. He responded to her whispered commands until he felt her shudder and the juices flow from her. He hadn't realized that a woman could secrete so much in lovemaking.

'Not bad . . . for the first time,' Penny said. Embarrassed, he looked up at her and was dazzled by the look in her eyes. She did love him and Anthony fell hopelessly and utterly in love with her.

Chapter Seven

————————— ◆ —————————

Rozia no longer slept at the hospital, Margaret was staying with her. She loved the little girl and she loved the sound of a child in the house.

She would stand at the window and watch her granddaughter swinging happily, backwards and forwards, her blonde hair flowing loose behind her like a curtain of silk, and for a moment she would remember Hannah as a child. Jerzy had built the swing for Margaret.

'We went to the hardware shop, we bought everything we needed, and Margaret helped me erect it. We are very proud of ourselves,' he had told Rozia and she hated herself for not being able to give him a child.

Visitors had started to come and see Hannah. Sybil was a particular pleasure, she brought her books and chocolates and sat and ate them herself. Once she even went into the swimming pool with her.

That was the day Hannah made the most progress, and they both giggled like little children.

Esther came every day; she, like Rozia, bullied her and wouldn't accept failure.

On the day Hannah walked across the room, Esther was there with Rozia. On the day Hannah hugged Margaret and told her she was coming home, Esther was also there.

After Rozia, triumphant and glowing, had taken Margaret home, Esther curled up in a chair by Hannah's bed.

Hannah was wearing a blue silk nightdress and peignoir that suited her – she looked very beautiful.

'Hannah,' Esther said, 'will you listen to me? In a few

months when you are well, get a job. And don't go back to teaching. Get a job in the real world – why not broadcasting? – your mother did that. And then you might start living again. You have become a bore – I almost feel sorry for Anthony.'

Hannah turned to look at her, amazed, and she felt her mouth drop open.

Anthony took her home from the hospital. She wore a new suit and nylons and a pretty blouse; she was tired of course, but excited, and the house was filled with flowers. Everyone was so kind, and even Margaret seemed pleased to see her. It was later though, when she was getting ready for bed, having taken off her clothes, that she noticed what she hadn't noticed in the hospital, her thigh, her left thigh was thinner than her right thigh, her left knee smaller than her right, her calf, her left calf, was smaller than her right calf. She was not lopsided, she did not walk with a brace, but her left leg was different and she would never be able to camouflage that. Hannah cried then, deep terrible tears. Anthony, who had been bringing her up a cup of tea, asked what was the matter and then Hannah saw him look at her leg, saw the look on his face and she covered her eyes and screamed.

The next day she told Rozia what Esther had said, and Rozia, without questioning her child, telephoned Professor Lindt, an old friend from the war years who was now head of the Polish section at the BBC. Whilst Rozia arranged her life, Hannah longed for her father. Again she yearned for the undefined man her mother had called a prince. What was it Rozia had said – that he loved the theatre? – well, so did she, perhaps she could do what he had not lived to do: become a director . . . But immediately she dismissed the thought, realizing it was unachievable.

Suddenly it came to her. She would make a radio programme about the Poles in exile. She knew what she would call it, for she had heard the expression often enough in her mother's café: 'the Silver Brigade', the nickname for those Poles who had once been the aristocracy, the generals, and the diplomats, who now waited on guests in London hotels, making beds, summoning taxis, cleaning boots, carrying luggage whilst they mourned their own lost inheritance.

After all, Hannah reasoned, the programme would be a natural progression of her own emerging fascination, and yet at the same time disassociation, with those with whom she shared a common heritage – she was their child, only orphaned from them by circumstance. Hannah was beginning to understand that she spanned two different cultures, but what she did not yet realize was that this very understanding would alienate her from an already unhappy marriage. She rationalized to herself that an exploration of her Polish heritage might enable her to learn to live with the England that was her home. It did not occur to her that this same journey into her past might well destroy her present.

But Hannah's dream did not materialize in quite the way she had thought it might. She went to work for the BBC, but as a copytaster in the news room. It was not a particularly interesting position, she had to filter all the news wires to establish if there was anything of particular interest to the Polish service, but it did allow her the opportunity to regain her strength – and to watch and learn. And Hannah watched and learnt quickly.

After about six months in the job she noticed an item about a pie that was being baked in Denby Dale, a village in the North of England, in honour of Queen Elizabeth's Coronation. It wasn't just a pie – it was the largest pie ever baked. Hannah knew that every aspect of the Coronation was being milked by the producers, but this story might well be something that they had overlooked. After all, it was probably not particularly apparent that a pie would make an interesting story, but Hannah knew she could exploit an English peculiarity in such a way as to bring a little pleasure into the bleak life of Poland. She suggested it to Professor Lindt who at first doubted her reasoning, but she did her research anyway and wrote a four-minute script. Pleased with her efforts, she nibbled her fingers and waited. Not for long; the professor took her off the news desk and let her produce the item on Denby Dale's pie. After that her job was changed; she became a researcher, but one who was allowed to produce her own inserts.

And that was Hannah's life until Esther had decided to go on a holiday to Israel.

'How long for?' she asked, trying to control the sudden panic at the thought of her friend being away from her.

'I don't know,' Esther replied, grinding a cigarette out with too much effort. They had met in one of those tea places off Regent Street that served bath buns and stodgy cream cakes.

'It's a man, it's always a man. I don't particularly want to talk about it. He's married and I want to end it, OK? And I won't end it if I stay here.'

'I understand,' Hannah said quietly, not understanding at all.

After she left Esther she took a bus to Rozia and Jerzy's house – she could not face going home right away. Rozia was not there but Jerzy was, he was making a doll's house for Margaret. It was a beautiful thing, more like a palace than a house, with tiny gilt chairs and even a little throne room.

'It's wonderful,' Hannah said as she watched him carefully gluing the tiny pieces of wood together.

'What's the matter?' Jerzy asked, intent on his task, not even looking at her.

Stunned, Hannah sat down. 'How do you know something is wrong?'

'It's the way you walk, your mother does it all the time. When you are upset, both of you, your heels click.'

'How extraordinary.'

'Not really – it's probably the way you tense your ankles so your feet go more quickly and they make more noise.'

'No one has ever remarked on that before,' she said slowly. Jerzy smiled. 'Perhaps no one has ever noticed it.'

'Esther is going to Israel,' Hannah admitted to him as she shrugged off her coat.

'Does that matter?' Jerzy was still sticking his pieces of wood together.

'I didn't quite realize how much.'

'Why?'

'I suppose it is because she is the only friend I have.' Hannah realized she had tears in her eyes. She didn't try to hide them.

Jerzy put the little chair and glue down on the table. 'I know that you and your mother have a complicated relationship, but surely your situation with Anthony is satisfying?'

'No, it isn't.' Hannah found she was crying openly now but it didn't bother her. 'Anthony and I have grown apart. The thing is, Jerzy, I realize that I am more Polish than I thought and there are certain things about Anthony that I just don't understand. I have no common background with him. It wouldn't matter if we shared our present, but we don't for various reasons.' She cleared her throat, suddenly embarrassed but unable to stop. 'And Esther and I do share a past, so I am going to miss her very much, and I am upset because I am not sure she is going to come back to England and it makes me feel very lonely.'

Jerzy did not try to touch her, he just let his voice, soft and kind, do the caring. 'What can you do to fill the gap?' he asked.

Hannah could feel Jerzy's affection for her; it made her

think of Jouk, of how kind her mother's men were – how unlike Anthony . . . Rozia made good choices.

Hannah thought once again of her real father whom she had never known – was he like Jerzy, was he like Jouk? Was he . . . and then she remembered her need to find out who she was.

'I could try to make my programme, that would help.' She could see Jerzy's questioning look. 'I wanted to make a radio programme about the Poles in exile,' she continued lamely.

'So do it,' he said, picking up his piece of wood again.

That night Hannah wrote directly to Desmond Langley, a serious producer who worked for the Third Programme, sending a careful synopsis of 'The Silver Brigade'. She suggested that it might be one of a series of six programmes on the lives of the allies in exile after the war. Langley sent her back a terse memo suggesting that they meet. Hannah was nervous. Langley's reputation for programme making was impeccable, but his impatience with incompetence was equally well known.

The interview was difficult. Langley was a tall man with receding black curly hair, and he smoked incessantly as he cross-questioned her, allowing her very little time for explanation in her replies: he wanted facts, nothing else.

'Why don't you do this for the Poles? Sounds like the right kind of thing for them.'

'I want to do it for the Third Programme. Perhaps the English can learn a bit more about the rest of the world.'

'Oh, you see it as an educational programme then!'

'I see it as an investigation,' Hannah snapped, and she was almost prepared to get up and leave. She hated Langley, and she remembered English chauvinism, her teaching days and her frustration with the single-mindedness of the system. Ridiculously, she wanted to cry.

She almost didn't hear Langley answer her, he had to repeat himself and she could see he was irritated.

'All right then.'

'What?'

'You'll have to deal with the channels, there'll probably be some flak. I'll take you on secondment – just to do this programme, then we'll see.'

He stood up and shuffled his papers around. Hannah still sat in her chair, unable to believe what she had just heard.

'Well, get on with it,' Langley said.

'Yes. Right.' Hannah stood up too; she didn't know whether to shake his hand or not, half offered her own and then turned and fled without even asking when she might start.

When Hannah got home that night, she went upstairs to her daughter. She found her asleep, her head on her arm, her long blonde hair trailing over the pillow. Gently, Hannah touched the hair. Margaret moved and she took her hand away. She turned out the bedside light and tiptoed out of the room, closing the door very quietly.

The Simpsons had an au pair girl called Martha. She was a big girl, blonde with a milk and cream complexion, and she seemed kind and caring. She cooked wholesome and nourishing food and loved Hannah – and Hannah responded to Martha's affection, she reminded her of Danuta.

Martha would collect Margaret from school every day and take her to Rozia's café. Rozia adored that, she would spoil her granddaughter, feeding her favourite cakes and delicacies, showing her off to her delighted customers, encouraging her to spend time with Jerzy.

Rozia was aware of her passing years; she would sit at her mirror and trace the little lines around her eyes, fearing the impact that they might have on her still young husband. She was now forty-eight; she knew that for her age she looked wonderful, but Jerzy was only forty-three. He was a charming man and she loved him, and she knew he loved her. But like her beloved Papa so long ago Jerzy was a dreamer, he talked of designing the most beautiful and the most extraordinary building. He actually worked with two local Polish building contractors supervising the conversion of old houses into modern flats, but he stretched himself as little as he could. It was not that he was lazy, but Jerzy had lived a different kind of life in Poland to the one that even Jouk had known.

Before their wedding, she had discovered that he was a real prince. His childhood had been spent on one of the family's many estates in the north of Poland. He had worshipped his beautiful mother with her long red hair and her slender waist. He had married into his own class; he still had a photograph of his wife – a raven-haired countess who loved to hunt. She had borne him children, sons. Jerzy had taken his architectural degree because he wanted to understand the kind of restoration work that he needed to undertake on his estates, and his wife's. With the outbreak of war he had joined his regiment. His Countess Elizabeth had returned with the children and the servants to Warsaw where, in the bombing, she and they had lost their lives.

When Rozia wept because she could not bear him a child, Jerzy told her, caressing her still lovely body, 'I don't want them now, there is nothing for them to inherit. Don't judge me harshly for that, Rozia. I am not a dilettante, it is just that I have never been taught differently.'

Rozia knew he did his best to cope with the change in his fortunes – but it was when she saw him with younger women that her heart burned and her eyes ached. He knew her fears, and he never tired of reassuring her. 'I love you. I loved you from the moment I met you. Of course I have regrets for the past, and so do you. But now we have each other and we are not alone. I have no wish for anyone else,' and Rozia believed him. But still she hated to see him in the company of women. She couldn't rationalize the hurt, nor did she try to push it away. Sometimes she wondered if she welcomed it, perhaps as proof of her own inadequacies.

Anthony had not been pleased with Hannah's return to work. He had tried to stop her but, faced with her implacable determination and reasoned argument that it was only shift work, not the nine to five variety, he had capitulated, but he wasn't a happy man in defeat. He didn't like coming home to a meal that Martha had prepared, nor the fact that Margaret spent her afternoons at Rozia's café, but eventually he realized that it fitted his lifestyle.

He saw more and more of Penny, taking extraordinary risks just to touch her, enticing her with the tip of his tongue. He couldn't resist her. Everything else faded from him, as if the rest of his life was at a distance, somewhere beyond the immediacy of Penny.

But then he had remembered his ambitions. It happened over dinner with Justice Hunter, the head of his chambers. Knowing that he was a close, if unpublicized friend of those in power within the Conservative Party, Anthony remarked that he would be interested in a political career.

It took several months, but eventually Justice Hunter summoned him to his rooms. 'Wednesday week, six-thirty, Smith Square,' he said. 'It'll just be a drink with one or two people to get to know them – you know the form.'

It wasn't that he fell out of love with Penny, but suddenly his other priority re-asserted itself. And when she next crept up to him and kissed him, she was rewarded with cold lips and a curt, 'Control yourself, we must be careful. We will see each other soon, I promise,' but the hand that could not bear not to touch a curved buttock allowed itself a quick caress.

Since then he had pursued an even-handed course, enjoying Penny but ensuring that he cultivated his political ambitions much as he might water and feed a precious and

311

well-loved garden, careful not to do too much too quickly, or too little too late.

Anthony was determined that his flowers should bloom at their best, at the right season. It didn't bother him that he had no firm political convictions and that once he had been a socialist. He felt no guilt about Hannah; he reasoned that his passionate couplings with Penny hadn't damaged his marriage – it was Hannah who had done that when she went back to work.

Hannah, of course, knew about Penny. She had long since discovered the existence of the other woman. It had happened one afternoon in the spring. She had seen them together in the Strand. They were in a taxi, and Hannah was waiting to cross the road at the traffic lights. She still didn't know what made her look into the taxi, but her first thought was how in love the girl was, how she looked at the man as he spoke, how she put out a tentative hand to his tie. He must be married Hannah thought, the girl's gesture was not proprietorial, and then she saw that the man was Anthony. Her only concern at the time was that he should not see her. Later, casually, she asked if there were any women in his chambers.

'Mrs Jenkins and of course Penny who types,' he said and Hannah knew by the slight softness in his voice that the girl was 'Penny who types'. The only shock was that she did not mind. Far from lamenting Anthony's physical disinterest in her she welcomed it, alone in her single bed, grateful for the distance that separated her from him. She had put her body to sleep; she neither craved nor shunned sex. It was as if it didn't exist. Her thin leg seemed to have ended any such needs.

But she worried about how often her work took her away from home. The separation from Margaret was beginning to disturb her. Her five-year-old daughter was so restrained with her – sometimes Hannah wanted to grab her in her arms and cuddle her, but Margaret was always so formal. Recently she had noticed that Margaret hugged Martha and Rozia often – that hurt. She wondered what was wrong with their relationship. Had she established guidelines that she had learnt from Rozia?

It was on the night before Hannah began work on her programme that she thought about the child, remembering how cold Rozia had been with her, how different she was with Margaret. Perhaps it was because she was happy now, because a man loved her? Hannah went into her bedroom and slowly took her clothes off. She looked at her body and realized she didn't know anything about it – where her orgasms came from. She knew it was somewhere between her legs, but where exactly? At the thought, her thighs tightened and she saw that her nipples had hardened slightly. Hannah opened her legs and touched herself, finding the little mound of flesh and beginning to rub it. She found herself getting warmer, and within what seemed pleasurable moments she had an orgasm. It had been so long since she felt anything at all that she began to touch herself again, liking it, not feeling pressurized, feeling nice.

Hannah prepared her programme around Rozia's café, using it as the base where all the Poles came to recapture their lost Poland. On the night of its broadcast the café was filled with the Poles, with BBC people, with the family – including Sybil and Martin who were part of the family, Rozia teased Sybil that she had become almost Polish. Sybil enjoyed that. She and Rozia shared a kind of peace now, and they both loved Hannah. Bernice had gone her own way – that was the way it was.

Hannah was beautiful on the night of her broadcast. She glowed with happiness. Desmond Langley, taciturn but pleased, shared a table with her, squeezing her hand and laughing as the accordionist, once a major, serenaded them.

Jerzy carried Margaret around as if she were his own grand-daughter; the food in austerity Britain was luscious, the drink generous, the laughter and the celebration everywhere.

Anthony didn't drink vodka, he drank whisky and watched as Langley invited Hannah to dance, and whirled her around and around. He glanced at Hannah's legs; no one else seemed to have noticed that one was thinner than the other – was it just him? he wondered – because it had affected him.

Penny was no longer in his life, she needed too much. He had told her that he didn't want her any more, that it wasn't fair because he would never marry her. She had taken it badly – she loved Anthony.

On the day she left chambers he felt relieved and to a certain extent happy that the double life was over, but she kept telephoning him, day after day the calls came and he invented excuses for not taking them – the excuses were not for Penny, they were for himself.

The clerks were laughing at him, he knew that and he was very angry with her for putting them both in that position. One night she was waiting outside his office; she looked terrible – haunted almost – he couldn't bear it. She started to cry and begged him to call her. Anthony was with Hunter so he ignored her, staring at his feet as the judge waved down a taxi. Penny stood on the kerb, watching them get in, and then she stepped into the road. Anthony thought they might run over her – he could see her tears in the street lights. Now, at Hannah's party, he wondered what had become of her.

He glanced over to his wife, surrounded by her Poles and her BBC people, and he remembered how he had felt about her when he had first seen her at the tennis club; how young, how lovely she had been, moving around the tennis court after her shots, aware of herself but still somehow shy. Hannah wasn't shy now; she held the limelight, enjoying it, proud of it. Suddenly he realized that her behaviour just wasn't English – yes, that's what it was, that was what had gone wrong. Hannah had offered herself to him as a shy young Englishwoman and he had married that Hannah, but this Hannah was foreign, different – she just wasn't the same as him. It wasn't that he was better, his behaviour and needs were different to hers. As he poured himself another whisky he thought of all their years together and he felt very lonely.

Rozia too had her thoughts. As she watched Hannah revel in her success she felt proud, but involuntarily Samuel came into her mind, and she felt an ache for the father she had lost which burnt her throat and her eyes. She hadn't achieved her dreams, neither had he, but Hannah the grandchild he would have spurned had done it. Suddenly Rozia longed for Samuel, for Hannah the mother and Jonathon the brother, but mostly, agonizingly, it was Booba she craved; and then she looked back at Hannah and she saw that Booba, by a freak of light, was there – but it was a Booba coloured by Stefan, moulded by Jouk and reared by Rozia.

In pain Rozia tore her eyes away, and saw that Jerzy was watching her as if he could read her mind – she realized how much she loved him, she reached out for his hand, and as she clasped it Rozia found she didn't ache quite as much.

Hannah was finally bathed and healed. Success had beaten polio. She pulled Margaret on to her lap and cuddled her, feeling her close – she shut her eyes for a moment, savouring her joy.

'You must have a holiday now, before the next programme,' Desmond said, lighting a cigarette.

'Where would I go?' Hannah asked.

'Israel,' Jerzy replied, quickly squeezing Rozia's hand, 'to Esther, to your friend. That is where you belong now.' He smiled at Hannah, sharing intimacies.

Rozia cleared her throat, remembering Jouk's relationship with Hannah, feeling momentarily excluded by Jerzy. Then she thought about Shosha and Mordechai, they were not dead . . . perhaps? No, she dismissed the idea as soon as it came into her mind, they were part of her past and she should be happy that Hannah and Jerzy shared a love, she must not feel excluded by them.

'I don't think I desperately want to go to Israel,' Anthony said loudly.

'Well, you don't have to, I shall go on my own. Jerzy is right, I do need time with Esther.' Hannah knew her voice was sharp.

Anthony was stung . . . even Esther was more important than he to Hannah . . . what kind of marriage did they have, did they share? It was a farce – but what could he do to change their lives? Hannah was so far away from him. She just didn't care any more.

Chapter Eight

———————◆———————

Israel in 1955 was a land of Jews, but a land isolated and aware of its own vulnerability.

After the euphoria of independence Israel was attacked, and attacked back. Emigration was higher than immigration, conditions were difficult, there were few luxuries, but to those who were Zionists the fight for their land would never be abandoned.

For Hannah Simpson, the wife of an Englishman, the daughter of a Polish woman who had once been a Jew, the prospect of three weeks in Israel was enhanced by the possibility of finding her mother's past. After Jerzy's surprise suggestion, Hannah had considered it carefully; she was tired, the thought of a holiday without Anthony was not something she contemplated with pleasure but she did miss Esther, a trip to Esther was something pleasurable in itself – and, as Desmond said, 'If there is a story – we'll take it.' So she told Rozia, 'I have decided to go.'

Rozia was quiet on the subject for several weeks. She didn't even speak to Jerzy about it despite his various hints that she might like to talk. Rozia always dealt with herself by herself. Even Hannah had no idea as to what her feelings were until she telephoned her.

'I had a friend, a very good friend, her name was Shosha – she married a man called Mordechai Chalavie, also a friend. They emigrated to Israel in 1924, find them for me, please . . .'

'Did they know my father?' Hannah asked.

'No, but they saw him once,' Rozia admitted, remembering the ghost-like face and the shiver of a premonition on that night in Marshalkowska as surely as if she were there at that very moment, instead of sitting in her fringed and tasselled salon.

Anthony had been less than enthusiastic about the trip, but then it seemed to Hannah that Anthony was less than enthusiastic about anything that she did – so she tried not to care. Martha had promised to take great care of Margaret and she knew that Rozia would never neglect her grandchild – and the thought of the sun was so pleasurable.

Hannah had never really been curious about Judaism as such; it meant nothing to her except of course as the faith of Esther and her family.

She decided to fly by the Israeli national airline, El Al, because Desmond Langley had said, 'You'll get more colour that way.' At first she regretted her decision; there were Jews praying, ones with big hats and white faces and long side curls. Others in skull caps harangued each other in the aisles, whilst their wives gossiped. She thought for a minute that she was back at Esther's brother's bar mitzvah, but then the plane began its descent to Lodd airport and the mood changed, the atmosphere moved from disordered if friendly chaos into a shared emotion as those on the plane began to sing, softly at first, then louder, the Israeli national anthem – they cried, some of them, others were proud – the few non-Jews watched amazed as these peculiar people merged into one.

Hannah felt none of their emotion in the nightmare of Lodd airport. She longed for the organization of London, but instead there was a lot of shouting and pushing and queuing whilst passports were checked and luggage located. If it hadn't been for a rather nice American who had shouldered his way through the mass of people towards her, she would have stayed just where she was – maybe for hours.

'Can I help you?' he asked.

She shuddered, the kind of shudder that registers instant attraction – it made her nervous so she merely nodded. He picked up her case and pushed her through. Hannah saw that he was carrying cameras and a tape recorder. He must be a journalist, she thought, but she hadn't the courage to acknowledge his kindness in any way other than to say thank you. Esther was there, she was kissing her, holding her, and everything was all right again.

'Who was the dish?' Esther asked.

Hannah giggled, young again. 'I would like to know.' She saw a man, small and wiry with dark curly hair, hovering behind her friend, and Esther saw her looking at him.

'Yaacov, this is Hannah,' she said.

'Hello,' he said, offering a hand. Hannah felt thick gnarled flesh – his hand felt so strong that for a moment she shut her eyes and wanted to throw herself into this man's arms, to feel him hold her. Instead she looked at Esther. Esther nodded. 'I felt that way too,' she said, 'when I first met him.'

Yaacov grinned. 'You women, you women – you talk of a man as if he isn't there.'

'And you men,' Esther said, 'do the same.' Whilst they bantered Hannah had a chance to register her friend. Esther wore shorts and a tee-shirt, her hair was short, bleached lighter by the sun, her skin brown – she looked healthy and so happy.

Hannah knew her own appearance was a dramatic contrast. True, she was wearing a nice grey suit, and a little hat topped the gold hair which curled around her shoulders, but her face was white and strained and there was no strength in her. Her leg ached; it always ached when she was tired.

They drove to Esther's kibbutz. The air was warm and dry; Hannah took her jacket off and her hat, but her blouse stuck to her – she longed to take her nylons off. Yaacov was driving the truck – 'We usually use it to transport livestock or fruit,' Esther said. Hannah sniffed: yes, she thought, they used it to transport livestock. She was very tired, she couldn't see much, the night blocked out any sights. She went to the small room that Esther had prepared for her. It was bare – just a bed – but there was a bowl of flowers.

'Sleep,' Esther told her, offering a hot cup of precious cocoa – it was her one luxury, she admitted, cocoa from England. Hannah noticed she didn't say cocoa from home.

Hannah slept late, and when she awoke the following morning the sun shone bright and hot. No one was around, just gentle slopes of grass and some trees. Over to the side was a big building. She showered, using a hose that was put up outside her room – she didn't need the towel Esther had left her, the heat dried her off – and then she made her way towards the building. Inside was a vast cafeteria, if that was the right word for lots of tables and chairs, and a big hatch which led to the kitchens. Hannah couldn't help but notice how clean they were – potatoes had been peeled, chicken was ready for cooking; there were tomatoes and cucumbers and endless large bowls of apple purée.

'Hannah.'

Hearing her name, she spun on her heel. Yaacov was walking towards her, carrying a mug and a big plate with some bread and cheese.

'Breakfast,' he said.

Embarrassed, Hannah looked at her watch.

'At twelve-thirty?'

'So OK. Lunch then.'

She smiled and sat down in the sun, grateful for something to eat. The heat warmed her and she lay back in the grass.

'We'll take you to the beach – later, when Esther has finished.'

'Where is she?'

'Chickens,' he said.

'Oh.'

Hannah offered a piece of bread to Yaacov who sat easily by her, his knees bronzed and hardened. As he took it she noticed a number on the outside of his wrist. Unable to stop herself she gently reached out and touched it.

'Dachau,' he said.

And Hannah remembered Dr Weinstein.

They walked to the beach which was down a steep hill. Hannah wondered how her leg would cope with the climb back, but she said nothing. The sand was white, and the water clean.

'Don't get red,' Esther instructed. And mindful of her fair skin, Hannah retreated under a tree.

Just as they were gathering their things for the return to the kibbutz Hannah saw a van arrive. She glanced over at Esther. Her face was impassive, but Hannah knew her friend too well, she had obviously asked someone to collect them.

That night the kibbutzniks had a party for Hannah; they laughed and sang, someone played an accordion, and there was a lot of dancing.

'My mother was Jewish,' Hannah told Yaacov. He looked quizzical. 'She was born in Warsaw to a Jewish family. She fell out with them when she met my real father who was a Polish student. He was killed in some sort of student riot and she converted to Catholicism and married my stepfather. But she has some friends here in Israel and I would like to try and find them for her.'

'I came from Poland,' Yaacov said quietly. 'My name was Jacob, we lived in Gdansk. In 1943 we were all of us due to be sent to Auschwitz, my parents, my grandparents, my uncles, my aunts, my cousins, they all went. But I didn't. I was eight years of age. A non-Jewish friend hid me in his house until a neighbour betrayed us all. Somehow I ended up in Dachau, alone except for the other living dead.'

'I can only imagine what it must have been like,' Hannah said. 'I went with my parents to Poland in 1938 to try and bring about a rapprochement between my mother and her family. On the way,' she was aware now that others were listening, 'we had to cross the German border. I made friends with this Polish doctor, "friends" – he was an elderly man and I was a little girl. They tried to take him off the train, it was terrible.'

No one spoke, no one said anything – it was a moment for the lost millions.

Two days later Hannah went with Esther to the central kibbutz office in Tel Aviv.

They found Mordechai Chalavie.

The kibbutz where he lived was not far from Esther's, called 'Yad Mordechai' – 'The Hand of Mordechai' (named after a young Jewish fighter who had been killed in the Warsaw uprising). It was actually on the Egyptian border – there were raids in that area, bad raids.

'When do you want to go?' Esther asked.

'Tomorrow?'

'Tomorrow I work. Today,' Esther said, and drove the van out of the city fast and hard to Yad Mordechai. Hannah was surprised to find she was nervous. What would this woman be like? She remembered Bashela, the old woman she had met with Rozia in the Warsaw ghetto. It was funny to think that she had probably seen Shosha's mother long after Shosha had last seen her.

Hannah listened to Esther gabbling, as she called it, in that funny language which seemed to bear no relation to a European tongue.

'Why should it?' Esther asked. 'It's Semitic, because we Jews are a Semitic people, that is what is so bloody stupid about the whole thing. We and the Arabs are cousins.'

'Don't tell me, Esther, it's an inter-family war.'

'Don't be so English, Hannah. According to us you are Jewish.'

'What are you talking about?'

'Your mother was Jewish, that makes you Jewish too, and your daughter.'

'Anthony wouldn't think that was anything to be particularly pleased about,' Hannah said, realizing that it was the first time she had thought of Anthony, or even Margaret for that matter, in three days. She wondered – a little concerned – why she didn't miss them.

'That is one good reason for me personally to tell Anthony,' Esther said.

'You really don't like him?'

'No.'

They drove in silence, companionable and comfortable, for a while.

'It's wonderful, isn't it?' Esther said.

'No, it's flat terrain, and there isn't a lot to see.'

'Wait, we are going to take you to Tiberius, just you wait. And Caesarea and –'

'OK, Esther, OK,' Hannah interrupted. 'I didn't say I didn't like it.'

They arrived at the kibbutz at around six-thirty in the evening. A young boy went to find the Chalavies and he came back with a woman with grey curly hair, and a strong kind face. The woman was running – Hannah couldn't imagine Rozia running any more. The woman stopped in front of her. She was crying. Silently she reached out a hand. Hannah stood still, not knowing what to say. Esther pushed her in the small of her back and she almost stumbled into the woman's arms. She felt herself being hugged and patted.

'Come,' the woman said in Hebrew.

She took them to her little house; bread and cake and wine and lemon tea were suddenly produced. Children were presented. Where was the man, Mordechai? Hannah wondered. She asked Esther to find out. Her jaw ached from smiling.

'He died two years ago.'

'Ask her what my mother was like,' Hannah said, hoping she wasn't being too forward.

With Esther as translator Shosha described the cajoling, flirting, ambitious and powerful Rozia of the Warsaw years. She talked of Samuel and Hannah Mezeurski. Hannah had no idea she was named after her grandmother. She talked of Booba and Jonathon. When she had finished, Hannah knew about her mother. Quietly, almost embarrassed, she offered a photograph of Rozia on her wedding day, a beautiful elegant Rozia, so far removed from the rough little lady with the warm face who sat opposite her. Shosha smiled, touched the photograph and asked if she might keep it.

'You like father,' Shosha said in bad English, pointing to Hannah.

'Did you know him? My mother said you saw him once.'

'Yes,' Shosha answered in Hebrew, and Esther translated how, as a young girl, she had seen the handsome prince who had claimed her friend's heart all those years ago across a wide street on a cold Warsaw night. It hurt Hannah to hear it – so near, yet so untouchable – and again she longed for Stefan Gordanski.

Shosha wrote a letter to Rozia, and Hannah promised to give it to her. They kissed and hugged before they left, and Hannah took a photograph so Rozia would know what Shosha looked like.

Yaacov and Esther took her to Yad Vashem, the memorial to the six million. A friend, Ahron Eshhol, an archaeologist by nature and a pilot officer by profession, came with them. They took her to Tiberius with its rich green country and Hannah thought of Jesus and the miracle of the fish; they took her to Caesarea and she sat amongst the Roman ruins and listened to the sea. Hannah didn't know that the sun had tanned her, that her leg no longer felt tired. Hannah didn't know that in Israel she had become beautiful.

As she sat in the soft breeze of the quiet night, Ahron watched her.

'Have you been to Massada?' he asked.

'No,' Hannah said.

'Then I will take you.' He held out a hand . . . 'We will go now,' he said.

'Now.'

And that was the way it was. Hannah drove off in a jeep in the night air whilst Esther hugged Yaacov and thanked whatever it was up there for bringing her friend to Israel.

As Hannah drove through the hot Israeli night, she watched the extraordinary young man beside her with his tanned skin and almost navy blue eyes, his thick black hair, his straight nose and the full mouth which allowed the arrogance of perfection. And Rozia sat in London, crying over her daughter. There had been a raid on Yad Mordechai that day – people had been killed. Forgetting which kibbutz Hannah was in and fearing, quite ridiculously she told herself, that something might have happened, Rozia rang Esther's mother and obtained the telephone number of Esther's kibbutz. Whoever answered the phone said, 'Oh yes, Hannah went to Yad Mordechai with Esther, they went to see some friends of Hannah's mother.' And the black bird of terror plucked at Rozia's heart again. The Jews had killed her Stefan, and now they had killed Hannah.

Jerzy held her, he slapped her and bullied her, but still Rozia sat and mourned and cried . . . even though they did not know for sure.

Whilst Rozia wept, Hannah Simpson climbed the hill to Massada. As the sun rose the young Israeli took away her dress, took off her shoes, kissed her feet and her breasts. Hannah pulled him on to her, feeling him move into her, and she swung over on top of him and let her hunger out as she rode, and screamed and begged . . .

Later, when the sun was up, Ahron took her again.

'You know nothing of loving, Hannah,' he whispered, as he touched her and caressed her. 'Don't be afraid to let someone give to you.' Hannah heard him and she opened her legs and she let him love her.

'Here,' he said, when they sat up and smoked a cigarette together, 'here the last Jews committed suicide rather than live under Roman rule. You know we have a saying, Hannah, "Massada shall never fall again".'

When Hannah returned to the kibbutz she felt whole and strong. She bid farewell to Ahron, and as she walked over to Esther, realized she hadn't even asked if he had a girl-friend, or a wife, or children. She hadn't wanted to know. For those few hours he had been hers, and she his. The rest didn't matter.

She spoke to Rozia on the telephone . . . and heard her anguish.

'I am coming home,' she told her.

She hugged Esther hard at Lodd airport, knowing it might be a long time before she saw her again. When she arrived at London airport her mother and her daughter were there to meet her. Hannah hugged them both, seeing them both perhaps for the first time.

When she saw Anthony that night, he asked what it was like in Israel.

'It's a hot land that smells of olives and citrus fruit,' she said quietly.

'What did you say?' he answered as he walked up to bed.

Chapter Nine

——— ◆ ———

On her return Hannah thought everything would be different, because she felt different . . . It took her just a few days to see that everything was just the same. The realization that she couldn't effect the changes, that she couldn't wave a wand and bring in warmth and love where there was no warmth and love was painful.

She resolved to battle through – to try.

The first change must be Anthony. On her second night home she prepared herself for bed, knowing that her tanned legs were no longer as dissimilar as they used to be. He was already in bed, waiting to put out the light. He wore striped pyjamas, and as she looked at his pale skin she couldn't help but think of Ahron. She fought his memory off – that would have been too difficult to cope with. Hannah made herself give to Anthony, she felt his tongue push into her mouth and she knew she would have to like it.

The next was Margaret. She tried to bridge the gap with her child by spending all her time with her at the weekends. She knew it was unsatisfactory, but the only alternative was to give up her work and that would have been to give up the only part of her life that belonged to her – if she was judged as selfish for that, then so be it.

Her Polish programme had been reviewed in the best journals and newspapers and she was accepted by her peers – that made her feel marvellous. 'It's like being in a permanently warm bath; I know someone will take the plug out eventually but at the moment it feels so good,' she told Desmond Langley.

Saturdays were easy: they shopped. On Sundays they strolled around the Natural History Museum, the Museum of Mankind, the Science Museum. Anthony seemed to enjoy these outings; he would hold Margaret's hand and they would stare at an exhibit for what seemed like hours to Hannah who was somehow always holding the coats, hers, Margaret's and Anthony's. Once she suggested a film instead – they both, father and daughter, looked at her as if she were deliberately trying to spoil their day. She smiled quickly. 'I only thought it would make a change,' she said, and went back to looking at the remains of dead butterflies and dried bones. She planned a complete new anthology series on the role of the old within society, redesigned her house and even revamped her entire wardrobe on those Sundays.

The third was Rozia. She gave her Shosha's letter immediately on her return.

'Thank you,' Rozia said, holding the note in her hand lightly as if it were a flower.

'Mordechai has died, I am afraid,' Hannah said as quietly as she could.

'In a way I hoped Shosha was dead too,' Rozia replied.

And Hannah understood.

Jerzy was with Rozia when she read the little note from Shosha, asking her to write, telling her of her three children, of Mordechai's death, of her peace and happiness in Israel.

'I hope you too are happy, Rozia,' she had written.

'What will you reply?' Jerzy asked, sure of her response.

It was not an easy letter to write, but she did it, accomplishing the task without emotion, detailing Jouk's death, her re-marriage to Jerzy, the birth of Margaret, how she started her little café.

There was nothing of herself in the letter – now that there was a possibility Rozia had no wish to re-open her past, and Shosha was her past. With Jouk's death she wanted it to be over. Her wish that Hannah try to find Shosha had been a frivolous one, she hadn't thought she would actually ever manage to do so.

It was quite a deliberate omission on her part that there was no address at the top of her notepaper.

Not long after Jerzy had built the swing for Margaret, he gave up all pretence of working.

'I can't adapt myself to building places that have no beauty. I realize it is not very practical but utilitarianism is unappealing to me. Forgive me, Rozia, if I am a disappointment to you, but that is the way it is.'

Rozia tried not to mind, she told herself it didn't matter, but she was aware of a slight shift in her focus: she no longer thought of Jerzy as the focal point of her life. It was not a dramatic decision, more a gradual thing. She realized that Margaret's arrival from school was the pinnacle of her day – it was not that she fell out of love with Jerzy, it was just that Rozia found it harder to live with a flawed dream than with the expectation of another's possibility. And the possibility was Margaret. It wasn't that she didn't love Hannah either, it took her illness and possible death to know quite how much her daughter meant to her, but Hannah wasn't there. In a rare honest moment she told Sybil that Hannah was possibly the only unselfish love she had. 'I just wish I could show her quite what she means to me,' she said.

'Have you ever tried to say I love you?' Sybil asked. Her age now showed, her fingers were bent with arthritis, but the only inconvenience she admitted to was that Martin now had to brew the tea.

Rozia looked at Sybil, and her voice almost broke as she said, 'I don't know how to. I never have – you see. Hannah is the reason why everything changed in my life – and even now I still can't come to terms with it.'

'Why?' Sybil asked. 'I have had to learn to deal with Rosemary's death.'

'You don't bear the guilt.'

'That's insensitive. Of course I blame myself.'

'It's not just Hannah,' Rozia said, 'it's everyone else too. I can't deal with it, Sybil, and I won't.'

And so she turned to Margaret. Whilst Hannah was in Israel Rozia told her that once she had wanted to be a biochemist.

'I want to be a doctor,' Margaret said suddenly, without thinking.

'That would make me very happy,' Rozia told her.

On Margaret's nineth birthday, the family assembled at Rozia's flat for a celebration high tea. Rozia had prepared a special birthday cake, *Sacher Torte*, an extravagance of chocolate and sugar which Jerzy loved. As he watched her ice the cake, and put little candles around it in a circle, he praised her. Unaware that a smudge of chocolate had marked her chin, just below the lip, and that her normally tidy hair, now fashionably short again, was dishevelled, she looked up and smiled at him. 'She could have been ours,' she said.

'But she isn't,' he said gently and Rozia felt so sad, and the blood rose to the surface of her otherwise smooth white skin.

Jerzy saw the sudden flush. He knew Rozia felt that they should have had a child of their own but he had never regretted that they couldn't. He had lost his children and his wife, he missed them, sometimes even wondered what they would have been like in their later years, but he had no liking for remorse – for what might have been.

Later, after a loving that surprised and moved her, Rozia went back to the cake – she used white icing to make a little lake and then she put two figures and a dog on it, as if they were skating. She felt Jerzy as if he were still inside her – how different it was to their first coupling which she remembered now only with embarrassment.

She had been awkward, scared almost. She had insisted that the lights were off, worried by the little white fish-like flashes that had marked her stomach since Hannah's birth. Jerzy had been gentle at first and then the hunger and the years of wanting had overcome him and he had entered her, pulling her to him, unable to contain himself. 'I don't mind,' she had said.

The next time Rozia felt him hard against her she eased herself on to him, begging him to touch her. Uncaring of his needs she kept him in her, desperate for that release. She bent backwards, holding his ankles, gasping and groaning, not realizing that the force had gone out of him. When she felt him slip from her she touched herself and brought herself to a climax that left her shaking and tearful. Only then did she know that Jerzy had not come.

He would not talk about it, and she feared so deeply that he might not want her again; he did not approach her the next night, nor the next. She knew she had to reach out for him, and so on the third night she touched him, and whispered her fears.

'It is more so for me, Rozia, I am the man – perhaps I may fail you again, perhaps I cannot please you. I feel so ashamed.'

A fear so deep-surfaced, so childish. 'No,' she wanted to shout, 'not again, not again.' But as the wail surfaced, she crushed it down. She loved Jerzy, she would help him, together they would learn – instinctively and with great care for him Rozia reached out and touched his flaccid penis, she felt him stiffen and she turned on her back and pulled him into her, thrusting and moving with him, and suddenly she wasn't anxious any more and it was good.

When Margaret arrived back from school she hugged her grandmother, oohing and aahing over her birthday cake. But then she excused herself and went up to the little spare room that Jerzy had prepared as her own. She had caught a

331

fly at school and placed it in a matchbox. Going into her grandmother's room she removed the tweezers from the make-up case which Rozia kept on her dressing table. In the privacy of her own room Margaret opened the box and managed to imprison the fly between the thumb and first finger of her left hand. Using the tweezers very carefully, she slowly removed its wing. She wanted to know how it was attached to the body.

Whilst Margaret dissected the fly, Hannah was shopping for her daughter. She was the only member of her family to acknowledge the arrival of the rock culture – at thirty-four Hannah was too old to be part of the generation that gyrated and jived, but Presley promised a promiscuity that inflamed her.

Alter the hooped skirts of Alma Coogan, the irreverent new music makers matched Hannah's release from the coyness, prudery and whimsey of post-war England.

She bought Margaret three rock records – and a record player in a smart blue and white carrying case.

When she arrived, laden with presents, the greeting she gave Rozia and Jerzy was perfunctory – she wanted Margaret.

When she had awoken that morning Hannah had remembered it was Margaret's birthday. As she lay in her bed in those first moments of the day she recalled her birth – it had been cold and lonely, she had been so frightened in that big white room, she had wanted Anthony, but he wasn't with her, no one was there. She had help at the right time, medically speaking, and it was kind, but rushed – no one had thought to be careful of Hannah and her child. She didn't remember the actual pain, but she knew it had riven her, overwhelmed her – she had wanted to die. She knew that she held on to that memory, cherishing it, but for Margaret the only appeasement against the shock of that first great battle for life was its erasure from her consciousness. But Hannah still felt the bond of that shared fight and she burst into her child's bedroom that morning, disturbing her from sleep, wanting to hold her. She was shocked at the resistance in the small body.

As if sensing her mother's needs, Margaret came into the hall as soon as she heard her voice.

'What have you been doing?' Hannah asked her, the tenderness in her voice obvious.

'Dissecting a fly,' came the reply.

'Dissecting what?' she said laughingly.

'A fly, I told you.'

Hannah smoothed Margaret's hair away from her eyes, she didn't try to hold her. 'Come, let me show you what I've brought you. I know you said you wanted to wait until Grandma gave you her presents, but wouldn't it be nice not to have them altogether?'

'OK.'

Hannah watched as Margaret unwrapped the big box. She opened it, and looking at the record player, smiled her thanks. There were the records, tortoiseshell hair slides, lace handkerchiefs, and a tiny bottle of perfume, *Je Reviens*. Hannah knew that really Margaret was too young for that, but she thought she might like an acknowledgement of her femininity.

'Thank you,' Margaret said, 'they are all lovely.' She piled the packages up haphazardly, and carried them into her bedroom. Hannah saw her drop them on to the bed without looking where they fell.

The little perfume bottle fell out of its blue box and rolled on to the floor. Hannah saw that Margaret hadn't noticed. She went into the room after her and picked it up. She said nothing, just put it back in its box. She could see that Margaret was gazing intently at something on the white shiny dressing table underneath the window. She hoped it wasn't the fly, and then Margaret said, 'Do you want to see the wing?'

Hannah watched in horror as she showed her the fly, now back in its box with its wing still trapped in the tweezers. She listened as Margaret explained.

'It's really a question of the wrist movement, a jerk, then you have it. The art is to ensure that the creature is still alive.'

'But it will die anyway – without a wing, it can't fly. How will it get its food?'

'I suppose so – I don't know, supposing I fed it?'

'It wouldn't be free.'

'Well, it won't be free now anyway will it? Without its wing.'

Margaret turned the box upside down on the shiny surface. The little black insect rubbed its tiny legs, and turned round and round in circles – Hannah couldn't stand flies, or the noises they made, but this seemed to her like a cry of pain. She picked up the dressing table mirror that obviously belonged to Rozia, with its gold handle and gold edges, and picture on the back of a little girl in blue flounces and big petticoats; Hannah slammed it on top of the fly. There was the sound of cracking glass; she picked the mirror up and saw a great gash, like a cut, as a splinter fell out on to the table, and then she saw that the fly was still alive. She looked at Margaret.

'You shouldn't be so dramatic, Mum,' her daughter said as she squashed the fly with the palm of her hand.

Anthony arrived late, he had been to a meeting at Smith Square – the prize had come at last. He had been offered the chance to fight a seat at a forthcoming by-election.

'She's rather attractive and he is in the right image – they've got a child too. Whilst of course we could never be as naive as the Americans, one can't ignore that Kennedy bandwagon and its effect. Issues can become clogged in the voters' minds, but a good-looking MP is never forgotten,' Hunter had said when he proposed Anthony, who of course was told none of that.

Anthony waited until the tea was over before he revealed his news. He was not surprised when Hannah immediately offered her support in every way.

'It's important for you that Margaret and I do our bit, and so we will.'

'You won't drag Margaret around with you,' Rozia said, and there was no question in her tone.

'Of course she will want to support her Daddy, it's a chance for us to be a family, together.'

That night after Margaret had gone to bed, Hannah decided that in keeping with her role as the involved wife she should find out about Anthony's policies – she realized she knew nothing of his attitudes. She went into his study to talk to him, but found him slumped in his reading chair. He looked like a crumpled sack, and she could see quite clearly that he had gained weight. His mouth was open, and he was snoring a little.

She noticed the draft of a speech on the side table and started to read it – her immediate reaction was of disgust; Anthony was a capitalist, committed to preserving the values of old England, and as a socialist of the new order Hannah realized quite how much she was going to have to compromise herself. His speech was a prediction of what the welfare state would be like in forty years' time – he argued that it would breed parasites living off the system, taking dole money because it would be more advantageous than getting a job. Hannah swallowed quickly, feeling quite hot, and then she noticed a little white sheet of paper. On it were the words 'Sally Phillips Hampstead 1898' with hearts drawn all around them. It wasn't Anthony's writing. Oh God she thought, not now, not when I am really trying to make the marriage work.

Inadvertently she glanced at Anthony, who was watching her.

'I am reading your speech,' she said lamely.

'And you don't like it.'

'I like this even less,' she said, holding the note in her open palm.

'What's that?' he asked.

'A lady's telephone number.'

'Well, what's my room mate David Smith up to? I borrowed the pad from him, he must have hidden it between the pages.'

Anthony got up and came over to Hannah; he bent down and kissed her, letting his hand slide under her bra, working her nipples. Hannah tried not to think of David Smith with his corpulent bachelor body which had never seemed to her to offer the kind of sensual delights that this note obviously planned, but her heart told her that Anthony wouldn't cheat on her now – not now – and she arched her back and opened her mouth to take his tongue.

After his adoption, Anthony went up to his prospective constituency every week. He stayed with the chairman of the local Conservative Party, Sir Alec Rose and his wife Joan. Anthony rather liked Joan, a big blonde who responded nicely to his innuendoes. It was just enough to keep his spirits up; he found that he didn't miss Hannah.

Hannah knew she should spend the times when Anthony was away with Margaret, but she was working on a new programme about British rock and roll stars so her daughter stayed instead with Rozia and Jerzy whilst she courted Tommy Steele, Lonnie Donnegan and the like – she rather enjoyed it. She tried to tell Margaret about the music and the fans and the discipline, but she was never interested.

The were all just getting used to the new pattern of their lives when Alec Rose telephoned Anthony to say that he felt the family should be seen together at a local garden party.

'We are a small town, Anthony, gone this way and that

in elections because of the foundry and the brickworks. Whichever way folks vote they do like a family, so it wouldn't hurt to have the wife and child there.' So it was agreed that Anthony would go up on Thursday evening, and Hannah and Margaret would follow on Friday afternoon. Anthony was quite pleased with that arrangement. It would give him some hours with Joan before Hannah arrived. Alec always went to bed at ten-thirty.

Rozia delivered Margaret, all shiny and pretty in her navy school coat and a smocked dress that Rozia herself had bought her, to Hannah in the reception of the BBC.

'Is this where you work?' Margaret asked.

Hannah could see she was nervous and she wondered why. 'Yes, would you like to see my office?' she asked.

'Yes.'

'Come on then.'

'And Grandma?'

'No, Grandma's going,' Rozia said, giving her a kiss.

Margaret shot a worried look towards Rozia and then stood on her tiptoes and hung her arms around her grandmother's neck.

'Have a lovely weekend. Give my love to Jerzy and don't let him eat all the cheesecake – leave some for me.' The intimacies flowed from Margaret to Rozia, and Hannah felt left out.

She kissed her mother perfunctorily. 'Thanks,' she said, scooping Margaret up and propelling her towards the lift.

When she got to the office she showed Margaret where she sat, which telephones she used, Desmond said 'hello' and then there was nothing else for them to see.

'Shall we go?' she said.

Margaret nodded and let her mother take her hand. Hannah felt ridiculous.

They took a taxi to King's Cross. Hannah glanced at Margaret and saw that the little girl was drawing patterns

337

on the window of the cab. She thought of herself at thirteen, and she tried to remember her feelings.

'I used to do that,' she said. 'Grandma used to be irritated.'

Margaret felt lost without Rozia and Jerzy. She loved him, not as much as Rozia of course, but he was so kind to her — she hadn't forgotten how much time and trouble he had taken in making her swing, she thought those were the best hours they had ever spent together.

And now she was with her mother. Their Saturdays were easy, they had a lot to do. Sundays were best, on Sundays Daddy was there, and they went to museums and did interesting things. It was a shame that Mummy always looked so bored.

But this weekend was different. She'd been pushed into her best clothes and told it was important that she behaved well. The thought of having to meet strangers terrified her.

Hannah noticed tears in her child's eyes. She wanted to help Margaret, she put her hand on her arm. 'Come and sit next to me,' she said. 'I am a little scared too.'

When they arrived at the station, Anthony was waiting for them. He rushed over and kissed them both, Hannah on the lips, Margaret on the cheek. He took Margaret's hand and Hannah noticed with a pang that her fingers curled around his, gripping them tight.

The weekend passed in a whirl of being nice to people, of people being nice back. But Hannah felt as if she were an interloper into someone else's life. She watched herself shaking hands, pushing Margaret forward, saying the right things, and she was surprised at how good she was at it. The night she arrived she and Anthony had intercourse, using each other for their own individual pleasure. How selfish we are, Hannah thought in a moment of clarity. Neither of us gives, so how can we expect Margaret to be any different?

The following morning they shared the breakfast table with their daughter in the large draughty dining room of the old-fashioned hotel which was to be their home that weekend.

The food was awful: lukewarm tea, soggy bread, and greasy eggs.

'Uughhh!' Margaret said for all of them.

'You don't have to eat it,' Hannah said.

'You'd better. Wait till you taste Joan's lunch,' Anthony said morosely.

Hannah was aware of Joan's hostility immediately, and she understood Anthony's relationship with the woman. She hoped Joan wouldn't read too much into it. 'I am his wife,' she wanted to say, 'I am the one who is permanent. I have to be.'

She didn't say anything, but rode the other woman's unkind assessment easily, and turned her own not inconsiderable charm on to Alec Rose.

'Your wife is absolutely delightful,' she overheard him tell Anthony.

Joan overheard too. 'We ought to get ready for the garden party,' she said. 'Would you like to use my bedroom?' she offered unwillingly.

'Thank you,' Hannah said. She took Margaret up with her.

They both stood in the doorway, awed by the two enormous mahogany beds that sat square side by side. There was a large mahogany wardrobe, a tallboy and a very large dressing table. Margaret got up on to the stool and looked at herself in the mirror.

'Do I really look like Daddy?' she asked.

'Yes,' Hannah answered. She came near to her daughter, so that Margaret could examine her own long fair hair, her brown eyes, different in shape to the child's, the little nose, the full mouth, the wide flat cheekbones.

'See, your face is thin, slender – Daddy's bone structure. Mine is flatter.'

Hannah took Margaret's hands and put them over her face, making her feel the bones, the structure, and then she put her child's hand on her own face.

'I understand,' Margaret said gravely, and took her hand away.

Hannah pulled her hair up from her neck. 'It's easier to see without hair,' she said. 'I know what I'll do. I'll find a photograph of Daddy when he was your age, before he matured, then you'll understand it.'

'Do you have a photograph of yourself?' Margaret asked.

'Yes, I do,' Hannah said quickly. She could feel her heart beating. 'Would you like to have it?' she asked.

'I would like to see it,' Margaret answered.

Mother and daughter stared at each other in the mirror, both of them wanting to hold on to the moment.

Joan Rose burst into her bedroom. 'Are you finished?' she asked.

Hannah and Margaret were both dressed in blue. Margaret looked beautiful. She wore a blue taffeta party dress that Rozia had made. Hannah had to admire her mother's skills. She wore a pale blue suit. She'd bought it especially.

Margaret was the centre of attention. And Anthony played her for all she was worth, showing her off at the penny dip and on the roundabout.

Margaret found to her utter amazement that she didn't miss Rozia, her parents were being so nice to her. She loved the attention they lavished on her. It was just the other people who bothered her.

On Sunday they went to church. Margaret noticed that her mother didn't say any of the prayers. She wondered why. Lunch was at the hotel. The table was large, there were twelve people seated at it, all eating more of the disgusting food. She tried to eat the Brussels sprouts but they weren't crisp like at home. They were wet and tasteless.

She tried to attract Anthony's attention, but he was talking to that awful woman Joan something. And Mummy was involved with the woman's husband. She decided to prod Anthony under the table, and share the miseries of the Brussels sprouts with him. She lifted the tablecloth a little so that she could position her foot nearer her father's. She noticed shiny black shoes, Daddy's shoes, but between both his feet was a white one and the white shoe was rubbing at his trouser leg. She wouldn't be able to get her own small foot anywhere near his. She sat back on her chair; suddenly she missed Rozia terribly, and she couldn't help crying.

Hannah saw her daughter's tears and then she noticed Joan's hand in Anthony's lap – pressing into him. She recalled the note she had found in his speech and she knew it hadn't been sent to David Smith. She saw her body cleaving to Anthony's on the floor of the study whilst that note had lain on the table. It hadn't been there the next day; had he rung the lady when he got to his chambers? Had he done to her what he had done to Hannah the night before? Had his hand and mouth moved in the same way on that other skin as they had moved on hers? And Joan, was she fondled as Hannah had been fondled? Her palms were wet and she felt sick.

Hannah knew it was over then, over and done with. It wasn't just Anthony's infidelities, it was her too, she didn't fit in, she wasn't like Anthony, she was different. With perfect clarity she saw the dinner Rozia had prepared for Anthony when they had got engaged. She remembered her embarrassment at the obvious differences between Anthony and her parents, how she had wanted to be like Anthony – but she wasn't like him at all. She was the outsider, just like Rozia. She wanted to cry, but she held the tears back, this was not the time. The peach had been split, straight down the centre, it had been easy to cut through the flesh but the hard kernel was another thing, and now Anthony had done it for her.

341

She said nothing over the lunch, forcing herself to swallow the tasteless food, but later, as they walked away from the hotel, she said to Anthony quietly enough, 'Immediately this election is over I shall be getting a divorce.'

—PART 2—
A Single Woman

A SHADOW FROM...

Chapter Ten

———◆———

The reality of the divorce hit Hannah hard. She suddenly found herself a single woman. And after all the years of marriage, albeit an inadequate one, the realities were awesome. But mostly it was the bitterness that horrified her. There were moments, in the early months, when she might have changed her mind, but Anthony's hatred made sure she could not. Sometimes too there was regret and remorse, but she couldn't do anything about that.

For a while she and Anthony lived on in the same house, but separately. That was bad, but finally she was able to find herself a flat in Maida Vale. It was on the ground floor of a large Edwardian house. It had four rooms and an enormous kitchen. The lounge had large French windows that opened on to a small messy garden that smelt of honeysuckle in the right season.

It was easier after she moved, she took pleasure in organizing her flat. It didn't have the formality of the house. She had a squashy couch and comfortable chairs, and she liked to have her flowers heaped together in large vases. Her books were piled up on the floor in the lounge, and her desk was always littered with her work.

But there was no one to change a plug. If she wanted to take off a bottle top and it was stuck, there was no one with greater physical strength to do it. The long nights after the crowded days were not the solace she had expected. At first it was comfortable to be alone, not to have to make conversation with a disinterested partner, but soon she realized that unless she made plans when Margaret was not there, she wouldn't hear another human voice until the child returned.

Anthony had been elected to Parliament. Hannah was very pleased for him – even though he told her he had won to spite her for leaving him.

One time, when he came to collect Margaret – they tried to keep those times unacrimonious, but it wasn't always easy, one or the other had right on their side, one or the other was resentful, and their roles changed as if they were on a seesaw – Hannah tried to explain that his promiscuity had broken her. As he left, Anthony asked her if she had ever wondered why he had gone to other women – it certainly wasn't because he didn't love her.

Hannah was deeply shaken.

Later that evening she wrote to her lawyer and reiterated her previous instructions that she wanted no money from Anthony, just support for Margaret . . . they had sold the house, she had half, enough to buy the flat. As she sealed the envelope she wondered about her motives. At first she had said, 'I work, it would be wrong to take money,' but was the real truth that she did feel ultimately responsible? She had refused to sue for adultery – so it would have to be the long-drawn-out process of desertion.

Margaret, of course, had to change schools. Hannah had been extremely worried until she met the assistant head teacher, Sally Harcourt. She had long black hair and fair skin that had an almost translucent quality about it. She wore no make-up, and on the day they met, was dressed quite plainly in a fawn sweater and matching skirt. Hannah was quite taken with her.

She changed her job, moving into television – it took a lot of energy, and a lot of nerve. Hannah was not quite as confident as she needed to be, and there was a lot of resistance to a sound radio producer. At first she worked as an assistant, but after two years, and a proven record as a member of the National Union of Journalists, she was allowed to make her first programme – the subject was alcoholism.

Hannah needed a secretary and she found a small red-headed dynamo called Natalie. They connected immediately. Natalie had been employed in the television casting department, but she was bored with anxious actors and omnipotent casting directors, she told Hannah. Natalie's boyfriend Peter was immediately informed that he would have to take second place to her work until the programme was 'in the can'. Hannah was impressed not only by the vernacular, but also by her very honest priorities – she had been like that with Anthony. Her director was Michael Chester, young, anxious and good . . . at least he assured Hannah that he was good.

She reined herself in and prepared for work, having arranged for Margaret, yet again, to stay with Rozia during the week. She felt badly about that, but there was no way she couldn't. Hannah knew she ought to talk to Margaret about it, so that she would know how she felt – it was just that she didn't have the time right then.

She went to King's Cross late at night, braving hostility and fumes to talk to the drunks whose only homes were the pavements. She found sleeping hostels where despair was normality, and she persuaded these men and women to appear on the screen with their vulnerabilities and weaknesses exposed to view. She cajoled housewives in pubs and supermarkets, she pushed their husbands and their boyfriends into volunteering guilty secrets and her coup was to trap those who believed themselves to be the captains, the reformed and reformers, into public admissions. When she had finished her programme its content was formidable and she was exhausted. She had not stopped except to eat a snatched egg or bowl of cereal, and to sleep.

She didn't listen to Rozia's complaints and tried not to see Margaret's withdrawal.

'It's only for about three weeks,' she would say when she rushed in for her statutory half-hour before work every day.

The film crew eyed her suspiciously; she was a woman. They were shocked at her filming schedule, but homemade soup, brewed late at night whilst she checked the script, her charm, and her heavy quota of overtime brought a thaw in their attitude. They began to respect her work, they made her one of them. When a drunk threatened, one of their number would move in and protect her. When her feet ached Michael would rub them, and when she wanted to cry with tiredness Natalie comforted and urged her on, as she did the others.

The head of documentaries, David Lawley, questioned her on the overtime, but when he saw the first rushes he said nothing – Hannah had come up with a masterpiece.

It was the BBC's official entry at Montreux – it won.

After her triumph, Hannah found that the initial discomforts faded and her life took on a new pattern. She entertained a lot, she had a wide circle of acquaintances, a few of them close, but she missed Esther. She got used to Margaret staying with Anthony every other weekend, admitting only to herself that she had actually begun to enjoy the times of solitude. It was certainly easier to entertain when Margaret wasn't there. She could enjoy an extra glass of wine or smoke the obligatory joint without the worry of having to get up in the morning.

But she was beginning to worry about Rozia. To both their distress Sybil had become quite ill with her arthritis and couldn't get out very much. Martin cared for her as much as he was able, but they bickered now. Rozia did what she could too, but she admitted she found her visits there very depressing.

Rozia was preoccupied with other things. She had noticed

that Jerzy now spent a lot of time with a pretty Hungarian countess with short blonde hair and a little dog – they talked of hunting and reminisced about experiences that they had not actually shared.

She did admit to Hannah that she was feeling very tired, but she could not tell her daughter that her mind was playing outrageous tricks. She saw the Hungarian countess, she saw her husband, she saw the intimacies between them – and she agonized over the image of familiar tendernesses offered to another body.

Hannah knew nothing of her mother's anguish, but she saw her loneliness and for the first time in many years she wished Jouk had not died. She felt guilty – she had not mourned him as she should have done, but had forgotten him in the longing for her own father.

Once, when Hannah visited, Jerzy was not there at all. Rozia said, 'He's been out all day working with the countess. He is designing some flats for her. She has a very large house and she wants to convert it. Of course I am glad he is working again, he likes restoring beautiful houses.'

With unexpected care Hannah knelt and eased her mother's shoes from her feet. She placed them on the small tapestry pouf that Rozia had made when they visited Poland. Hannah had always wondered at the significance of her mother turning such a beautiful piece of work into a place for feet – originally it had been the seat of a chair.

'On the first morning in Poland I saw Jouk help his father on with his shoes. I was shocked to see him do such a thing for another man.'

'And now you do this for me,' Rozia said quietly.

'Yes,' Hannah answered her.

After the success of the alcohol documentary Hannah produced a series on the young, on Eichmann's trial, the changing face of the Commonwealth, and post-austerity England.

And after the plethora there was nothing . . . 'The brain cells are dead,' she told Natalie. 'I have slots to fill and not a thought in my head.'

'Look around you,' her secretary said comfortably.

'Look around me – there is Kennedy and Mrs Kennedy and Kennedy and all the other Kennedys.'

'Then do the Poles again, this time in Poland.'

'Not a bad idea,' she expostulated. Natalie was filing her nails, a habit Hannah hated normally.

'I've got to go to Michael Chester's showing of his new Hollywood movie. I don't think I'm going to enjoy it, so I can sit there and quietly plan my own programme in my head.'

The viewing theatre was crowded by the time Hannah got there. There were groups sitting and talking animatedly. A few guests stood by the door clinging to glasses of rough wine and stale cheese sandwiches as if they might never eat again. It seemed to Hannah as if everyone was talking to someone. They all knew each other, but Hannah couldn't see anybody she knew.

She found an empty seat and sat down gratefully, clutching her handbag on her knees. She glanced around and saw Michael surrounded by his peers who were here to judge him, and perhaps condemn him.

'Who honestly loves a rival's success?' one of the better known reviewers said, his voice carrying above the throng.

Michael came over and greeted her. 'Sorry I can't stay with you, pet,' 'pet' was an addition to his vocabulary that Hannah didn't recognize, 'but I've got to be seen doing my bit at the chat. Are you all right on your own? I thought you might have brought someone.' Hannah smiled at Michael. She had forgotten how much she liked him.

'I'm fine,' she said. 'I'll watch your film, love it and go home.'

'You may not love it. Frankly I –'

'Michael, how wonderful to see you,' said a fat man with a cigar and a moon face which should have been generous – but for his thin lips. She saw another man beside him, tall, slender with a slight almost imperceptible stoop.

'Marvellous,' she heard Michael say as he embraced the newcomer. He turned back to Hannah. 'Brian Webster, this is Hannah Simpson. Look after each other – Brian's American.'

Hannah didn't want to look after anyone, especially an American.

'Michael thinks we should sit together.' The man's voice was light.

'Yes,' Hannah said. Suddenly she felt uncomfortable.

'But there is no place next to you,' he said.

'No, there isn't. Why don't you sit over there?' she pointed to a seat on the other side of the small viewing theatre.

'But then I don't get to sit with you.'

'That doesn't matter.'

'But Michael said we should keep each other company.'

'I don't think he means that we . . .' Hannah bit her words back. She realized she was being rude to a total stranger. 'I am sorry,' she continued, forcing a small amount of charm, 'but I don't see two seats together.'

'Over there,' he said. 'Come on, let's make the director happy . . . if it doesn't bother you.'

Hannah got up and tripped over a step. He steadied her arm whilst inwardly she cursed her clumsiness.

'It's difficult to see in this light,' he said.

Muted pastels of stylized long shots, blurred enlargements of the human form sharpened by harsh dialogue – an indulgence of topical protest skilfully portrayed without substance moved across the screen with agonizing slowness. But indulgence with tantalizing flesh entangled in a montage of eroticism unnerved Hannah. She felt the man next to her, smelt him almost. Embarrassed, she tightened her thighs. She tried to concentrate but she knew his eyes were on her not the screen – analytical, lustful? she didn't know which. She couldn't look back at him.

A screech of pain and blood filled the screen, red tomato ketchup spreading out like a poppy in the field, staining pretty pink flesh . . . and then blackness.

'Wonderful, wonderful,' the voices erupted. 'A success.' Hand clapping, foot stomping. The lights were on. Michael Chester was a star.

'It was shit,' Brian said softly.

He took her for a drink, acidic red wine in a crowded pub near to closing time.

'But it's better than that place,' he said.

'Yes,' Hannah had to agree.

She examined him. He had a broad, almost flat face, rather beautiful grey-green eyes, and his hair was thick, and dark – but she could not stop looking at his mouth. It was a very sensual mouth.

He looked familiar; it was ridiculous, but she was sure she had seen him before.

'Are you here on holiday, or are you working?'

'Sabbatical. Away from the family.'

'Oh, do you have a big family?' How ridiculous, how could she be disappointed – everyone was married.

'Just normal. A wife and two children.' Was he looking at her too hard?

'How long are you staying?'

'I don't know.'

'Time please, ladies and gentlemen. Drink up.'

Brian looked confused.

'You've obviously just arrived. Licensing hours,' Hannah said by way of explanation. 'The pubs close at eleven. He's warning everyone.'

'You mean we have to leave?'

'Yes.'

They found an Italian restaurant which served imitation spaghetti and weak coffee on flowered tablecloths. There were candles stuck into wine bottles and waiters making a lot of noise for atmosphere.

'Eat. It isn't bad,' he said, digging his fork into the pasta.

'No,' Hannah agreed, and concentrated on shovelling the food into her throat. 'How do you know Michael?' she asked.

'We met when he covered the Democratic Party convention in 1960.'

'Will you tell him what you think of his film?'

'Yes.'

Hannah smiled. He was lucky, what would she say? Criticism never came easily to her.

'You're a producer.'

'Yes, documentaries, but then you know that.'

'Yes. I have seen one of your programmes . . . on alcoholism. It was good.'

'Thank you.' Hannah flushed up from the praise.

'Well, you know I am married with two kids. What about you?'

'A modern lady. Divorced with one kid.'

'That's modern?'

They walked after the meal. London at night in spring was a soft city. Without traffic the streets were less harsh, less masculine. The parks, with the trees sporting their new leaves, made strange patterns against the sky, almost like giant doodles on a blue/black pad. There was a moon, stars, streetlamps making silvery indents against the night. They didn't talk, their feet moved in unison. Hannah wanted to stroke him.

Instead she said, 'It's late. I need a taxi.'

He hailed one, declined the offer of a lift, ushered her in. 'Good night. Thank you for a nice evening.' He slammed the cab door shut and was gone. And she was in the little black box, speeding back to the child who had expected her hours before. She had arranged a babysitter. She didn't like asking Rozia to babysit at night. Bernice Adams had died just a few months previously, it had jolted Hannah for she had suddenly realized that Rozia was fifty-seven years of age, that in three years' time she would be sixty.

By the time Hannah settled down in her bed, it was two-fifteen. She wasn't tired, and she touched her tingling body. Damn that American, she didn't want to feel open. She masturbated often, normally orgasm was quick – but tonight it was different, and she turned into the pillow aching to hold the man.

Unable to sleep, she watched the sky change from black/blue to ink/blue, to dust-grey. It started to rain. In the small hours Hannah's failures lined themselves up. She saw herself through the stages of her life: the child, the adolescent, the young woman and now – in her prime. A woman of her age, she told herself, should be established, set in the pattern of her life; she shouldn't expect change. And yet Hannah did expect it, she had been gearing her life towards that end. She had followed the wrong paths, had made a catastrophic error of judgement in her marriage, but the desire had always been there. What right had she to imagine that she was any different from millions of other women who accepted their lot? What arrogance to evaluate her own life as different? She had pursued her career, left her daughter with her mother, broken her marriage, because she had believed it was right for her. And what were the results of that labour? A lonely child, and a lonely woman. He body still stung with its longing.

She got up and went into the kitchen. She made coffee, enjoying the smell of the ground beans as the water filtered through . . . drip, drip, into the pot.

She had let Rozia take over responsibility for Margaret without understanding the full implications. Hannah made herself think back to Margaret's babyhood. She faced herself as unsatisfactory mother; she saw her daughter emotionally crippled by her own lack of caring. She pulled herself back from over-dramatization. That in itself was a solace. Mental flagellation is as comfort-giving and pointless as the confessional box, she told herself.

Hannah found herself observing her thirteen-year-old daughter at breakfast. She noticed that her daughter was pale, that there were black shadows under her eyes. It was extraordinary how one could observe just such a physical sign of stress even in a loved one and feel sympathy, but it never reached into the guts in quite the same way as when one observed it with a child.

'Aren't you having cereal?' Hannah asked. She always set out packets on the table, far too many for just two people, but habits are hard to break.

'No. Not today.' Margaret was buttering herself some toast.

'You look tired.'

'I am a bit.'

'Are you sleeping?'

'Yes.' The response was clipped, irritated.

Hannah reached for a slice of toast herself. She always made several slices and put them in a toast rack. Anthony had insisted on a toast rack. He said that if you laid bread down it went soggy.

She buttered the toast and then spread it liberally with honey. She took a bite, hearing the noise the crunch made. She was even aware of herself chewing.

'How are you getting on at your new school?' she asked.

'Fine.'

'Margaret, I am getting monosyllabic responses,' Hannah said carefully. 'Have you made friends?'

'Yes, but it isn't the same is it?'

'It will be.'

'Will it?'

355

Neither of them spoke. Hannah glanced around her kitchen. It was a large room, painted white with a wooden floor. She had a couch at one end and bookshelves. There were flowers, herbs and pots of 'interesting' food. It had a comfortable feel about it.

'I love this room,' she said.

'You are obviously very happy in the flat,' Margaret answered.

Hannah wanted to say something, but she could think of nothing appropriate. She felt terribly responsible for her daughter's unhappiness and she didn't know what to do about it.

Rozia's life with Jerzy had a pattern – she opened the café while he made the breakfast – but on that particular morning he left early before she had awoken. He was doing some work for the countess. They had to go across London to look at a house she wanted to convert into flats. 'We need to be there by nine,' she had said.

'I won't disturb you,' Jerzy had told Rozia, 'but I will have to leave at seven.'

So when she awoke at eight o'clock he had already gone, but he had left a note: 'I will be back by five o'clock. We will have dinner, I shall cook, it is already in the refrigerator half-prepared. And then perhaps we will listen to Chopin.'

Rozia couldn't help but look inside the refrigerator. She found chicken paprika – she popped a finger in the sauce and licked it, the taste was good.

She dressed in a favourite blouse and a black skirt. She ruffled her now short hair with her hands – she knew it was going grey, but at fifty-seven she thought it appropriate. She checked her make-up and went down to open the café.

She liked the mornings best; a few regular English customers came, drank her coffee and left, but mostly there were the expatriates who kissed her hand in the old way, played chess and discussed the latest play or concert with such a passion that they might have been talking of personal affairs, but then music and literature and politics and science were matters to be treated with passion. Rozia felt comfortable with them.

Later, after she cleared up, she realized that it was five-thirty and Jerzy was not home. She was tired so she sat down in her favourite chair, and she must have fallen asleep because he woke her when he came in at seven-fifteen.

'I am sorry, Rozia, but the builder is a Pole, we started to talk and –'

'Yes,' she said, interrupting him, suddenly not wanting to hear the excuses – she could see him with the countess and he was breaking her heart, the pain was terrible.

Jerzy went over to the gramophone and put on a record. He had realized for some time, of course, what was going on inside Rozia's head and he was very angry. He had resolved to say nothing, to wait until she saw that her accusations were unjust, but now, as much as he disliked confrontation, he knew he had to challenge Rozia – there was no question of another woman, he had told the countess that when she had betrayed an interest.

He turned back to Rozia. 'I realize that you believe there is something going on between the countess and myself and it disturbs me that you could think such a thing. If I didn't appreciate how little self-confidence you have in yourself, I should be extremly distressed. You have to stop it, Rozia, there is nothing for you to agonize over. You are putting both of us, you and me, into a position of distrust . . . and it is all in your mind.'

He squatted in front of her, took her hands into his, feeling how cold they were and clammy. 'I am a weak man, in some ways, but I am not a disloyal one. I love you and your doubt of me is a sickness that could hurt us both if you do not deal with it now.'

Rozia wanted to believe Jerzy. She noticed that his normally clean shirt cuffs were grimy – he had obviously been working in dust – and she would have touched him, but inside the pain was still there; she could see the truth in what he was saying, so why wouldn't the pain stop?

Chapter Eleven

━━━◆━━━

Hannah's day took her over. An editing session with a difficult director, planning meetings for a new documentary series on the youth culture, and then, unexpectedly, a call from the director of programmes.

'Hannah. Come up to the office will you?'

'Oh God. What does he want?' Hannah said to Natalie.

'Another brilliant esoteric idea that won't work on the screen or perhaps he might actually give you an answer on the Polish proposal,' Natalie replied without looking at Hannah. She was concentrating on her typing. She had to, she wasn't very good at it.

Hannah walked out of her office and down the corridor to the swing doors that separated management from programming. There was a different carpet on the other side, green instead of brown, and it was of a thicker texture. There was a different atmosphere too – quieter, they murdered you without the shouting. She supposed it was the same in every industry. At least she knew not to fight the system, just to diplomatically sidetrack it where possible.

'Ah Hannah . . . there you are.' The director of programmes was a small, stocky man once renowned for his innovative ideas, but now lassoed and neatly tied by the role of administrator.

'Poland,' he said, finishing the dregs of a cup of coffee. 'It's a good idea – do it.'

'Bear in mind I'm interested in the implications of the Church as the symbol of resistance against the state. The Church and Poland are intertwined – doesn't matter what totalitarianism tries to do, the agnostic will ally himself with Rome in order to register his protest – it doesn't matter against whom as long as there is a cause to fight for.'

'Errum . . . Well, all right then.'

Hannah got up and walked to the door.

'Oh, by the way,' he added, 'this came in this morning. Bloody good journalist. I know his work. He got a Pulitzer for covering the Bay of Pigs. Like to use him. Perhaps he might have an idea for this. John would be too light and I think we need a face on the screen. Anyway, meet him. See if you get on . . .'

Hannah know even before the letter was in her hand who it was from.

She asked Natalie to ring him and make an appointment.

'What day?' her secretary asked, leaning over her diary.

'Whenever . . .' Hannah tried not to listen as her secretary arranged for Brian Webster to come and see her at three o'clock the next day.

He was already waiting in her office when she got back from a quick liquid lunch with a friend in the script department, and it flustered her to find him leaning over her desk. He wasn't due until three o'clock. She quickly glanced at her watch . . . it was two-fifteen.

'I'm early,' he said. 'I had hoped to invite you to lunch, but you had already gone.'

'You've been here since one o'clock?'

'No, one-fifteen. I was late.'

Hannah moved towards her side of the desk, feeling more comfortable behind its bulk.

'Thank you for the nice time the other evening. I honestly didn't think we'd meet again.'

'I knew you were working for Tristar. That gave me an unfair advantage. I knew where to reach you without you knowing that I did. I could think over whether I should call you or not.'

'You needed to think about it?' Hannah said lightly.

'I am married,' he said with a shrug, 'and I like my wife. Can I get a coffee?' he asked.

'Of course,' she said quickly, embarrassed. 'But it's quite disgusting. It comes from a machine.'

As if on demand, Natalie arrived back from her lunch. She collected the cups she kept in her drawer and carried them down to the machine in the corridor.

'Natalie doesn't like paper mugs,' Hannah said by way of explanation. 'Why do you want to work here?'

'It gives me an excuse,' he said quietly, 'not to go back for a while. I told you, I like my wife, but I am just not ready to take up the reins again. At least not for a while.'

Hannah watched the calm face carefully. There was little to read in it.

'Everyone is doing Germany – why not look at a country which has been Communist since '47?' she said quickly. She looked down at her desk, ruffled through a file. 'How about Poland, and what it means for a Catholic people under an atheist regime. But you have to understand, Brian, what I mean by Catholic. The Church is more than a religion.'

'I'd like to look at some material. On the surface it doesn't seem to be my kind of thing.'

'Well, I . . .'

'But attacking the Soviets might make my homecoming a little more acceptable to middle America.'

'Oh. The Administration doesn't like your style of reporting?'

'The Administration doesn't bother me. But my father-in-law bothers my wife.'

'And your father-in-law is middle America,' Hannah said.

Brian smiled at her. He held his hand out for her. 'I'll look into your project and I'll call you.'

'Wouldn't you like us to provide you with research facilities?' Hannah asked.

'No, thank you. I'll do my own and let you know whether I think I'm your man or not.'

'Don't we get a chance to look at you and see if you are right for us?' Hannah said quickly.

'Of course. ABC have my material. You can make your evaluations too.'

Hannah coloured up. She knew she had been stupid, the director of programmes had already made it clear he wanted Brian, and knowing the director of programmes the deal was probably already done. But she didn't want him to leave, she wanted him to stay all afternoon, to agree to do the programme – she wanted to know him better. He left before Natalie came back with the coffee.

Brian walked away from the Tristar building deep in thought. Of course he wanted to do the Polish programme, but there was something about Hannah Simpson. He was disturbed by her – he knew he was attracted to her, but he had a feeling that now was not the time to dabble. It might have repercussions that he couldn't deal with, not now . . .

Brian Webster was born in Oklahoma City in the State of Oklahoma in 1928. The Depression had never touched his family. They didn't invest in stocks – nor were they in trade. Just middle-class Americans who prided themselves on their pursuit of good values. Good values meant the worship of flag and country along with God . . . in that order. He was the child of middle-aged parents who believed in the maxim of a child being seen but not heard. They brought him up to know that America was a special nation – more favoured than any other. Isolationism was comfortable – they had what was rightfully theirs. They had no needs that were not nourished from their own land. Europe was very far away.

George Webster was a lawyer. He was sure that he could have run for public office. He would most certainly have been elected. After all, everyone liked him; but what they didn't know was that at times he was beset by such anxiety that in the quietness of his home, when the mental stress was just too much to bear, he would turn on Emily, his wife, and beat her in a desperate attempt to establish control of all that assailed him. He never hit her on the face. He concentrated on her back, and the constant barrage had left her with a damaged spine. Neither Emily nor George understood what caused his violence and it didn't occur to them to find out why George hurt. Emily never went to the hospital about her back. The doctors would realize how it had been caused and she wouldn't have been able to stand the humiliation. So they were tied, George and Emily, irrevocably, and the shame was borne by both of them.

But they felt nothing but pride for their only son. He was a pleasing child who never caused a sleepless night. He crawled when he should, walked when he should, and his first intelligible words were uttered in keeping with the national average. He was neither embarrassingly bright nor worryingly slow. His grades put him into the top half of the class, and when he was sixteen he was selected to swim for the school. George was so pleased about it that he didn't beat Emily for a while. Emily for her part doted on her son. She would have liked another child, but she had only conceived once. She didn't talk about her feelings. She didn't think there was any point – who would have wanted to listen? She always shopped cautiously and Brian would know the day of the week by the menu. But there were always cakes. Emily enjoyed making them. She would spend hours titivating the swirls on her chocolate fudge cake. Sometimes, if she were icing, she would practise on spare pieces of paper. She was always careful to throw the telltale evidence away. George didn't approve of waste. Leftovers were always turned into unimaginative dishes to appease his sense of economy. Emily didn't care that they were unappetizing, she was much more interested in her cakes.

When the local boys came home from the war, Emily and George were at the railway station to add their greetings to those of the rest of the townsfolk. Brian always remembered that day: the bunting, the flag, the music, the cheering – and mostly the pride. He burst with love for the brave men who marched and waved. He wanted to be one of them, his chest bedecked with ribbons and medals. He wanted the crowd's approbation as much as he wanted to give it.

'One day, Dad, I'll go and fight for America too,' he said to his father.

'That's right son. You will and we'll welcome you back with a parade just as big and just as good as this one 'cause what you do for America, America will never forget.'

'Pray God he doesn't have to, George,' Emily muttered quietly.

'Why do you say that, Emily? If he has to go, he'll go like we all do.'

And so Brian grew up believing that America could never shame itself.

To the Websters' great joy, when Brian began to date girls he chose Barbara Maguire, the daughter of the local newspaper magnate. They were a match – Brian and Barbara – the town knew that. The lean, handsome young man and the pretty blonde princess who lived in a big house on Winchester Avenue, the smartest road in the town.

They came together quite naturally without gaucheness or pain. And when the hesitant hands on flesh grew curious, it was a mutual thing and their bodies found each other with anguish.

Their courtship was not only smiled upon by the Websters, but also by the Maguires. He was the mid-American blueprint – an athlete, a reasonable scholar, above all a WASP.

When Brian and Barbara were separated by their respective colleges they filled their lonely hours with anxious and loving letters and in their third year they announced, to the respective parents, their desire to wed. The Maguires invited the Websters to cocktails.

'Bourbon,' Erskine said, pouring George a large glass.

George didn't like bourbon. He preferred martini, but he didn't like to mention it so he took his glass and drank the contents as if they were medicine. Emily asked for a sherry.

'An English drink,' her host said. Neither she nor George knew if it was a compliment or not.

Emily tried to engage Mrs Maguire in conversation but her hostess, attired in a lemon dress and lemon shoes which almost matched the upholstery of her drawing room furniture but did little for her complexion, only responded with a nod or a no to Emily's cautious little forays into the social niceties.

'Well, let's get on with what we all know we are here to discuss,' the newspaper magnate said, alleviating Emily's conversational pressure. She admired his forthright manner. George would have circumvented the issue until, unable to avoid it, he would have had to acknowledge it. 'Of course, they are too young, but what can you do with them, George?' he continued. 'I think they should marry after college next year. I'll take Brian into my office. He can learn newspapers. And we'll buy their house. Can't have them living in a shack.'

George and Emily shared a look. It was beyond all they had hoped for. Erskine didn't mind. He didn't have a son. Barbara was his only and much loved child and if she wanted Brian then she would have him – just like the pony he had bought her when she was sixteen. That animal had served her well. No need to think otherwise of Brian.

But Brian didn't want to go into Erskine's business. He wanted to be a journalist and Barbara knew that. She waited in a coffee bar over the road when he went to see the editor of the Oklahoma journal who agreed, after reading the college magazine that Brian edited, to offer him employment.

'A hack reporter,' screamed the magnate. 'What kind of profession is that? How are you going to keep my daughter?'

'I am going to work too, Dad,' his daughter told him. She had no fear of her father, unlike her timid mother who had once, a long time ago, wanted to work herself.

'And what, pray, do you intend to do?' thundered Erskine.

'I am going to work as a children's counsellor.'

'And what about your own children?'

'We choose not to have them yet . . .' she said.

But Barbara found herself with child some two months before her wedding. 'I'll bring up your son and then I'll work,' she told Brian.

Of course it meant compromise. Brian had to change newspaper – accept his father-in-law's patronage and work for his establishment. But Brian loved Barbara and he loved the child growing within her.

Their marriage was a joyous occasion. The large house in Winchester Avenue smiled upon them and the lovers were joined in a union which they had both longed for. Emily wore grey silk and her back was healing quite nicely now. She had confided her pleasure in the art of cake-making to Barbara and to her trepidation and delight she had been requested to make and ice the wedding cake. Erskine hadn't been pleased – a homemade affair was hardly what he had in mind for his precious little girl – but when she sat upon his knee and whispered that it would be a benevolent gesture to the Websters and to Oklahoma City he had acquiesced willingly. However, even he had been stunned by Emily's skills. She had made three tiers and iced it lovingly, white on white. Lovebirds and lovers' knots encircled each tier and the top was crowned in iced roses. The years of practice had not gone to waste. She had hoped that George would say that he liked it, but he didn't. After the wedding, for some inexplicable reason he hit her. He said something about

366

her hogging the limelight. She didn't like being hurt again.

She took the car and drove it a little too fast along the highway. No one saw it crash. They wouldn't have known it was her if her diary hadn't been thrown clear of the flames.

They didn't tell Brian until he came back from his honeymoon. He cried for the woman who had held him and loved him. And Barbara understood even though her mother had never held or loved her.

They christened their son Emile Eugene. And not long after that Brian became deputy editor of the paper. He wrote a by-line every week on what was happening in Washington. He travelled backwards and forwards to the capital, and although Washington offered a lot of inducements Brian kept faith with his wife – he had no need of any other. Her body excited him, her mind stimulated him and she was his best friend. With the advent of the Kennedy years Brian was offered a job in Washington. He took it. He was a success and had regular television slots. Barbara, happily ensconced in an affluent suburb, presented him with a daughter – they called her Camille. Brian was now quite well known. Erskine still worked, but George had retired. He drank a bit, but everyone tolerated it. After all he did miss his wife so much.

For Brian and Barbara the life and the loving were good.

But all that was before Brian went to Vietnam. He had gone on an extended fact-finding mission. The collapse didn't take long. He had been in Vietnam for just eleven weeks. The stench of death, the corruption, the human suffering took their toll in his despair. His reports were not printed. His editors asked him for different information. The country did not want to know of the defeats or the surrenders. They wanted tales of bravery supported by tub-thumping patriotism. Brian could not give that to them. He saw the other side of politics. His assignment was cancelled.

He was ashamed of his collapse, seeing it as unforgivable weakness. He did not regret his stand, he had no complaint with his punishment, but he chose not to go back to America. He thought he might work in London for a while – and then he would go back.

He found a small bare flat in Hampstead where he kept photographs of his wife and his children by his bedside along with the letters they had written to him week after week since he had last seen them.

Barbara no longer asked him when he was coming home. She just let him know that he would be welcome whenever and however he wished. But then Barbara was a good woman, Brian knew that. At this moment he resented her strengths, he couldn't live with her. He had been tested and he had failed. She wouldn't have done.

So Hannah Simpson was out of the question. He wouldn't do the programme. He'd leave the project. There were other ideas, other television companies.

It was at the end of the day that Hannah found herself dialling Brian's telephone number – he had stayed in her head, almost as if he haunted her. She had to see him again.

'I have to drive north,' she heard herself saying, she hoped her voice didn't sound as unnatural to him as it did to her. 'Could I see you? I am sure I could excite you about Poland. I know the country well, I've been there – and my mother is Polish.' Was she being too pushy? – she hoped not.

'All right,' he said, and his tone was even, but not unwelcoming. 'Come for a drink now, if you like.'

It was a warm evening. The air in London was soft. Hannah let down the roof of her car, turned on her radio and drove up to Hampstead.

Brian saw her arrive, he had been watching for her. Somehow he had known as soon as he got back to his flat that she would call, and he knew as soon as he heard her voice that he would invite her to his flat. He waited for her to ring the doorbell, and still he waited for a moment. Then he let her in.

As she stood on the doorstep Hannah was suddenly very nervous, it was ridiculous of her to have come to this man's flat to talk about Poland – she could have seen him at the office. Whatever had possessed her to be so impulsive? She was angry with herself. She told herself to leave . . . and then he opened the door.

His flat was small – almost monk-like in its simplicity. A small double bed covered with a multicoloured rug was pushed in the corner. There was a table with a typewriter on it. A cream couch and armchair formed a right angle in front of an open fireplace. Three of the walls were lined with shelves. There were some books piled haphazardly, and others positioned neatly with their spines facing outwards. On the shelf nearest the typewriter Hannah could see typing and carbon paper. On the other wall was a large map of Vietnam.

On a small table close to the bed were a number of photographs of a woman and two children. Their frames were slightly facing the room. Hannah absorbed the positioning.

She sat down on the couch.

'Coffee?' Brian asked.

'Yes, thank you. At least I'll get mine,' she laughed.

'Yes, and it will be fresh. Excuse me a moment,' he said. He went out of the room into what Hannah assumed was the kitchen. She didn't follow him. She glanced up at the map. It was obviously an old one, the paper had buckled in its frame, and there was a small tear in one of the corners. She got up from the couch and walked over to it. It was French Vietnam, divided into its older territories of Tonkin, Annam and Cochin China. Hannah had a sick feeling as she studied it, almost as if she were looking at something dead. Like Europe before the war.

'That map was in my apartment in Saigon.'

'I have been told it is a beautiful city.'

'Was . . . A city full of the children of war, corruption, vice, squalor and dissipation is how I see Saigon. And it'll get worse. We will never defeat the VC, Hannah, simply because the Vietnamese don't want us to. They don't care. Can you imagine looking into a face and seeing nothing but eyes, mouth, nose . . . no emotion, no feeling? It's like looking into the faces of the dead. We are going to commit more and more men to that country, and eventually we are going to be fighting that war. Our government doesn't realize we can never win. The side we are with were the ones that fought with the French. The peasants, the people of the country, see them as the enemy. The Viet Cong are their own.'

'Your views can't be very popular in America.'

'No, they are not. But they are going to gain ground. The young, they'll start it. We already have the beginning, stemming from the civil rights movement. The protests are beginning, and God knows where they will end . . . Our standards, our double standards are unacceptable. We'll start with genuine and honest gut reaction to the lies, and then it'll grow until it becomes political and in itself manipulative.'

'How long have you felt like this?' Hannah asked.

'Since I was in Vietnam. I went there as an innocent. Do you know, you can take a taxi to the war? A driver for the right amount of money will heave you into his cab and take you to see the "game". But before I filed the reports that weren't popular the army used to transport me in helicopters. You got breakfast before you went. And as you took off you saw scenery that was touched by magic – rice fields, perfect in symmetry, trees, golden skies, no cable wires to cut across the view. It was perfection. And then you'd get to the front and you'd hit the ground and your legs would start to move fast, like pistons, getting you behind cover, because if you stayed out in the warm gentle sun, a hard cold bullet would knock your head off. I tasted fear. And then, after a day watching the battle that wasn't a battle, because the South Vietnamese soldiers didn't want to fight, I'd go back to Saigon and I'd have a delicious meal in a French restaurant. And there would be a willing, soft smelling girl if I wanted.'

His face was wrinkled suddenly, like an old man's. Hannah went over to him, she ran her hands over his, up his arms, wanting only to comfort, to ease the pain. She felt his hands on her neck, touching her hair, and then they were on her lips, prising them open, and his mouth was on hers. She wound her arms around his neck and smelt his heat. His hands opened her blouse and found her breasts and she arched towards him.

Brian pulled away from her and shook his head but then, unable to control anything but the wanting, he pulled her to him.

Her breasts were full and soft and tingling and hard. She felt his fingers digging into her back. They stumbled together to the bed. He took away her clothes, slowly. He paused only to fondle or caress each new part of her that was open to him. Then, watching her, slowly he dropped his own clothes on to the floor. Hannah could see his penis rising hard against his body. Suddenly she felt shy. He reached out and took her hand and put it on him. She closed her fingers around him and caressed him a little. He put his mouth to her breasts and began to lick and bite them. He rolled on top of her, kissed her and entered her. She lay back, feeling him in her, moving with him, enjoying his pleasure, anticipating his climax. But he came out of her and bent down on her, kissing her between her legs, using his tongue, and she felt as if she were drowning and she couldn't breathe. She wanted him to stop, but she couldn't have borne it if he had. And then there was the pain that wasn't a pain and she felt as if she were exploding. He turned her over on her back and she felt him in her again, and there were spasms of pleasure as she came again.

'I don't have to fight for it,' she whispered.

He looked hard into her eyes. 'I always have to fight, it's like climbing a mountain and wanting desperately to come down on the other side but you can't quite get over the top unless you push.'

Hannah reached up and pulled his head down to her and she pushed her tongue deep into his mouth. He bit her and drove hard into her and she wound her legs around him, across his back, pulling him closer. They rode hard, their skins making a sucking noise as they stuck together. Their breathing was fast and faster. She felt as if she couldn't stand the sensations any more and then, she first, he immediately after, they climaxed.

They held each other, they touched each other's faces and bodies and then he was inside her again, but it was gentle, unhurried and to Hannah's amazement she found herself surrendering to her body again, and she pulled Brian closer, holding him tightly, feeling his penis flash in and out of her, and she started to tremble.

'Look at me. I want to see you when you come,' he said.

'How could I? How could you . . . I?' Hannah whispered, curling into him.

'We did,' he interrupted, 'and I knew we would, the moment I first saw you. And I knew it would be like this. That's why I tried not to . . .'

'I am sorry, I –'

'No, don't say that. It is wonderful.' His hands touched her eyes, her nose, her mouth, her lips. They strayed down to her breasts and then over her stomach and down between her legs. 'You are incredible,' he said softly.

He got up from the bed, went into the bathroom and came back with some Kleenex and he cleaned her carefully.

She held out her arms to him, but he said 'bath'. And then she heard that the tap was already running. Brian picked her up in his arms and carried her into the little hall to his old-fashioned bathroom. He put her into the water and then got in with her. They soaped each other, taking their time. He cupped her face in his hands.

'Hannah, you have wonderful soft, caring eyes,' he said.

'So do you,' she said. She had thought they were grey, but now they looked almost blue/green. 'And you have obscenely long eyelashes,' she added, her fingers straying over his lips, soft and full-shaped, almost like a cupid's bow. She hated thin mouths, they denoted meanness, she was sure of that. Involuntarily her hand strayed to her own. What was it like?

'A tempting mouth, generous, open,' he said, and he let his fingers go between her lips, 'like those between your legs, so beautiful,' and his hands went down and he pulled open her thighs slightly and put his finger inside her, and using the pressure of the water with his other hand he gave her unbelievable pleasure. Hannah lay back in the bath, her hair hanging down into the water, her arms flung back over her head to let him have free run over her body, not wanting to do anything but just feel.

She glanced down into the water and saw him erect and hard. She reached out her hand and touched him wonderingly. Instinctively she bent down and took him into her mouth, rubbing her lips over him, nipping a little with her teeth and then she plunged him straight into her mouth, pushing him almost down her throat, and then she released him a little, letting her teeth and tongue work on him. She heard him moan from pleasure and she drank from him eagerly, swallowing, wanting to feed from him.

'I've never done that before. I mean I've never wanted to,' she finished lamely.

'Thank you. It was beautiful, special. Something very precious.'

For a moment they were still, close, touching each other with their breath. And then he smiled, his eyes wrinkling up at the corners.

'It's cold now, in the water.' Brian reached for a towel and helped her out of the bath. He wrapped her in it, winding it around her as if she were a child. He dried her and then he dried himself. He kissed her full on the mouth and held out his hand.

'Come.' She took it and they went back into the lounge. 'Don't dress. I want to see you. Like that,' he said.

Hannah remembered her leg then – but suddenly it really didn't matter any more. She smiled. 'I think I was dead before this evening.'

'I think I was too.'

They sat on the couch, naked together, and held each other.

They talked new lovers' talk.

She told him everything about her marriage, about her illness, even about Poland. She cried a little when she described how Rozia had let her know that Jouk wasn't her father.

Brian stroked her hair. 'I'll go back with you,' he said, 'and we will bury your past.'

Hannah smiled at him, she wanted to believe him, but she just said, 'Perhaps.'

Chapter Twelve

———— ◆ ————

Since the night he had come home late Rozia had withdrawn even further from Jerzy. She could not even respond when he touched her neck. However hard she tried she could not rid herself of the gnawing belief that he had been unfaithful.

Jerzy could not cope with her coldness, so he spoke with her again, this time without anger for he felt none. He was saddened by what was happening to him and Rozia. He wanted it to stop.

'I can't share you,' she said.

'But you aren't.'

'That woman.'

'I have told you she is a client. I knew you were unhappy when I wasn't working, don't deny it. It was that look of disapproval – even when I helped in the café it was there; so when the opportunity for the kind of work you approved of presented itself, I took it. To please you, to get back your respect.'

'I don't care about that any more.'

'But you did.'

'Yes.'

'I would like to continue, it's the quality of work I want to do.'

'Give it up.'

Jerzy sighed. 'If it will quieten your fears, then I will.'

Rozia was shocked; had she wanted to discover an infidelity so that perhaps she could blame another's disloyalty for her own failure as a wife? She saw Jerzy looking at her with such incredible tenderness that she had to avert her eyes.

Hannah's life took a new pattern. She worked, and she worked well, but it was no longer the centre of her existence. Brian took over that role. She woke to the thought of him, she dressed with a new kind of sensuality, even selecting underwear that she knew would please him. She anticipated his presence with the longing that comes only from loving.

He came into the office every day. She would watch him as he wrote, watch him on the telephone, and watch whilst he talked. They worked together, talked together, were silent together, ate together, but only slept together occasionally. Margaret was the reason.

'Hannah, I know she is only thirteen, but you and I are a fact. I think she ought to get used to that,' Brian told her one evening after they had finished work.

'I know. But I am worried that when you meet my family you'll be so appalled that you won't ever want to see me again.'

'I love you. I don't give a damn about your mother and your daughter. And I want to be with you, not just a couple of times a week.'

Hannah felt a hot flush. Did he mean that? What about his family? They'd never spoken about his wife and children. Hannah didn't even know how to bring them into the conversation. She felt she should, and yet she felt she had no right to do so.

And then suddenly there was darkness.

'I am living in a fool's paradise, Hannah. I get my letters. I reply to them. At those moments I can contain what I feel for you. And then I think about you and I know I can't. You devour me. When I am not with you I ache for you. I am tormented by the need for, by the sight and smell of you. You've cut across my life. I know it's unfair, but I chose not to think of the implications. I want you, I want us. I want to hold on to the joy you've given me.

'But of course it means eventual pain, and really it's pointless and we shouldn't continue to see each other, but I don't want to let go of the happiness, not until I have to.'

'If those are your real feelings, I can't understand why you should want to see my daughter,' Hannah found herself saying coldly. She hadn't thought of their relationship in terms of pain, and she found the reality of such a truth almost unbearable.

'Because I love you. Because she is part of you. Because I want to be with you all the time. Because she prevents it.'

'No, Margaret doesn't prevent it.' For the first time in more than a month Hannah felt the floor beneath her feet. And it hurt.

'Yes, you're probably right.' Brian spoke very quietly. Hannah couldn't look at him. 'I never wanted this to happen. I told you that I tried to withdraw from the programme because I sensed what would be, what you and I would mean to each other. But at the same time I love my family and I can't pretend to you that I don't. I never promised you a future. Even if I wanted to I can't change the priorities. All I can give you is now, but I should have listened to myself. The price is too high.' He picked up his briefcase, packed his papers and walked out of the office.

Hannah sat at her desk dry-eyed. She felt numb. Had it all gone? All the joy . . . soured by the reality that had never been hidden, and the inevitability of endings.

She walked – maybe for hours, she didn't know. Margaret wasn't at home – she was with Anthony. What would she do? She should have to get used to it – after all, he would have gone back to America anyway – but she could have had him till he left. She wanted him, she wanted to be with him – she couldn't bear not to see him – it was ridiculous of course. But what was it he had said? *I don't want to let go of the happiness – not until I have to.*

She almost ran back to her car, jerked the door open, started the engine, fumbling with the key in her haste.

She drove as fast as she could, swerving round cars, taking enormous risks, until she screeched to a halt outside the flat. She ran to the door, pushed it. Brian normally left it open. But it was shut. She rang the bell, there was no reply.

Disconcerted and feeling a little sick she sat in the driving seat. She would wait. Hannah watched the hands of the clock move round five minutes, ten minutes, fifteen minutes. The waiting was terrible. Would he come? Would he be glad to see her? Maybe he wouldn't want her. She started up the ignition. She'd go. It was better that way. It was too humiliating to wait outside the flat. But then she couldn't bear to go. She had to see him. She turned the engine off. Half an hour, an hour. Where was he? Hannah knew his movements. When he wasn't with her, he was home. Where had he gone?

She cried. Great tears of self-pity. An hour and a half. She had to go – where was her pride? She started the car again. It choked and spluttered and stopped. She tried again. But then Hannah saw him driving slowly around the corner. He saw her immediately, and stopped his car, a hired VW. But he didn't get out of his car. She went to him. Brian didn't say anything. He didn't move towards her. He didn't make it easy for her.

'Can I have you for as long as we have?' she asked.

'I can't leave them, Hannah.'

'I know,' she said, her fingers reaching for him.

Whilst Hannah loved Brian, Margaret had dinner with her father and he told her he was going to get married.

'We're organizing a little lunch after the ceremony. And er . . . Susan's young friend Roger will be here. We've invited him specially. He is sixteen. I've met him. Nice chap. Hoping to go to Cambridge.'

Margaret fidgeted with her napkin. She didn't like the idea of arranged meetings with boys. She didn't like boys. They had spotty skins and they groped, using wet flabby tongues inexpertly and messily. She shivered. And the wedding. The thought of her father married to someone else was difficult. Margaret had always known that she was the most important person in his life, but now there was someone else. Susan. She hadn't minded her when she was a friend, but now she was to be his wife, her stepmother.

Susan was very big, fleshy, dark, she had heavy breasts and ample hips. She seemed to tower over Margaret's slender father despite his small pot belly. They made an odd couple. Susan cooked a great deal, listened to music and played the piano, lulling Anthony to sleep with her interpretations of Mozart and Beethoven. Margaret thought she was a sloppy dresser. Like her mother and her grandmother she herself was a neat, fine person, taller than both of them, but there was nothing overt or crude about Margaret. And she was, if she was honest, slightly offended by Susan's obvious sexuality. Margaret was quite unaware of how much Rozia and Hannah had shaped her preferences. And if it had been pointed out to Margaret that some of her judgements might well have been tinged by jealousy, she would have flushed up and insisted that no such emotion coloured her view, but still she found it difficult to swallow her dinner.

Hannah insisted on buying her a new dress for the wedding and even Margaret had to acknowledge that it looked nice. It was pale blue with a boat-shaped neckline, a tight waist and a full skirt. As she stared at herself in the mirror on the morning of the wedding, Margaret caught sight of her femininity and for once it pleased her. She brushed her hair until it shone. She wore it loose and flowing and caught up by two slides that matched her dress exactly. Rozia had bound them in the same colour. But despite her pleasure at her looks she was a little tearful. She didn't know why but there was a strange feeling in her stomach, like a lump that wouldn't go away.

Hannah drove her to the block of flats where her father lived – she hadn't wanted Hannah to take her, but her mother had insisted. Margaret wondered how she would spend the day, she liked to think that she might cry a little.

She wished her friends Lucille and Alison were with her – they'd formed a group, they did everything together. Margaret felt so alone. She got into the lift and pressed the bell to her father's floor. As soon as she got out she heard the sounds of jollity.

'Darling, you look marvellous. I've been waiting for you.' Her father's face thrust itself up at her. He smelt a bit of whisky and she withdrew slightly. She didn't like the smell of alcohol.

'Susan, what a beautiful stepdaughter you have,' Margaret heard someone say.

'Yes, isn't she? She looks like her mother,' Anthony replied.

There was a brief silence, the kind you can cut. Margaret giggled a little. She suddenly forgot her antipathy towards Hannah. At least her mother wasn't fat, she thought. She glanced at Susan, who was wearing a tight pink dress that did nothing to conceal the outlines of her body.

There were a lot of people in the room, some Margaret recognized. People from her father's chambers and quite a few from his constituency, two or three of them well-known faces, including the chairman of the party. Others she did not know; she presumed they were members of Susan's family. Someone stuck a glass of champagne in her hand. Margaret sipped, but she didn't like it. Her father kept dragging her off to meet people. He was slightly drunk and kept muttering that Roger would be here soon. Margaret was tempted to tell him that she didn't care whether Roger came or not, but she realized there was no point – he wouldn't listen anyway. Susan hadn't come anywhere near him since his outburst about Hannah. After her initial amusement Margaret felt quite sorry for her.

Anthony was pouring himself another drink when Susan found him.

'There you are,' she said.

'Lost me in the crowd, did you?'

'I love you, Anthony. I know you loved her, but she didn't want you so you're stuck with me.'

She turned away on her heel, not wanting to look at him.

After about half an hour Margaret thought she ought to go and see if Susan was all right; she didn't seem to be in the room and Anthony had been unkind. She found her standing alone in the kitchen, drinking champagne. Her make-up seemed slightly smudged, and Margaret wondered if she had been crying.

'Congratulations,' she said. 'I didn't say it before and you look really nice.'

'Thank you, Margaret,' Susan replied.

'Look,' she said suddenly, 'don't worry about Daddy's comment. It's just that a marriage is hard to forget. Once you've been with him for a few years, he won't even remember the times with my mother.'

'I hope you're right, Margaret. Unfortunately for me, he thinks quite a lot of her.'

'Why unfortunately? She has someone else anyway . . .'

'Oh, does she?' Susan brightened visibly. 'Oh look, Roger's arrived. Anthony's bringing him over.' Margaret glanced at her. She was suddenly positively bristling with pleasure.

'Of course, one can't ignore the fact that my father did love my mother very much. It must be hard for both of them to forget that,' Margaret said, her voice as sweet as it had been a moment before. Susan turned to her – the hurt was as obvious as if she had kicked a dog. She turned away.

'Darling, meet Roger.' Her father's speech was blurred, one word flowing into the other.

Margaret looked at her escort. Her worst fears were confirmed. He had spots and a weak mouth. She could have conceded that he had nice eyes.

'Sorry I'm late,' he said, 'but I played in a rugby match this morning.'

Susan had taken her father's arm and walked off with him.

'Oh, there's champagne.' Roger grabbed a glass from a passing waiter.

Momentarily Margaret was amused, she thought the waiter looked like a penguin – all black with a white front and white gloves. She thought he even walked like one, with little jerky movements and stiff arms. She glanced at Roger – should she share the thought? Then she realized there was no point. He wouldn't have appreciated it.

'Well, everyone, now is the hour,' shouted a man Margaret knew . . . Tom Jackson, a lawyer friend of her father's. 'Let's go to the registry office. It's on the corner of the next street. We can all walk.'

Margaret wished there was someone she knew well. Someone she could stand with and not have to talk to. She didn't want to talk. There was the lump inside her, it was no longer small – it seemed to swamp her.

'Here, have a quick drink. You look a bit pale,' Roger said, offering her a glass of champagne from a tray. 'Go on,' he added, 'you may not like the taste but it will help. I imagine that it can't be easy, seeing a parent marrying. I don't suppose I would like it much.'

Margaret looked up at him, suddenly grateful for his understanding. She wanted to cry but she fought back the tears. 'I don't understand really. I mean I like Susan, and my parents were really unhappy together. I suppose it's change really.'

'Whatever it is, the champagne will help,' Roger said.

Margaret drank the glass very quickly. She felt quite light-headed and a little sick, but it wasn't unpleasant . . . and the lump wasn't quite as big as it had been.

She and Roger walked to the registry office together. She had to cling on to his arm because she couldn't manage too well on her high heels. They reached the registry office a little after everyone else. Her father seemed to be making a great fuss about having her near him. Margaret shuffled towards the front, embarrassed. She sat immediately behind her father, and throughout the brief ceremony tried to concentrate on the small thinning patch just on the crown of his head. The scalp looked quite pink under the thin strands of hair. She felt oddly disappointed by it – a reminder of human vulnerability. And in particular her father's.

She drank more champagne when she got back to the flat. She didn't want to talk to Susan, so she avoided her.

Her father held her tight and told her that he loved her. She realized it was the first time he had ever said it.

Roger talked a great deal. She listened. It was all quite easy, there was no effort required. He didn't need much fuelling. He just went on and on about his exams, about his rugby, and about how he liked her. Would she come to a party next week? She didn't think she answered but even if she did say yes, well, why not? Everything seemed to be at a distance, as if she were removed, listening to herself speak, watching herself move.

Margaret saw him – Roger – take her into another room. She felt tired. She watched herself lie down on the bed, falling on top of coats and furs. She seemed to be giggling. She saw herself stick her head inside a fur stole, and the hairs tickled her nose. It was funny. She felt sick. But then the sick feeling went away again, and it was nice. Roger was looking at her feet, taking off her nice shoes, and he was playing with the stole, wrapping it around his shoulders.

Did the hair tickle his ears? She asked him, she heard herself ask him, and it was so funny when he said no.

And then he came nearer, looming over her, and suddenly it wasn't funny because she was back inside her own body, and she could see eyes that were bloodshot. And she started to try to get up, but she couldn't. He was on top of her, and his tongue was trying to get into her mouth; his hands were pulling at her skirt and he was trying to touch her there. She heard her scream from far away, but then it was muffled, his hand was over her mouth, and he was hitting her, telling her to be quiet. That it was nice. That he wanted her because he loved her. She could feel him fiddling with himself with one hand whilst he held her down with the other and suddenly there was a stem of flesh being thrust at her mouth. She gagged. She could smell urine and perspiration, and she could taste it. She bit hard, and he screamed, rolling off her. She ran into the lounge. She heard her father, but she didn't want him. She wanted Hannah . . .

'Mummy, Mummy!' she cried, and her heart broke because Mummy wasn't there.

When Margaret came to she found herself tucked up tight in a bed. She looked around Anthony's bedroom, but there were no coats, nothing to remind her of the horror of just a few hours before, but she remembered it. She began to sob again, wanting Hannah, needing her. And then suddenly, miraculously, Hannah was there, holding her, cuddling her.

'Mummy, Mummy.'

'No darling, it isn't Mummy. We rang the flat and left a message. She wasn't expecting you until late so she's probably out.'

Jolted, Margaret moved away from the stranger – it was Susan.

'I am all right,' she said, pushing back the tears.

'No you are not. And neither would I be,' Susan said softly, 'but I am glad to say you hurt him, he had to be taken to hospital.'

'Oh.'

'Yes, you drew blood.' She was smiling.

'Did I?' Margaret's voice was quiet and then she said, 'Good, he smelt disgusting.'

'Would you like some tea?' Susan asked.

'Yes, thank you.' Margaret moved back under the covers. She noticed that Susan had taken off the pink dress, that now she wore a soft blue one and she looked much nicer. And then Margaret remembered how she had spoken to her before the wedding.

'I am sorry I said what I said,' she volunteered.

'Said about what?' Susan asked.

Hannah came a little later. She rushed into the bedroom and tried to touch Margaret – but it was too late. Margaret didn't need her by then. She pushed her away.

'I am all right.' The words were the same as she had used to Susan, but the tone was different.

'I wouldn't be.' Susan's words were now said by Hannah.

'No, wouldn't you? Well I am not you and I am fine now. Are we going home?'

'Whenever you want.'

'Right.' Margaret pushed the sheets back. She felt quite shaky, but she didn't want Hannah to see. She looked down at herself, her nice blue dress was creased. Picking up some of the skirt, she rubbed it with her fingers. For a moment Margaret wanted to cry, but she set her lips and looked at her mother. 'Come on then.'

She walked out of the bedroom. She couldn't look at her father – he disgusted her, he had smelt of drink too. Margaret went over and kissed Susan on the cheek.

'Take care darling. See you soon,' Susan said.

She turned back to her mother and then she noticed that

there was another man in the room. He was tall, dressed in jeans.

'Hello, Margaret,' he said. 'I am Brian, a friend of your mother's.'

He was an American – now she knew what her mother had done on her father's wedding day.

Anthony got up from where he had been slouching on the sofa.

''Bye darling, I'll call you as soon as I get back from my honeymoon.'

'We, and our,' she corrected him, 'or isn't Susan going with you?'

Margaret walked out of the flat without looking back. Pressing the lift button, she ignored the whispered exchanges between her parents. She noticed that Brian had walked out immediately after her. She waited for him to say something, but he didn't.

She felt her mother reach out and touch her neck. Margaret tried to ignore the warm fingers, but they did feel nice and she allowed the intimacy just until the lift arrived.

When they got back to the flat Margaret excused herself and went straight to her bedroom. In the safety of her familiar room she threw herself on to her bed, and suddenly feeling wretched and sick, she sobbed loudly. She heard Hannah come in but she shouted, 'Go away, don't you understand, I don't want you.'

She snatched at her towel and almost ran to the bathroom. She locked the door behind her and ran a hot tub. The hottest she could bear. She didn't look in any of the mirrors that Hannah had hung on the three walls, in heavy ornate gold frames that were shown to their best advantage against the white walls. Margaret got into the bath, ignoring how it stung her delicate skin. She scrubbed and scrubbed, bringing herself up in red weals, grateful for the physical discomfort. She washed her hair, even though she'd done so that morning. She rubbed her scalp almost viciously and made it bleed.

Towelling herself dry, she belted her bathrobe tightly and let herself out of the bathroom. She was aware that Hannah and the man were sitting in the lounge. She called out a token 'Good night.'

Hannah came to the door. 'I would like to talk to you,' she said rather gently.

'I've nothing to say,' Margaret replied.

'I am sorry I wasn't there when you needed me.'

'Well, you never were anyway. So I am used to it.'

Hannah drew in her breath sharply. 'Don't hate me,' she said.

'I don't hate you, I just don't need you.'

'Do you want Rozia?'

'No! I don't want any of you!'

The thirteen-year-old girl who was no longer a child pushed her mother out of her room, shut the door on her and turned the key.

It was later that same evening, after drinking wine – a lot of it – that Brian said, 'I am getting letters asking me when I am coming home.'

'I am going to lose you,' Hannah said, 'and I can't bear it. I should feel guilty. I should feel bad about what exists between us. You are another woman's husband, and the father of her children. The only way I can cope with that is to think of you in the singular. I know adultery is wrong, it means pain for everyone. But I love you. And there is nothing I wish to do about that. I want us to go to Poland together – perhaps not yet, but later, when you are back with your wife, I'll pay the price for the trip.'

Hannah told them all, a surly Margaret, an anxious Anthony, and a careful Rozia, that she and Brian were going to Poland. She made no excuses, offered no explanations.

Margaret seemed disinterested. All she said was, 'I suppose I will have to stay with my father.' But Hannah could see a flare of something like happiness in her daughter's eyes.

Rozia seemed nervous. 'It's funny to think of you going to Poland after all this time. I wouldn't like to go – not now.'

Hannah smiled at her, she touched her hair – she often touched Rozia now. It was as if she had become the parent and Rozia the child.

Martin had died suddenly – Sybil was in a home. Esther was in Israel. They only had each other now. Oh, of course they had their men, except that Rozia didn't believe she had Jerzy, and Hannah knew she didn't have Brian. And Margaret was Anthony's now – they both knew that. They had their acquaintances, their good-time friends, but really it was just the two of them, as it probably always had been.

Anthony said, 'Just be careful, but I can't say I am sorry to have the opportunity of having Margaret with me. I feel very bad, I realize I have neglected her. I must do what I can now, and hope it isn't too late.'

'You are softer, Anthony.'

'I've lost something very precious, Hannah, and I am having to learn to live with that.'

As she put the telephone down Hannah realized that she was crying, and she wasn't surprised.

Chapter Thirteen

———◆———

The airport sprawled over several acres, easily swallowing the giant planes as if they were toys. Cars, buses and taxis disgorged their occupants at appropriate electronic doors. The travellers took their multicoloured travel documents and bustled through passport control into the departure lounges where they gobbled up their allocation of duty-free spirits and perfume like hungry children set loose in a free sweet shop.

But even the utilitarianism of travel did little to submerge the excitement of the coming and going. And Hannah drank it all in, remembering the anticipations of a thirteen-year-old on a station platform. The family holidays in France and Italy – even the business trips abroad had been conducted with an air of normality, but this was different. This was a journey back to another life. One that perhaps even she didn't know, but it was part of her, something that somehow she had never been able to diffuse. Hannah noticed that she had pointed her toes and that her shoes were making little circular movements which could have left a pattern if the floor had not been covered in carpet.

Brian had gone to get some coffee, and she sat in one of the black plastic chairs with padded backs and bottoms that seemed to be the badge for airports everywhere. Their hand luggage was at her feet. A brown leather holdall, Brian's, which was covered with different travel labels. Hannah glanced up to see if she could see him. She didn't want to be seen to be prying, but she was curious to know where he had been, Vietnam, Singapore, Hong Kong, Australia,

South America, Israel – and suddenly she remembered the man at Lodd airport and of course it had been Brian – so they were fated to be together, the gods had decided.

Hannah felt warm and good, and so happy. She had a momentary mirage of foreign places and foreign tongues, and she recalled how she had dreamed in the treehouse. To hear different sounds, to smell different smells, to see different sights. She shivered and fantasized for a moment. She saw them together, their faces superimposed on fantastic images, always together, always loving. And then she looked again. Her eye caught the small label that was attached permanently to the handle. Mr and Mrs Brian Webster, 1018 South Canyon Drive. She didn't read any more. There wasn't any fantasy or mirage left.

'Coffee? It looks disgusting, but it's wet,' Brian said, holding two paper cups in his hands.

'Thanks,' Hannah said. She didn't look at him. 'How much time till the flight?'

'Not long.'

'I wonder how it will be. At least I can go back and see the places, if not the people,' she said, her voice unnaturally bright.

Brian looked at her carefully. She looked back at him. She noticed the little lines, like crisscrosses made by a fine pen, around his eyes. He started to say something, but then he stopped. 'Drink your coffee,' was all he managed.

'BEA announce the departure of flight BE 601 for Warsaw. Embarkation at Gate Seven.' The thin clear voice repeated the message in French and Polish. Hannah and Brian stood up, collected their luggage and walked silently towards the embarkation point. They were so close their hips almost touched . . . but they were silent and it wasn't a comfortable silence.

Brian saw Barbara, his children. He heard their laughter as if they were with him, the clatter of skis carried out of the house for the last holiday before he went to Vietnam, the feel of a warm wet mouth that he kissed so unashamedly in front of the children. Would he ever be able to kiss that mouth again? He remembered the comfort of Barbara's thighs as they clung and surrounded him. How could he hurt that softness, how could he split open that gentle and insistent place where he had lodged his seed and made his children? Would he ever be able to go back and pretend it was all still the same? And Hannah, how could he leave her – the joy of her, the special longing, the feeling of being whole with her? He had told himself that the trip was their present. He would not think of the future. But he had known when he got back with the coffee that Hannah was thinking of Barbara. Brian was torn in two, one part of him belonging to his family, and the other to Hannah. Each part bound by pledges of loyalty and love.

Hannah tried not to think of the unknown woman who had rights over her lover. She tried not to think of the children who called him Daddy. All she could have was momentary. She reached over and clung to Brian's arm. He looked down at her, briefly touched her hair and pulled her closer. He kissed her full on the mouth.

Far away in America the woman who occupied so many thoughts dialled a number in London.

'Why don't you go over, Barbara?' her friend, a woman called Cecile who envied Barbara's marriage, had said. 'Go as a surprise.'

'I'll go, but I won't surprise him. I'll call the television company.'

It was Natalie who took the call. 'I'm sorry, he's in Poland,' she said. 'No, I don't know where,' she replied, looking at the itinerary. 'We just know he'll be back in about three weeks.'

'He's gone to Poland. I'll plan to be in London, at his flat, when he gets back. Will you take care of the kids for me, Cecile?' Barbara said.

An aeroplane is a fatter tube than a train, and the rows of seats don't allow for privacy as the older trains used to. There were no little compartments with half-shaded lights, just a dark blue interior with piped music and little square holes for windows. Plastic had replaced ormolu, and a little piece of magic was gone.

Hannah tried to concentrate on the miracle of flying through the air, but it compared poorly to the pleasure of hurtling through towns and villages on a railway track. Travel demeaned the journey now, she thought. She glanced around at their fellow travellers. They were faceless, much like her and Brian, she supposed. The younger ones chose blue jeans, the uniform of the egalitarian society. Others wore suits and dresses, but there was no glamour.

'Do you know that my mother travelled to Warsaw in crêpe de Chine and a hat?' Hannah said to Brian.

'Was she as beautiful as you?'

Hannah smiled. 'More so. She was perfect. But untouchable.'

'Well, you are very touchable,' he whispered, running the tip of his finger over her breast. She smiled at the tightening of her nipple.

Hannah stuck her nose up close to the window. The little green square of England was all visible: the inlets of water, the silver threads of the roadways.

'You are like a child today,' Brian told her.

'Am I?' she said. 'I suppose that whatever we do in terms of dehumanizing ourselves, there is still some magic in adventure.'

More plastic appeared when the food tray was offered, cellophane-wrapped stewed coffee. Hannah couldn't help remembering the silver tray and the little fly-like attendant.

The smell of the country welcomed her back. There was nostalgia and a longing for her roots that had been implanted by a memory that wasn't hers, and yet it marked her because it was her inheritance. An exile from a country she had never known and which she could never claim. She had a strange sense of familiarity that disturbed her.

'In one sense I feel as if I have come home and in another I am totally alien,' she told Brian. 'I have no place.'

'I understand that,' Brian said sharply.

Hannah looked at him. 'You feel that way because you think America has let you down?'

'Yes.'

'It is painful for you. But you are not part of an amorphous mass. You are an individual. You think, you feel, you are. You have the right of dissent.'

As she spoke, Hannah knew that she was not reaching Brian's pain. It was just words. She felt inadequate.

They got into a taxi and drove into Warsaw. They saw little of the horrors of the war, just a few bomb sites, but for the most part they saw wide roads and large blocks of flats. There were queues of people waiting at bus stops, outside shops, everywhere. Hannah tried to remember the Warsaw of her childhood, to find a likeness. She remembered the hustle and the crowded streets. Now everything seemed empty.

The Forum Hotel was like all international hotels. It could have been a native of any culture. But the check-in was different. There were anxious-looking men searching for wealthy tourists to change their money. Pretty girls with red and blonde hair who sat around the reception area. Any foreigner would do. It all meant a little better food, a little more money. There was no welcoming porter or friendly receptionist. There was just a faceless person who could have been a policeman, or woman.

Hannah didn't like it.

When they got to their bedroom Hannah threw her case on the floor and knelt down to look under the bed, running her hand along the edge of the carpet.

'What are you doing?' asked Brian.

'I am looking for bugs.'

'Bugs?'

'Listening devices manned by secret agents ready to report our every move.'

Brian burst out laughing. He got down on the floor. 'Let's give them a cabaret from the West,' he said. He pulled her to him, nuzzling her ear. Her hands went into his hair and they loved noisily.

They had dinner in the hotel restaurant. They were tired, their limbs ached after their loving, and their heads were full of each other. They had no desire to explore little 'interesting' places. They wanted nourishment, a bath, and each other again, before sleeping.

The restaurant was crowded, and they were seated at a small square table set for four. Water was poured into glasses but there was no ice. They were given a card which offered several choices for each course. Hannah chose beetroot borscht, remembering Rozia's light pink sweet and sour soup with the little boiled potatoes floating in it. There was also escalope on the menu. Hannah decided to have that for her main course. Brian asked for cucumber soup and cabbage rolls.

Whilst they waited for their food they were quiet, just touching each other, aware of their passion being held in abeyance. The waiter came back with two borschts. It was heavier than Rozia's with more of a meat flavour and there were litle dumplings in it. Hannah wrinkled up her nose.

'Don't you like it?' Brian asked.

'It's all right, but it isn't like my mother used to make,' Hannah smiled. 'Funny, at the time I never appreciated her food but in retrospect it was delicious.'

She didn't get her escalope. She got stuffed cabbage rolls. They were dry but they were served with the most delicious mushrooms in a cream sauce.

'This is good,' Hannah said, mopping up her sauce enthusiastically with the surprisingly good bread that had been put on the table with the meal.

'I think I would have preferred a hamburger,' Brian muttered moodily.

'And ketchup?'

'And ketchup.'

The waiter overheard them talking in English. He looked hard at them. For a moment Hannah was worried. Could it be wrong to criticize the food? she wondered nervously, then dismissed the thought as ludicrous. Or was it . . . He was coming over to them.

'American?' the waiter asked Brian.

'Yes,' he answered.

'I am English,' Hannah said, suddenly full of chauvinism.

'You speak Polish?' the waiter said.

'My parents are Polish. I was last here in 1938.'

The waiter clapped his hands and embraced her. 'You were with us before the Nazis, before the Russians. When Poland was for the Poles.'

He was speaking quite loudly. Hannah looked around nervously. She certainly didn't want anyone to overhear that remark. The waiter disappeared to his serving table and came back with a bottle of vodka which he poured into three glasses. He toasted Brian, he toasted Hannah. No one seemed to mind.

Hannah and Brian reciprocated his toasts but firmly declined another drink. Other diners were staring at them. After a few moments of intensive conversation, a man from a neighbouring table got up and came over to them. He took Hannah's hand in his and kissed the inside of her wrist, bowing low in order to do so. He spoke good English.

'My name is Tom Staniewicz. I overheard our inebriated friend here say that you are English and American.'

'Yes,' Brian said.

'I would like to welcome you to Warsaw. Some friends and I are dining here. Will you perhaps join us for a vodka or some tea? I would not recommend the coffee. It is disgusting.'

The Pole preceded them to his table. His companions, two other men, stood up and, following the same procedure, kissed the inside of Hannah's wrist. They introduced themselves as Julius Marcin and Alek Szymanski. They were all journalists, they said.

Brian responded by introducing Hannah and himself and explaining that they were in Poland to prepare a television programme on the millennium of Poland as a Christian state. 'We are here to absorb, to learn – the vernacular is to do a "recce".'

Julius Marcin smiled. 'To understand Poland is to understand that Christianity is indivisible from the state, whatever the Communists say. Even the agnostics, atheists and Jews pray to the Virgin Mary as the mother of the land.'

'Are there any Jews left?' Hannah asked.

'Just a few. I am one,' Szymanski answered.

'How did you survive?'

'I fought in the Polish underground. I was taken in by a Christian family. Of course my family died, but a lot of Jews managed to get into Russia and perhaps were interned in a local camp or in some cases even avoided that. Some of us were lucky.'

'My mother's family were Jewish,' Hannah told him.

'Do you know what happened to them?'

'No, she lost contact with them in 1924. I came here with my parents in 1938. My father wanted to persuade his own parents to come to England. But they wouldn't. Still, they were fortunate, they died of old age. My mother's parents wouldn't see her – she had become a Catholic.'

'Aren't you curious about your mother's family?' Julius Marcin asked.

'Yes I am. But I don't know anything about them. I just know that the family name is Mezeurski. It's funny how one's memory holds on to some things. I was told the name just once by my father. That was the first time I discovered that my mother had been Jewish. She converted in Poland.' Hannah found herself exposing her family story in a way she would never have done in England. She was amazed at herself. The men were total strangers.

'But you know, the incredible coincidence is that the name Mezeurski is quite well-known to us,' Julius Marcin said.

Hannah sat up. She could feel a tightening in her stomach. 'What do you mean?' Her voice was a little breathless.

'Jonathon Mezeurski is a professor at Warsaw University. He is now a sick man. He has cancer, but he still writes on his subject . . . physics.'

'And in the underground press. He is a staunch critic of the government. He says he is going to die anyway, so what the hell . . .' Szymanski interjected.

'He doesn't live far from here. We could telephone him. Find out if he is a relative. It isn't late,' Marcin said.

Brian held her wrist, rubbing her skin. 'It would be wonderful for you to find out,' he said. 'For your mother . . .'

'She had a brother called Jonathon,' Hannah said very quietly.

'Would you call him?' Brian asked.

Hannah didn't hear him. She suddenly remembered Rozia's breakdown. She heard her mother screaming, she put her hand up to her breast, trying to calm her heart which seemed to be leaping in twists and turns, stopping her from even breathing.

'Can you give me any information about your mother's family?' Marcin leaned towards Hannah.

'My mother's name is Rozia. She was a student in chemistry at Warsaw University,' she told him.

As he left the table to make the telephone call, Hannah found herself drinking another glass of vodka. 'I'm scared,' she heard herself saying.

'Of course you are,' Brian said.

Hannah knew even before Marcin returned to the table that Jonathon Mezeurski was her uncle. The suppressed excitement in the Pole's face said everything.

'Come. Mezeurski is waiting for you.'

'Now, but –'

'Now,' Marcin said.

They took a taxi. Hannah felt as if a time span had gone. She was a little girl again, going to meet her family. She glanced down at her shoes. Black, shiny patent court shoes, but they could have been buckles over white socks – but she wasn't a child now, and Hannah the woman was aware of the irrevocability of this step. By going to Mezeurski's flat, she was filling in the missing gaps in her life. She would discover the spinning wheel that had woven the thread of her life even before the fabric had been made up.

The taxi stopped at a modern block of flats. Hannah was jolted. A woman was standing by the open door. It reminded her of their arrival at another apartment building in Warsaw, and another woman who had stood waiting, all those years ago.

'Hannah, Hannah?' she said.

'Yes.'

'My name is Lily. I am Professor Mezeurski's daughter. Please come up.'

Hannah walked into the harsh light of the entrance hall to the block.

A grey, utilitarian block with steel eyes that housed two

lifts. She turned to look at the woman. They shared the same blonde hair.

The steel eyes opened to a little box. They all crowded in. Hannah could hear the questions. How was Mezeurski? The polite replies. Brian touched her neck. She smiled at him.

They were taken into a tiny flat, furnished with spindly modern pieces that looked as if they would never last ten years. A man sat swathed in blankets by the window. He had white hair and the haggard face of one who knows his time has come.

He turned as they came in. He had been looking out of the window. Hannah was embarrassed. He was not dressed, but wore only a dressing gown and pyjamas. He greeted his friends with a kiss on both cheeks. He called for vodka for them. He would have tea, with lemon.

'And now where is Hannah?' he said in English. Hannah was surprised. She walked towards him. 'Come nearer, so I can look at you. An old man's privilege,' he said.

Hannah knelt down and he turned an angle-poise lamp towards her, carefully shading the glare away from her eyes. And then he looked at her. He ran his hands over her face as a blind man might, touching the nose and the chin, touching her hair.

'Rozia, Rozia . . . Oh my God.' He began to cry. Taking time over the tears, not hiding them, nor explaining them.

Hannah sat back on her haunches, watching him.

'Lily, bring me my photographs.' A box was handed to him. A hand went on Hannah's shoulder. Mezeurski riffled through the box and selected what he wanted. He handed a photograph to Hannah. She didn't look at it for a moment, and then she did. It was Rozia, but a Rozia she had never seen, who was looking up adoringly at a man who held her hand. A sombre man who wore a skull cap and a full beard.

'Your grandfather – Samuel Mezeurski,' Jonathon said, and then he took her in his arms and embraced her. She could feel the bony shoulders and the thin body, so wasted by disease. 'We have so much to say. You will come back tomorrow. For lunch. We will talk then. Now we must entertain our friends and thank them.' Lily brought a tray with vodka and tea, and the sticky porto that Jouk had drunk. There were the same little cakes. Hannah felt as if she had come home.

Hannah was not expected to visit Jonathon until one o'clock, so she spent the following morning with Brian, trying to concentrate on television business. It was hard – she wanted to pursue her mother's history and she was excited about meeting Jonathon. Would he be like Rozia? She doubted it, he was far too open, far too emotional.

She and Brian met Juliana Satafim, a Polish documentary producer whom Hannah had met at the Montreux Television Festival. She was filming at the Palace of Culture, Stalin's present to the Polish people; the tallest building in Warsaw, its message to the Poles was unmistakable. Hannah and Brian watched, amused at Juliana's sardonic observations.

'We must not miss such a beautiful brick structure. After all, this one we can definitely sell to Russian television. Can you imagine a better way to spend an evening,' she said directly to Brian whilst she lit a new cigarette from the butt of the old one, 'than a detailed evaluation of the gift from Stalin to Poland?' She gave a short laugh, and drew them away from the camera crew. 'Shall we walk a little?'

She led the way down towards a large street crowded with trams. They crossed over to the other side and sat on one of the rows of benches in front of a small square.

'I'll introduce you to Smeltovkia. He is the head of my department and a Communist. You will need to study all the literature on current Polish feeling in the underground press. I will make sure that it will be given to you. I have told him that the programme is about religious experience. I thought it better.'

'In other words we should be careful of what we say.'

'You will find him doctrinaire.'

'And you?' Hannah was thinking of Jonathon and the three men they had met last night.

'Expediency is my passport,' Juliana answered shortly. 'Come on,' she said. 'I only have the crew for the rest of the morning. If you want, you can go off and meet me for lunch later.'

'I will stay with you,' Brian said, 'but Hannah has other things to do.'

She took a taxi to the Mezeurski apartment. She was slightly disconcerted by the number of people standing around in the hall, talking quietly amongst themselves. Anxiously she walked inside. The atmosphere was unmistakable. Death had laid claim, leaving its trail of unhappiness and loneliness that knows no boundaries of culture, country or faith, political and religious. Communists, Catholics and Jews, all Poles mourning a friend, had come together in a grief that excluded Hannah. She didn't know Jonathon Mezeurski and his passing should have meant nothing to her, but it did; she accepted it, but there was a rage inside her. He was the one man who could have found her an identity and now he was gone – stolen in the moment of discovery. She had to write a note of condolence, leave a message or something. She glanced around her. Of course she knew no one.

A big-boned man with a ruddy face and a shock of black hair spoke to her. 'You are the English cousin?'

'Yes,' Hannah answered. 'I didn't know. I mean perhaps I should have telephoned before I came. I am very sad.'

'Lily will want to see you,' the man said, ignoring her stuttered sentences. Hannah was aware that she was being examined – the foreign woman. Inadvertently she glanced down at the navy dress she was wearing. It was sleeveless, in fine wool, with a jacket over the top. Even though the colour was sombre enough, it seemed to scream of a style that was unacceptable in that room. She wanted to sit down but there was nowhere available.

The man was back, guiding her arm. 'Come,' he said. He took her through the closed door. Hannah found herself in a small bedroom dominated by an enormous double bed. She was shocked. Under the covers there was a form, a human form, its lines shrouded by white sheets. She couldn't take her eyes away from it and yet there was something so intrusive about her staring.

'I am glad you are here,' Lily said.

'I am so sorry,' was all Hannah could manage.

She saw that Lily was wearing a black skirt with a checked top. It strained slightly over her figure betraying that the weight was newly acquired. Her face was blotched, her eyes were red. She had a handkerchief twisted around her fingers. 'I will miss him,' she said. She straightened the sheets on the bed, as she must have done so many evenings when the man was still alive.

'I don't want to intrude,' Hannah said softly.

'No, you are not. You are my cousin. My only relative. Funny, we are strangers and yet the bonds of family reach out.'

'I wonder how Rozia would feel,' Hannah said, 'knowing that I am here now.'

'Perhaps this will help her.' Lily reached behind her and handed Hannah a box. It seemed to be an old chocolate box, battered and damaged. Hannah opened it. Inside she saw photographs and letters and a diary. She closed it quickly. 'However curious I am about her, I can't pry.'

Lily nodded.

'It is up to her to tell me,' Hannah said, as if to remind herself of her place.

She stayed with Lily throughout the rest of the day. She thought of Jouk's funeral, how formal and disciplined it had been. People cried here without shame.

Chapter Fourteen

———— ◆ ————

Hannah and Brian decided to stay in Krakow for one night and then go to the Tatra Mountains, to the memories of Hannah's youth. She told Brian she wanted to find poppy fields and green apples, pink hams and soured milk. She wanted to walk with him by the clear streams and lie with him in the fields. She was determined to find her grandfather's house – or what was left of it. She had discovered that it was now a collective farm.

Brian drove an old Ford, the kind he would have had, Hannah thought, when he was at college. The window on her side of the car was open. She could feel the warm wind caressing her arm, bringing up the little white hairs so the sun could touch them. Hannah did not know if it was because it was the same time of year, but the dry stinging heat that had made her want to remove all her clothes all those years ago cloaked her body again. She saw the stiff old lady dressed in black, her nervous mother, the courtly old man . . . and Jouk, beloved Jouk who had helped to weave the fairytale of her youth.

But she had other grandparents and suddenly she knew she had to remember them too. 'I want to go to Auschwitz,' she said.

Brian drove into the small town of Oswiecim. Suddenly it seemed colder. Hannah knew the camp had been built on marshland so that the sun would somehow be diffused, but there seemed to her to be a more obvious coldness than pure logistics.

As they drove up to the iron gates with their hideous

message 'Arbeit Macht Frei', a cattle truck was drawing up. It was as if they were witnessing some hideous replay of a scene from twenty years before.

She had come to honour the dead. Anaesthetized by the comforts of her life in England she had assumed she would be able to cope, but the reality was too much. She grabbed Brian's hand. His fingers curled over hers. They clung to each other.

There were green fields and trees. Were there trees twenty years before? What had it looked like to Samuel and Hannah Mezeurski, to Jonathon Mezeurski? She felt their terror, and in her head she heard Esther's voice, 'Your mother was Jewish, that makes you Jewish too, and your daughter.' And Hannah knew that Auschwitz was no more a memorial to others, it could have been her grave.

Once it had been a Polish army barracks. The buildings were pleasant red brick, with small leaded windows. Inside they saw thousands of suitcases, piled one on top of the other, the names clearly marked – did she see Weinstein? Did she see Mezeurski? There were thousands of little wire spectacles. And there were shoes, caked with brown mud; occasionally there was a splash of red, or blue – even some high heels.

They moved past the display cases with their catalogue of horror, gazing at artificial limbs, cooking utensils, at the tins of make-up. The Nazis had plaited the hair before they processed it. The colours were dulled now. The neatly stacked piles of tresses looked like some obscene hairdressers. Hannah saw the children's clothes, little garments, some even trimmed with lace. She cried then.

The sun was high in the sky, but it could not warm the cold stones which reeked of the viciousness perpetrated there. Hannah and Brian walked over the earth that had felt the feet of the doomed. It was brown earth and it sprouted green grass, but it stank of pain.

As Hannah walked through that dreadful place she felt unquenchable fear. It was as if she was naked and running from the Nazi tormentors, her child torn from her breast, as if her Englishness was being ripped from her like a fragile, flimsy cloak, once covered with shiny sparkling sequins to hide her nakedness – but taken from her it was no more an armour against hate than the flimsy disguise it had proved to be.

For Hannah knew she belonged there, in that soil – not in her England, an England of dreams.

She was a Pole and by accident of birth she had escaped the death she should have had and it terrified her; for surely that death, that horrific destiny, would come back and claim her and her child, as surely as it had claimed her grandparents and cousins, her kith and kin. Rozia might have escaped, but Hannah would not – she was one of them. The guilt of survival aimed its mark at Hannah Oberska Simpson.

She couldn't speak to Brian. She felt him, but she couldn't look at him. They walked past the tour buses crammed with visitors. They ignored the ice-cream vendor who had set up a stall just by the entrance. They pushed through the queues of people talking and laughing as they sucked at the white globules. Brian drove directly to their hotel in the middle of Krakow. They registered, going through the usual rituals involving their custom declaration forms, their passports.

When they got to their bedroom, another unattractive anonymous room, Brian took off all of Hannah's clothes. There was nothing sensual in his movements. He took off his own clothes too and chucked them all into a corner of the room. He took her by the hand, and led her, almost as if she were a child, into the bathroom. He turned on the tap, switching the outlet over so that it ran through the shower head. He helped Hannah into the bath and stood by her, letting the water run through every part of her, and then himself. They stood together, feeling the wet running over their skin, through their hair, between their legs. It was Hannah who finally picked up the soap – a tiny piece of green that could boast little relationship with the creamy blocks sold so salivatingly in their square boxes in the affluent West. She worked it in her hand – rubbing it against Brian's skin, running it over his neck, his chest, his legs. He took it from her and cleaned her too.

They fell asleep like small children, exhausted. They lay on their beds, separately at first, but somehow their bodies reached out and they interlinked one with the other – Hannah curled into Brian, her legs over his, and his arms drew her close.

They must have slept for three hours. When they woke they were hungry.

'It seems almost obscene to think about my stomach,' Hannah said, pulling open her case and searching for stockings.

'That's a fatuous comment.'

'Pardon?'

'It's stupid. Just because you have been to a concentration camp there is no need to identify with it. You can't. Sympathize, abhor, but you aren't part of it so you can't know.'

'I am!' she screamed at him – 'I am. My grandparents died there. You don't have a copyright on suffering just because of Vietnam.'

'You didn't know your grandparents and I didn't suffer in Vietnam. But I had to stand and watch whilst others did.'

'And I stood and watched today.'

'You saw a memorial –'

'I saw the place where it happened. And I felt it, all of it. I wasn't as fortunate as you. I can't actually say I was a voyeur . . .' Hannah bit her lip.

Brian threw his hands up in the air in mock surrender. 'Stop it. We're going to say things that hurt.'

'Nothing can hurt as much as the fact that you have a wife . . .' Hannah found herself saying and she was appalled.

'It seems somewhat unfair to compare Barbara to the horrors of Auschwitz and Vietnam.'

'I didn't mean her specifically.'

Brian sat on the bed. He was half dressed, in jeans, socks, and shoes. Hannah wanted to put her arms around him but he held her away by his look.

'I love you. I am married to someone else. Do you want to deal with it now or when we get back from Poland?'

'Poland is mine, we agreed that.'

'Yes. But we are carrying an extra passenger whether we like it or not.'

The journey to the former Oberski family home took just two hours. It was smaller than Hannah remembered. A large truck packed full of apples was parked close to the house on the spot where Jouk had once sat in his rocking chair and smoked his pipe. The little garden no longer existed. It all looked strange and yet at the same time there was a familiarity that was so intensely personal that the presence of the truck was hurtful. It was a reminder that the house was no longer anything to do with Hannah. And yet it was so much part of her childhood that she still claimed it as her own. It was ludicrous. She could see that it was part of the collective farm. But the languid atmosphere that had embraced her, and she remembered, had bored her, was still there. There was no sense of urgency. No pressure.

Hannah glanced at Brian. She felt awkward with him. Yesterday night they had slept apart, without touching, curled into the pillows of their twin beds. Tiredness and the pain of Auschwitz had been the shared excuse. She had tattled over breakfast, comparing the slightly stale bread to the soft, melting concoctions that Danuta had offered to start the day. Brian had taken her mood and offered nothing to jar it. He knew that neither of them had slept, but he couldn't reach out to her. What was the point? Not until he had made up his mind what he was going to do.

'Do you want to go in?' he asked her, wondering how she was feeling.

'Yes.'

Hannah led the way into the house. She was wearing a blue shirt. He remembered that they hadn't made love for two days.

There were no doors any more. And the salon was used to store apples. Hannah suddenly remembered, standing in the doorway, how the shaft of sunlight had cut through the haze. She could almost see Jouk as he had been the day the priest came to pay his visit. But now there were just apples. Angrily she kicked at one.

'Please don't damage the crop.' A dark wiry man stood on the other side of the hall.

Hannah turned to him. 'I am sorry. My foot must have slipped.'

'That looked like a deliberate kick to me,' the man insisted. 'What are you doing here?' His voice was angry.

'I came to see the house. I stayed here as a child. My grandparents used to own it.'

'I understand now. You'll stay and eat with us.' It wasn't a question.

Hannah looked at Brian who stood waiting in the shadows of the staircase. 'He wants to know if we will eat here.'

'Yes.'

'Your husband?' the man asked.

'No,' she replied, 'my friend.'

'Look around,' the Pole invited. 'Walk – you'll see changes. We eat at six.'

Hannah's little white bedroom no longer existed. The upstairs of the house had been completely gutted. There was nothing left to remind her that it had once been a home.

Anxious to be out of its cloying atmosphere and the smell of apples, Hannah and Brian went to find the treehouse. The tree stood exactly as it had done when Hannah had climbed its branches. But there was no house. The platform had long since rotted.

They walked to the river. There were no more poppy fields. The entire area was given over to apple trees. But the stepping stones were still in the river, and silver fish sprinting this way and that in the clear water. Hannah took off her shoes and waded in. Brian laughed at her as she jumped across the little stones. She slipped. The water came up to her waist. As she clambered out of the river she could feel the weight of it pulling at her skirt, plastering it to her body, sticking to her legs. Brian touched her. His hand moulding the V between her legs. And there by the river in the warmth of the Polish sun, they loved each other. Hannah felt Brian ride high into her and she arched her back and curled her legs around him. She felt him come, pouring his sperm into her, and she asked for his child.

Dinner, Hannah and Brian discovered, was an excuse for a party. All the members of the collective gathered together and toasted the foreign visitors. The lovers were separated, cornered at different ends of the large room at the local inn which had been commandeered for the evening. Those with relatives in America forced vodka on to Brian, and those who remembered the Oberskis clung to Hannah. A small, rather sombre trio played Polish folk songs whilst salt herring and Polish ham were devoured at incredible speed. All the men wanted to dance with Hannah. And she swirled to the music, feeling her now dry skirt swish her legs. The vodka helped the loving and she danced for Brian as if they were alone.

Brian didn't dance, he watched her and he knew that he loved her. That night he told her that he would never leave her.

'What about your family?'

'It will be hard, very hard, and there may be times when I will hate you, but I will never not love you.'

Hannah drew him close. She understood that there would be hurt, she was sorry for that but guilt was not a luxury she could allow herself. She wanted Brian. She wanted the years of emptiness to be over. She touched his hair, feeling his breath on her skin, his thigh on her thigh. She knew him, she was him as he was her. She felt as if they were part of the same whole and all their lives they had been waiting for the coming together. Momentarily she was aware of tears pricking at her eyelids, and she wanted to cry. But she didn't, he was sleeping and she didn't want to wake him.

Hannah was disappointed by Czestochowa, there was no magic there. But when they got to the monastery it all changed. She began to feel the power of the Catholic Church. On the little hill above the ordinary town the Black Madonna, the symbol of Poland, drew them in.

It was as if the yearnings and the prayers of millions of pilgrims had built themselves into the walls. She allowed herself to be swept into the fervour and for the first time in her adult life she knelt and prayed, thanking whoever it was for Brian, for happiness.

They returned to Warsaw as a couple. They met with Juliana Satafim. She came to their hotel and they sat in the bar and talked television.

'You look better,' the Polish woman told Hannah. 'You were strained when you first arrived.'

'I was tired, and I had just met my mother's brother. It was quite emotional.'

'I am sure it was,' Juliana said quietly. She stubbed out her cigarette. 'Will you take him back with you?'

'Unfortunately he died whilst I was here.'

'That's sad, but at least you found each other.'

'It will be very sad for my mother,' Hannah said, suddenly

realizing for the first time the magnitude of her discovery. She thought of the little box that Jonathon had given her. She hadn't allowed herself to open it. It was for Rozia.

Lily came to dinner with them. She and her husband. She said she was coping, but her face was still set with sadness. Hannah held her hand throughout the dinner. Her husband, Wadjek, was quiet, a worried man with tired eyes. He was a lecturer in mathematics at the University.

'I doubt if you will ever be able to film your programme,' he said.

'I don't want to lose you, Hannah,' Lily said. 'You are my only family.'

'You won't. And you will come and visit us in England.'

'And meet the legendary Rozia,' Wadjek said, laughing. 'I am not sure I can cope.'

'She isn't that bad,' Hannah said.

'Can you imagine the impact she made on my father's life? His beautiful sister going to the University, falling in love with a dashing young gentile . . .'

'Do you know, the most extraordinary thing is that after Jouk, my stepfather, died, I longed to know about my real father. I think I sort of fell in love with him, or rather the image I made of him.'

'And now that you are talking about him, how do you feel?'

'A sense of loss of course, because I never knew him. But I am not in love with him, I don't need to be.'

After a tearful farewell to Lily, Hannah and Brian went to their room. On the dressing table was the little tin box designated for Rozia. Hannah touched it briefly and shivered.

'Open it,' Brian said.

'No . . . it isn't for me.'

'It's about your father, your real father. Listen to me, Hannah.' He took her shoulders, drawing her close to him.

'This trip was your pilgrimage to your past. When we go, that past has to be over, you won't have any more baggage to carry. What you do now you do for yourself – you won't be able to hide behind someone else's mistakes. Open the box – then it can be over.'

Hannah got up from the bed, she took the little box and prised off its lid. Inside were diaries, letters. Hannah ignored them, even the one addressed in neat writing to Rozia Oberska which was sealed. She shivered though, when she saw the envelope. On the back was written *Samuel Mezeurski 1942.*

'God knows what he was thinking when he wrote that,' she whispered.

Brian nodded. He took the tin from her hands, and emptied the contents on to the floor. There were photographs. One seemed to separate itself from the others, it was of a young man in military cadet uniform. She turned it over and saw the writing on the back. There was a name printed in capital letters. STEFAN GORDANSKI, and a date: August, 1923.

'Mourn him,' Brian told her, 'and then think of what your mother has gone through all these years – look at your face, Hannah, and then look at his.'

Hannah stood up, she propped the photograph up on the mirror and then pulled her hair away from her face, and she understood even more about Rozia.

Chapter Fifteen

———————◆———————

Throughout the journey back to England Hannah clung to Brian. She hadn't told him, but she had a dreadful feeling in her stomach that all was not as it should be. She kept telling herself not to be silly. Brian would probably have to go back to America and see his wife, but then he would come to her, and there was nothing to fear. He loved her, she knew that. Margaret liked him. She was dealing with fancies.

Brian touched her hair. 'Hey,' he whispered, 'could I have my hand back for a minute? You're squeezing my fingers so hard there is no blood left in them.'

'Oh, sorry. I didn't realize . . .'

'Yes, you did. You're gripping on for dear life. What is it?'

'I don't know.'

'Premonitions. I believe in those.' He touched her stomach gently.

'Well I don't,' Hannah replied. 'It's just that I can't bear the thought of being apart from you tonight.'

'Well, you won't be. I'll come to your home. I'll drive past my place on the way to collect the mail,' he said lightly.

'Fine.'

'And there will be some letters from Barbara. And that will hurt you, but less than the realization that I love you is going to hurt her.'

'Of course. And you know that I'll do everything I possibly can to be as supportive –' Hannah bit her lip – 'that's a stupid thing to say. I am the cause of it . . .'

'I don't know whether you are or not. I didn't go home to her after Vietnam. I stayed here alone. I can't imagine that I wouldn't have come back to you. But equally I wouldn't have left her.' Brian's hands were curled into his palms. Hannah leaned over to him and gently opened his fingers.

They had left Hannah's car at the airport. They argued good-naturedly over who should drive.

'All right, I'll drive to your place and then you can drive to mine,' Hannah said, throwing her bag on to the back seat.

'That means I get to drive in the rush hour.'

'You'll be going the opposite way to the traffic.'

Brian put the roof down whilst she fiddled with the radio. *Madame Butterfly* was on one of the stations. She winced. She didn't want to hear about love's failures.

'No, leave that on,' Brian said as he got into the car. 'I like it . . . pop opera.'

'I just wish he'd come up that bloody hill a bit earlier,' Hannah muttered as she swung into the traffic.

'You're a romantic.'

'Yes . . .'

Brian turned the radio down so that the voices could just be heard mouthing their sentiments of love and longing. 'When are you going to give Rozia her box?'

'Pandora's box, you mean.'

Brian laughed. 'As long as hope is left in it, she'll be all right.'

Hannah glanced at him out of the corner of her eye. She felt her stomach contract. Maybe that was why she was so fearful. *As long as hope is left in it . . .* She drove silently, and with a new-found confidence she turned the radio up and listened to the Humming Chorus – comfortable, with Brian's hand on her knee.

They turned into his road. Hannah was reversing into a convenient spot when the front door was flung open. A tanned woman with thick dark hair that hung to her shoulders ran down the steps and threw herself towards Brian. Hannah could see that his face was blank.

The woman in her obvious joy saw nothing. 'Darling, darling. I am so happy to see you.'

'Barbara.' He turned briefly towards Hannah before he put his arms around her. He hugged her quickly and then stepped back. 'I'd like you to meet Hannah Simpson,' he said.

'I am delighted to meet you.' Barbara extended her hand. She kept her other arm around her husband's waist. Hannah took the hand. She hoped it didn't show that she was shaking.

'What are you doing here?' Hannah could hear the strain in Brian's voice, but Barbara showed nothing.

'I wanted to surprise you. We want you back,' she looked up into his face, 'so I came for you. The children are so excited. We've missed you, Brian.'

Hannah tried to concentrate on the driving, but her head was full of the wide American face that had claimed her man. She felt numb, but at the same time there was a pain inside her that was almost too terrible to bear. She didn't know how she got home. She just threw herself into the flat, fell on to the floor and cried as if her heart were breaking. She heard the telephone ring but she didn't answer. Eventually it stopped.

After some time she went into the bathroom. Her make-up was smeared down her face, her eyes were red from weeping. She washed herself and bathed her sore eyes. Then she heard the doorbell. Hannah sighed. She wouldn't answer it. No one knew exactly what time she was coming back. But the bell wouldn't stop. It went on and on. Incessantly ringing, reverberating in her head. She had to answer it. It was Brian.

'Why are you here?' she said. 'Shouldn't you be in bed with your wife or something?'

He hit her then. A dry stinging slap that set her staggering backwards – and then he grabbed her, pushed her back on to the floor and loved her violently. She tried not to respond, but then her loving matched his and they beat each other with their knuckles, bringing each other to a pitch of emotion that they had never felt before. They came together, thrusting at each other with their legs, their buttocks and their arms.

Afterwards, quite a long time afterwards, Brian said, 'I've told her.'

'What did she say?'

'She said she knew as soon as she saw you. Apparently I always liked blondes.' The small attempt at a joke fell flat.

'How is she?'

'How were you?'

'Terrible, when I thought I'd lost you.'

Brian left her soon afterwards. He had to go back to Barbara. 'You don't wrap up a marriage after twenty years and two children in one afternoon,' he said.

Hannah knew she had to go and see Rozia. Wearily she climbed into her car and drove to the Finchley Road. Rozia had already gone upstairs, and Jerzy was clearing up in the café. She hugged him.

'Was it good?' he asked.

'I found Jonathon, Rozia's brother. There are letters in here for her, she will need you later.'

Jerzy nodded. 'I'll be here,' he said.

'I am tired,' Hannah told Rozia as they went into the salon, 'it has been an exhausting trip and quite an emotional one. And when we got back Brian's wife was waiting for him at his flat.'

'Quite a shock I would have thought,' Rozia said tartly.

'Yes, but we have decided to be together. He's told his wife.'

'Poor woman.'

Hannah nodded, she could understand Barbara's pain and

anger. She knew she would have to think about that, but later, she had other things to do first.

'I have something for you,' she said to Rozia.

'A present from Poland?'

'In a way. I think I ought to tell you about it first.' Hannah faced her mother, she wanted to sit down but she didn't know whether she should. It was funny, she felt very young and very old. 'We have never been particularly close, you and I, for all sorts of reasons. I am sorry about that now because I am going to open a lot of wounds.' She concentrated on her feet, and the tufted carpet. 'I found your brother.'

'You can't have done, he must be dead.' The response was fast.

'No. But he is now. He died whilst I was in Poland.' Hannah forced herself to look at her mother. Her face was quite white. 'I met some men and I told them that I had a Polish mother. They asked for your surname. I remembered it to be Mezeurski. They told me about Jonathon. They rang him and I went to see him. He was very emotional, he told me he loved you very much.'

The cry came from the back of her throat. It was like the strangled note of a clarinet . . . elongated, but clamped by a shut mouth. 'What do you mean he is dead now?' Hannah didn't know how Rozia had managed to even speak.

'I was due to see him the next day. When I went back he had died in the night – it was cancer. His daughter, Lily, gave me a box for you. Inside is a letter from your father to you. Mummy, I am sorry.' How long was it since she had called her Mummy?

Rozia nodded. Hannah put the box into her lap. 'Jonathon kept this with him, he escaped from the cattle truck and went to Russia where he was interned. That's where he met his wife.'

'He has a child?' Rozia said almost conversationally, as if to put off the moment of opening the box.

'Yes, Lily. She is married.'

'He was pleased to see you?' Rozia asked. She looked up at Hannah, her eyes were brimming over but there was no sound.

'Yes,' Hannah said.

Rozia started to open the lid, but her fingers were trembling. 'I can't,' she said, 'will you?'

Hannah opened it. 'Can I stay with you, or do you want to be alone?'

Rozia nodded. Hannah didn't know what she meant, but then her mother gave her the envelope. 'Read it to me,' she said.

Hannah slit open the envelope and took out two single sheets of paper. She smoothed them out, and trying not to think, she began –

My darling little Rozia.

You will always be my little Rozia and if there is one thing to be gained from this nightmare, at least I know you are safe in England. My darling girl, I have never forgotten you and on this last journey I beg your forgiveness. I know you have a child. Kiss her for me. I pray that you and Jonathon will survive. He has to get out of this transport to another life. I hope, I pray . . . I cannot write. There is too much and too little time.

Are you a chemist? I hope so. Stefan Gordanski's mother is with us. I enclose her letter that brought us together. We embrace you.

Papa.

At the bottom of the paper was a scrawl. It was spiky, almost illegible. Hannah read it carefully. '*I love you. Mama.*'

She took the other letter and read it quickly – unable to look at Rozia – her own heart was beating too quickly.

My dear Mr Mezeurski,
My name is Sonia Gordanska. My son was Stefan, and he

*and your daughter were lovers. Joseph Oberski contacted me
to inform me that Rozia had a little girl, and that the child
was my son's.*

*Stefan was a Jew. My beloved husband died when he was
a baby. I lived in a small stetl community – we were Jews
living with Jews, the law is that the widow marries the brother.
My brother-in-law was an unkind man. I ran away
from him, took off my wig. I lived amongst the goyim –
if I had gone to the Jews they would have sent me back, so
I pretended to be a Catholic. I was so frightened of what
they would do to me if they discovered that we were Jews
so I let Stefan believe that he was a Catholic, but he
was never baptized. How terrible that you did not know this
before.*

*We might, you, your dear wife, and I – have known the
joy of our children's child, but through fear and hatred the
truth was hidden. I will not impose myself on you. Perhaps
if you wish, you will contact me.*

Hannah looked at her mother then.

Rozia was crying now, quite openly. 'I am sorry,' she
said, 'I know it is very selfish, you must be feeling very
strange yourself, but would you mind leaving me – for just
a little while?'

Hannah nodded, she got up. 'It's funny, but I knew who
I was at Auschwitz, I didn't need any letters.' She stopped,
bent and kissed Rozia's forehead.

On her way out she told Jerzy the contents of the letters.
She wanted Brian.

Rozia herself sat quietly for several hours – sometimes she
walked a little and then she sat down again and took up the
photographs.

The faces came back, bringing with them their own particular kind of memory. A little girl with long red hair, was
that her? She couldn't believe it. *I was another person . . .*

but there was a familiar face, Papa . . . beloved Papa . . . and Mama, and Booba, and her beautiful young prince. It was now so long ago – it was hard even to remember the passion.

When the time was right, she called for Jerzy.

'What happens now?' he asked.

'Now?'

'Yes, you and Hannah, and you and Margaret.'

'There is no change, Jerzy. That is our tragedy – it is too late for us, we are strangers to each other, a Family of Strangers.'

Whilst Hannah digested the realities of her birth, Brian was killing his marriage. Barbara sat on a chair, her legs tucked up under her; her eyes were red, but she was controlled. Brian held a glass of whisky in his hand. He drank intermittently. The bottle was by his chair.

'Look,' Barbara suddenly said, twisting slightly on the chair, 'if you want time to be with this woman, to burn her out of your system, I'll hurt, but I'll accept it.'

'It isn't like that,' Brian said.

'You mean it's true love.' Her voice was bitter.

'You are my past. You are part of me. You are a good woman. I respect you. I love you, but . . .'

'But?'

'Look, I don't want to cause you more pain. You'd be better off with someone else. Someone who can love you the way you deserve to be loved.'

'That's a cop-out.'

'OK.' Brian leaned towards her. His fingers interlocked with each other. 'Hannah is my future. She makes me feel that there is nothing I cannot do, nothing I can't achieve.'

'And didn't I make you feel like that?'

Brian shook his head.

Barbara bit her lip. 'And the children. What about them?'

'I am still their father.'

'Here. While they are in America. Some father.'

Brian winced. 'That's the bad part.'

'Yeah. They didn't ask to be born. And suddenly their Dad has fallen in love with some cheap whore –'

'She isn't a whore, but if it helps you to call her that . . .'

'No, it doesn't help. She doesn't look like a whore. She looks like a thoroughly nice woman, but she's stolen my husband, God dammit.' Barbara's face screwed up into a thousand little creases.

Brian got up and went to sit next to her. He put his hand on her arm.

'Don't touch me!' she screamed at him. 'Don't touch me.'

Barbara went back to America the next day, she wouldn't let Brian see her off. He went to Hannah. She told him what was in the letters and he held her.

Later he asked about Margaret.

'She is with Anthony. I rang her and said I was back, but that I was very tired. She said it didn't matter, she would stay where she was. I spoke to Anthony too, he told me he doesn't know how to get through to her, but apparently she seems to like Susan. They go to museums together.'

On the morning of the fourteenth day after Hannah and Brian had returned from Poland, Brian made her breakfast and brought it to her in bed. There was tea, little pieces of toast and marmalade.

'Rozia made me breakfast like this the day I got married,' Hannah said.

'There is no answer to that,' he replied. 'How are you?'

'Now that you ask, shitty.' Hannah pulled herself up in the bed and lay propped against the pine headboard; her pretty white lace cushions were strewn around her, and her blonde hair tumbled down to her shoulders. She watched as he moved around her overtly feminine bedroom with ease; he was dressing for work, the jeans and the shirt were on, the feet still bare.

He came to sit next to her, his hand went to the neck of her nightgown which had fallen open, and he moved it and cupped one of her breasts. Hannah winced, it hurt.

'Your breasts, they've grown.'

'What . . .?'

'Look, they have little blue veins and your nipples are a different shape. I never noticed that before. Does it always happen before your period?'

'I haven't had a period . . .' Hannah spoke before she could think about the implications, 'I haven't had a period since Poland, two weeks before we went to be exact.'

Brian looked into her face. 'You could be –'

She put her hand over his mouth. 'Don't say it.'

'Why not? Pregnant. Do you mind?'

'Do you?' She noticed that he was breathing harder.

He moved away from her as if to give himself a moment to think. Hannah clung on to the bedclothes. She remembered how she'd asked for his child, there in Poland, by the stream. And now, perhaps . . . How would he feel? She was frightened, she might lose him after all. Perhaps she was too old.

He turned back to her. There was a light in his face, and his eyes seemed brighter. 'It would be wonderful.'

'What about your children?'

'And what about your child?'

'Oh God . . .' Hannah whispered quietly.

'Thank you, God,' Brian whispered back. They clung to each other. 'When can you take a test?' Brian asked.

'I'll see the doctor today.'

'But you would only be four weeks pregnant.'

'You mean I have to wait?'

'You have to wait . . . And so do I.'

He went out then, leaving her in her bed. As he walked down the path he felt himself tremble. Was it happiness? He didn't know. He'd made the decision to leave two children. And now he and Hannah had perhaps made another, Hannah's son. He had no doubt that it would be a son, his son; he felt a tingling inside him, and saw the tiny foetus, smaller than his own fingernail, and then he knew joy.

Brian brought Hannah flowers, long-stemmed velvet red roses. As he walked back to the flat he thought about his children. He had written to them, separately, painful letters trying to explain what had happened. He had been more blunt with Emile.

How can I make it easier? he had said. *I've met someone who gives me something I have never known before. She makes me feel there is nothing I cannot do, nowhere I cannot go. I love you, Emile. In your eyes perhaps not enough because I am leaving your mother. I can't alter that truth. I can give you all kinds of clichés, that you'll love Hannah; you'll come and visit. But I am here in England and you are there in America. But will you come to me, next vacation, so at least we can talk?*

The letter to his brown-eyed button of a daughter who so resembled her mother was shorter, simpler.

I love you. I will never stop loving you. In a way I love Mummy, but without Hannah I have no life.

He hadn't told Hannah of the anguish he had felt when he told Barbara he was leaving her. She'd said, 'I'll never divorce you. I believe in the sanctity of marriage. Live with your whore.'

Brian decided to ring his children that night, each one tucked in their own private school – he had to hear their voices, he ached for them.

Hannah was still in bed when he got back. 'How will all the children feel?' she asked, as if reading his mind.

'Maybe they'll hate us, even Margaret. We can only try and work for their forgiveness.'

'Do we have to sacrifice them for our new life?'

'We did that, Hannah, you and I, if you want to look at it that way, the first time we loved each other.'

Hannah was silent for a while, then she said, 'But at least we can tell them we never lied.'

—Epilogue—

December 13th, 1981

Rozia stood in her tiny lemon and white kitchen preparing a dinner for her whole family. The little *pierogi* stuffed with cheese were waiting to be steamed, a duck soup simmered on top of the stove, its rich aroma scenting the tiny bungalow with an enticing but heavy invitation that promised overfilled stomachs and lack-lustre sleep. A goose sizzled in the oven, the crisp roast potatoes soaked in its rich fat, and the cauliflower awaited the hard-boiled eggs and breadcrumbs that would turn it from a sensible vegetable into a dietician's nightmare. A cheesecake with too many raisins waited on the sideboard in the dining end of Rozia and Jerzy's retirement cottage, as they chose to call it.

All this had been achieved by Rozia, a not inconsiderable task for someone who was now seventy-six years of age. She and Jerzy had sold their Finchley Road house for a considerable sum to a property developer, and had purchased this little bungalow near Esher, just off the A3. It had a beautiful garden with a lush green lawn, masses of standard roses, and mature cherry trees, apple and pear trees. The interior had been quiet and unremarkable. Rozia put in glass doors between the dining and the sitting end of the lounge. She covered the walls in red felt and hung photographs and paintings. Green plants and red roses, whatever time of the year, were her extravagance.

A heavy, frameless mirror dominated the dining room. Her little fringed lights and opulent cabinets were comfortable in their new surroundings. Jerzy loved the garden, he cared for it himself, content to leave the house to Rozia.

Now at seventy-one he was older in his ways than his wife, he liked to sit and read, or listen to his beloved Chopin on a wonderful new music centre that Brian had given him.

Rozia was particularly happy that day. She sang a little tuneless song to herself as she re-arranged her leaves, so much a feature of her table decorations, for the umpteenth time. Margaret was coming too. She did not see much of her beloved granddaughter. She found her life style so disturbing, despite the fact that she had achieved the professional ambitions that Rozia had set for her. Margaret was a fellow in the field of genetics. She wore her pale blonde hair cut close to her neck, and her usual clothes were jeans and a neat blouse and a V-neck jumper. There was a ring, a heavy silver band on her wedding finger. It had been there since Emma moved in. Rozia had never met Emma, Margaret's flatmate, as she chose to call her.

Hannah did not look her fifty-seven years. Her hair was still grey-blonde, although it was aided now by a hairdresser. Her skin was good, her eyes had a fire not normally associated with her age, and the sensuality she enjoyed showed in her walk.

Rozia stirred her soup and thought about her family. It had taken her a long time to come to term's with Hannah's divorce and re-marriage, but now she had to admit that Brian was the right man for Hannah – her daughter was beautiful, the ravages of polio long gone. She made award-winning documentaries and she had her son, Matthew. Rozia's eyes softened as she thought of him – now at eighteen the young prince, her Stefan come alive again, with Brian's grey-green eyes.

How they all loved Matthew. He was a gentle boy with a powerful imagination and almost a lust for life. Even Brian's American children adored him, the boy especially – he and Matthew were very close. What was strangest of all to Rozia was that Emile seemed to love Hannah too. The girl was like her mother, of course. At least she had re-married. Rozia had been pleased when she heard that, she had often wondered about Brian's wife and how she had coped when another woman destroyed her family.

Rozia was always amazed at Hannah's lack of guilt. She had told her that she herself could never have built her happiness on someone' else's unhappiness. She could still feel the force of Hannah's fury – even now, nineteen years later. She remembered how Hannah's eyes had fired with anger: 'I think it is worse to continue to be unhappy. By building on that unhappiness you damage so much more because of the basic lie to yourself. Look at you, look at what it did to you and to me, and to Margaret. I am not going to carry on in the same way. I am going to reach out for love – it's there for me and I am damn well not going to let it go. And anyway, you can't judge me because *you* reached out for your happiness, all those years ago, in Warsaw.'

Now, in her seventy-seventh year, Rozia realized that Hannah was right. The only true freedom was the freedom that Hannah had insisted on as her right. It was strange, but now that she thought about it she realized it had been Hannah who had actually managed to help her break a rule, flout a convention, and marry a man so much younger than herself. And that had given her the greatest happiness she had ever known; she loved Jerzy deeply, and she regretted that her jealousy had clouded the joy.

Her sadness was that Hannah didn't understand that there was a God and Jesus was His Son who died on the Cross for mankind.

'You are dreaming again over the soup,' Jerzy said.

Rozia looked up at him, ready to deny any such activity, but then she just smiled. 'Why don't you put on the news?' she said. 'We have not heard it today and listening to the news is one of our rituals.'

'Perhaps today we should break a ritual.'

'No, why should we?' Rozia went over to the radio in the corner of the kitchen and turned it on. She heard the car in the drive; she would have gone to meet the family but there was something on the news about Poland – Martial Law, internment . . . what was internment?

She turned to ask Jerzy – but then she felt a pain, and it hurt so much she couldn't even cry out.

Was that Hannah looking down at her? Why was she looking down . . . She had the white dress on, the one she wore in the Tatra Mountains, and she was carrying the red poppies. This time, this time it would be different – because she had her chance again, she would thank her for the flowers. The long hair, the white dress, the flowers – the strong sun creating a nimbus around her daughter's head . . .

'Thank you,' Rozia whispered, inside herself, because she couldn't speak. 'I can say thank you now.' She wanted to lift up her hand, to touch her, but she couldn't. Hannah was staring at her now, with her big eyes; she wanted to say, 'I love you,' but Hannah was getting nearer and bigger, she wanted to kiss her, to tell her . . . to say to her . . .

Hannah let the red carnations drop to the floor when she realized her mother was dying. She bent close to her, wanting to hold her – she was sure she had seen her lips move.

'Brian,' she whispered, 'I think she said, "Hannah, I love you."'